THE COLLECTED
EROTICA

THE COLLECTED EROTICA

An Illustrated Celebration of Human Sexuality Through the Ages

CARROLL & GRAF PUBLISHERS

NEW YORK

THE COLLECTED EROTICA
An Illustrated Celebration of Human Sexuality Through the Ages

Carroll & Graf Publishers
An Imprint of Avalon Publishing Group Inc.
245 West 17th Street
11th Floor
New York, NY 10011

AVALON
publishing group incorporated

This edition copyright © 2007 Eddison Sadd Editions

First Carroll & Graf edition 2007

The material in *The Collected Erotica* is an edited version of that first published by
Carroll & Graf in the United States in three volumes as
Erotica (1992), *Erotica II* (1993) *and Erotica III* (1996).

Library of Congress Cataloging-in-Publication Data is available.

ISBN-13: 978-0-78671-885-6
ISBN-10: 0-7867-1885-4

9 8 7 6 5 4 3 2 1

AN EDDISON•SADD EDITION
Edited, designed and produced by
Eddison Sadd Editions Limited
St Chad's House, 148 King's Cross Road
London WC1X 9DH

Phototypeset in New Aster and Gill Sans using QuarkXPress on Apple Macintosh
Printed in Singapore
Distributed by Publishers Group West

CONTENTS

PART ONE

The Maze

So far as we know, this is the first book of its kind: an illustrated anthology of erotica, taking as its source material the sexual art and literature of both East and West. We believe it is the first of its kind, but we are mindful of Marie Antoinette's milliner, who was moved to point out to her demanding client one day: 'Nothing is new, ma'am, only what has been forgotten.'

Human sexuality is a vast subject. Although it is only comparatively recently that our culture has come of age and decided that erotic literature can be made available to the general public, it has always been written, and the world's great libraries have whole sections devoted to it. Erotic art has always been produced – either for wealthy patrons or for the amusement of the artists themselves or their close circle – but has seldom seen the light of day. Even great art, even the religious icons of other cultures, will often languish unseen in the vaults of museums if it is sexually explicit.

The whole subject of erotica is a maze. The authors of erotic literature are often anonymous or pseudonymous. The works frequently appear in several versions, having been pirated, translated, re-translated and bowdlerized by pseudonymous publishers. Today, some important erotica is being re-published by major publishing houses. However, much remains in

OPPOSITE *'Donna che solleva la Gonna' by Giovanni Zuin.*

Zeus, the male principle and Father of the Gods, on one of his frequent missions to that end. School of David, France, eighteenth century.

national libraries and institutions which are sometimes ambivalent about the material: it may not be properly catalogued, access can be made difficult and even the basic conservation of books, prints and drawings may be neglected, depending on the attitude of individual curators. At the same time, much erotic art and literature is in the hands of private collectors, some of whom are very generous about making rare items available for copying and photography, while others are less so.

Thanks to some pioneer publishing since the Second World War, some parts of this maze of erotica will already be familiar to most readers. This book opens up much more of the maze to the general public – and provides a guide. As a guide, the book makes no claim to being comprehensive or definitive; it is an exploration.

Sadly, following the liberalization of the laws governing the publication of sexual material, a great deal of second-rate, ugly and pernicious stuff has also become available. This was inevitable but it does not argue for suppression. Indeed, it makes it vital for good erotica to be published, so that we can see for ourselves the difference between the life-enhancing, and the sordid and destructive. Until sex takes its proper place on our bookshelves, it will be difficult for it to take its proper place in our lives. Women-haters and those who are addicted to cruelty and violence must look elsewhere – there is nothing in this book for you.

All anthologies involve selection, and readers need to know what principles have governed the process. This part is an exploration of mainstream sexuality as revealed in writing and images that were, until comparatively recently, forbidden, banned or privately distributed. For that reason there is little from the second half of the twentieth century, when the cultural climate began to change and the restrictions on writing openly about sex were relaxed. Since the historic obscenity trials of the 1960s (of *Lady Chatterley's Lover* and *Fanny Hill* in the UK and *Tropic of Cancer* in the USA), writers and artists of every type, and every quality, have been able to deal with sex in an increasingly explicit way.

Erotic art is found among the very earliest evidence we have of human culture. This stone figure, popularly known as the Venus of Willendorf, after the place in Austria where it was discovered, was carved in the Paleolithic period around 30,000 BCE. Her newly acquired name is not inappropriate. She is clearly an object of worship: an idealized woman, a celebration of female sexuality and fecundity.

Another, unknown, artist looks at the auto-erotic.

There have been regrettable anachronisms (the Oz trial in the UK, for example) but in general writers and artists no longer have to look over their shoulders or fear a knock at the door if their chosen subject is sex. This part is concerned with the forbidden. Whatever their motives for producing the work, many of the writers and artists included here were pushing out the frontiers and risked penalties ranging from loss of reputation, position and income, to fines, imprisonment or banishment. There are exceptions, and to round off the work there are quotations and illustrations from many other sources, but this is essentially material that has, in its time, been forbidden by Western culture.

This part is predominantly Western but it also contains material from the older, wiser civilizations of the East, which have regarded sex as an important (and largely guiltless) subject for thousands of years. In order to publish these texts in the West (and avoid prosecution) subterfuge was necessary. *Kama Sutra, Ananga-Ranga* and *The Perfumed Garden* were produced and distributed by Sir Richard Burton and others under the auspices of the 'Kama Shastra Society – London and Benares', which was only a blind.

The writers included in this part – with a few notable exceptions from all periods and cultures – are men. This is unavoidable, as historically most writers (certainly most writers of erotica) were men. We are pleased to say that this is changing now. But this male bias does not mean that there is nothing here of interest to women. Perhaps it is significant that much of the best erotic writing (*Fanny Hill* or *Satyra Sotadica*, for example) uses the device of the first-person narrative, with a woman as the narrator!

This is not a literary collection in the normal sense – it is an erotic collection. The illustrations are just as important as the text, and the extracts which make up the greater part of the text have been selected not primarily for their literary value, but because they have something to tell us about sexuality.

Lay your sleeping head, my love,
Human on my faithless arm;
Time and fevers burn away
Individual beauty from
Thoughtful children, and the grave
Proves the child ephemeral:
But in my arms till break of day
Let the living creature lie,
Mortal, guilty, but to me
The entirely beautiful.

FROM *LULLABY*
W. H. AUDEN

In compiling this part we have not so much sorted the sheep from the goats as penned a wide selection of both beasts together in order to make comparisons and enjoy the variety.

This involves putting minor writers with the great and the good; the lewd and the bawdy with the sublime and the religious. The illustrations are similarly diverse, ranging from the fine and delicate to the rude and disgraceful. We are sorry if some of these juxtapositions are surprising. Sex has many aspects.

An anthology of this kind is not so much a book as a group encounter. Nobody can leave their sexuality at home: here we all are, writers, researchers, editors, artists, designers and, of course, you, the reader, all with our own erotic experiences and appetites, our own aesthetic and moral opinions, all involved in an extraordinary bring and buy sale. Freud wrote in one of his letters, 'I am accustoming myself to the idea of regarding every sexual act as a process in which four persons are involved. We shall have a lot to discuss about that.' In which case, like one of Cecil B. De Mille's epics, this collection has a cast of thousands.

This is not a solemn book, but it does have a serious subject. Sex is important and if you are unhappy about it for any reason you should seek advice. If your doctor is unsympathetic (or stupid) ask to be referred to a sex counsellor or look in the telephone book for self-help organizations.

Eros, the Greek god of love, gave his name to this 'erotic' anthology. Gods are used to having their names taken in vain, of course – Love more than most – but we would like to get it right. He appears in the book from time to time, often in unlikely places, but do these fleeting glimpses justify the title? We think so. After all, without him it is all nothing but empty shadow-play.

Here, Eros attending is Venus in a painting by an unknown twentieth-century artist.

CHAPTER ONE
The Moment of Desire

The moment of desire! the moment of desire!
*   the virgin*
That pines for man shall awaken her womb to
*   enormous joys*
In the secret shadows of her chamber: the youth
*   shut up from*
The lustful joy shall forget to generate and create
an amorous image
In the shadows of his curtains and in the folds
of his silent pillow

FROM *Visions of the Daughters of Albion*

WILLIAM BLAKE

How fortunate to have been a young person reaching sexual maturity in India 2,000 years ago! Sex was guiltless, openly discussed, and the sage Vatsyayana had just completed his *Kama Sutra*. This great work collated all the sexual wisdom of previous centuries and presented it as an easily understood guide. Vatsyayana wrote the book as a religious duty: his intention was to enable young people to avoid the shocks and pitfalls of sex and to enjoy its wonders. Included was guidance on every aspect of the relationship between men and women, together with a no-nonsense manual of sexual instruction covering everything from biting and scratching to fellatio and love-making postures. The following extract gives the flavour of the work.

A gust of wind will blow open the petals of a poppy that is slow in blossoming. Love suddenly brings the spirit of a girl to flower.

FROM THE *SANSKRIT*
AMARU, C. 800 AD.

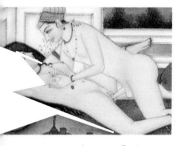

ABOVE and OPPOSITE *Erotic miniatures from Rajasthan, painted in the Mughal manner. The age-old tradition of Indian miniature painting – which includes a wide diversity of styles – has always involved copying. This means that dating the art can sometimes be a problem, although these paintings are late nineteenth- or early twentieth-century.*

When a woman sees her lover is fatigued by con-stant congress, without having his desire satisfied, she should, with his permission, lay him down upon his back, and give him assistance by acting his part. She may also do this to satisfy the curios-ity of her lover, or her own desire of novelty.

There are two ways of doing this, the first is when during congress she turns round, and gets on the top of her lover, in such a manner as to continue the congress, without obstructing the pleasure of it; and the other is when she acts the man's part from the beginning. At such a time, with flowers in her hair hanging loose, and her smiles broken by hard breathings, she should press upon her lover's bosom with her own breasts, and lowering her head frequently, should do in return the same actions which he used to do before, returning his blows and chaffing him, should say, 'I was laid down by you, and fatigued with hard congress, I shall now therefore lay you down in return.' She should then again manifest her own bashfulness, her fatigue, and her desire of stopping the congress.

Earlier in the *Kama Sutra* Vatsyayana explains the importance of both wooing and foreplay to young men and counsels them to be tender and gentle in their initial approach:

Women, being of a tender nature, want tender beginnings, and when they are forcibly approached by men with whom they are but slightly acquainted, they sometimes suddenly become haters of sexual connection, and some-times even haters of the male sex.

Nearly 2,000 years after the Kama Sutra was written – at a time when India was the 'jewel in the crown' of the British Empire, but its ancient wisdom largely ignored – the young Frank Harris was receiving his sex education in the usual Western manner.

A week later Strangways astonished us both by telling how he had made up to the nursemaid of his younger sisters and got into her bed at night. The first time she wouldn't let him do anything, it appeared, but, after a night or two, he managed to touch her sex and assured us it was all covered with silky hairs. A little later he told us how she had locked her door and how the next day he had taken off the lock and got into bed with her again.

ABOVE and OPPOSITE *The artist who produced these fine charcoal drawings was obliged to remain anonymous, signing his work 'A I'. They were taken from the series entitled 'Claire Obscure' first published in Vienna in 1935. These are skilful confections: suggestive shadows from which naked flesh shines like an erotic beacon.*

At first she was cross, or pretended to be, he said, but he kept on kissing and begging her, and bit by bit she yielded, and he touched her sex again. 'It was a slit,' he said. A few nights later, he told us he had put his prick into her and, 'Oh! by gum, it was wonderful, wonderful!'

'But how did you do it?' we wanted to know, and he gave us his whole experience.

'Girls love kissing,' he said, 'and so I kissed and kissed her and put my leg on her, and her hand on my cock and I kept touching her breasts and her cunny (that's what she calls it) and at last I got on her between her legs and she guided my prick into her cunt (God, it was wonderful!) and now I go with her every night and often in the day as well. She likes her cunt touched, but very gently,' he added; 'she showed me how to do it with one finger like this,' and he suited the action to the word.

Strangways in a moment became to us not only a hero but a miracle-man; we pretended not to believe him in order to make him tell us the truth and we were almost crazy with breathless desire.

I got him to invite me up to the vicarage and I saw Mary the nurse-girl there, and she seemed to me almost a woman and spoke to him as 'Master Will' and he kissed her, though she frowned and said, 'Leave-off' and 'Behave yourself,' very angrily; but I felt that her anger was put on to prevent my guessing the truth. I was aflame with desire and when I told Howard, he, too, burned with lust, and took me out for a walk and questioned me all over again, and under a haystack in the country we gave ourselves to a bout of frigging, which for the first time thrilled me with pleasure.

All the time we were playing with ourselves, I

kept thinking of Mary's hot slit, as Strangways had described it, and, at length, a real orgasm came and shook me; the imagining had intensified my delight.

Nothing in my life up to that moment was comparable in joy to that story of sexual pleasure as described, and acted for us, by Strangways.

Frank Harris published the first volume of *My Life and Loves* in 1922, when he was sixty-eight and 'half-drowned in the brackish flood of old age'. He wanted it to be the most honest autobiography ever written. It would record his contacts with the important people of his time (and he had indeed met most of them), but it would also be truthful about sex. In the foreword he wrote: 'Nine men and women out of ten go through life without realizing their own special nature: they cannot lose their souls, for they have never found them. That's why I love this book in spite of all its shortcomings and all its faults...' Unfortunately, the book marked his downfall – the world was still not ready for 'Frankness' of this sort.

Frank Harris was a curious amalgam. He was one of the greatest editors of his time (notably of the *Saturday Review*), the staunch friend and biographer of Oscar Wilde who dedicated *An Ideal Husband* to him, a lifelong romantic and fierce radical. He was a notorious seducer but genuinely loved women for themselves. When those men he had offended had their revenge after the publication of *My Life and Loves* it was for radical onslaughts like this one against the Anglo-Saxon male: 'He has made of his wife a meek upper servant or slave... who has hardly any intellectual

ABOVE and OPPOSITE *During the
endless sunset of the Austro-
Hungarian Empire, its splendidly
decadent capital, Vienna, produced
a wealth of erotic art. When A1's
'wanton' (above) first enjoyed the
attention of her young lover in
1935, her painted bronze sister
(opposite) had already had her
skirt lifted by inquisitive fingers
for nearly 40 years.*

interests and whose spiritual being only finds a narrow outlet in her mother instincts!'

George Bernard Shaw, a friend for more than forty years, wrote of Harris: 'He blazed through London like a comet, leaving a trail of deeply annoyed persons behind him, and like a meteor through America... I think I know pretty well all the grievances his detractors had against him; but if I had to write his epitaph it should run "Here lies a man of letters who hated cruelty and injustice and bad art, and never spared them in his own interest. RIP."'

We shall hear Frank's voice (a remarkable basso profundo which one of his mistresses confessed 'made her sex open and shut' whenever she heard it) from time to time in this part. He recalled his own first sexual encounter with clarity.

Before every church festival there was a good deal of practice with the organist, and girls from neighbouring houses joined in our classes. One girl alone sang alto and she and I were separated from the other boys; and girls; the upright piano was put across the corner of the room; and we two sat or stood behind it, almost out of sight of all the other singers, the organist, of course, being seated in front of the piano. The girl E..., who sang alto with me, was about my own age; she was very pretty, or seemed so to me, with golden hair and blue eyes, and I always made up to her as well as I could, in my boyish way. One day while the organist was explaining something, E... stood up on the chair and leant over the back of the piano to hear better or see more. Seated in my chair behind her, I caught sight of her legs, for her dress rucked up behind as she leaned over; at once my breath stuck in my throat. Her legs were lovely, I thought, and the temptation came to touch them; for no one could see.

I got up immediately and stood by the chair she was standing on. Casually I let my hand fall against her left leg. She didn't draw her leg away or seem to feel my hand, so I touched her more boldly. She never moved, though now I knew must have felt my hand. I began to slide my hand up her leg and suddenly my fingers felt the warm flesh on her thigh where the stocking ended above the

An oil painting on canvas which is attributed to Lovis Corinth (1858–1925). The painting's subtly pervasive eroticism comes from the woman's expression: we admire the breasts, the long flank, but always seek the face again. It is the whole woman who is erotic.

knee. The feel of her warm flesh made me literally choke with emotion: my hand went on up, warmer and warmer, when suddenly I touched her sex; there was soft down on it. The heart-pulse throbbed in my throat. I have no words to describe the intensity of my sensations.

Thank God, E... did not move or show any sign of distaste. Curiosity was stronger even than desire in me and I felt her sex all over, and at once the idea came into my head that it was like a fig (the Italians, I learned later, called it familiarly *fica*); it opened at my touches and I inserted my finger gently, as Strangways had told me that Mary had taught him to do; still E... did not move. Gently I rubbed the front part of her sex with my finger. I could have kissed her a thousand times out of gratitude.

Suddenly, as I went on, I felt her move, and then again; plainly she was showing me where my touch gave her most pleasure: I could have died for her in thanks; again she moved and I could feel a little mound or small button of flesh right in the front of her sex, above the junction of the inner lips; of course it was her clitoris. I had forgotten all the old Methodist doctor's books till that moment; this fragment of long forgotten knowledge came back to me: gently I rubbed the clitoris and at once she pressed down on my finger for a moment or two. I tried to insert my finger into the vagina; but she drew away at once and quickly, closing her sex as if hurt, so I went back to caressing her tickler.

Suddenly the miracle ceased. The cursed organist had finished his explanation of the new plain chant, and as he touched the first notes on the piano, E... drew her legs together; I took away my hand and she stepped down from the chair. 'You darling, darling,' I whispered, but she frowned, and then just gave me a smile out of the corner of her eye to show me she was not displeased.

Ah, how lovely, how seductive she seemed to me now, a thousand times lovelier and more desirable than ever before. As we stood up to sing again, I whispered to her: 'I love you, love you, dear, dear!'

I can never express the passion of gratitude I felt to her for her goodness, her sweetness in letting me touch her sex. E... it was who opened the Gates of Paradise to me and let me first taste the hidden mysteries of sexual delight. Still after more than fifty years I feel the thrill of the joy she gave me by her response, and the passionate reverence of my gratitude is still alive in me.

This experience with E... had the most important and unlooked for results. The mere fact that girls could feel sex pleasure 'just as boys do' increased my liking for them and lifted the whole sexual intercourse to a higher plane in my thought. The excitement and pleasure were so much more intense than anything I had experienced before that I resolved to keep myself for this higher joy. No more self-abuse for me; I knew something infinitely better. One kiss was better, one touch of a girl's sex.

H enry Miller's attitude towards sexuality and women is very different from Frank Harris's – he does not romanticize the one and idealize the other. On the contrary, he goes out of his way to strip away pretensions and to shock in doing so, but (only in his best writing) goes on to show you a new beauty in what remains. It is not

may i feel said he
(i'll squeal said she
just once said he)
it's fun said she

(may i touch said he
how much said she
a lot said he)
why not said she

(let's go said he
not too far said she
what's too far said he
where you are said she)

may i stay said he
(which way said she
like this said he
if you kiss said she

may i move said he
is it love said she)
if you're willing said he
(but you're killing said she

but it's life said he
but your wife said she
now said he)
ow said she

(tiptop said he
don't stop said she
oh no said he)
go slow said she

(cccome? said he
ummm said she)
you're divine! said he
(you are Mine said she)

E. E. CUMMINGS
(1894–1962)

A watercolour (right) on paper by
'Fay D', a Hungarian artist working
in Paris in the 1920s. The bronze
reliefs (opposite) are from the same
period but produced in Germany.

'reality' any more than Frank Harris's writing is – they both involve literary artifice – but it is a fundamental difference in both attitude and approach. There are extracts from his best work later in this book. The fire and poetry of *Tropic of Cancer* and *Tropic of Capricorn* were never again achieved, but the later writing has its memorable incidents. This account of Miller's early sexual explorations from *Plexus* would be a bleak little episode were it not for the strangely touching impulse of the girl Kitty at the end.

One day George drew me aside to tell me something confidential... There was a young country girl he wanted me to meet. We could find her down near the bridge, toward dark, with the right signal.

'She looks twenty, though she's only a kid,' said George, as we hastened toward the spot. 'A virgin, of course, but a dirty little devil. You can't get much more than a good feel, Hen. I've tried everything, but it's no go.'

Kitty was her name. It suited her. A plain-looking girl, but full of sap and curiosity. Hump for the monkeys.

'Hello,' says George, as we sidle up to her. 'How's tricks? Want you to meet a friend of mine, from the city.'

Her hand was tingling with warmth and desire. It seemed to me she was blushing, hut it may have been simply the abundant health which was bursting through her cheeks.

'Give him a hug and squeeze.'

Kitty flung her arms about me and pressed her warm body tight to mine. In a moment her tongue was down my throat. She bit my lips, my ear lobes, my neck. I put my hand under her skirt and through the slit in her flannel drawers. No protest. She began to groan and murmur. Finally she had an orgasm.

'How was it, Hen? What did I tell you?'

We chatted a while to give Kitty a breathing spell, then George locked horns with her. It was cold and wet under the bridge, but the three of us were on fire. Again George tried to get it in, but Kitty managed to wriggle away.

The most he could do was to put it between her legs, where she held it like a vice.

As we were walking back toward the road Kitty asked if she couldn't visit us sometime – when we got back to the city. She had never been to New York.

'Sure,' said George, 'let Herbie bring you. He knows his way around.'

'But I won't have any money,' said Kitty.

'Don't worry about that,' said big-hearted George, 'we'll take care of you.'

'Do you think your mother would trust you?' I asked.

You were ashamed
of the soft down on your bottom,
I of my member's
huge-bulbed gracelessness:
delicately I caressed
that delicate bottom;
graciously you rewarded
gracelessness.

Never were two more suited,
each one's shame
answered with, first, affection,
then desire:
now I lie sleepless
dwelling on your shame,
and shamelessly desiring
your desire.

BECAUSE OF LOVE
ROBIN SKELTON (1925–)

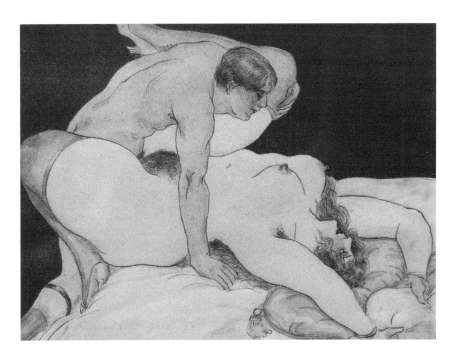

This astonishing watercolour is from a series of 33 produced by an anonymous Czech artist at the turn of the twentieth century.

Kitty replied that her mother didn't give a damn what she did.

'It's the old man: he tries to work me to the bone.'

'Never mind,' said George, 'leave it to me.'

In parting she lifted her dress, of her own accord, and invited us to give her a last good feel.

'Maybe I won't be so shy,' she said, 'when I get to the city.'

Then, impulsively, she reached into our flies, took out our cocks, and kissed them – almost reverently. 'I'll dream about you tonight,' she whispered. She was almost on the point of tears.

For reality in sexual autobiography – plainly expressed and stripped of charm – there is no more remarkable book than *My Secret Life*, written by the unknown Victorian Englishman who called himself 'Walter'. Printed privately in eleven volumes – of which only six complete sets have been traced – it is one of the most extraordinary social documents from that period. The author diarizes, in obsessive detail, each of his sexual encounters (more than 1,500) from youth to late middle age, a period spanning most of the Victorian era. The style is often awkward and crude, some of the incidents cruel and exploitative (nothing compared with, for example, the violent and sadistic passages which feature in the fashionable erotica of Anaïs Nin, but that is fantasy) yet *My Secret Life* has the unmistakable ring of truth about it. In this early episode in an eventful sex life Walter completes his seduction of his mother's maid, Charlotte. On her day off they go to an 'accommodation house'.

One of a series of engravings for 'Les Diaboliques' by the French artist Léon Richet.

It was a gentleman's house, although the room cost but five shillings: red curtains, looking-glasses, wax lights, clean linen, a huge chair, a large bed, and a cheval-glass, large enough for the biggest couple to be reflected in, were all there. I examined all with the greatest curiosity, but my curiosity was greater for other things; of all the delicious, voluptuous recollections, that day stands among the brightest; for the first time in my life I saw all a woman's charms, and exposed my own manhood to one; both of us knew but little of the opposite sex. With difficulty I got her to undress to her chemise, then with but my shirt on, how I revelled

One of a series of highly mannered erotic illustrations drawn in 1922 by Viennese artist Joseph Ortloff.

in her nakedness, feeling from her neck to her ankles, lingering with my fingers in every crack and cranny of her body; from armpits to cunt, all was new to me. With what fierce eyes, after modest struggles, and objections to prevent, and I had forced open her reluctant thighs, did I gloat on her cunt; wondering at its hairy outer covering and lips, its red inner flaps, at the hole so closed up, and so much lower down and hidden than I thought it to be; soon, at its look and feel, impatience got the better of me; hurriedly I covered it with my body and shed my sperm in it. Then with what curiosity I paddled my finger in it afterwards, again to stiffen, thrust, wriggle, and spend. All this I recollect as if it occurred but yesterday, I shall recollect it to the last day of my life, for it was a honey-moon of novelty; years afterwards I often thought of it when fucking other women.

We fell asleep, and must have been in the room some hours, when we awakened about three o'clock. We had eaten nothing that day, and both were hungry, she objected to wash before me, or to piddle; how charming it was to overcome that needless modesty, what a treat to me to see that simple operation. We dressed and left, went to a quietish public-house, and had some simple food and beer, which set me up, I was ready to do all over again, and so was she. We went back to the house and again to bed; the woman smiled when she saw us; the feeling, looking, titillating, baudy inciting, and kissing recommenced. With what pleasure she felt and handled my prick, nor did she make objection to my investigations into her privates, though saying she would not let me. Her thighs opened, showing the red-lipped, hairy slit; I kissed it, she kissed my cock, nature taught us both what to do. Again we fucked, I found it a longish operation, and when I tried later again, was surprised to find that it would not stiffen for more than a minute, and an insertion failed. I found out that day that there were limits to my powers. Both tired out, our day's pleasure over, we rose and took a hackney coach towards home.

Exploration of another, and the novelty of doing so for the first time, is, of course, one of the wonders of sex. But there are pitfalls for the inexperienced, and all too often in our culture the young have been left groping – both literally and metaphorically – in the dark. In the West, until comparatively recently, there was no proper information available on sex even for adults. Armed with tales from their peers, which were frequently full of absurd notions, and driven only by instinct, the young were pitched straight into the practical with little or no theoretical knowledge – often with tragic results. In matters of sex education, the Dark Ages continued until well into the twentieth century in the West. In eighth-century Japan – while Europe was still enjoying all other aspects of the Dark Ages – well produced sexual textbooks and manuals, and elegant erotic novels, were already widely available. There was also a translation of a third-century Chinese medical text book, the *Pao P'u*

In a soft box of plushy fluff,
Black, but with glints of copper-red
And edges crinkly like a ruff,
Lies the great god of gems in bed.

Throbbing with sap and life, and sends
In wafts the best news ever sent,
A perfume his ecstatic friends
Think stolen from each element.

But contemplate this temple, contemplate,
then get your breath, and kiss
The jewel having fits in front,
The ruby grinning for its bliss,

Flowers of the inner court, kid brother
So mad about the taller one
It kisses till they both hay-smother
And puff, then pulse, in unison...

FROM *ANOINTED VESSEL*
PAUL VERLAINE (1844–96)

Tzu, dealing with sex. Only towards the end of the nineteenth century was anything comparable published in the West. Nor was Havelock Ellis's monumental and long overdue *Studies in the Psychology' of Sex* greeted with enthusiasm by Victorian society, worthy and well-intentioned though it was. In Japan, the idea of sex education is not only time-honoured but it is a concept enshrined in the country's creation myths. Who could find anything objectionable or unseemly

BELOW and OPPOSITE *All three works are by the Japanese master of the coloured woodcut Utamaro Utagawa (1753–1806). The* Song of the Pillow *is considered by many to be his masterpiece.*

in sex education when every child is taught that Japan's mythical founders, Izanami and Izanaji, received instruction in lovemaking from two shepherdesses?

Given the thinness of the paper walls in the traditional Japanese house it is just as well that children learned about sex before having to draw their own conclusions. The childish interpretation of the sexual act is generally to regard it as a violent attack on the mother by the father.

Louis Morin was born in Brussels in 1851. The eroticism in his work is usually lightened by humour, as in this wonderfully idealized naval engagement.

This trauma has been used by Freudians to explain behavioural problems in some adults, notably the more morbid obsessions of poor, tormented Edgar Allan Poe who spent his formative years in the close confines of theatrical lodgings with his parents. Mercifully, Japan has been spared a succession of Edgar Allan Poe, although its literature is not without its violence and morbidity.

Lovers who are overlooked, voyeuristically, is a common theme in *shunga* – the erotic prints of Japan. The same motif is popular in Western erotica, often presented as a 'first lesson in love'.

Although watching others making love may be genuinely instructive, in erotic literature, such episodes arc generally confections designed to titillate. This lively example comes from the *Voluptuous Confessions of a French Lady of Fashion*, published in the beautifully-produced Victorian underground magazine *The Boudoir*. The heroine is watching her young aunt with her fiancé from a hiding place in the grounds of her grandmother's estate.

I applied my eye, as I held my breath, and was witness of what I am going to relate.

Bertha, hanging on the neck of Monsieur B., devoured him with kisses.

'Come,' she said, 'my darling, I was very unhappy to refuse you, but I was afraid. Here, at least, I am assured. This beautiful Mimi, what pleasure I am going to give him. Hold, I come already in thinking of it! But how shall we place ourselves?'

All right; but first let me see again my dear Bibi,

it is such a long time I have wanted her.'

You may guess what my thoughts were at this moment. But what were they going to do? I was not left long in suspense.

Monsieur B., going down on one knee, raised the skirts of Bertha. What charms he exposed! Under that fine cambric chemise were legs worthy of Venus, encased in silk stockings, secured above the knee by garters of the colour of fire; then two adorable thighs, white, round, and firm, which rejoined above, surmounted by a fleece of black and lustrous curls, the abundance and length of which were a great surprise to me, compared above all to the light chestnut moss which commenced to cover the same part in myself.

A gently satirical watercolour by the nineteenth-century Belgian artist Louis Morin.

'How I love it,' said Alfred. 'How beautiful and fresh it is! Open yourself a little, my angel, that I may kiss those adorable lips!'

Bertha did as he demanded; her thighs, in opening, made me see a rosy slit, upon which her lover glued his lips. Bertha seemed in ecstasy! Shutting her eyes, and speaking broken words; making a forward movement in response to this curious caress, which transported her so.

'Ah, you kill me... encore!... go on! It's coming... I... I.... I'm coming!... Ah, ah!'

What was she doing? Good God! I had never supposed that any pleasure pertained to that part. Yet, however, I began to feel myself in the same spot some particular titillations, which made me understand it.

Alfred got up, supporting Bertha, who appeared to have

And full her face was honey to my mouth,
And all her body pasture to mine eyes;
The long lithe arms and hotter hands than fire,
The quivering flanks, hair smelling of the south,
The bright light feet, the splendid supple thighs
And glittering eyelids of my soul's desire.

FROM *LOVE AND SLEEP*
ALGERNON CHARLES SWINBURNE (1837–1909)

An erotic postcard from the Belle Epoque.

lost all strength; but she soon recovered herself, and then embraced him with ardour.

'Come, now, let me put him in,' she said.

'But how are we going to do it?'

'Turn yourself, my dear, and incline over this unworthy seat; let me do it.'

Then, to my great surprise, Bertha, by rapid and excited movement, herself undid the trousers of Alfred, and lifting his shirt above his navel she exposed to my view such an extraordinary object, that I was almost surprised into a scream. What could be this unknown member, the head of which was so rosy and exalted, its length and thickness giving me a vertigo?

Bertha evidently did not share my fears, for she took this frightful instrument in her hand, caressed it a moment, and said: 'Let us begin, Monsieur Mimi, come into your little companion, and be sure not to go away too soon.'

She lifted up her clothes behind and exposed to the light of day two globes of dazzling whiteness, separated by a crack of which I could only see a slight trace; she then inclined herself, and, placing her hands on the wooden seat, presented her adorable bottom to her lover.

Alfred just behind her took his enormous instrument in hand, and wetting it with a little saliva commenced to introduce it between the two lips which I had perceived. Bertha did not flinch, and opened as much as possible the part which she presented, which seemed to open itself, and at length absorbed this long and thick machine, which appeared monstrous to me; however, it penetrated so well that it disappeared entirely, and the belly of its happy possessor came to be glued to the buttocks of my aunt.

There was then a conjunction of combined movements, followed by broken words – Ah!... I feel him... He is getting into me,' said Bertha. 'Push it all well into me... softly... let me come first. Ah!... I feel it... I'm coming!... Quicker! I come... stop... there you are! I die... I... I... Ah!'

As to Alfred, his eyes half closed, his hands holding the hips of my aunt, he seemed inexpressibly happy.

'Hold,' said he, 'my angel, my all, ah! How fine it is! Push well! Do come... there; it's coming, is it not! go on... go on... I feel you're coming... push well, my darling!'

A French postcard from the Belle Epoch. While some tourists preferred more explicit images, the romantic traveller could imagine himself in this idealized scene.

Both stopped a moment; my aunt appeared exhausted; but did not change her position; at length she lightly turned her head to give her lover a kiss, saying – 'Now, both together! You let me know when you are ready.'

The scene recommenced. At the end of some instants, Alfred, in turn, cried out – 'Ah!... I feel it coming... are you ready, my love? Yes... yes... there I am... push, again... go on... I spend... I am yours. I... I... Ah! What a pleasure... I... sp—... I spend!'

A long silence followed; Alfred seemed to have lost his strength, and ready to fall over Bertha, who was obliged to put her arms straight to bear him. Alfred recovered himself, and I again saw that marvellous instrument coming out of the crack, where he had been so well treated. But how changed he was. His size diminished to half, red

An unknown late nineteenth-century German artist is as cheerfully over the top as his subject.

and damp, and I saw something like a white and viscous pearl come from it and drop to the floor.

Alfred began to put his clothes in order; during which my aunt, who had got up, put her arms round the neck of her lover, and covered him with kisses. What had I been doing during this time? My imagination, excited to the highest degree, made me repeat one part of the pleasures which transported my actors.

At the critical moment I lifted petticoat and chemise, and my inexperienced hand contented itself by exploring that tender part. I thus assured myself that I was made the same as Bertha, but I knew not yet what use or consolation that hand could give. This very morning was to enlighten me.

After plenty of kissing, Bertha said to Monsieur B. – 'Listen, my dear, I have been thinking. You know that my apartment is quite isolated; without my *femme de chambre*, who sleeps in the anteroom, no one could know of our rendezvous, and we could pass some adorable nights together.

'Under a pretext of wanting something for my toilette, I will send Julie to Paris tomorrow afternoon, and after the evening we can join each other. Be on the look out, you can give me a sign during the day of the hour when you can slip away to me. I beg you to take the most minute precautions.'

It was then decided that Monsieur B. should go first. He was to take a walk out of the park, and during the time my aunt would regain her room by the private staircase. Monsieur B. went out, and I remained hidden in my brambles till he was sufficiently far off not to have any fear of being perceived by him. Observing that my aunt had not yet come out, I stopped and looked again. There was in the pavilion a chamber pot and wash basin; I saw Bertha fill the latter, lift up her petticoats, and stoop over it. She was placed right in front of me, and nothing could scape my view. As she did this her slit opened, it seemed to me a much more lively carnation, the interior and the edges, even up to the fleecy mound which surrounded it, seemed inundated with the same liquor which I had seen come from Monsieur B.

This German oil painting, together with the one opposite, takes the same journey as the saucy English seaside postcard, beyond grossness into a kind of celebratory and vulgar innocence.

Bertha commenced an ample ablution, and I was going away from my place as softly as possible when I remained fixed, glued to the spot. The hand of my aunt, refreshed with care all the parts which had been so well worked. All at once I saw her stop still, then a finger fixed upon a little eminence which showed itself prominently; this finger rubbed lightly at first, then with a kind of fury. At length Bertha gave the same symptoms of pleasure which I had often seen before.

I had seen enough of it! I understood it all! I retired and made haste to take a long tortuous path, which brought me to the chateau. My head was on fire, my bosom palpitated, and my steps tottered, but I was determined at once to play by myself the last act I had seen, and which required no partner.

I arrived in my room in a state of madness, threw my hat on the floor, shut and double locked the door, and put myself on the bed. I turned up my clothes to the waist, and, recollecting to the minutest details what Bertha had done with her hand, I placed mine between my legs. Some essays were at first fruitless, but I found at length the point I searched for. The rest was easy; I had too well observed to deceive myself. A delicious sensation seized me; I continued with fury, and soon fell into such an ecstasy that I lost consciousness.

When I came to myself I was in the same position, my hand all moistened by an unknown dew.

I sat up quite confused, and it was a long time before I entirely came to myself. It was nearly the hour of *déjeuner*, so I made haste to dress and went down.

My aunt was already in the salon with my grandmother. I looked at her on entering; she was beautiful and fresh, her colour in repose, her eyes brilliant, so that one would have sworn she had just risen from an excellent morning's sleep, her toilette, in exquisite and simple taste, set off her charming figure. As to me I cast down my eyes and felt myself blush.

The tedious male preoccupation with 'being the first' (wonderfully lampooned in the song 'She Lost Her Virginity at the Astor Club': 'they found one on a pillow, but it wasn't hers') supported a minor industry at one time. The ingenuity of prostitutes whose maidenheads could be resurrected indefinitely to please their clownish clients has a certain gruesome humour, but we will not dwell too long on the

OPPOSITE *An eighteenth-century coloured etching.*

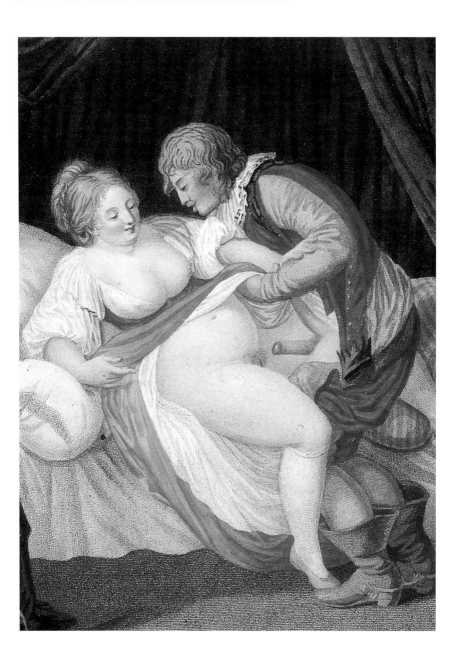

Artists employed to illustrate
the erotica of the Enlightenment
often went far beyond their texts,
employing a formidable armoury of
technical and psychological effects
to make the image as powerful
as possible. The young woman
here has not only been 'discovered',
but her solitary pleasure is also
conveniently lit by the candle
of her discoverer.

subject of deflowering. Octavia describes her initiation in one of the most famous erotic books of all time, Nicolas Chorier's *Satyra Sotadicu*, which appeared in numerous versions in many different languages from 1660 onwards. The vigour of the writing is typical of the seven dialogues between Octavia and her sexually experienced aunt Tullia.

Cavieco came on, blithe and joyous... He despoils me of my chemise, and his libertine hand touches my parts. He tells me to sit down again as I was seated before, and places a chair under either foot in such a way that my legs were lifted high in air, and the gate of my garden was wide open to the assaults I was expecting. He then slides his right hand under my buttocks and draws me a little closer to him. With his left he supported the weight of his spear. Then he laid himself down on me... put his battering-ram to my gate, inserted the head of his member into the outermost fissure, opening the lips of it with his fingers. But there he stopped, and for a while made no further attack. 'Octavia sweetest', he says, 'clasp me tightly, raise your right thigh and rest it on my side.' – 'I do not know what you want', I said. Hearing this he lifted my thigh with his own hand, and guided it round his loin, as he wished; finally he forced his arrow into the target of Venus. In the beginning he pushes in with gentle blows, then quicker, and at last with such force I could not doubt that I was in great danger. His member was hard as horn, and he forced it in so cruelly, that I cried out, 'You will tear me to pieces!' He stopped a moment from his work. 'I implore you to be quiet, my dear', he said, 'it can only be done this way; endure it without flinching'. Again his hand slid under my buttocks, drawing me nearer, for I had made a feint to draw back, and without more delay plied me with such fast and furious blows that I was near fainting away. With a violent effort he forced his spear right in, and the point fixed itself in the depths of the wound. I cry out... Cavieco spurted out his venerean exudation, and I felt irrigated by a burning rain... Just as Cavieco slackened, I experienced a sort of voluptuous itch as though I were making water; involuntarily I draw my buttocks back a little, and in an instant I felt with supreme pleasure something flowing from me which tickled me deliciously. My eyes failed me, my breath came thick, my face was on fire, and I felt my whole body melting. 'Ah! ah! ah! my Caviceo, I shall faint away', I cried; 'hold my soul – it is escaping from my body!'

The print entitled The Curious Wanton *by Thomas Rowlandson (1756–1827). Although erotic subjects formed only a small part of his output, many are unforgettable images offering us his own uniquely ribald insights into the sexual manners of Regency England.*

Seduction, not unexpectedly, is a recurring theme in erotic literature. For the real-life erotomane ('Walter' or Casanova) who dedicates most of his time and energy to sex, it is variety which is important: not so much variety in love-making, which is of more interest and relevance to the monogamous, but an endless variety of 'conquests'. Unable to sustain more than a shallow and inevitably unsatisfactory relationship, they move rapidly from one partner to another. There is, of course, an underlying homosexuality about these serial lovers, both men and women. The saying that 'a man who cannot find what he wants in a thousand women is looking for a man' is very perceptive; it is interesting how many of Casanova's sexual exploits involve

ABOVE *An etching by the German artist M. E. Phillipp.*

OPPOSITE *An unknown nineteenth-century artist (possibly Zichy or Charles de Beaumont) tries out some ideas for a study of fellatio. The vigour of the drawing and keenness of observation suggest that this – like Turner's erotic sketches tragically destroyed by Ruskin – may have been sketched from life.*

women who are dressed as men. Such careers tend not to have happy endings. The ageing Casanova, librarian to Count Waldstein in Dux, Bohemia, alone in the draughty room writing his famous *Memoirs*, is a rather pathetic figure. He never completed the work, but the *Memoirs* are a clever, apparently truthful account of his extraordinary life and times. Here he recalls one of his more imaginative seductions, where a theological debate with two girls is quickly turned to his advantage. Hedwig, though quick intellectually, is not familiar with the word 'erection'.

'What is that?'

'Give me your hand.'

'I feel it, and it is as I had imagined it would be; for without this phenomenon of nature man could not impregnate his spouse. And that fool of a theologian maintains that it is an imperfection!'

'Yes, for the phenomenon arises from desire; witness the fact that it would not have taken place in me, beautiful Hedwig, if I had not found you charming, and if what I see of you did not give me the most seductive idea of the beauties I do not see. Tell me frankly if, on your side, feeling this stiffness does not cause you a pleasant excitation?'

'I admit it, and precisely in the place you are pressing. Do not you, my dear Helena, feel as I do a certain itching here while you listen to the very sound discourse to which Monsieur is treating us?'

'Yes, I feel it, but I feel it very often where there is no discourse to excite it.'

'And then,' I said, 'does not Nature oblige you to relieve it in this fashion?'

'Certainly not.'

An untypically cheerful portrayal of the Devil by the Belgian etcher Félicien Rops. Rops lived and worked in France and belonged to the French school. For the Decadents, among whom Rops was a powerful force, Satan symbolized the ultimate freedom from convention. Rops was a brilliant artist, his work much in demand. Ironically it was neither absinthe nor syphilis that killed him in 1898 but that most bourgeois of all angels of death – overwork.

'But it does!' said Hedwig. 'Even in sleep our hand goes there instinctively; and without that relief, I have read, we should be subject to terrible maladies.'

Continuing this philosophical discussion, which the young theologian sustained in a masterly manner and which gave her cousin's beautiful complexion all the animation of voluptuous feeling, we arrived at the edge of a superb basin of water with a flight of marble stairs down which one went to bathe. Though it was chilly our heads were heated, and it occurred to me to ask them to dip their feet in the water, assuring them that it would do them good and that, if they would permit me, I would have the honor of taking off their shoes and stockings.

'Why not?' said the niece. 'I'd like it.'

'So should I,' said Helena.

'Then sit down, ladies, on the top step.' And they sit, and I, placing myself on the fourth step below, fall to taking off their shoes and stockings, praising the beauty of their legs, and for the moment showing no interest in seeing anything above the knee. I took them down to the water, and then there was nothing for it but that they should pull up their dresses, and I encouraged them to do so.

'Well,' said Hedwig, 'men have thighs too.'

Helena, who would have been ashamed to show less courage than her cousin, was not slow to follow her example.

'Come, my charming Naiads,' I said, 'that is enough; you might catch cold if you stay in the water longer.'

They came up the stairs backward, still holding up their skirts for fear of wetting them; and it was

my part to dry them with all the handkerchiefs I
had. This agreeable office allowed me to see and to
touch in perfect freedom, and the reader will not
need to have me swear that I made the most of the
opportunity. The beautiful niece told me that I was
too curious, but Helena accepted my ministrations
in a manner so tender and languishing that I had
to use all my will to keep from going further.
Finally, when I had put on their shoes and stockings, I said that I was in raptures at having seen
the secret beauties of the two most beautiful girls
in Geneva.

'What effect did it have on you?' Hedwig asked
me.

'I do not dare tell you to look; but feel, both of
you.'

'You must bathe too.'

'That is impossible, getting ready takes a man
too long.'

'But we still have two full hours to stay here with
no fear of anyone coming to join us.'

Her answer made me see all the good fortune
which awaited me; but I did not choose to expose
myself to an illness by entering the water in the
state I was in. Seeing a garden house a short distance away and certain that Monsieur Tronchin
would have left it unlocked, I took them there, not
letting them guess my intention.

The garden house was full of pot-pourri jars,
charming engravings, and so on; but what was best
of all was a fine, large couch ready for repose and
pleasure. Sitting on it between the two 'beauties
and lavishing caresses on them, I told them
I wanted to show them what they had never seen,
and, so saying, I exposed to their gaze the principal

*The ingenuity of this disgraceful
pair is matched only by that of the
engraver who manages to combine
a strong anti-clerical statement
with both humour and eroticism.*

*Much of eighteenth-century French
erotica was strongly anti-clerical in
tone. Authors, who were fired
with the new materialism of the
Enlightenment scattered their
novels liberally with lecherous
monks and debauched ecclesiastics.*

effective cause of humanity. They stood up to admire me; whereupon, taking them each by one hand, I gave them a factitious consummation; but in the course of my labors an abundant emission of liquid threw them into the greatest astonishment.

'It is the word,' I said, 'the great creator of mankind.'

'How delicious!' cried Helena, laughing at the designation 'word'.

'But I too,' said Hedwig, 'have the word, and I will show it to you if you will wait a moment.'

'Sit on my lap, beautiful Hedwig, and I will save you the trouble of making it come yourself, and I will do it better than you can.'

'I believe you, but I have never done it with a man.'

'Nor have I,' said Helena.

Having made them stand in front of me with their arms around me I made them faint again. Then we all sat down, and, while I explored their charms with my hands, I let them amuse themselves by touching me as they pleased, until I finally wet their hands with a second emission of the humid radical, which they curiously examined on their fingers.

After restoring ourselves to a state of decency, we spent another half hour exchanging kisses, then I told them they had made me half happy, but that to bring their work to completion I hoped they would think of a way to grant me their first favors. I then showed them the little protective bags which the English invented to free the fair sex from all fear. These little purses, whose use I explained to them,

With only himself to blame, Cupid's interruption of the proceedings in this wonderful photogravure print seems less than fair to the adventurous lovers.

aroused their admiration, and the beautiful theologian told her cousin that she would think about. Become intimate friends and well on the way to becoming something more, we made our way toward the house, where we found the pastor and Helena's mother strolling beside the lake.

To examine another aspect of sexual beginnings, we need to look at a literary form with a long pedigree including St Augustine and Jean-Jacques Rousseau. The confession, true or otherwise, is a natural vehicle for conveying erotic ideas because even those that are spurious often have an air of salacious intimacy about them. The anti-clerical erotica of the seventeenth and eighteenth centuries made use of the confession, straining the credulity of the reader, but this is mainly unpleasant stuff and will not be included. More interesting are the musings of the real-life

ABOVE and BELOW *These drawings were the creation of a pneumatic age: Zeppelin founded his factory at Friedrichshafen in the same year of 1900. The world had to wait more than a decade for Freud's 'Passing of the Oedipus Complex' and nearer seventy years for Beryl Cook.*

A study in erotic languor by
M. E. Phillipp, a German artist
much influenced by Beardsley
and the Decadents. Though most
did not themselves live to see it,
the world of the Old Europe the
Decadents so hated was about to
end. This etching w;is completed
just before the First World War.

*Give me chastity and
constancy, but not yet.*

FROM *CONFESSIONS*
ST AUGUSTINE
(354–430 AD)

'Walter' in the Prefaces to his extraordinary confession. The matter-of-fact tone displays honesty.

PREFACE

I began these memoirs when about twenty-five
years old, having from youth kept a diary of some
sort, which perhaps from habit made me think of
recording my inner and secret life.

When I began it, had scarcely read a baudy
book, none of which, excepting *Fanny Hill*,
appeared to me to be truthful: that did, and it does
so still; the others telling of récherché eroticisms
or of inordinate copulative powers, of the strange
twists, tricks, and fancies of matured voluptuousness and philosophical lewd frankness, seemed to
my comparative ignorance as baudy imaginings or
lying inventions, not worthy of belief; although
I now know, by experience, that they may be true
enough, however eccentric and improbable, they
may appear to the uninitiated.

Fanny Hill's was a woman's experience. Written
perhaps by a woman, where was a man's written
with equal truth? That book has no baudy word in
it; but baudy acts need the baudy ejaculations; the
erotic, full-flavored expressions, which even the
chastest indulge in when lust, or love, is in its full
tide of performance. So I determined to write my
private life freely as to fact, and in the spirit of the
lustful acts done by me, or witnessed; it is written
therefore with absolute truth and without any
regard whatever for what the world calls decency.
Decency and voluptuousness in its fullest acceptance
cannot exist together, one would kill the other; the
poetry of copulation I have only experienced with
a few women, which however neither prevented

them nor me from calling a spade a spade...

I had from youth an excellent memory, but about sexual matters a wonderful one. Women were the pleasure of my life. I loved cunt, but also who had it; I like the woman I fucked and not simply the cunt I fucked, and therein is a great difference. I recollect even now in a degree which astonishes me, the face, colour, stature, thighs, backside, and cunt, of well nigh every woman I have had, who was not a mere casual, and even of some who were. The clothes they wore, the houses and rooms in which I had them, were before me mentally as I wrote, the way the bed and furniture were placed, the side of the room the windows were on, I remembered perfectly; and all the important events I can fix as to time, sufficiently nearly by reference to my diary, in which the contemporaneous circumstances of my life are recorded.

I recollect also largely what we said and did, and generally our baudy amusements. Where I fail to have done so, I have left description blank, rather than attempt to make a story coherent by inserting what was merely probable. I could not now account for my course of action, or why I did this, or said that, my conduct seems strange, foolish, absurd, very frequently, that of some women equally so, but I can but state what did occur...

... this is intended to be a true history, and not a lie.

Intimate cosmetic articles, such as these combs, lend themselves to erotic decoration. Every time he combed his beard, the owner of these exquisite nineteenth-century ivory carvings was pleasantly reminded of the true purpose of grooming.

SECOND PREFACE

Some years have passed away since I penned the foregoing, and it is not printed... The manuscript has grown into unmanageable bulk; shall it, can it, be printed? What will be said or thought of me, what became of the manuscript if found when I am dead? Better to destroy the whole, it has fulfilled its purpose in amusing me, now let it go to the flames!

I have read my manuscript through; what reminiscences! I had actually forgotten some of the early ones; how true the detail strikes me as I read of my early experiences; had it not been written then it never could have been written now; has anybody but myself faithfully made such a record? It would be a sin to burn all this, whatever society may say, it is but a narrative of human life, perhaps the every day life of thousands, if the confession could be had...

Shall it be burnt or printed? How many years have passed in this indecision? why fear? it is for others' good and not my own if preserved.

An eighteenth-century French miniature painted on ivory, entitled Young Woman Asleep.

CHAPTER TWO

The Refinements of Passion

It was a night of sensual passion, in which she was a little startled and almost unwilling: yet pierced again with piercing thrills of sensuality, different, sharper, more terrible than the thrills of tenderness, but, at the moment, more desirable. Though a little frightened, she let him have his way, and the reckless, shameless sensuality shook her to her foundations, stripped her to the very last, and made a different woman of her. It was not really love. It was not voluptuousness. It was sensuality sharp and searing as fire, burning the soul to tinder.

Stone lovers from the Lakshmana Temple in Khajuraho, India, built in the tenth century CE.

Burning out the shames, the deepest, oldest shames, in the most secret places. It cost her an effort to let him have his way and his will of her. She had to be a passive, consenting thing, like a slave, a physical slave. Yet the passion licked round her, consuming, and when the sensual flame of it pressed through her bowels and breast, she really thought she was dying: yet a poignant, marvellous death.

She had often wondered what Abelard meant, when he said that in their year of love he and Heloise had passed through all the stages and refinements of passion. The same thing, a thousand years ago: ten thousand years ago! The same on the Greek vases, everywhere! The refinements of passion, the extravagances of sensuality!

From *Lady Chatterley's Lover* D. H. LAWRENCE

ALCIBIADE
ET GLYCERE.

*When Pope Clement VII
(1478–1534) was late in paying
an artist he unwittingly founded an
erotic industry. The artist, Giulio
Romano, allegedly retaliated by
drawing a series of explicit sexual
postures on the Vatican wall.
Legend has it that these were
then copied by Marcantonio
and described by Aretino. Artists
such as this sixteenth-century
engraver were to produce their
own versions of 'the postures'
for the next 300 years.*

In this extract, while reflecting on the nature of erotic love during her post-coital 'high', Connie seizes upon the medieval lovers Abelard and Héloïse to express her sense of timelessness and of identification with all the lovers of the past. In fact, there are other similarities between the experiences of the medieval lovers, which are expressed in their fascinating letters, and those of Lady Chatterley and her gamekeeper. It is just as well she kept her private thoughts from the unlettered Mellors, however, since he might have had a sleepless night. Peter Abelard (1079–1142) was a theologian who fell in love with his young pupil Héloïse. They had a child and married, which so infuriated her guardian that he had Abelard castrated. Following this disaster he became a monk, she a nun – the letters they later exchanged are among the jewels of European literature.

The conflict between sacred and 'profane' love is a Judaeo-Christian creation. In Hinduism, by way of contrast, sex is not regarded as tainted or disgraceful: in an everyday sense it is a pleasure to be enjoyed guiltlessly; theologically, the love-making of the God and Goddess, Shiva and Parvati, is the perfect expression of unity. In medieval India (and today in the subcontinent) male sexual organs – the lingam of Shiva – were worshipped; in medieval Europe, by contrast, they ran the risk of being cut off if they stepped out of line.

Christian theology recognizes that sacred and profane love come from the same spring – a nun is a 'bride of Christ' – but profane love must be transmuted, a process given expression in the figure of Mary Magdalene. This transmutation is not always perfect, however, and there are ambiguities. In describing her religious ecstasy St Theresa wrote that an angel bearing a long burning spear with a fiery tip 'plunged it into my deepest innards. When he drew it out, I thought my entrails would have been drawn out too, and when he left me I glowed in the hot fire of love for God. The pain was so strong, and the sweetness thereof was so passing great, that no one could ever wish to lose it.' Bernini's famous sculpture of her in the Church of Santa Maria della Vittoria in Rome captures the moment she describes (and its ambiguity) perfectly. This is an old chestnut, and one occasionally pulled out of the fire by art historians. Is the expression Bernini gives her the ecstasy of sacred or of profane love? 'Perhaps they look the same,' you may say. Perhaps they are the same.

A drawing by the Austrian artist A l.

Most Eastern religions avoid the painful riddle of sacred and profane love by regarding them as either the same, or aspects of the same phenomenon. Ikkyu was a Zen monk who achieved enlightenment at the age of twenty-six – there is a tradition that he was the illegitimate son of the Japanese emperor Gokomatsu. After the death of his spiritual mentor in 1428 Ikkyu began a life of wandering through a country experiencing the turmoil of civil war. For nearly half a century he devoted his considerable energies to Zen Buddhism and wine, women and song – in about equal measure.

Ikkyu's *Kyounshu*, a collection of poems written in Chinese, is among Japan's greatest works

Japanese coloured woodcuts from the 1830s, known as Ukiyo-e or 'pictures of the floating world'.

of literature. Much of his work was love poetry and many of these exquisite poems were written for Mori, the blind servant who became the greatest love of his life. It was a rather unconventional view, but for Ikkyu erotic passion and Zen were one and the same thing. The following four different examples will illustrate what we mean by this.

Whispers, bashfulness and a pledge
We sing of love and make promises for three lives
*   to come*
We may fall to the way of beasts while still alive
But I shall surpass in passion the horned abbot
*   of Kuei.*

Blind Mori night after night sings with me
Under the covers, like mandarin ducks,
*   new intimate talk*
Making promises to be together till the dawning
*   of Maitreya's salvation*
At the home of this old buddha all is spring.

Rinzai's disciples don't understand Zen,
The truth was passed down to this blind donkey.
Making love for three lifetimes, ten aeons;
One night's autumn breeze a thousand centuries.

An Indian miniature from
Rajasthan.

Dream-wandering in the garden of beautiful Mori,
A plum blossom in the bed, faith at the heart of
*   the flower.*
My mouth is filled with the pure fragrance of that
*   shallow stream*
Dusk and the shades of the moon as we make our
*   new song.*

Passionate love is one of the strongest emotions: it can move mountains and force kings into exile. The earth itself can move if Hemingway is to be believed (but who can feel the same about him after Gertrude Stein's savage put-down, 'false hair on the chest!'). If a Streetcar Named Desire hits you, what can be done? As always, the Hindu love manuals offer advice. Kalyana Malla wrote *Ananga-Ranga* a thousand years after *Kama Sutra*, although Vatsyayana's work is still quoted.

But there are ten changes in the natural state of men, which require to be taken into consideration. Firstly, when he is in a state of Dhyasa at a loss

to do anything except to see a particular woman; secondly, when he finds his mind wandering, as if he were about to lose his senses; thirdly, when he is ever losing himself in thought how to woo and win the woman in question; fourthly, when he passes restless nights without the refreshment of sleep; fifthly, when his looks become haggard and his body emaciated; sixthly, when he feels himself growing shameless and departing from all sense of decency and decorum; seventhly, when his riches take to themselves wings and fly; eighthly, when the state of mental intoxication verges upon madness; ninethly, when tainting fits come on; and tenthly, when he finds himself at the door of death.

That these states are produced by sexual passion may be illustrated by an instance borrowed from the history of bygone days. Once upon a time there was a king called Pururava, who was a devout man, and who entered upon such a course of mortification and austerities that Indra, Lord of the Lower Heaven, began to fear lest he himself might be dethroned. The god, therefore, in order to interrupt these penances and other religious acts, sent down from Svarga, his own heaven, Urvashi, the most lovely of the Apsaras (nymphs). The king no sooner saw her than he fell in love with her, thinking day and night of nothing but possessing her, till at last succeeding in his subject, both spent a long time in the pleasure of carnal connection. Presently Indra, happening to remember the Apsara, dispatched his messenger, one of the Gandharvas (heavenly minstrels), to the world of mortals, and recalled her. Immediately after her departure, the mind of Pururava began to wander; he could no longer concentrate his thoughts upon

While medieval stone carvers and woodcarvers in the West hid their erotic jokes in dark corners of Gothic cathedrals, the temple carts of India celebrated human sexuality in all its moods and paraded it in the sunshine.

OPPOSITE *The favourite of a maharaja, painted in the late nineteenth century.*

*Dust of dead flowers,
O tigress, has been spilled
smoothly on the body of
your breasts. It is a task
to praise your breasts,
for their lips are gilded like
the sun and red like sunset.*

FROM THE *SANSKRIT*
MAYURA, C. 800 AD

worship and he felt upon the point of death.

See, then, the state to which that king was reduced by thinking so much about Urvashi! When a man has allowed himself to be carried away captive of desire, he must consult a physician, and the books of medicine which treat upon the subject. And, if he come to the conclusion that unless he enjoy his neighbour's wife he will surely die, he should, for the sake of preserving his life, possess her once and once only. If, however, there be no such peremptory cause, he is by no means justified in enjoying the wife of another person, merely for the sake of pleasure and wanton gratification.

Moreover, the book of Vatsyayana, the Rishi, teaches us as follows: suppose that a woman, having reached the lusty vigour of her age, happen to become so inflamed with love for a man, and so heated by passion that she feels herself falling into the ten states before described, and likely to end in death attended with phrenzy, if her beloved refuse her sexual commerce. Under these circumstances, the man, after allowing himself to lie importuned for a time, should reflect that his refusal will cost her life; he should, therefore, enjoy her on one occasion, but not always.

*A twentieth-century oil painting
on canvas which was executed
by an unknown artist.*

Is passionate love a flower which is more likely to flourish in the gardens of others? There does seem to be a prevailing wind which often carries the seeds in that direction. In his wonderful poem, Lone Gentleman, the Chilean poet Pablo Neruda is uncompromising on the subject.

Young homosexuals and girls in love,
and widows gone to seed, sleepless, delirious,
and novice housewives pregnant some thirty hours,
the hoarse cats cruising across my garden's shadows
like a necklace of throbbing, sexual oysters
surround my solitary home
like enemies entrenched against my soul,
like conspirators in pyjamas
exchanging long, thick kisses on the sly.

A charcoal drawing by the Viennese illustrator A I.

The radiant summer entices lovers here
in melancholic regiments
made up of fat and flabby, gay and mournful
*   couples:*
under the graceful palm trees, along the moonlit beach,
there is a continual excitement of trousers and
*   petticoats,*
the crisp sound of stockings caressed,
women's breasts shining like eyes.

It's quite clear that the local clerk, bored to the hilt,
after his weekday tedium, cheap paperbacks in bed,
*   has managed to make his neighbour*
and he takes her to the miserable flea-pits
where the heroes are young stallions or passionate
*   princes:*
he caresses her legs downy with soft hair
with his wet, hot hands smelling of cigarillos.

Johannes Martini produced this
series of remarkable charcoal
drawings in Germany in 1915.
He seems to have used models
for the studies, but may have
worked from photographs.

Seducer's afternoons and strictly legal nights
fold together like a pair of sheets, burying me:
the siesta hours when young male and female
*   students*
as well as priests retire to masturbate,
and when animals screw outright,
and bees smell of blood and furious flies buzz,
and cousins play kinkily with their girl cousins,
and doctors glare angrily at their young patient's
*   husband*
and the professor, almost unconsciously, during the
*   morning hours,*
copes with his marital duties and then has break-
*   fast,*
and, later on, the adulterers who love each other
*   with real love,*
on beds as high and spacious as sea-going ships –
so for sure and for ever this great forest surrounds
*   me,*
breathing through flowers large as mouths chock
*   full of teeth,*
black-rooted in the shapes of hoofs and shoes.

Sexual passion is not controllable – it rules us.
It is no respecter of consequences, which is
why it is so often tragic and the stuff of which
great poetry is made. Thrones fall down like
ninepins before it: we will pay any price, however high. In Tennyson's magnificent retelling of
the Arthurian legend, *Idylls of the King*, we see
how the whole machinery of Courtly Love, specifically designed to contain passion, is in fact
destroyed by it. Sir Launcelot sacrifices honour
and friendship, Queen Guinevere loses her husband and her freedom. Arthur's tragedy is not

only the loss of his kingdom (and ultimately his life), but the fact that he still loves Guinevere. For us, of course, myths always embody truth. Saying his last farewell to Guinevere at the convent, the Queen's head bowed so that her long golden hair conceals her face, he whispers under his breath: 'Let no man dream but that I love thee still.'

Far away from Camelot, in their own Garden of Eden in Nottinghamshire, Lady Chatterley and Mellors have their first encounter with passion, or he does. Afterwards she admits to herself that she 'had not been conscious of much' while for Mellors it was 'the old connecting passion'.

An oil painting by the German artist Paul Paede who was born in Berlin in 1868 and died in Munich in 1929.

Connie crouched in front of the last coop. The three chicks had run in. But still their cheeky heads came poking sharply through the yellow feathers, then withdrawing, then only one beady little head eyeing forth from the vast mother-body.

'I'd love to touch them,' she said, putting her fingers gingerly through the bars of the coop. But the mother-hen pecked at her hand fiercely, and Connie drew back startled and frightened.

'How she pecks at me! She hates me!' she said in a wondering voice. 'But I wouldn't hurt them!'

The man standing above her laughed, and crouched down beside her, knees apart, and put his hand with quiet confidence slowly into the coop. The old hen pecked at him, but not so savagely. And slowly softly, with sure gentle fingers, he felt among the old bird's feathers and drew out a faintly-peeping chick in his closed hand.

'There!' he said, holding out his hand to her. She took the little drab thing between her hands, and

It's what the world would call very improper. But you know it's not really improper – I always labour at the same thing, to make the sex relation valid and precious, instead of shameful. And this novel is the furthest I've gone. To me it is beautiful and tender and frail as the naked self is.

ON
LADY CHATTERLEY'S LOVER
D. H. LAWRENCE
(1885–1930)

Listen, the darkness rings
As it circulates round our fire,
Take off your things.

Your shoulders, your bruised throat!
Your breasts, your nakedness!
This fiery coat!

As the darkness flickers and dips,
As the firelight falls and leaps
From your feet to your lips!

FROM *NEW YEAR'S EVE*
D. H. LAWRENCE

Charcoal drawing by the Viennese
artist known as 'A I'.

there it stood, on its impossible little stalks of legs, its atom of balancing life trembling through its almost weightless feet into Connie's hands. But it lifted its handsome, clean-shaped little head boldly, and looked sharply round, and gave a little 'peep'. 'So adorable! So cheeky!' she said softly.

The keeper, squatting beside her, was also watching with an amused face the bold little bird in her hands. Suddenly he saw a tear fall on to her wrist.

And he stood up. and stood away, moving to the other coop. For suddenly he was aware of the old flame shooting and leaping up in his loins, that he had hoped was quiescent for ever. He fought against it, turning his back to her. But it leapt, and leapt downwards, circling in his knees.

He turned again to look at her. She was kneeling and holding her two hands slowly forward, blindly, so that the chicken should run in to the mother-hen again. And there was something so mute and forlorn in her, compassion flamed in his bowels for her.

Without knowing, he came quickly towards her and crouched beside her again, taking the chick from her hands, because she was afraid of the hen, and putting it back in the coop. At the back of his loins the fire suddenly darted stronger.

He glanced apprehensively at her. Her face was averted, and she was crying blindly, in all the anguish of her generation's forlornness. His heart melted suddenly, like a drop of fire, and he put out his hand and laid his fingers on her knee.

'You shouldn't cry,' he said softly.

But then she put her hands over her face and felt

that really her heart was broken and nothing mattered any more.

He laid his hand on her shoulder, and softly, gently, it began to travel down the curve of her back, blindly, with a blind stroking motion, to the curve of her crouching loins. And there his hand softly, softly, stroked the curve of her flank, in the blind instinctive caress.

She had found her scrap of handkerchief and was blindly trying to dry her face.

'Shall you come to the hut?' he said, in a quiet, neutral voice.

And closing his hand softly on her upper arm, he drew her up and led her slowly to the hut, not letting go of her till she was inside. Then he cleared aside the chair and table, and took a brown soldier's blanket from the tool chest, spreading it slowly. She glanced at his face, as she stood motionless.

His face was pale and without expression, like that of a man submitting to fate.

'You lie there,' he said softly, and he shut the door, so that it was dark, quite dark.

With a queer obedience, she lay down on the blanket. Then she felt the soft, groping, helplessly desirous hand touching her body, feeling for her face. The hand stroked her face softly, softly, with infinite soothing and assurance, and at last there was the soft touch of a kiss on her cheek.

She lay quite still, in a sort of sleep, in a sort of dream. Then she quivered as she felt his hand groping softly, yet with queer thwarted clumsiness, among her clothing. Yet the hand knew, too, how to unclothe her where it wanted. He drew down the thin silk sheath, slowly, carefully, right down

Portrait of a young woman by an unknown artist, oil on canvas, Austria, c. 1930.

Illustrations from an eighteenth-century French erotic novel. These were widely read throughout Europe, although in England translations were usually available soon after publication.

and over her feet. Then with a quiver of exquisite pleasure he touched the warm soft body, and touched her navel for a moment in a kiss. And he had to come in to her at once, to enter the peace on earth of her soft, quiescent body. It was the moment of pure peace for him, the entry into the body of the woman.

She lay still, in a kind of sleep, always in a kind of sleep. The activity, the orgasm was his, all his; she could strive for herself no more. Even the tightness of his arms round her, even the intense movement of his body, and the springing of his seed in her, was a kind of sleep, from which she did not begin to rouse till he had finished and lay softly panting against her breast.

Then she wondered, just dimly wondered, why? Why was this necessary? Why had it lifted a great cloud from her and given her peace? Was it real? Was it real?

Her tormented modern-woman's brain still had no rest. Was it real? And she knew, if she gave herself to the man, it was real. But if she kept herself for herself, it was nothing. She was old; millions of years old, she felt. And at last, she could bear the burden of herself no more. She was to be had for the taking. To be had for the taking.

The man lay in a mysterious stillness. What was he feeling? What was he thinking? She did not know. He was a strange man to her, she did not know him. She must only wait, for she did not dare to break his mysterious stillness. He lay there with his arms round her, his body on hers, his wet body touching hers, so close. And completely unknown. Yet not unpeaceful. His very stillness was peaceful.

She knew that, when at last he roused and drew away from her. It was like an abandonment. He drew her dress in the darkness down over her knees and stood a few moments apparently adjusting his own clothing. Then he quietly opened the door and went out.

She saw a very brilliant little moon shining above the afterglow over the oaks. Quickly she got up and arranged herself; she was tidy. Then she went to the door of the hut.

All the lower wood was in shadow, almost darkness. Yet the sky overhead was crystal. But it shed hardly any light. He came through the lower shadow towards her, his face lifted like a pale blotch.

'Shall we go then?' he said.

'Where?'

'I'll go with you to the gate.'

He arranged things his own way. He locked the door of the hut and came after her.

'You aren't sorry, are you?' he asked, as he went at her side.

'No! No! Are you?' she said.

'For that! No!' he said. Then after a while he added: 'But there's the rest of things.'

'What rest of things?' she said.

'Sir Clifford. Other folks. All the complications.'

'Why complications?' she said, disappointed.

'It's always so. For you as well as for me. There's always complications.' He walked on steadily in the dark.

'And are you sorry?' she said.

An eighteenth-century engraving after the series Loves of the Gods by Agostino Carracci.

The drama of chiaroscuro, the effect of light and shade, is used to heighten the eroticism of this remarkable anonymous oil painting.

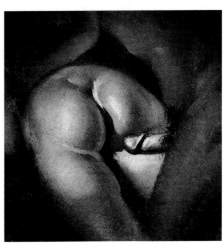

An anonymous French etching.

'In a way!' he replied, looking up at the sky. 'I thought I'd done with it all. Now I've begun again.'

'Begun what?'

'Life.'

'Life!' she re-echoed, with a queer thrill.

Recognition of her passion for Mellors, her husband's gamekeeper, comes later and suddenly to Lady Chatterley:

Ah, too lovely, too lovely! In the ebbing she realized all the loveliness. Now all her body clung with tender love to the unknown man, and blindly to the wilting penis, as it so tenderly, frailly, unknowingly withdrew, after the fierce thrust of its potency. As it drew out and left her body, the secret, sensitive thing, she gave an unconscious cry of pure loss, and she tried to put it back. It had been so perfect! And she loved it so!

And only now she became aware of the small, bud-like reticence and tenderness of the penis, and a little cry of wonder and poignancy escaped her again, her woman's heart crying out over the tender frailty of that which had been the power.

'It was so lovely!' she moaned. 'It was so lovely!' but he said nothing, only softly kissed her, lying still above her. And she moaned with a sort of bliss, as a sacrifice, and a newborn thing.

One-sided passion, or detachment on the part of one of the protagonists, makes for unsatisfactory erotic writing. This exuberant piece from *The Boudoir*, which makes no claim for authenticity and is pure Victorian melodrama, was written to excite the reader's erotic imagination: this is a kind of writing which is in itself a sexual act.

An anonymous etching made in Paris in the 1920s.

We were in a small reception room that served as my boudoir. F., who understood me, went out and waited for me in the big drawing room, whither I rejoined him, with an odd volume in my hand.

In an instant, he declared his passion. What he said – what I answered, I know not. I remember nothing.

I led him towards the hall, for fear we should be overheard. There was a double door between the drawing room and a little vestibule, where I could hear a servant. As we reached there, Monsieur F., beside himself, seized me in his arms, and a lingering kiss, a kiss of fire, a kiss that responded to my soul, arrested a shriek that I should not have been able to stifle.

At the same time, his prompt hand had lifted my petticoats, and was scientifically caressing my burning slit, that quick as lightning poured out upon his fingers palpable traces of the spendings that filled it to overflowing.

'Begone, … begone! … away,' I said, with stifled accents, 'do… To-morrow… three o'clock'; and I fled in a state which I cannot describe.

Happily, the lady who was waiting was not very clever, and did not notice my disordered state.

I shall not undertake to narrate my feelings till the next day. All that I can remember is, that I firmly resolved to satisfy my erotic longings.

My husband intended to absent himself for two or three days, and I arranged so as to send my servants on different errands. I dressed myself carefully and waited.

An illustration from Les Diaboliques (The Possessed), a savage satire on the foibles and sexual habits of French Second Empire society.

OPPOSITE One of a series of charming watercolours by the Belgian artist Louis Morin.

My dear F. arrived. I opened the door to him myself, and led him to my boudoir.

We sat down, much embarrassed. He was very respectful and asked my pardon for what he had done the day before, saying that he was unable to master the delirious rage that had seized him, and that his love for me was such that he would die if he was unable to enjoy me.

I knew not how to answer. Both our hearts were too full. He took my hand and kissed it. Shuddering, I rose. Our mouths met. I confess I made no more attempts at resistance. I had not the strength to do so.

I fully enjoyed this intense happiness. I felt that he was carrying me along – but to where? What were we to do? In my boudoir there were only a very narrow low sofa, some armchairs, and ordinary seats without arms.

F., still holding me in his arms, sat on a chair, so that I found myself in front of him, leaning over his head and face. I felt one of his arms loose my waist; soon my clothes were all up in front, and F. tried to pass his knees between my legs.

'Oh, no,' said I, between two sobs. 'No, ... I pray you, have pity.'

F. made efforts to pull me down, so as to straddle across him; but on instinctive feeling, although I longed for it, I still resisted, and stiffened myself against him. We soon became exhausted. At last, having dropped my eyes a little, I saw something that put an end to the struggle.

F. had taken out his instrument for the fray. Its ruby, haughty head stood up proudly. In length and thickness really uncommon, it vied even with that of Monsieur B. I had no strength to resist such

ABOVE and BELOW *In the preface to* Les Diaboliques, *published in 1873, the novel from which these illustrations are taken, the author explains the Decadent credo with heavy irony: '… real stories of this era of progress, of this civilization of ours which is so delicious and so divine that when one tries to write about it the Devil always seems to be dictating!'*

a sight; my thighs opened by themselves. I slid down hiding my face on my lover's shoulder, and I gave myself up to him, opening myself as much as possible, desiring, and yet fearing the entrance of such a handsome guest.

I soon felt the head between the lips of my grotto, that the thin tool of my husband had not accustomed to such a bountiful measure. I made a movement to help him, and had hardly introduced the point, when I felt myself flooded by a flaming jet of loving liquor that covered thighs and belly.

The prolonged wait, and his own passion, had made the precious dew pump up too quickly, and I had not been able to enjoy it as I should.

I could not help showing a little disappointment, but my lover, covering me with kisses, told me that I need wait but during a brief period of repose, and that I should soon be more satisfied with him.

We sat on the sofa, entwined in each other's arms, telling one another of our love and happiness; we had fallen in love at first sight, and both had given way to irresistible passion.

In a few moments I saw that my lover was ready to begin again, and I asked how we were going to do it. I did not wish to try again that posture that had turned out so badly for me, and I could see F. also looking about him.

An idea struck me. I rose, smiling, and toying with him; he rose too, I retreated, and he eagerly pursued me, till at last I went and leant with nonchalance upon the mantelpiece, presenting my crupper, that I wriggled like a cat, and at the same time I turned my head and threw him a provoking glance.

Ah! how he understood me. F. rushed upon me,

and kissed me, saying 'thank you.'

Then he got behind me, and threw my petticoats over my back. When he saw the beautiful shape of my bottom, he gave a loud cry of admiration. I expected as much, but did not dream of the homage he paid to it.

F. threw himself onto his knees, and after having covered my backside with kisses he drew them apart, just at the top of the thighs, and I could feel his lips, nay even his tongue. I shrieked out, and was overcome.

F. rose up, and began to put it in; his enormous instrument could not easily penetrate, in spite of our mutual efforts, so he drew it out, put a little saliva on the head and shaft, and I soon felt myself stabbed to the very vitals, filled and plugged tightly up, and in a state of unspeakable ecstasy.

My lover, leaning over me, glued his lips to mine, that I offered to him by turning my head; his tongue dallied with mine. I was beside myself. I felt myself going mad. The supreme moment arrived. I writhed about, uttering inarticulate words.

F., who was reserving himself, was delighted at my joy; he let me calm down, and then I felt his sweet movement again.

Ah, how he knew how to distil pleasure, and double it by a thousand delicate, subtle shades. Oh! that first lesson; I can feel it, as I write, between my thighs.

'Dear angel,' he said, 'tell me what you feel; it's so nice to enjoy each other's soft confidence, when we form but one body, as at this moment.'

Oh, how his speech made me happy; I, who had always wished to hear and say those words that had almost driven me wild, when my aunt was at

A woman on her knees –
Love only knows
What service she attends –
to heaven shows
The artless epic of her
* shining seat.*
Beauty's clear mirror, -
* where she loves to gaze,*
See and believe herself.
* O woman's arse,*
Roundly defeating man's
* in every class,*
O arse of arses: Glory!
Worship! Praise!

FROM *A BRIEF MORAL*
PAUL VERLAINE (1844–96)

The French watercolour (opposite) and etching (above) are both by anonymous artists working in Paris during the 1920s.

work! I did not hesitate an instant longer.

'I must do it again,' said I, 'it's coming – push in – again – right in – finish me – ah! I die!'

'My adored one, I'm coming too – it's bubbling up – Ah I spend!'

F. gave a push, and fell upon me. I felt his ejaculation, and nearly fainted under the jet.

How was it that I did not die during that embrace? Nothing that I had imagined at the sight of my aunt's sweet struggles could approach this reality! I remained overwhelmed, my head in my arms, my bosom heaving, incapable of movement.

F. drew out. I still spent. I kept on spending. I stopped as I was, without sense of shame, naked to the waist, trembling, mechanically continuing the movement of my bottom, and causing the overflow of liquid to fall to the ground.

F. took pity on me. After rapidly adjusting himself, he pulled down my petticoats, and taking me in his arms sat by my side on the sofa. I was delirious for a second. He calmed me; his sweet voice brought me to a little. I begged him to leave me to myself, and he went away.

Detachment, which as we have seen normally signals failure in the writing of erotica, is a key element in the highly individualistic style of Anaïs Nin. She somehow uses an artificial distancing to heighten the erotic effect, thereby turning her best short stories into something approaching erotic fables or fairy stories. The man for whom she wrote repeatedly told her to 'leave out the poetry', evoking a furious response – a letter that he would never have received, but

I have been a slave to my passions, but never to a man!

LA BELLE OTÉRO
THE FAMOUS COURTESAN OF THE
BELLE EPOQUE

which says some important things about the
male and female perceptions of erotica:

> Dear Collector: We hate you. Sex loses all its power
> and magic when it becomes explicit, mechanical,
> overdone, when it becomes a mechanistic obses-
> sion. It becomes a bore. You have taught us more
> than anyone I know how wrong it is not to mix it
> with emotion, hunger, desire, lust, whims,
> caprices, personal ties, deeper relationships that
> change its color, flavor, rhythms, intensities.
>
> You do not know what you are missing by your
> microscopic examination of sexual activity to the
> exclusion of aspects which are the fuel that ignites
> it. Intellectual, imaginative, romantic, emotional.
> This is what gives sex its surprising textures, its
> subtle transformations, its aphrodisiac elements.
> You are shrinking your world of sensations. You
> are withering it, starving it, draining its blood.
>
> If you nourished your sexual life with all the
> excitements and adventures which love injects into
> sensuality, you would be the most potent man in
> the world. The source of sexual power is curiosity,
> passion. You are watching its little flame die of
> asphyxiation. Sex docs not thrive on monotony.
> Without feeling, inventions, moods, no surprises
> in bed. Sex must be mixed with tears, laughter,
> words, promises, scenes, jealousy, envy, all the
> spices of fear, foreign travel, new faces, novels,
> stories, dreams, fantasies, music, dancing, opium,
> wine.
>
> How much do you lose by this periscope at the
> tip of your sex, when you could enjoy a harem of
> distinct and never-repeated wonders? No two hairs
> alike, but you will not let us waste words on a

A drawing executed by an unknown English artist.

description of hair; no two odors, but if we expand on this you cry Cut the poetry. No two skins with the same texture, and never the same light, temperature, shadows, never the same gesture; for a lover, when he is aroused by true love, can run the gamut of centuries of love lore. What a range, what changes of age, what variations of maturity and innocence, perversity and art...

We have sat around for hours and wondered how you look. If you have closed your senses upon silk, light, color, odor, character, temperament, you must be by now completely shriveled up. There are so many minor senses, all running like tributaries into the mainstream of sex, nourishing it. Only the united beat of sex and heart together can create ecstasy.

The erotica of Anaïs Nin, although among the best work in the genre and unusual for having been written by a woman, does not always live up to her aspirations for it. Some of this must be laid at the door of her literary tormentor ('leave out the poetry!'); but compare this extract from her short story *Elena* with the piece from *Lady Chatterley's Lover* which follows it and is similarly isolated from its context.

Where there is real sex there is the underlying passion for fidelity...

D. H. LAWRENCE
(1855–1930)

These were the external feelings of the bodies discovering each other. From so much touching they grew drugged. Their gestures were slow and dreamlike. Their hands were heavy. His mouth never closed.

How the honey flowed from her. He dipped his fingers in it lingeringly, then his sex, then he moved her so that she lay on him, her legs thrown over his legs, and as he took her, he could see himself entering into her, and she could see him too. They saw their bodies undulate together, seeking their climax. He was waiting for her, watching her movements.

Because she did not quicken her movements, he changed her position, making her lie back. He crouched over so that he could take her with more force, touching the very bottom of her womb, touching the very flesh walls again and again, and then she experienced the sensation that within her womb some new cells awakened, new fingers, new mouths, that they responded to his entrance and joined in the rhythmic motion, that this suction was becoming gradually more and more pleasurable, as if the friction had aroused new layers of enjoyment. She moved quicker to bring the climax, and when he saw this, he hastened his motions inside of her and incited her to come with him, with words, with his hands caressing her, and finally with his mouth soldered to hers, so that the tongues moved in the same rhythm as the womb and penis, and the climax was spreading between her mouth and her sex, in cross-currents of increasing pleasure, until she cried out, half sob and half laughter, from the overflow of joy through her body.

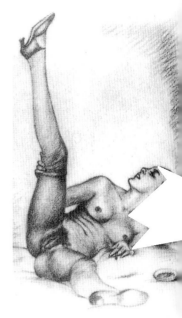

An etching by 'Rainier, E.', the pseudonym of Carl Breuer-Courth, Germany, c.1920.

He too had bared the front part of his body and she felt his naked flesh against her as he came into her. For a moment he was still inside her, turgid there and quivering. Then as he began to move, in the sudden helpless orgasm, there awoke in her new strange thrills rippling inside her. Rippling, rippling, rippling, like a flapping overlapping of soft flames, soft as feathers, running to points of brilliance, exquisite, exquisite and melting her all

The delights of soixante-neuf
captured in watercolour by
Hellmuth Stockmann, 1920.

molten inside. It was like bells rippling up and up to a culmination. She lay unconscious of the wild little cries she uttered at the last. But it was over too soon, too soon, and she could no longer force her own conclusion with her own activity. This was different, different. She could do nothing. She could no longer harden and grip for her own satisfaction upon him. She could only wait, wait and moan in spirit as she felt him withdrawing, withdrawing and contracting, coming to the terrible moment when he would slip out of her and be gone. Whilst all her womb was open and soft, and softly clamouring, like a sea-anemone under the tide, clamouring for him to come in again and make a fulfilment for her. She clung to him unconscious in passion, and he never quite slipped from her, and she felt the soft bud of him within her stirring, and strange rhythms flushing up into her with a strange rhythmic growing motion, swelling and swelling till it filled all her cleaving consciousness, and then began again the unspeakable motion that was not really motion, but pure deepening whirlpools of sensation swirling deeper and deeper through all her tissue and consciousness, till she was one perfect concentric fluid of feeling, and she lay there crying in unconscious inarticulate cries. The voice out of the uttermost night, the life! The man heard it beneath him with a kind of awe, as his life sprang out into her. And as it subsided, he subsided too and lay utterly still, unknowing, while her grip on him slowly relaxed, and she lay inert. And they lay and knew nothing, not even of each other, both lost.

The last word on language and passion in erotic writing has to come from Henry Miller. Whatever the shortcomings of his later work, *Tropic of Cancer* and *Tropic of Capricorn* are powerful and unforgettable novels. In this extract it is not only the shocking images and words which are so remarkable, making a kind of surprising beauty out of ugliness, but the rhythm of the language, following one crescendo with another. The second part of the extract comes after the diatribe in the novel and is included because you may need a quiet walk on the Left Bank afterwards.

A charcoal drawing by A I.

Tania is a fever, too – *les voies urinaires*, Cafe de la Liberté, Place des Vosges, bright neckties on the Boulevard Montparnasse, dark bathrooms, Porto Sec, Abdullah cigarettes, the adagio sonata *Pathétique*, aural amplificators, anecdotal seances, burnt sienna breasts, heavy garters, what time is it, golden pheasants stuffed with chestnuts, taffeta fingers, vaporish twilights turning to ilex, acromegaly, cancer and delirium, warm veils, poker chips, carpets of blood and soft thighs. Tania says so that every one may hear: 'I love him!' And while Boris scalds himself with whisky she says: 'Sit down here! O Bori... Russia... what'll I do? I'm bursting with it!'

An Indian ink drawing made by Theo van Elsen who worked in Paris during the 1930s.

At night when I look at Boris' goatee lying on the pillow I get hysterical. O Tania, where now is that warm cunt of yours, those fat, heavy garters, those soft, bulging thighs? There is a bone in my prick six inches long. I will ream out every wrinkle in your cunt, Tania, big with seed. I will send you home to your Sylvester with an ache in your belly

A woman pleasures her lover
'à l'espagnol' in this charcoal
drawing by A1.

Caress my breasts with your fingers,
they are small and you have
neglected them. Enough! Now set
your mouth just there immediately.

FROM THE SANSKRIT
AMARU, C. 800 AD

and your womb turned inside out. Your Sylvester!
Yes, he knows how to build a fire, but I know how
to inflame a cunt. I shoot hot bolts into you, Tania,
I make your ovaries incandescent. Your Sylvester
is a little jealous now? He feels something, does
he? He feels the remnants of my big prick. I have
set the shores a little wider, I have ironed out the
wrinkles. After me you can take on stallions, bulls,
rams, drakes, St. Bernards.

You can stuff toads, bats, lizards up your rec-
tum. You can shit arpeggios if you like, or string a
zither across your navel. I am fucking you, Tania,
so that you'll stay fucked. And if you are afraid of
being fucked publicly I will fuck you privately. I
will tear off a few hairs from your cunt and paste
them on Boris' chin. I will bite into your clitoris
and spit out two franc pieces...

Indigo sky swept clear of fleecy clouds, gaunt
trees infinitely extended, their black boughs gestic-
ulating like a sleepwalker. Somber, spectral trees,
their trunks pale as cigar ash. A silence supreme
and altogether European. Shutters drawn, shops
barred. A red glow here and there to mark a tryst.
Brusque the facades, almost forbidding; immacu-
late except for the splotches of shadow cast by the
trees. Passing by the Orangerie I am reminded of
another Paris, the Paris of Maugham, of Gauguin,
Paris of George Moore. I think of that terrible
Spaniard who was then startling the world
with his acrobatic leaps from style to style. I
think of Spengler and of his terrible pronun-
ciamentos, and I wonder if style, style in the
grand manner, is done for. I say that my
mind is occupied with these thoughts, but it
is not true; it is only later, after I have crossed

the Seine, after I have put behind me the carnival of lights, that I allow my mind to play with these ideas. For the moment I can think of nothing – except that I am a sentient being stabbed by the miracle of these waters that reflect a forgotten world. All along the banks the trees lean heavily

For centuries the workshops of India produced erotic miniatures for the amusement of wealthy patrons and their ladies.

Food, drink, narcotics, carpets and furnishings, gardens and exotic pets, all help to exalt lovemaking to the greatest pleasure human beings can know. These are Indian miniatures, from the late eighteenth century.

over the tarnished mirror; when the wind rises and fills them with a rustling murmur they will shed a few tears and shiver as the water swirls by. I am suffocated by it. No one to whom I can communicate even a fraction of my feelings...

When the flames of passion die back to a steady glow, the great love manuals of the East encourage men and women to perfect a variety of sexual techniques that will keep boredom from the bedroom. At the conclusion of *Ananga-Ranga* ('State of the Bodiless One'), Kalyana Malla, who has an unsentimental view of human relationships, gives this advice:

The chief reason for the separation between the married couple and the cause, which drives the husband to the embraces of strange women, and the wife to the arms of strange men, is the want of varied pleasures and the monotony which follows possession. There is no doubt about it. Monotony begets satiety, and satiety distaste for congress, especially in one or the other; malicious feelings arc engendered, the husband or the wife yields to temptation, and the other follows, being driven by jealousy. For it seldom happens that the two love each other equally, and in exact proportion, therefore is the one more easily seduced by passion than the other. From such separations result polygamy, adulteries, abortions, and every manner of vice, and not only do the erring husband and wife fall into the pit, but they also drag down the names of their deceased ancestors from the place of beautiful mortals, either to hell or back again upon this

world. Fully understanding the way in which
such quarrels arise, I have in this book shown
how the husband, by varying the enjoyment of
his wife, may live with her as with thirty-two different women, ever varying the enjoyment of her,
and rendering satiety impossible.

The classical *Kama Sutra*, the love manuals of
the Middle Ages (*Ananga-Ranga* and *Koka
Shastra* notably) and numerous later Indian
texts all teach that a variety of lovemaking positions is essential if the thrill and excitement of
sex is to be maintained. These positions were
given evocative names and described so that
they could easily be learned by heart.

A Japanese woodcut by Utamaro,
one of the greatest artists to work
in that medium.

The coloured woodcut (top) is by Utamaro (1753–1806). the beautifully executed painting on fabric (above) is from the second half of the nineteenth century. The artist is uknown.

If you lift the girl by passing your elbows under her knees and enjoy her as she hangs trembling with her arms garlanding your neck, it is called *Janukurpura*, the Knee-Elbow.

If your lustful lover buries her face in the pillow and goes on all fours like an animal and you rut upon her from behind as though you were a wild beast, this coupling is *Harina*, the Deer.

When, straightening her legs, she grips and milks your penis with her vagina, as a mare holds a stallion, it is *Vadavaka*, the Mare, which is not learned without practice.

If, lying with her face turned away, the fawn-eyed girl offers you her buttocks and your penis enters the house of love, this is *Nagabandha*, the coupling of the Cobra.

Japanese erotic texts, in common with the Hindu love manuals, regard sex as a sacrament rather than a subject for shame. 'The union of male and female, of man and woman, symbolizes the union of the gods themselves at the moment when the world was created. The gods smile upon your lovemaking, enjoying your pleasure! For this reason both husband and wife must strive to please each other and themselves when they embrace. If you are both satisfied, the gods will be satisfied... good sex brings more honour to Daikoku than a well-tended altar.'

These words of wisdom come from the *Pillow Book*, which was written during the Kamakura period (1192–1333) by an aristocratic lady for the education of young women. It was the forerunner of many pillow books, all small and unillustrated since they were designed to be kept, together with combs and make-up, in the lacquered wooden pillow or *makura* which Japanese ladies slept on to preserve their elaborate coiffure.

The original *Pillow Book* was nothing if not direct: all problems were attacked with the same attention to detail. Homosexuality was common among the samurai (as in many elite fighting brotherhoods: the Sacred Bands of ancient Greece; the imperial Turkish Janissaries; Oliver Cromwell's Model Army) and if the relationship with a husband whose tastes tended that way were to be preserved, 'the young wife should offer him her anus from time to time. She should pay scrupulous attention to hygiene and prepare herself carefully with lubricating cream.'

The *Pillow Book* offered psychological as well as physical advice. Newly married wives are told to find subtle ways of praising their husband's penis. When it is flaccid, sly comments such as 'how huge your penis is, my love, so much larger than I remember my father's when he went naked to the bath-house' are suggested. In erection she should try, 'I cannot believe how big your penis is, my love. Is it possible that I can accommodate such a wonder? Fill me now!' Lastly, this inspired medieval sex counsellor exhorts women to miss no opportunity of telling their husbands 'how manly you are, how fortunate I am to have such a man!'

Shung prints by Koriusai (above) and from a pillow book (top).

Although the *Pillow Book* and most of its later imitators were unillustrated (or at best poorly illustrated), Japan did produce some of the most extraordinary erotic art the world has ever seen

– shunga. Early shunga prints were often commissioned by the owners of the great bordellos or 'green houses' as advertisements. One set from 1660 shows forty-eight different sexual positions, almost rivalling the Hindu tradition in imagination. When he saw shunga prints for the first time, the nineteenth-century French writer Edmond dc Goncourt was clearly both shocked and excited: 'The animal frenzies of the flesh... the fury of copulation as if transported by rage!'

Shunga was the art of 'the floating world' or the 'city without night'. This referred to the pleasure districts of Japan's great cities, where in the eighteenth and nineteenth centuries every kind of aesthetic and sensual delight was available. Here, poets and artists lived side bv side with the cultured and refined courtesans of the 'green houses'. These were greenhouses indeed, steamy hotbeds of political and cultural radicalism where masters of the four-colour woodblock print like Harunobu, Utamaro and Hokusai created unforgettable and often very amusing erotic images.

Shunga prints are indeed the fireworks of erotic art, featuring penises enlarged to erupting roman candles, vulvas like Catherine wheels, the image alive with movement and vibrant with colour and pattern.

Chinese nineteenth-century rosewood toilet box with eleven concealed miniatures.

In China the 'refinement of passion' finds expression in the elaborate symbolism of Taoism. In the religious text known as *I Ching* ('The Book of Changes') dating from around 1200 BCE, Tao (the whole, perfection, cosmic order) is shown to come from the interaction of Yin (male) and Yang (female). This interaction occurs in all things. The sky is Yin, the earth is Yang; mountains are Yin, valleys Yang, and so on. In this sexualized cosmos it follows that lovemaking is central: the *I Ching* goes so far as to say that 'the sexual union of man and woman gives life to all things'.

A painting on silk, c. 1730.

Taoist sages produced love manuals at a very early date. Centuries later these texts formed the basis for the Japanese tradition of erotology. The Taoist manuals gave evocative names to the various lovemaking positions such as 'Galloping Horse' and 'Monkey Facing Tree'. Successive waves of censorship under Confucianism have meant that visual erotic art in China, even at its best, cannot compare with Japanese or Indian erotic art: the principles of proportion and subtleties of anatomy were never mastered by the Chinese artists. Instead, eroticism found expression in the symbolism of landscape painting and in the great erotic novels of the Ming Period such as *Chin P'ing Mei* ('Metal Vase Plum Blossom').

Confucian restrictions meant that Chinese artists were never really allowed to master either anatomy or perspective. This painting was executed on silk.

In both art forms we need to understand the symbolism in order to release the erotic meaning. The title of *Chin P'ing Mei* contains 'vase', a female symbol, and 'plum', a male one: if this subtlety is lost we miss the whole point of Chinese erotic writing (see also the poems of Ikkyu on page 52). However, given this key, we begin to understand that the *Chin P'ing Mei* is like an erotic concerto.

Pear Blossom poured wine for Lady Ping and her guest, Hsi-Men, and left the pair to their guilty pleasures. Believing themselves alone, how quickly the lovers undressed one another with urgent fingers and gasps of pleasure: he at the scented arbors of her armpits and belly and the secret fruits ripe and luscious. She at the jade stalk risen up and the heavy purse of pleasure. But what is this? Pear Blossom the sly one has made a hole in the paper of the wall so that she can spy upon the lovers at their games. This shameless girl is near enough to feel the gusts of breath from her mistress as he opens the scented field of cinnabar with his tongue. The maid is so close she can even hear the music of the jade flute as it slips over the tongue and lips of her mistress.

What wild scene is this? Now the glistening gateway of jade is offered to him, and the leaping white tiger crosses the fields of snow. The pace is furious now and the lovers call out to each other, Mistress Ping noisy from both mouths as the purple plum moves between her lips. She turns to spur on the rider, her heavy hair dancing about her temples. And who can remain dry in such a storm as this? Pear Blossom's own cup is full and her fingers dance in the moisture.

All are lost now. Hsi-Men shouts as his fire juices spurt, Lady Ping moans as the thunder shakes her thighs and outside in the cold a little one shudders.

In ancient China, novel writing was not regarded as a worthy occupation for a serious man of letters and none of the time-honoured literary conventions applied. For this reason much of *Chin P'ing Mei* was written in a spare colloquial style, perfectly captured in the scholarly and accurate translation by Clement Egerton. This version, published in 1939, was entitled *The Golden Lotus* and the numerous sexual descriptions (for example, of fellatio in this extract) had to be rendered in Latin to avoid prosecution.

Hsi-mên Ch'ing and his ladies made merry in the Hibiscus Arbour. They drank till it was late, and then went to their own apartments. Hsi-mên Ch'ing went to Golden Lotus's room. He was already half drunk, and soon wished to enjoy the delights of love with his new lady. Golden Lotus hastily burned incense, and they took off their clothes and went to bed. But Hsi-mên Ch'ing would not allow her to go too fast. He knew that she played the flute exquisitely. He sat down behind the curtains of the bed, and set her before him. Then Golden Lotus daintily pushed back the golden bracelets from her wrists and mentulam ad

Last night a peach petal was wetted by the rain,
And when a girl
After her toilet said:
Which is the more bountiful,
I or the peach petal?'
And he said:
'Peach petal wetted by the rain is incomparable,'
There were tears and a tearing of flowers.

To taste the living flower
Tonight would be quite a good night, my lord,
If so you wish.

DEAD FLOWER, OR LIVING?
GEISHA SONG, LATE EIGHTEENTH CENTURY

A small ivory carving of lovers,
dating from the nineteenth century.

sua labra adposuit [brought his jade stalk to her lips], while he leaned forward to enjoy the delight of her movements. She continued for a long time, and all the while his delight grew greater. He called Plum Blossom to bring in some tea. Golden Lotus was afraid that her maid would see her, and hastily pulled down the bed curtains.

'What are you afraid of?' Hsi-mên said. 'Our neighbour Hua has two excellent maids. One of them, the younger, brought us those flowers today, but there is another about as old as Plum Blossom. Brother Hua has already taken her virginity. Indeed wherever her mistress is, she is too. She is really very pretty, and of course no one can tell what a man like Brother Hua may do in the privacy of his own home.'

Golden Lotus looked at him.

'You are a strange creature, but I will not scold you,' she said. 'If you wish to have this girl, have her and be done with it. Why go beating about the bush, pointing at a mountain when you really are thinking about something quite different. I know you would like to have somebody else to compare with me, but I am not jealous. She is not actually my maid. Tomorrow, I will go to the garden to rest for a while, and that will give you a chance. You can call her into this room and do what you like with her. Will that satisfy you?'

Hsi-mên Ch'ing was delighted. 'You understand me so well!' he said, 'how can I help loving you?' So these two agreed, and their delight in each other and in their love could not have been greater. After she had played the flute, they kissed each other, and went to sleep.

The next day Golden Lotus went to the apartments

of Tower of Jade, and Hsi-mên Ch'ing called Plum Blossom to his room, and had his pleasure of her.

From that day, Golden Lotus showered favours on this girl. She would not allow her to go and wait at the kitchen, but kept her to attend to her bedroom, and serve her with tea. She chose beautiful clothes and ornaments for her, and bound her feet very tightly.

Fragment of a hand-written, illuminated love manual.

The Islamic world is rich in erotic literature, from the wonders of Persian poetry to the dazzling collection of stories known as *The Arabian Nights*. There have been numerous translations of the *Nights* into Western languages but Sir Richard Burton's version is incomparable. Burton was sympathetic towards Arab culture and managed to capture the rhythm of the poetry in English: 'She hath breasts like two globes of ivory, like golden pomegranates, beautifully upright, arched and rounded, firm as stone to the touch, with nipples erect and outward jutting. She hath thighs like unto pillars of alabaster, and between them, there vaunts a secret place, a sachet of musk, that swells, that throbs, that is moist and avid.'

Sir Richard Burton also translated the most famous of the Arab love manuals, *The Perfumed Garden* of Sheikh Nefzawi. When he died he had just completed a revised version which included the missing chapter on homosexual practices. Unfortunately this was burned by Isabel, his wife, in one of the most notorious bonfires in literary history. Homosexual incidents feature in *The Arabian Nights*, and many of the Arab sex

*An Arabian Nights scene of lovers
enjoying one another on a Persian
carpet under the stars.*

manuals give advice on the subject. *The Book of Counsel* of the eleventh-century Emir Kai-Ka'us ibn Iskander recommends, mysteriously, that the reader should 'in summer devote himself to boys, in winter to women'.

The Perfumed Garden is an urbane, world-ly-wise book, full of wicked humour and very different in tone from the Hindu love manuals. The author, writing to ingratiate himself with the Grand Vizier of Tunis, but not above slyly sending up his patron admits that the Hindus had more lovemaking positions but enumerates what he judges the basic ones. He begins with foreplay.

Concerning all that is favourable to coition

Know, oh Vizier, (God's mercy be with you!) that if you wish to experience an agreeable copulation, one that gives equal satisfaction and pleasure to both parties, it is necessary to frolic with the woman and excite her with nibbling, kissing, and caressing. Turn her over on the bed, sometimes on her back, sometimes on her belly, until you see by her eyes that the moment of pleasure has arrived, as I have described in the previous chapter, and, on my honour! I have not stinted the descriptions.

When, therefore, you see a woman's lips tremble and redden, and her eyes become languishing and her sighs profound, know that she desires coition; then is the time to get between her thighs and pen-etrate her. If you have followed my advice you will both enjoy a delightful copulation which will leave a delicious memory. Someone has said: 'If you desire to copulate, place the woman on the ground, embrace her closely and put your lips on hers; then clasp her, suck her, bite her; kiss her neck, her breasts, her belly and her flanks; strain her to you until she lies limp with desire. When you see her in this state, introduce your member. If you act thus your enjoyment will be simultaneous, and that is the secret of pleasure. But if you neglect this plan the woman will not satisfy your desires, and she herself will gain no enjoyment.'

Concerning the different postures for coition
The ways of uniting with a woman are numerous and varied, and the time has arrived when you should learn the different postures...

According to your taste you may choose the posture which pleases you most, provided always that intercourse takes place through the appointed organ: the vulva.

FIRST POSTURE the woman on her back and raise her thighs; then, getting between her legs, introduce your member. Gripping the ground with your toes, you will be able to move in a suitable manner. This posture is a good one for those who have long members.

Line illustrations from the 1850 French translation of The Perfumed Garden.

SECOND POSTURE If your member is short, lay the woman on her back and raise her legs in the air so that her toes touch her ears. Her buttocks being thus raised, the vulva is thrown forward. Now introduce your member.

THIRD POSTURE Lay the woman on the ground and get between her thighs; then, putting one of her legs on your shoulder and the other under your arm, penetrate her.

The sun begins to bleed
On the spikes of the palm trees
and now he falls
a bursting crimson pomegranate
from all the branches;
your mat is the world tonight
and you are the sun setting
and I am the darkness
coming down over you.

HER SONG, FRAGMENTARY POEM
FROM FRENCH INDO-CHINA,
NINETEENTH CENTURY

A pencil drawing by an anonymous
Italian artist active in the 1880s.

FOURTH POSTURE Stretch the woman on the ground and put her legs on your shoulders; in that position your member will be exactly opposite her vulva which will be lifted off the ground. That is the moment for introducing your member.

FIFTH POSTURE Let the woman lie on her side on the ground; then, lying down yourself and getting between her thighs, introduce your member. This posture is apt to give rise to rheumatic or sciatic pains.

SIXTH POSTURE Let the woman rest on her knees and elbows in the position for prayer. In this posture the vulva stands out behind. Attack her thus.

SEVENTH POSTURE Lay the woman on her side, and then you yourself sitting on your heels will place her top leg on your nearest shoulder and her other leg against your thighs. She will keep on her side and you will be between her legs. Introduce your member and move her backwards and forwards with your hands.

EIGHTH POSTURE Lay the woman on her back and kneel astride her.

NINTH POSTURE Place the woman so that she rests, either face forward or the reverse, against a slightly raised platform, her feet remaining on the ground and her body projecting in front. She will thus present her vulva to your member which you will introduce.

TENTH POSTURE Place the woman on a rather low divan and let her grasp the woodwork with her hands; then, placing her legs on your hips and telling her to grip your body with them, you will introduce your member, at the same time grasping the divan. When you begin to work, let your movements keep time.

ELEVENTH POSTURE Lay the woman on her back and let her buttocks be raised by a cushion placed under them. Let her put the soles of her feet together: now get between her thighs.

Roman writers discussed different sexual positions, but there is none of the subtlety and insight of Hindu commentators and little concern for the feelings of the woman. The best of them was Ovid, whose *Ars Amatoria* ('The Art of Love'), written at the time of Christ, does at least address itself to women as well as to men: 'Reckon up each of your charms, and take your posture according to your beauty. One and the same mode docs not become every woman. If you are especially attractive of face – lie on your back... Let her press the bed with her knees, the neck slightly bowed, she whose chief beauty is her shapely flank...'

Rear-entry lovemaking, 'the posterior Venus', and the position known as 'the horse of Hector' where the woman rides the man, seem to have been especially popular in Classical times. They may seem plain fare compared with the infinite possibilities offered by Eastern authorities, but in our culture they have stood the test of time. To end this section on the refinements of passion we will follow these two basic sexual postures, or motifs, down through the ages.

Aristophanes, the great Greek comic dramatist writing in the fifth to fourth centuries BCE, refers to rear-entry lovemaking both in *The Peace* and in *Lysistrata*, the heroine of which complains: 'I will not squat on all fours like a lioness!' Athenacus, writing in the second century CE,

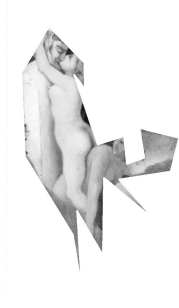

An Offering to the God Priapus, *which was painted by an unknown French artist at the end of the eighteenth century.*

There on the vulgar on the humble bed
I add the body of love, I had the lips,
The sensuous, the rosy lips of wine,
Rosy with such a wine, that even now
Here as I write, after so many years,
In my solitary house, I am drunk again.

FROM *ONE NIGHT*
C. P. CAVAFY (1863–1933)

makes it clear that the 'posterior Venus' was still popular throughout the Greek world. He records that a famous courtesan allowed herself to be mounted five times in succession in that, her favourite, posture by a dirty but handsome travelling tinker who caught her eye. News of this reached the market place and when she was reproached by her protector she made the ingenious excuse that she could not possibly have allowed such a dirty, low-born rogue to touch her breasts and make them sooty!

The beauty of female buttocks was so admired by the ancient Greeks that they held public competitions in which girls revealed their 'derrières' to a panel of judges. Indeed, Athenaeus tells the story of two sisters who lived near Syracuse who had often won prizes for their magnificent behinds, but they quarrelled over whose was the most splendid.

To resolve matters they exposed themselves simultaneously to an unsuspecting youth on the highway (thus anticipating 'mooning' by about 2,000 years). He fell for the elder sister (or rather her bottom) and married her, but not before his younger brother had decided to make it a double ceremony. The chronicler records that the sisters were known by the inhabitants of Syracuse as Callipygi because, although they were of lowly birth, their posteriors served them for a dowry. Full of gratitude, the newly rich sisters dedicated a temple to Venus, under the title of Venus Callipygos (Venus of the beauteous buttocks).

The Romans were no less fond of the 'posterior Venus' and the well-preserved frescoes of the Pompeii brothel show that it was one of the main attractions of the establishment. After the fall of the Roman empire the practice evidently did not go out of fashion, because at the dawning of the Renaissance Boccaccio tells this delightful bawdy tale (or tail) in which the artful priest Dom Gianni contrives to enjoy Gossip Pietro's buxom wife Gemmata in his favourite manner.

A nineteenth-century heliogravure illustration for the 'Postures' of Aretino.

Gossip Pietro on his part, albeit he was very poor and had but a little cot at Tresanti that scarce sufficed for himself, his fair, young wife, and their ass, nevertheless, whenever Dom Gianni arrived at Tresanti, made him welcome, and did him the honours of his house as best he might, in requital of the hospitality which he received at Barletta. However, as Gossip Pietro had but one little bed, in which he slept with his fair wife, 'twas not in his power to lodge Dom Gianni as comfortably as he would have liked; but the priest's mare being quartered beside the ass in a little stable, the priest himself must needs lie beside her on the straw. Many a time when the priest came, the wife, knowing how honourably he entreated her husband at Barletta, would fain have gone to sleep with a neighbour, one Zita Garapresa di Giudice Leo, that the priest might share the bed with her husband, and many a time had she told the priest so: howbeit he would never agree to it, and on one occasion: – 'Gossip Gemmata,' quoth he, 'trouble not

A drawing by the highly gifted
German artist and illustrator Franz
von Bayros (1866–1924). Clearly
influenced by Beardsley and the
Decadents, von Bayros – whose
work was almost exclusively erotic
– was obliged to move from one
European capital to another as
each outrageous new work was
banned by the authorities.

An illustration from a French erotic
manual published during the Age
of Enlightenment.

thyself about me; I am well lodged; for, when I am so minded, I turn the mare into a fine lass and dally with her, and then, when I would, I turn her back into a mare; wherefore I could ill brook to part from her.' The young woman, wandering but believing, told her husband what the priest had said, adding: – 'If he is even such a friend as thou sayst, why dost thou not get him to teach thee the enchantment, so that thou mayst turn me into a mare, and have both ass and mare for thine occasions? We should then make twice as much gain as we do, and thou wouldst turn me back into a woman when we came home at night.'

Gossip Pietro, whose wit was somewhat blunt, believed that 'twas as she said, approved her counsel, and began adjuring Dom Gianni, as persuasively as he might, to teach him the incantation. Dom Gianni did his best to wean him of his folly; but as all was in vain: – 'Lo, now,' quoth he, 'as you are both bent on it, we will be up, as is our wont, before the sun to-morrow morning, and I will shew you how 'tis done. The truth is that 'tis in the attachment of the tail that the great difficulty lies, as thou wilt see.' Scarce a wink of sleep had either Gossip Pietro or Gossip Gemmata that night, so great was their anxiety; and towards daybreak up they got, and called Dom Gianni; who, being risen, came in his shirt into Gossip Pietro's little bedroom, and: – 'I know not,' quoth he, 'that there is another soul in the world for whom I would do this, save you, my gossips; however, as you will have it so, I will do it, but it behoves you to do exactly as I bid you, if you would have the enchantment work.' They promised obedience, and Dom Gianni thereupon took a light, which he

handed to Gossip Pietro, saying: – 'Let nought that
I shall do or say escape thee; and have a care, so
thou wouldst not ruin all, to say never a word,
whatever thou mayst see or hear; and pray God
that the tail may be securely attached.' So Gossip
Pietro took the light, and again promised obedience; Dom Gianni caused Gossip Gemmata to
strip herself stark naked, and stand on all fours
like a mare, at the same time strictly charging her
that, whatever might happen, she must utter no
word. Then, touching her head and face: – 'Be this
a fine head of a mare,' quoth he; in like manner
touching her hair, he said: – 'Be this a fine mane of
a mare;' touching her arms: – 'Be these fine legs
and fine hooves of a mare;' then, as he touched her
breast and felt its firm roundness, and there awoke
and arose one that was not called: – 'And be this a
fine breast of a mare,' quoth he; and in like manner he dealt with her back, belly, croup, thighs,
and legs. Last of all, the work being complete save
for the tail, he lifted his shirt and took in his hand
the tool with which he was used to plant men, and
forthwith thrust it into the furrow made for it, saying: – 'And be this a fine tail of a mare.' Whereat
Gossip Pietro, who had followed everything very
heedfully to that point, disapproving that last particular, exclaimed: – 'No! Dom Gianni, I'll have no
tail, I'll have no tail.' The essential juice, by which
all plants are propagated, was already discharged,
when Dom Gianni withdrew the tool, saying: –
'Alas! Gossip Pietro, what hast thou done? Did I
not tell thee to say never a word, no matter what
thou mightst see? The mare was all but made; but
by speaking thou hast spoiled all; and 'tis not possible to repeat the enchantment.' 'Well and good,'

*Mihály Zichy (1827–1906)
worked in Budapest, Vienna and
Paris, and was successively Court
Painter at St Petersburg and in
Moscow for Czar Alexander II. It
was not a happy life and even the
most erotic of his superb drawings
have a melancholy air.*

Some further illustrations from the erotic manual shown on page 94.

replied Gossip Pietro, 'I would have none of that tail. Why saidst thou not to me: – "Make it thou"? And besides, thou wast attaching it too low.' 'Twas because,' returned Dom Gianni, 'thou wouldst not have known, on the first essay, how to attach it so well as I.' Whereupon the young woman stood up, and in all good faith said to her husband: – 'Fool that thou art, wherefore hast thou brought to nought what had been for the good of us both? When didst thou ever see mare without a tail? So help me God, poor as thou art, thou deservest to be poorer still.' So, after Gossip Pietro's ill-timed speech, there being no way left of returning the young woman into a mare, downcast and melancholy she resumed her clothes; and Gossip Pietro plied his old trade with his ass, and went with Dom Gianni to the fair of Bitonto, and never asked him so to serve him again.

Before following 'Hector's horse' (or at least the sexual posture known by that endearing name in the Classical world) through the darker byways of literature, it is valuable to look through the stud book. In India the sexual posture in which the woman rides the man has always had a special significance. Even today, traders in the bazaar will show those erotic miniatures to potential customers first because they are 'naughtier'. The reasons for this are obscure, but may have something to do with the reversal of the normal order in a society which is traditionally male-dominated. It may even be risqué because it symbolizes the hermetic Tantric concept of an all-powerful Goddess. This position is described in the *Ratikallolini*: 'She whose dark eyes are like fallen lotus petals takes your penis and guides it into her vulva, then clings tight to you and shakes her buttocks, this is Charunarik-shita, Lovely Lady in Charge.'

The Chinese and Japanese call this position 'Wailing Monkey Climbing a Tree', an interesting but less homely name for it than 'Hector's horse'. Quite how the idea started that Andromache was fond of making love to the Trojan hero in this way is unknown. Martial conjures up a colourful domestic scene. 'Behind the doors the Phrygian slaves would be masturbating, every time Andromache mounted her Hector horse fashion.' Ovid disagrees on technical grounds that do not seem to make much sense. A little woman may get astride her horse; but tall and majestic as she was, the Theban bride never mounted the Hectorean horse.' Horace describes a prostitute who 'naked in the lamplight, plied with wanton wiles and moving buttocks the horse beneath her'. Four centuries earlier Aristophanes has Lysistrata remark, 'Women love to get on horseback and to stay there!' And in *The Wasps* the Greek playwright even makes a double entendre. When Xanthias asks his lover to ride him, she puns on the name of a former tyrant and the Greek for horse: 'Shall you revive the tyranny of Hippias then?'

The 'horse of Hector' was well known in the Renaissance. The lustful abbot uses it in the fourth story of Boccaccio's *Decameron*.

Miniature painting from the Ganges Valley, India, early nineteenth century.

'Who will know? No one will ever know; and sin that is hidden is half forgiven; this chance may never come again; so, methinks, it were the part of

One of a series of 20 nineteenth-century German erotic 'medallions' based on Renaissance and Classical visual and textual sources.

Infinite wealth and leisure in a polygamous society can lead to some strange inventions. Whether this nineteenth-century painting from Jaipur is an amusing invention of the artist or the record of an experiment is not known.

wisdom to take the boon which God bestows.' So musing, with an altogether different purpose from that with which he had come, he drew near the girl, and softly bade her to be comforted, and besought her not to weep; and so little by little he came at last to show her what he would be at. The girl, being made neither of iron nor of adamant, was readily induced to gratify the abbot, who after bestowing upon her many an embrace and kiss, got upon the monk's bed, where, being sensible, perhaps, of the disparity between his reverend portliness and her tender youth, and fearing to injure her by his excessive weight, he refrained from lying upon her, but laid her upon him, and in that manner disported himself with her for a long time.

CHAPTER THREE
Forbidden Fruit

'Did you miss me?
Come and kiss me.
Never mind my bruises,
Hug me, kiss me, suck my juices
Squeezed from goblin fruits for you,
Goblin pulp and goblin dew.
Eat me, drink me, love me;
Laura, make much of me:
For your sake I have braved the glen
And had to do with goblin merchant men.'

Laura started from her chair,
Flung her arms up in the air,
Clutched her hair:

'Lizzie, Lizzie, have you tasted
For my sake the fruit forbidden?
Must your light like mine he hidden,
Your young life like mine be wasted,
Undone in mine undoing
And ruined in my ruin,
Thirsty, cankered, goblin-ridden?'

An etching made by the Belgian
artist Martin van Maele to
illustrate Histoire Comique
de Francion.

FROM *GOBLIN MARKET,*
CHRISTINA ROSSETTI

The forbidden fruit was always sex: that was the apple which Eve gave to Adam, a symbol of her sexuality (the serpent can speak for himself – he usually does). Writers in every culture

Orgy of Bacchantes by Jaques
Philippe Caresme. Appropriately
enough, the artist chose
watercolour as the medium.

have used fruit metaphors to describe sex.
Nature has aided and abetted the poets in this
lascivious idea; a banana is much like a penis,
the inside of the apple resembles the vulva, nipples are berries, peaches buttocks, and so on.
The world's erotic literature drips with fruit juice
(and wine and honey).

Eating fruit is an enjoyable oral experience
and orality is of course an important part of our
sexuality. The eating of fruit and oral sex are
both pleasurable and sufficiently similar to work
as metaphors of each other. Fellatio and cunnilingus are potentially still more pleasurable, of
course, because they involve genital as well as
oral stimulation (so far as we know, fruit does
not enjoy being eaten).

All this explains why men and women (and poets) can enjoy fruit and oral sex; but it raises two questions. Why should fruit (pleasure) be forbidden? And why should oral sex be in this chapter of the book which is concerned with the forbidden? This is not the place to attempt to answer the first question at length. All we need to know is that the sinfulness of pleasure – sex in particular – is a Judaeo-Christian concept. Sex is wrapped around with taboos and controlled with regulations in all human societies: the innocent Pacific island of our imagination is as much a myth as the Garden of Eden (in fact, it is the same myth). What is important is how, and how much, this powerful thing is controlled. It is to be regretted that misogynistic Biblical lawmakers from Ezekiel to St Paul hit upon the idea of making sex sinful in order to control it.

Royal lovers enjoying the lovemaking posture known as Kakila, the Crow Position. Bundi, India, eighteenth century.

This explains forbidden fruit. But since this entire book concerns forbidden fruit – and this section of it that which has been most forbidden – why is oral sex dealt with here? We cannot blame this on the Judaeo-Christian tradition. Listen to the Roman writer Martial, a pagan and not noted for his shyness in sexual matters: 'All night long I possessed a lewd young woman, I never knew anyone so licentious. Tired of a thousand postures, I asked for the puerile service [sodomy]; before I had done asking, she turned at once in compliance. Laughing and blushing I asked for something worse than that – the wanton consented instantly.'

We, nowadays, may find it strange to think of oral sex as being more unusual or wicked than sodomy, but that was certainly the view of Roman and Greek society, a view to which the works of numerous writers testify. It is too con-venient to blame Old Testament prophets for everything. Why do we make such distinctions? Here is a later Jewish prophet, Sigmund Freud, having a joke about sodomy.

It is disgust which stamps that sexual aim as a per-version. I hope, however, I shall not lie accused of partisanship when I assert that people who try to account for this disgust by saying that the organ in question serves the function and comes in contact with excrement... are not much more to the point than hysterical girls who account for their disgust of the male genital by saying that it serves to void urine.

Greek and Roman writers regarded oral sex as very exotic sexual fare, although this does not seem to have inhibited the revellers depicted below on this Attic cup attributed to the artist Skythes.

Vatsyayana in his *Kama Sutra* is offhand about 'congress in the anus' but says love-making in water 'is improper because forbidden by religious law'. He has surprises for those with fixed ideas on oral lovemaking.

The male servants of some men carry on the mouth congress with their masters. It is also practised by some citizens, who know each other well, among themselves. Some women of the harem, when they are amorous, do the acts of the mouth on the yonis of one another, and some men do the same thing with women. The way of doing this (i.e. of kissing the yoni) should be known from kissing the mouth. When a man and woman lie down in an inverted order, i.e. with the head of the one towards the feet of the other and carry on this congress, it is called the 'congress of a crow'.

In ancient India fellatio was enjoyed by heterosexual men but was normally performed by male eunuchs and only rarely by 'unchaste and wanton women'. Vatsyayana's entire section on technique concerns male fellators.

Of the Auparishtaka or Mouth Congress
There are two kinds of eunuchs, those that are disguised as males, and those that are disguised as females. Eunuchs disguised as females imitate their dress, speech, gestures, tenderness, timidity, simplicity, softness and hashfulness... These eunuchs derive their imaginable pleasure, and tlieir livelihood from this kind of congress, and they lead the life of courtesans...

Suavely the wine pouring from your lower lips has called the gold swarm. It is a crimson fruit and has called the bees. The boy who has sucked that carmine fruit is drunken, and I am drunken, and the gilded bees.

FROM THE *SANSKRIT* MAYURA, c. 800 CE.

Although research suggests that oral sex was less popular in the West at the beginning of the century than now, it was evidently part of the generous fare offered at this Czech establishment.

Eunuchs disguised as males keep their desires secret, and when they wish to do anything they lead the life of shampooers. Under the pretence of shampooing, a eunuch of this kind embraces and draws towards himself the thighs of the man whom he is shampooing, and after this he touches the joints of his thighs and his jaghana, or central portions of his body. Then, if he finds the lingam of the man erect, he presses it with his hands and chaffs him for getting into that state. If after this, and after knowing his intention, the man does not tell the eunuch to proceed, then the latter does it of his own accord and begins the congress...

The following eight things are then done by the eunuch one after the other:

The nominal congress

Biting the sides

Pressing outside

Pressing inside

Kissing

Rubbing

Sucking a mango fruit

Swallowing up

At the end of each of these, the eunuch expresses his wish to stop, but when one of them is finished, the man desires him to do another, and after that is done, then the one that follows it, and so on.

When, holding the man's lingam with his hand, and placing it between his lips, the eunuch moves about his mouth, it is called the 'nominal congress'.

When, covering the end of the lingam with his fingers collected together like the bud of a plant or flower, the eunuch presses the sides of it with his lips, using his teeth also, it is called 'biting the sides'.

When, being desired to proceed, the eunuch presses the end of the lingam with his lips closed together, and kisses it as if he were drawing it out, it is called the 'outside pressing'.

When, being asked to go on, he puts the lingam further into his mouth, and presses it with his lips and then takes it out, it is called the 'inside pressing'.

When, holding the lingam in his hand, the eunuch kisses it as if he were kissing the lower lip, it is called 'kissing'.

When, after kissing it, he touches it with his tongue everywhere, and passes the tongue over the end of it, it is called 'rubbing'.

When, in the same way, he puts the half of it into his mouth, and forcibly kisses and sucks it, this is called 'sucking a mango fruit'.

And lastly, when, with the consent of the man, the eunuch puts the whole lingam into his mouth, and presses it to the very end, as if he were going to swallow it up, it is called 'swallowing up'.

Two of the artist Johannes Martini's sitters exploring the possibilities of 'soixante-neuf'.

The Viennese artist A I uses his chosen medium of charcoal to capture a moment of intimacy charged with the same amalgam of melancholy and excitement as the city inhabited by both the artist and his subjects.

As we are concerned with forbidden fruit here, we will need to come back to the questions raised by this. First, it is interesting to look at attitudes towards oral sex in other cultures and periods. In China and Japan all forms of oral sex have been enjoyed since the earliest times. The great courtesans were skilled in 'playing the Jade Flute' (fellatio) and most of the manuals include it. Cunnilingus ('drinking at the Jade Fountain') was also considered vital for complete enjoyment.

Although Fellatio and Cunnilingus sound rather like characters from the Italian *commedia*

Different styles, but similar fantasies are depicted by Theo van Elsen (above) and Aubrey Beardsley (below).

dell'arte of the seventeenth and eighteenth centuries, at that time (and indeed up to the nineteenth century) this particular forbidden fruit was not as popular as – for example – sodomy, judging by the number of pages of erotic literature devoted to it. Arctino was certainly much more interested in sodomy. Nicolas Chorier gives equal, and relatively slight, attention to both. John Cleland puts no detailed description of cither in *Fanny Hill*, while devoting an entire passage to flagellation. Flagellation literature and flagellation were all the rage in the seventeenth, eighteenth and nineteenth centuries in Europe. But although some fine minds were addicted to it (Jean-Jacques Rousseau, Algernon Swinburne), we will not be examining that particular forbidden fruit, since it has the blight known as psychopathology.

No doubt it has always had its followers, but by the nineteenth century oral sex was back in fashion, though not displacing its old rival until the twentieth. We will look at fellatio first. This is the last time we will hear from Mrs Mayhew, Frank Harris's 'sad sibyl'.

'Here is something new,' she exclaimed, 'food for your vanity from my love! Mad as you make me with your love-thrusts, for at one moment I am hot and dry with desire, the next moment wet with passion, bathed in love, I could live with you all my life without having you, if you wished it, or if it would do you good. Do you believe me?'

'Yes,' I replied, continuing the love-game, but occasionally withdrawing to rub her clitoris with my sex and then slowly burying him in her cunt again to the hilt.

'We women have no souls but love,' she said faintly, her eyes dying as she spoke.

'I torture myself to think of some new pleasure for you, and yet you'll leave me, I feel you will, for some silly girl who can't feel a tithe of what I feel or give you what I give –' She began here to breathe quickly. 'I've been thinking how to give you more pleasure; let me try. Your seed, darling, is dear to me: I don't want it in my sex; I want to feel you thrill and so I want your sex in my mouth, I want to drink your essence and I will –' and suiting the action to the word, she slipped down in the bed and took my sex in her mouth and began rubbing it up and down till my seed spirted in long jets, filling her mouth while she swallowed it greedily.

In this whimsical lithograph of 1908 by Henry Lemort, a bemused Priapus – half rigid flesh, half stone – tries to understand his worshipper's evident delight in an accoutrement he has always rather taken for granted.

'Now do I love you, Sir!' she exclaimed, drawing herself upon me again and nestling against me. 'Wait till some girl does that to you and you'll know she loves you to distraction or, better still, to self-destruction.'

'Why do you talk of any other girl?' I chided her. 'I don't imagine you going with another man; why should you torment yourself just as causelessly?'

She shook her head. 'My fears are prophetic,' she sighed. 'I'm willing to believe it hasn't happened yet, though – Ah, God, the torturing thought! The mere dread of you going with another drives me crazy; I could kill her, the bitch: why doesn't she get a man of her own? How dare she even look at you?' and she clasped me tightly to her. Nothing loath, I pushed my sex into her again and began the slow movement that excited her so quickly and me so gradually for, even while using my skill to give her the utmost pleasure, I could not help com-

Zichy's wonderful drawing is as much an exploration of the depressive personality as it is of impromptu fellatio.

paring and I realized surely enough that Kate's pussy was smaller and firmer and gave me infinitely more pleasure; still I kept on for her delight. And now again she began to pant and choke and, as I continued ploughing her body and touching her womb with every slow thrust, she began to cry inarticulately with little short cries growing higher in intensity till suddenly she squealed like a shot rabbit and then shrieked with laughter, breaking down in a storm of sighs and sobs and floods of tears.

Cunnilingus's first Western prophet, apostle (and ultimately martyr) was Frank Harris. His success as a maker of love (his own accounts were well-attested by women) may have had not a little to do with his skill in this delicate art. This is Frank's first lesson.

As we turned off towards our bedrooms on the left, I saw that her face was glowing. At her door I stopped her. 'My kiss,' I said, and as in a dream she kissed me: *l'heure du berger* had struck.

'Won't you come to me tonight?' I whispered. 'That door leads into my room.' She looked at me with that inscrutable woman's glance, and for the first time her eyes gave themselves. That night I went to bed early and moved away the sofa, which on my side barred her door. I tried the lock but found it closed on her side, worse luck!

As I lay in bed that night about eleven o'clock, I heard and saw the handle of the door move. At once I blew out the light, but the blinds were not drawn and the room was

My hands
Open the curtains of your being
Clothe you in a further nudity
Uncover the bodies of your body
Invent another body for your body

TOUCH
OCTAVIO PAZ (1914–)

A drawing by Johannes Martini.

alight with moonshine.

'May I come in?' she asked.

'May you?' I was out of bed in a jiffy and had taken her adorable soft round form in my arms. 'You darling sweet,' I cried, and lifted her into my bed. She had dropped her dressing-gown, had only a nightie on, and in one moment my hands were all over her lovely body. The next moment I was with her in bed and on her, but she moved aside and away from me.

'No, let's talk,' she said.

I began kissing her, but acquiesced, 'Let's talk.' To my amazement, she began: 'Have you read Zola's latest book, *Nana*?'

'Yes,' I replied.

'Well,' she said, 'you know what the girl did to Nana?'

'Yes,' I replied, with sinking heart.

'Well,' she went on, 'why not do that to me? I'm desperately afraid of getting a child; you would be too in my place; why not love each other without fear?' A moment's thought told me that all roads lead to Rome and so I assented and soon I slipped

A French watercolour, anonymous.

down between her legs. 'Tell me please how to give you most pleasure,' I said, and gently I opened the lips of her sex and put my lips on it and my tongue against her clitoris. There was nothing repulsive in it; it was another and more sensitive mouth. Hardly had I kissed it twice when she slid lower down in the bed with a sigh, whispering, 'That's it; that's heavenly!'

Thus encouraged I naturally continued: soon her little lump swelled out so that I could take it in my lips and each time I sucked it, her body moved convulsively, and soon she opened her legs further and drew them up to let me in to the uttermost. Now I

A charcoal drawing by A1.

varied the movement by tonguing the rest of her sex and thrusting my tongue into her as far as possible; her movements quickened and her breathing grew more and more spasmodic, and when I went back to the clitoris again and took it in my lips and sucked it while pushing my forefinger back and forth into her sex, her movements became wilder and she began suddenly to cry in French, '*Oh, c'est fou! Oh, c'est fou!* Oh! Oh!' And suddenly she lifted me up, took my head in both her hands, and crushed my mouth with hers, as if she wanted to hurt me.

The next moment my head was between her legs again and the game went on. Little by little I felt that my finger rubbing the top of her sex while I tongued her clitoris gave her the most pleasure, and after another ten minutes of this delightful practice she cried: 'Frank, Frank, stop! Kiss me! Stop and kiss me, I can't stand any more, I am rigid with passion and want to bite or pinch you.'

Naturally I did as I was told and her body melted itself against mine while our lips met. 'You dear,' she said, 'I love you so, and oh how wonder-

A coloured print by an unknown
artist.

fully you kiss.'

'You've taught me,' I said. 'I'm your pupil.'

The last word on this comes from the *Story of O*.
Written by the mysterious 'Pauline Réage', it first
appeared in Paris in 1954.

The weather was less warm that day than it had
been hitherto. René, who had spent part of the
morning swimming, was napping on the couch in
a cool ground-floor room. Annoyed to see that he
preferred to sleep, Jacqueline had joined O in her
alcove. The sea and the sun had rendered her blon-
der than ever: her hair, her eyebrows, her lashes,
the fur between her thighs and under her arms
seemed powdered with silver, and as she was wearing no make-up at all, her mouth was the same
pink as the pink flesh of her open sex. In order that
Sir Stephen – whose presence, O said to herself,
she would surely have divined, noticed, somehow

sensed, had she been in
Jacqueline's place –
could see every bit of her,
O took care to flex
Jacqueline's knees and to
maintain her legs wide
apart for a while and in
the full light of the lamp

> Today in the afternoon love passed
> Over his perfect flesh, and on his lips.
> Over his flesh, which is the mould
> Of beauty, passed love's fever, uncontrolled
> By any ridiculous shame for the form of the enjoyment...
>
> FROM *HE CAME TO READ*
> C. P. CAVAFY (1863–1933)

she had turned on at the bedside. The shutters
were drawn, the room was almost dark despite the
slivers of light that penetrated between cracks in
the wood. For nigh on to an hour Jacqueline
moaned under O's caresses, and finally, her nipples
erected, her arms flung over her head, clutching
the wooden bars at the head of her bed, she began
to scream when O, dividing the lips fringed with
pale hair, set quietly and slowly to biting the tiny
inflamed morsel of flesh protruding from the cowl
formed by the juncture of those sweet and delicate
little labia. O felt it heat and rise under her tongue,
and, nipping mercilessly, fetched cry after cry from
Jacqueline until she broke like a pane of glass, and
relaxed, soaked from joy. Then O sent her into her
room, where she went to sleep; she was awake
again and ready when at five René came to take
her and Nathalie down to the water for a sail; they
used to go sailing in the late afternoon, when a bit
of breeze usually rose.

This last extract is full of ambiguities which
need to be explored. It was written by a
woman to please men. The fact that it is a lesbian scene does not detract from (indeed even
enhances) its appeal for men. Like the voyeuristic Sir Stephen, the heterosexual male is happy

A French drawing in ink over pencil
dating from 1930.

to look on. The heterosexual female
response to the extract would generally
be neutral, or possibly marginally positive since it is well-written and explicitly
erotic. Would the heterosexual male
response to a well-written male homosexual encounter be the same? And would a
woman find it positively erotic as men do
lesbian scenes? Here is a chance to find
out. The novel *Teleny*, or *The Reverse of
the Medal*, was printed as a private edition in 1893. It is the work of several
hands; there is good evidence that Oscar
Wilde was among them.

'I love you!' he whispered, 'I love you madly! I
cannot live without you any longer.'

'Nor can I,' said I faintly; 'I have struggled
against my passion in vain, and now I yield to it,
not tamely, but eagerly, gladly. I am yours, Teleny!
Happy to be yours, yours for ever and yours alone!'

For all answer there was a stifled hoarse cry
from his innermost breast; his eyes were lighted
up with a flash of fire; his craving amounted to
rage; it was that of a wild beast seizing his prey;
that of the lonely male finding at last a mate. Still
his intense eagerness was more than that; it was
also a soul issuing forth to meet another soul. It
was a longing of the senses, and a mad intoxication of the brain.

Could this burning, unquenchable fire that consumed our bodies be called lust? We clung as hungrily to one another as the famished animal does
when it fastens on the food it devours; and as we
kissed each other with ever-increasing greed, my

fingers were feeling his curly hair, or paddling the soft skin of his neck. Our legs being clasped together, his phallus, in strong erection, was rubbing against mine no less stiff and stark. We were, however, always shifting our position, so as to get every part of our bodies in as close contact as possible; and thus feeling, clasping, hugging, kissing, and biting each other, we must have looked, on that bridge amid the thickening fog, like two damned souls suffering eternal torment.

The hand of Time had stopped; and I think we should have continued goading each other in our mad desire until we had quite lost our senses – for we were both on the verge of madness – had we not been stopped by a trifling incident.

A drawing by the German artist Franz van Bayros, a follower of Beardsley and one of the last prophets of Decadence.

A belated cab – wearied by the day's toil – was slowly trudging its way homeward. The driver was sleeping on his box; the poor, broken-down jade, with its head drooping almost between its knees, was likewise slumbering – dreaming, perhaps, of unbroken rest, of new-mown hay, of the fresh and flowery pastures of its youth; even the slow rumbling of the wheels had a sleepy, purring, snoring sound in its irksome sameness.

'Come home with me,' said Teleny, in a low, nervous and trembling voice; 'come and sleep with me,' added he, in the soft, hushed and pleading tone of the lover who would fain be understood without words.

I pressed his hands for all answer.

'Will you come?'

'Yes,' I whispered, almost inaudibly.

This low, hardly-articulate sound was the hot breath of vehement desire; this lisped monosyllable was the willing consent to his eagerest wish.

Then he hailed the passing cab, but it was some moments before the driver could be awakened and made to understand what was wanted of him.

As I stepped in the vehicle, my first thought was that in a few minutes Teleny would belong to me. This thought acted upon my nerves as an electric current, making me shiver from head to foot.

My lips had to articulate the words 'Teleny will be mine,' for me to believe it. He seemed to hear the noiseless murmur of my lips, for he clasped my head between his hands, and kissed me again and again.

Then, as if feeling a pang of remorse – 'You do not repent, do you?' he asked.

'How can I?'

'And you will be mine – mine alone?'

'I never was any other man's, nor ever shall be.'

'You will love me for ever?'

'And ever.'

'This will be our oath and our act of possession,' added he.

Thereupon he put his arms around me and clasped me to his breast. I entwined my arms round him. By the glimmering, dim light of the cab-lamps I saw his eyes kindle with the fire of madness. His lips – parched with the thirst of long-suppressed desire, of the pent-up craving of possession – pouted towards mine with a painful expression of dull suffering. We were again sucking up each other's being in a kiss – a kiss more intense, if possible, than the former one. What a kiss that was!

The flesh, the blood, the brain, and that unde-

OPPOSITE *Study of a nude boy by a contemporary artist.*

A drawing from Aubrey Beardsley's Lysistrata which had to be published underground following the Oscar Wilde scandal of 1895.

fined subtler part of our being seemed all to melt together in an ineffable embrace.

A kiss is something more than the first sensual contact of two bodies; it is the breathing forth of two enamoured souls.

But a criminal kiss long withstood and fought against, and therefore long yearned after, is beyond this; it is as luscious as forbidden fruit; it is a glowing coal set upon the lips; a fiery brand that burns deep, and changes the blood into molten lead or scalding quicksilver.

Teleny's kiss was really galvanic, for I could taste its sapidity upon my palate. Was an oath needed, when we had given ourselves to one another with such a kiss? An oath is a lip-promise which can be, and is, often forgotten. Such a kiss follows you to the grave.

Whilst our lips clung together, his hand slowly, imperceptibly, unbuttoned my trousers, and stealthily slipped within the aperture, turning every obstacle in its way instinctively aside, then it lay hold of my hard, stiff, and aching phallus which was glowing like a burning coal.

This grasp was as soft as a child's, as expert as a whore's, as strong as a fencer's...

Some people, as we all know, are more magnetic than others. Moreover, while some attract, others repel us. Teleny had – for me, at least – a supple, mesmeric, pleasure-giving fluid in his fingers. Nay, the simple contact of his skin thrilled me with delight.

My own hand hesitatingly followed the lead his hand had given, and I must confess the pleasure I felt in paddling him was really delightful.

Our fingers hardly moved the skin of the penis;

but our nerves were so strained, our excitement had reached such a pitch, and the seminal ducts were so full, that we felt them overflowing. There was, for a moment, an intense pain, somewhere about the root of the penis – or rather, within the very core and centre of the reins, after which the sap of life began to move slowly, slowly, from within the seminal glands; it mounted up the bulb of the urethra, and up the narrow column, somewhat like mercury within the tube of a thermometer – or rather, like the scalding and scathing lava within the crater of a volcano.

It finally reached the apex; then the slit gaped, the tiny lips parted, and the pearly, creamy fluid oozed out – not all at once in a gushing jet, but at intervals, and in huge, burning tears.

Roman and Greek writers (like the Arab erotologists) wrote extensively about homosexuality. There were those for whom it was a lifetime's passion, of course, like the general (and later emperor) Galba of whom Suetonius wrote:

A hand-coloured etching by the German artist Carl Breuer-Courth dated 1920.

A French lithograph of 1925.

'He was much given to the intercourse between men... it is said that when Icelus, one of his old bedfellows, came to Spain to tell him of Nero's death, he kissed him closely before everyone present and asked him at once to be depilated...!'

For other males in Classical times, homosexuality was a passing phase in their life. The Greeks have indeed given us a name for this relationship: Socratic love. In return for education and board and lodging, a youth would grant his tutor/protector sexual favours, but on reaching a certain age they would part, often with tears, the young man to marry, his mentor to face loneliness or perhaps to find another companion.

Bisexuality and homosexuality were common among the Roman patrician class in the first century CE and a favourite target for Martial and Juvenal. Many of Martial's epigrams were savage; this is among the milder ones: 'Pluck out the hair from breast and legs and arms; keep your member cropped and ringed with short hair; all this, we know, you do for your mistress' sake, Labienus. But for whom do you depilate your posteriors?' His attacks on the lesbian secret societies of Rome were no less harsh.

Our society has moved on since it destroyed Oscar Wilde – it needed to. Now the tragedy of AIDS has rekindled the flames of prejudice. Our greatest playwright, Shakespeare, had a homosexual love affair and wrote about it in the Sonnets. He also wrote *Twelfth Night*, in which a boy actor plays a girl, who dresses as a boy, who falls in love with a man, who... a comedy with a message which they tend to leave out of the

If the unexpurgated version of the Diary *is ever published, this feminine point of view will be established more clearly. It will show that women (and I, in the* Diary*) have never separated sex from feeling, from love of the whole man.*

ANAÏS NIN (1903–77)

notes in school editions: that gender is less important than we might suppose. To end this topic, here is a heady cocktail of orality, anality and ambiguity from Anaïs Nin.

French watercolour by an unknown artist in Paris in 1925.

Under their feet was a big white fur. They fell on this, the three bodies in accord, moving against each other to feel breast against breast and belly against belly. They ceased to be three bodies. They became all mouths and fingers and tongues and

*Another watercolour by the
unknown French artist whose work
is already featured on page 121.*

OPPOSITE *An etching of an
unconventional barre exercise by
the French artist Marcel Vértes
(1895–1961).*

senses. Their mouths sought another mouth, a nipple, a clitoris. They lay entangled, moving very slowly. They kissed until the kissing became a torture and the body grew restless. Their hands always found yielding flesh, an opening. The fur they lay on gave off an animal odor, which mingled with the odors of sex.

Elena sought the fuller body of Bijou. Leila was more aggressive. She had Bijou lying on her side, with one leg thrown over Leila's shoulder, and she was kissing Bijou between the legs. Now and then Bijou jerked backwards, away from the stinging kisses and bites, the tongue that was as hard as a man's sex.

When she moved thus, her buttocks were thrown fully against Elena's face. With her hands Elena had been enjoying the shape of them, and now she inserted her finger into the tight little aperture. There she could feel every contraction caused by Leila's kisses, as if she were touching the wall against which Leila moved her tongue. Bijou, withdrawing from the tongue that searched her, moved into a finger which gave her joy. Her pleasure was expressed in melodious ripples of her voice, and now and then, like a savage being taunted, she bared her teeth and tried to bite the one who was tantalizing her.

When she was about to come and could no longer defend herself against her pleasure, Leila stopped kissing her, leaving Bijou halfway on the peak of an excruciating sensation, half-crazed. Elena had stopped at the same moment.

Uncontrollable now, like some magnificent maniac, Bijou threw herself over Elena's body, parted her legs, placed herself between them,

glued her sex to Elena's, and moved, moved with desperation. Like a man now, she thumped against Elena, to feel the two sexes meeting, soldering. Then as she felt her pleasure coming she stopped herself, to prolong it, fell backwards and opened her mouth to Leila's breast, to burning nipples that were seeking to be caressed.

Elena was now also in the frenzy before orgasm. She felt a hand under her, a hand she could rub against. She wanted to throw herself on this hand until it made her come, but she also wanted to prolong her pleasure. And she ceased moving. The hand pursued her. She stood up, and the hand again traveled towards her sex. Then she felt Bijou standing against her back, panting. She felt the pointed breasts, the brushing of Bijou's sexual hair against her buttocks. Bijou rubbed against her, and then slid up and down, slowly, knowing the friction would force Elena to turn so as to feel this on her breasts, sex and belly. Hands, hands every-

Watercolour by an unknown artist, Italy, c. 1930.

where at once. Leila's pointed nails buried in the softest part of Elena's shoulder, between her breast and underarm, hurting, a delicious pain, the tigress taking hold of her, mangling her. Elena's body so burning hot that she feared one more touch would set off the explosion. Leila sensed this, and they separated.

All three of them fell on the couch. They ceased touching and looked at each other, admiring their disorder, and seeing the moisture glistening along their beautiful legs.

But they could not keep their hands away from each other, and now Elena and Leila together attacked Bijou, intent on drawing from her the ultimate sensation. Bijou was surrounded, enveloped, covered, licked, kissed, bitten, rolled again on the fur rug, tormented with a million hands and tongues. She was begging now to be satisfied, spread her legs, sought to satisfy herself by friction against the others' bodies. They would not let her. With tongues and fingers they pryed into her, back and front, sometimes stopping to touch each other's tongue – Elena and Leila, mouth to mouth, tongues curled together, over Bijou's spread legs. Bijou raised herself to receive a kiss that would end her suspense. Elena and Leila, forgetting her, concentrated all their feelings in their tongues, flicking at each other. Bijou, impatient, madly aroused, began to stroke herself, then Leila and Elena pushed her hand away and fell upon her. Bijou's orgasm came like an exquisite torment. At each spasm she moved as if she were being stabbed. She almost cried to have it end.

Over her prone body, Elena and Leila took up their tongue-kissing again, hands drunkenly searching each other, penetrating everywhere, until Elena cried out. Leila's fingers had found her rhythm, and Elena clung to her, waiting for the pleasure to burst, while her own hands sought to give Leila the same pleasure. They tried to come in unison, but Elena came first, falling in a heap, detached from Leila's hand, struck down by the violence of her orgasm. Leila fell beside her, offering her sex to Elena's mouth. As Elena's pleasure grew fainter, rolling away, dying off, she gave Leila her tongue, flicking in the sex's mouth until Leila contracted and moaned. She bit into Leila's tender flesh. In the paroxysm of her pleasure, Leila did

Watercolour by an unknown artist, Italy circa 1930.

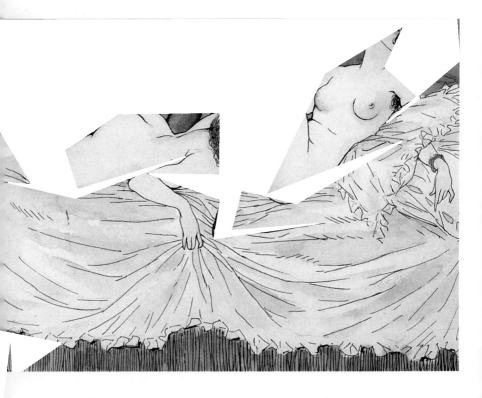

not feel the teeth buried there.

Elena now understood why some Spanish husbands refused to initiate their wives to all the possibilities of lovemaking – to avoid the risk of awakening in them an insatiable passion.

The old rogue Sheikh Nefzawi has the final word on forbidden fruit in this cautionary tale from his *Perfumed Garden*. The ingenious, if

A beautifully observed eighteenth-century painting from India of harem women enjoying one another. Pragmatic and enlightened men regarded such liaisons as inevitable and exciting to observe.

A young woman leaves her lover in no doubt as to the quality of his lovemaking. This is an early twentieth-century Indian miniature.

uncomfortable scheme demonstrates that lust – if not love – will always find a way...

There was once a man who had a wife whose beauty was like that of the moon at its full. He was very jealous, for he knew all the tricks that people play. That being so, he never went out without locking the doors of the house and terrasses. One day his wife said to him:

'Why do you do that?'

'Because I know your tricks and habits.'

'What you are doing is no good; when a woman wants a thing, all precautions are useless.'

'Perhaps so! but for all that I'll fasten the doors.'

'Locking a door is no good if a woman has made up her mind to get what you are thinking of.'

'Well! if you can do anything, do it!'

As soon as her husband had gone out, the woman went to the top of the house and made a hole in the wall so that she could see who was passing. At that moment a young man was going along the street; he raised his eyes, saw the woman, and desired to possess her. He asked how he could get to her. She told him he could not enter as all the doors were fastened.

'But how can we meet?' he asked.

'I will make a hole in the house door; you, when you see my husband returning from evening prayer, will wait until he has got inside the house, and then push your member through the hole in the door, opposite which I will put my vulva. In that way we can copulate – any other way will be impossible.'

So the young man watched for the husband's return and, as soon as he had seen him enter the house and close the door behind him, he went to the hole which had been cut in the door and put his member through it. The woman was also on the lookout; hardly had her husband entered, and while he was still in the courtyard, she went to the

A latter-day Pyramus and Thisbe by Paul Gavarni (1804–1866).

OPPOSITE *Stone relief, India, eleventh century CE.*

Ivory comb, India, from the nineteenth century.

door under the pretext of seeing if it were fastened; then, hastening to put her vulva opposite the member which was sticking through the hole, she introduced it entirely into her vagina.

That done, she put out her lamp and called to her husband to bring her a light.

'Why?' he asked.

'I have dropped the jewel I wear on my breast and cannot find it.'

So the husband brought a lamp. The young man's member was still in the woman's vulva and it had just ejaculated.

'Where did your jewel fall?' asked the husband.

'There it is!' she cried; and she drew back quickly, leaving uncovered her lover's member, which was withdrawn from the vulva all wet with sperm.

At sight of this the husband fell on the ground in a violent rage and, when he got up, his wife asked:

'Well, what about your precautions?'

'May God make me repent!' was his reply.

The final word in this part has to come from D. H. Lawrence.

And when, throughout all the wild orgasms of love slowly a gem forms, in the ancient, once-more-molten rocks of two human hearts, two ancient rocks, a man's heart and a woman's, that is the crystal of peace, the slow hard jewel of trust, the sapphire of fidelity. The gem of mutual peace emerging from the wild chaos of love.

PART TWO

The Essence of Desire

Erotica should be read aloud, in bed, by one lover to another: that is the ideal. The critic Marghanita Laski said at the time of the prosecution of Mayflower Books over the publication of *Fanny Hill* that she could find nothing wrong with the novel provided one had a companion at the time of reading it. There is nothing wrong with the solitary reading of erotic literature either, but we should not lose sight of its main intention: to excite the imagination and to start that reciprocal inflammation of body and mind which is sexual desire. A. P. Herbert expressed all this more succinctly, saying that the purpose of erotica was to make us 'as randy as possible as quickly as possible'. But the best erotic writing (in common with all the best fiction) draws on springs deep in the writer's unconscious and is not simply the creation of conscious intelligence. This may explain why characters in erotic fiction who have no business to be anything more than two-dimensional cardboard cut-outs, for all the attention the writer has given their characterization, sometimes come alarmingly to life.

Erotica is seldom great literature (much is barely literature at all), but there is a down-to-earth reason why the writing is often unexpectedly good. Wealthy patrons and entrepreneurial printers and booksellers have always been

OPPOSITE *A coloured engraving from Verlaine's Oeuvres Libres, artist unknown.*

prepared to pay handsomely for erotica. John Cleland wrote *Fanny Hill* to clear his debts; Anaïs Nin produced her erotic stories in order to support herself, and her circle of friends, in Paris. And many others – sometimes great writers have contributed to the genre for straight forward financial reasons. Anyone with the inclination could spend years of research attempting to attribute the many anonymous Victorian erotic novels to the leading literary figures of that age.

Erotic art and photography work on our imagination more directly than does literature. Biologically we are programmed to respond to certain visual erotic stimuli. Taste and preference come into this, of course, but give us the right signal – in stone, paint or photographic emulsion – and as sexual beings we cannot help but respond. Erotic images make such a strong and direct appeal that they can, fetishistically, become sexual icons: themselves the object of our awakened eroticism. The youth who violated Praxiteles' statue of Aphrodite personified this one aspect of human sexuality as surely as the goddess personifies them all.

If erotica excites, it also educates. In India, China and Japan this was always the dual intention of much erotic literature and art. There is still a surprising amount of ignorance about sexual matters: another reason why the publication of good erotica is important in a civilized society. Instruction manuals are all very well, but how much more we learn from a good erotic novel.

Producing erotic anthologies is also educative. Having made the decision to include some photographs in this part of the book, we were given

A nineteenth-century erotic figurine in carnival costume.

an opportunity to see one of the largest archives of sexual photographs in the world, spanning the entire history of photography. Presumably because they have not passed through the filter of an artist's mind and are taken directly from the life, sexually explicit photographs attract more attention from censors and regulators than do works of art. For that reason, all but a small handful of images were simply unpublishable.

We sorted through the archive – categorizing the photographs roughly – in order to gain some insights into this secret and illegal market which is shaped by supply and demand. There were few surprises in the 'specialist' categories, which ranged from the revolting through sad to the bizarre. The surprises came among the highly explicit photographs of mainstream sexuality which were taken from 1850 to the present day: a significant minority of these love's labours lost were astonishingly beautiful.

Had the subjects simply transcended the mercenary purpose of the photographer? Had what was observed drawn some response from the photographer that was far bigger than his petty intentions? The answer to both questions is 'yes'; we are better than we think. What the camera recorded in those ordinary rooms in Vienna and Los Angeles, Montmartre and Soho was both special and commonplace. It is an inheritance that no one can take from us: a fact central to our humanity. Sex is beautiful.

CHAPTER FOUR
The Watchers and the Watched

Far back in time, at a period so remote that we have only palaeontologists and geneticists for our guides, the human race consisted of a few small groups of hominids living in the African Rift Valley. This beautiful country was the real Garden of Eden. As these beings were, quite literally, the mothers and fathers of us all, it seems faintly indecent to speculate about their sexual behaviour. However, from zoological studies of our nearest animal relatives we can be certain of some general characteristics. For example, when one pair – let us call them Adam and Eve – began to enjoy one another it is likely to have started an explosive sexual chain reaction among the other adults of the group. This is the way human beings were before the dawn of time, and it is the way we still are: communal and imitative.

This imitative faculty is the foundation of our ability to learn which has given us our ascendancy over the rest of creation. It also makes us highly suggestible. Upon this convenient rock the advertising executives have built a mighty industry. Show us our favourite food and we want to eat it, we begin to salivate, sometimes we can almost scent it. Our voyeuristic attitude towards sex functions in much the same way. Voyeurism is not only the mainspring of erotica, it is the subject of much of it.

Some psychologists seek to explain voyeurism as an attempt, to witness the 'primal scene' of

Erotic silhouettes are extremely rare. This is surprising since the technique is strongly suggestive of shadows cast against a blind: intimate scenes observed voyeuristically by an unsuspected third party – us.

OPPOSITE *However charming or erotic Victorian photographs are, whatever magic contemporary chemicals and lenses have made of flesh tones, they always have a poignant quality. These were people who once lived, who crimped their hair, who tried not to laugh at the photographer's props. Now they are symbols of the fin-de-siècle: a reminder of the 'great vital constants' – sex and death.*

ABOVE and OPPOSITE *Silhouettes from the collection 'Er und Sie' (He and She) published in Vienna in 1922. The artist exploits the intimate, personal quality of the medium, which we associate with portraits, to enhance the erotic effect.*

our own conception. Most of us are content to hope that, like Edmund in *King Lear*, there was 'good sport' at our making. Laura in Mirabeau's *The Lifted Curtain*, a case study for Freudians, as was its brilliant author, is prompted by jealousy and curiosity to spy on her father.

One evening after supper, we retired to a salon where my father had coffee and liqueurs served. In less than half an hour, Lucette was sound asleep. At that, my father took me up in his arms and carried me to my room where he put me to bed. Surprised at this new arrangement, my curiosity was instantly aroused. I got up a few moments later and tiptoed to the glass door, whose velvet curtain I slightly pushed aside so that I could look into the salon.

I was astonished to see Lucette's bosom completely uncovered. What charming breasts she possessed! They were two hemispheres as white as snow and firm as marble in the centre of which rose two little strawberries. The only movement they showed was from her regular breathing. My father was fondling them, kissing them and sucking them. In spite of his actions, she continued slumbering. Soon he began to remove all of her clothing, placing it on the edge of the bed. When he took off her shift, I saw two plump rounded thighs of alabaster which he spread apart. Then I made out a little vermilion slit adorned with a chestnut-brown tuft of hair. This he half opened, inserting his fingers which he vigorously manipulated in and out. Nothing roused her out of her lethargy.

Excited by the sight and instructed by the example, I imitated on myself the movements I saw and experienced sensations hitherto unknown to me.

Laying her on the bed, my father came to the glass door to close it. I saved myself by hastening to the couch on which he had placed me. As soon as I was stretched out on the sheets, I began my rubbing, pondering what I had just viewed and profiting from what I had learned. I was on fire. The sensation I was undergoing increased in intensity, reaching such a height that it seemed my entire body and soul were concentrated in that one spot. Finally, I sank back in a state of exhausted ecstasy that enchanted me.

Returning to my senses, I was astonished to find myself almost soaked between my thighs. At first, I was very worried, but this anxiety was dispelled by the remembrance of the bliss I had just enjoyed.

... I took advantage of my father's absence to satisfy my burning curiosity. While Lucette was engaged in some task in another part of the house, I punctured a little hole in the silken curtain of the glass door.

I had not long to wait to profit from my stratagem.

On my father's return, he immediately donned a flimsy dressing-gown and led to his room Lucette, who was in equally casual attire. They were careful to close the door and draw the curtain, but my preparations frustrated their precautions, at least in part. As soon as they were in the room, I was at the door with my face glued to the glass by the lifted curtain. The first person to meet my eyes was Lucette with her magnificent bosom completely bare. It was so seductive that I could not blame my father for immediately covering it with quick, eager kisses. Unable to hold himself back he tore off her clothing, and in a twinkling of the eye,

My father compounded with my mother under the dragon's tail, and my nativity was under Ursa Major; so that it follows I am rough and lecherous.

FROM *KING LEAR*
WILLIAM SHAKESPEARE
(1564–1616)

A sinuous lithograph by Margit Gaal, 1921.

skirt, corset and chemise were on the floor. How temptingly lovely she was in her natural state! I could not tear my eyes from her. She possessed all the charms and freshness of youth. Feminine beauty has a singular power and attraction for those of the same sex. My arms yearned to embrace those divine contours.

My father was soon in a state similar to his partner's. My eyes were fixed on him, because I had never seen him that way before. Now he placed her on the divan, which I could not see from my observation post.

Devoured by curiosity, I threw caution to the winds. I lifted the curtain until I could see everything. Not a detail escaped my eyes, and they spared themselves not the slightest voluptuousness.

I was able to perceive clearly Lucette stretched out on the couch and her fully expanded slit between the two chubby eminences. My father displayed a veritable jewel, a big member, stiff, surrounded by hair at the root below which dangled two balls. The tip was scarlet red. I saw it enter Lucette's slit, lose itself there, and then reappear. This in-and-out movement continued for some time. From the fiery kisses they exchanged, I surmised that they were in raptures. Finally, I noticed the organ completely emerge. From the carmine tip which was all wet spurted a white fluid on Lucette's flat belly.

How the sight aroused me! I was so excited and carried away by desires I had not yet known that I attempted, at least partially, to participate in their delirium.

So entranced was I by the tableau that I remained too long and my imprudence betrayed me. My father, who had been too preoccupied with Lucette, now disengaging himself from Lucette's arms, saw the partially lifted curtain.

Comte Gabriel Honoré Riqueti de Mirabeau (1749–91), the greatest orator of the French Revolution, was imprisoned four times for 'wildness' on the orders of his father, the Marquis. These periods of confinement gave Mirabeau – the libertine, the resented son, the eternal outsider and 'voyeur' on society – time to write a good deal of high-quality erotica, much of it politically motivated. His enemies used the fact to blacken his reputation, but the people loved him all the same and he became a successful politician. Who better than the alienated Mirabeau to bridge two worlds? His reward is to rest with France's heroes in the Pantheon.

A woodcut by the artist Italo Zetti, which was designed to be used as a bookplate.

In her cool prose, Anaïs Nin controls characters who are little more than marionettes with the icy detachment of a puppetmaster, relying on her powers of description for the erotic charge. This is one of those short stories where all is not made clear until the end, at which point we have the distinct sense that the writer has manipulated us.

She murmured, 'Take your clothes off.'

He undressed. Naked, he knew his power. He was more at ease naked than clothed because he had been an athlete, a swimmer, a walker, a mountain climber. And he knew then that he could please her.

She looked at him.

Was she pleased? When he bent over her, was she more responsive? He could not tell. By now he desired her so much that he could not wait to touch her with the tip of his sex, but she stopped him. She wanted to kiss and fondle it. She set about this with so much eagerness that he found himself with her full backside near his face and able to kiss and fondle her to his content.

By now he was taken with the desire to explore and touch every nook of her body. He parted the opening of her sex with his two fingers, he feasted his eyes on the glowing skin, the delicate flow of honey, the hair curling around his fingers. His mouth grew more and more avid, as if it had become a sex organ in itself, capable of so enjoying her that if he continued to fondle her flesh with his

OPPOSITE *She both holds and frames the seat of her affections. The gesture is proprietorial, protective – the image unexpectedly beautiful.*

BELOW *Humour and pathos are frequently uninvited guests at the studios of pornographic photographers.*

Why, Jenny, as I watch you there –
For all your wealth of loosened hair,
Your silk ungirdled and unlaced
And warm sweets open to the waist,
All golden in the lamplight's gleam –
You know not what a book you seem,
Half-read by lightning in a dream!

FROM *JENNY*
DANTE GABRIEL ROSSETTI (1828–82)

tongue he would reach some absolutely unknown pleasure. As he bit into her flesh with such a delicious sensation, he felt again in her a quiver of pleasure. Now he forced her away from his sex, for fear she might experience all her pleasure merely kissing him and that he would be cheated of feeling himself inside of her womb. It was as if they both had become ravenously hungry for the taste of flesh. And now their two mouths melted into each other, seeking the leaping tongues.

Her blood was fired now. By his slowness he seemed to have done this, at last. Her eyes shone brilliantly, her mouth could not leave his body. And finally he took her, as she offered herself, opening her vulva with her lovely fingers, as if she could no longer wait. Even then they suspended their pleasure, and she felt him quietly, enclosed.

Then she pointed to the mirror and said, laughing, 'Look, it appears as if we were not making love, as if I were merely sitting on your knees, and you, you rascal, you have had it inside me all the time, and you're even quivering. Ah, I can't bear it any longer, this pretending I have nothing inside. It's burning me up. Move now, move!'

She threw herself over him so that she could gyrate around his erect penis, deriving from this erotic dance a pleasure which made her cry out. And at the same time a lightning flash of ecstasy tore through George's body.

Despite the intensity of their lovemaking, when he left, she did not ask him his name, she did not ask him to return. She gave him a light kiss on his almost painful lips and sent him away. For months

OPPOSITE *A contemporary erotic icon by an unknown artist.*

An illustration from Casanova's History of My Life.

the memory of this night haunted him and he could not repeat the experience with any woman.

One day he encountered a friend who had just been paid lavishly for some articles and invited him to have a drink. He told George the spectacular story of a scene he had witnessed. He was spending money freely in a bar when a very distinguished man approached him and suggested a pleasant pastime, observing a magnificent love scene, and as George's friend happened to be a confirmed voyeur, the suggestion met with instant acceptance. He had been taken to a mysterious house, into a sumptuous apartment, and concealed in a dark room, where he had seen a nymphomaniac making love with an especially gifted and potent man.

George's heart stood still. 'Describe her,' he said.

His friend described the woman George had made love to, even to the satin dress. He also described the canopied bed, the mirrors, everything. George's friend had paid one hundred dollars for the spectacle, but it had been worthwhile and had lasted for hours.

The aphrodisiac effects of voyeurism are exploited in this humorous piece from *Memoirs of a Venetian Courtesan*. The heroine – depressed after the death of her husband – enjoys some therapeutic theatre arranged by her friend, the opera singer Faustolla.

For several weeks Faustolla has insisted that I must take a lover. She understands my reluctance but reminds me that she does not talk of 'love' in fact, but of recreation. To make her point she asks whether I prefer the other options open to me, for she sees only two: Veniero or the madness which afflicts those nuns who cannot divert their desires but merely deny them.

Arriving at her rooms today (a special concession from my protector who will no doubt exact a price for it) I was conducted immediately to the bedroom. Here she gave me a great glass of wine and had me sit on a chair in her dressing room. To my amazement she then closed the doors on me leaving only a chink between. In front of this she placed a screen. 'The Theatre of Saint Angela. You cannot be seen but that is of little consequence since the performers expect no applause. The opera's libretto is an imaginative re-working of an old theme for which I make no apologies since my whole purpose is to recall it to your mind.'

With this Faustolla swept out, leaving my head spinning. By the time the full import of what she had said had dawned upon me I could already hear voices approaching.

A young man was praising her latest performance. As they entered the room I recognized Faustolla's lover, Fabrizio. Foolishly I made as if to greet him, having forgotten for the moment my status as hidden audience.

Faustolla had not forgotten her role. First she introduced the central character to fix him in the mind of the audience (a convention quite unnecessary in this case!). I do not mean Fabrizio but his gigantic cock. Falling to her knees before my hiding place, so close I feared to breathe, she took this prodigy from the young man's breeches. With a sideways glance to me – which somehow made her actions more disturbing – she began to lick, stroke

and suck this giant sweetmeat.

While she made her noisy feast, Fabrizio tore at his clothes until he was quite nude. Erected before me, and rising majestically from his belly, was the campanile. The architect had made some changes. This edifice was pale for most of its length and red at the end rather than the reverse, and the great bells were hung at the base, but the scale was similar!

Rising from her understandable homage, Faustolla now removed her garments. While she accomplished this her eyes never left his cock. The shining end was like a roof tile that has had rain upon it. The long column was veined white marble. The balls had the brown-red of weathered bricks. When eyes were not enough, and she was impelled to caress Fabrizio with her fingers, his cock moved like a man who has been startled.

As each of Faustolla's charms were revealed her lover explored it, first with eyes and then with hands. I could enjoy the perfect white of her heavy breasts and their scarlet teats; but I could not lift the weight of them or stiffen the nipples between my finger tips as he did. I envied too the exploring fingers in the moist cleft between her thighs and the hands which stroked the twin alabaster globes of her bottom.

And how I envied Faustolla when she turned and leaned forward over the bed: cunt open to receive her lover.

Reds and whites Faustolla, no browns or ochre. Her sex was crimson. Fabrizio lowered the head of his cock and nuzzled the glistening portal. I heard her gasp 'Yes, Yes.'

He pushed slowly into her. Then stopped again. Her call more urgent this time, as if all she wanted in the world was his cock in her: 'Yes! Yes!'

Again he pushed, pushed until I saw his dark balls rest against her pale skin. Now she was silent as he began to move in and out of her. The gusts of their breath the only sound.

He moved against her like the clapper of a great bell. I could see the rhythm of the ponderous movement, but I could only guess at the vibrations and their tone.

Perhaps guessing this – though I think for the time Faustolla had forgotten her audience in the passion of the part – she became suddenly vocal. But in the excitement of the quickening rhythm these sounds were not from her usual repertoire but shrieks and gasps.

These animal sounds spurred Fabrizio to such a fury of fucking that I knew the crisis must be close. It came

> I wish I were the wind, and you, walking along the seashore, would uncover your breasts and let me touch them as I blow.
>
> ANONYMOUS GREEK EPIGRAM
> (BEFORE FIFTH CENTURY AD)

to her first when she shouted a great 'Yes' of confirmation. This was the cue for her partner who gave a long, dying groan and collapsed on her back.

I thought my loins had turned to water, so wet was I. Yet Faustolla was wetter. When her gallant slipped to the floor behind her, the crimson landscape was awash with spume. A string of pearls cascaded down on to he who had so recently bestowed them.

All quiet. Two swooning on the bed as if dead. Another sipping from a glass of wine with trembling hands.

The second act. Placing her lover so that his head was away from me and between her legs, Faustolla smiled at me. From this kneeling position she

An engraving by an unknown artist which was made to illustrate the Sonetti Lusuriosi (Lewd Sonnets) *of Pietro Aretino.*

leaned forward and took hold of his penis. Since he was busy with his tongue in her sex, his face buried between the cheeks of her arse, she was free to make a direct appeal to her audience.

First she commends his penis to me, moving it in such a way as to show off all its features. Then, with mime of course, she asked if I would like it? Feigning disappointment at my supposed rejection of this generous offer she affects to comfort the cock. It must have been greatly offended by my coldness (coldness!) because it begins to thrash about: throwing itself from side to side in despair.

This moves Faustolla and she gives the cock sanctuary in her mouth. Strictly speaking only one third can be said to be truly closeted from the cruelties of the world but it is a sympathetic and imaginative audience. The pathos of this moment deeply affects Faustolla. As she rocks her mouth up and down to warm and comfort her guest, I can see real tears in her eyes.

Soon the cock is ready to take on the world again. Perhaps he is too full of his own importance because she begins to wave the great shining thing about. There is something in this stiff dance which brings an involuntary gasp from the audience. This causes a smile on stage just as the curtain is lowered.

I am wet again as I recall the lustful celebration which I then witnessed: a beautiful woman pleasuring herself on a cock of truly theatrical proportions. More than that: her every action, though

The moth's kiss, first!
Kiss me as if you made believe
You were not sure, this eve,
How my face, your flower, had pursed
Its petals up; so, here and there
You brush it, till I grow aware
Who wants me, and wide ope I burst.

FROM *IN A GONDOLA*
ROBERT BROWNING (1812–89)

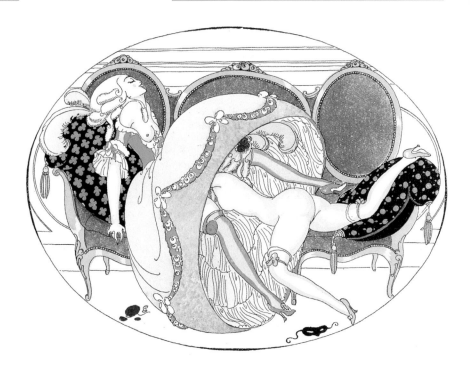

ABOVE and OPPOSITE *Coloured
stencil engravings which were
first published in 1917.*

intended for his pleasure and hers, was addressed
also to me. I believe my presence intensified her
pleasure just as I am sure that the knowledge that
this was being done for me, made what I witnessed
all the more affecting.

Her auburn hair danced about her white shoulders as she rose and fell. Sometimes she leaned
forward on him so that the weight of her hair and
breasts took them away from her body. Their
movement was different then and slower. When
she leaned back her breasts flattened and the
points of the nipples moved quickly.

Fabrizio was a long time in reaching his crisis.
Sometimes she turned away from me and her sex
was hidden, a mystery somewhere deep within

her haunches. All I could see was the long shaft of his cock appearing and disappearing between her buttocks.

When she turned to face me again, knees drawn up, I could see everything: his penis disappearing into the froth of hair as she pushed down onto it; her lips holding it as she pulled up.

At those times when she faced me and leaned back I could see her clitoris. Sometimes she reached down to the crimson bud and touched it, moving her finger quickly. Then she always sought my eyes.

That was how it was when Fabrizio began to groan with his orgasm. This time she must follow. Faustolla sought my eyes in vain. Then closed hers. A moment later she made a sound in the back of her throat and began to gasp like one drowning as each wave of pleasure broke.

Afterwards, when Fabrizio had gone, she opened the doors of my torture chamber and smiled. I did not have to ask her. She led me to the bed and pushed me back.

I felt her fingers in the damp hair, then opening my lips. The crisis came moments after I felt her tongue for the first time.

The voyeurism implicit in all erotic fiction is enhanced when voyeurism is also the subject of that fiction. The lubricity is further increased when one of the participants is aware that they are being watched, as in this episode involving an alternative 'Charlie's Aunt'.

'For God's sake fuck me – fuck me!'

Of course my cock was bursting to do so; with one shove he was sheathed to the cods; my loved mistress spent with that alone, so highly was she excited, not only by the preparations, but as she herself acknowledged to me, by the idea of the instantaneous infidelity to her husband, at the moment after he had just fucked her – such is the wild imagination of women when they give way to every libidinous thought. It would have been exactly the same if some equally fortunate lover had been awaiting my retiring from the field. The idea of success in deception is a passion with them, and they would almost sacrifice any thing to obtain it. Before I could arrive at the grand crisis, she was again ready, and we died away in an agony of blissful lubricity – she held me, as usual, so tight that I never thought of withdrawing from the folds of her delicious cunt, but lay still enjoying the never ceasing compressions of its velvety folds, which sometimes really had almost the force of a vice. I was rapidly ready for a second bout, which, like the first, ended in extatic joys, beyond the power of description. My charming mistress thought I ought now to desist, but pleading my forty hours' fast (for, of course, she knew nothing of my fucking Mary), I begged her to allow me to run one more course.

'Then, my darling Charlie, you must let me turn on my side, for I am so heated with your weight and my husband's that I must have some relief, but there is no occasion for you to

Et qui remonte et redescend
Et rebondit sur mes roustons
En sauts où mon vit à tâtons
Pris d'un vertigo incandescent

Parmi des foutres et des mouilles
Meurt, puis revit, plus meurt encore,
Revit, remeurt, revit encore
Par tout ce foutre et que de mouilles!

Cependant que mes doigts, non sans
Te faire un tas de postillons,
Légers comme des papillons
Mais profondement caressants,

Et que mes paumes, de tes fesses
Froides modérément tout juste
Remontent lento vers le buste
Tiède sous leurs chaudes caresses.

withdraw, leave me to manage it.'

With an art quite her own, she accomplished her object, her splendid buttocks' pressing before my eyes against my belly fired me immediately. My cock swelled and stood firm as ever. Then passing an arm round her body, I used my fingers on her excited and stiffly projecting clitoris. We had a much longer and more voluptuous fuck than before; nothing could exceed the delicious movements of my divine mistress; she twisted her body so, that I could suck one of her bubbies, while I fucked and frigged her; she spent with such a scream of delight that I am sure she must have been heard in the house, had it not been for the inner baize door to the room. She continued throbbing so deliciously on my prick that I began to flatter myself I should obtain a fourth favour, but she suddenly bolted out of my arms and out of bed. Turning round, and taking my whole prick into her mouth, and giving it a voluptuous suck, she said –

'No, my loved boy, we must be prudent if we mean to have a repetition of these most exquisite interviews. You have given me most extatic pleasure, and by moderation, and running no risk in too long indulgence of our passions, we may safely manage to enjoy similar interviews every day. Get into the dressing-room, remain there until I leave my room and pass your door. After I have seen that no one is near, I will cough twice, wait a minute longer,

And lifting up and dropping back
To land on bollocks with a bump,
And bouncing where my white-hot stump
Dizzily feeling round the crack

Among the juices and the come
Dies and revives and dies again,
Retools, and dies, and tools again,
Through so much juice and all that come.

My fingers meanwhile, which full-pelt
Were tapping light quick commentaries
On your unguarded orifice,
Butterflies, but profoundly felt,

Leave the glen slowly for their calm
Long climb from buttocks' moderate chill
Around toward each tremulous hill,
Warm in the hot and hollowed palm.

FROM *THE WAY THE LADIES RIDE*
PAUL VERLAINE (1844–96)

*An engraving made in the late
nineteenth century.*

then quietly leave and descend by the back stairs.'

All was happily effected, and for the week longer they remained with us, I found means to repeat the charming lesson every day, without raising suspicion in any one's mind.

The preceding episode – 'A Peep-Hole Aftermath' – is taken from *The Romance of Lust*, one of the most popular erotic novels of the Victorian period. Having persuaded his aunt to allow him to watch her with his uncle, the hero then enjoys the effects of this aphrodisiac aperitif. *The Romance of Lust* was published in four volumes between 1873 and 1876. It appears to have been written by several people, but was edited by William Simpson Potter.

The novel is in the picaresque tradition. It has no real plot but it is well written and nicely paced, which is just as well for the reader, who is led through a bewildering forest of sexual encounters. *The Romance of Lust* is a truly alternative novel: the shadow of contemporary convention. Its hero Charlie seduces not only aunts but also sisters and uncles – indeed, everyone and anyone. His sexual tastes are catholic, although he does have a marked preference for the alternative sexual venue: indeed, the novel could just as easily have been called the 'romance of sodomy'.

The pastiche novel *Passion's Apprentice* makes use of the voyeur motif in an unusual way, combining sex with farce. We join the hero and unwilling voyeur – William Ashton – in the rooms of a Paris milliner.

It seemed the difficult business of millinery did not in itself provide Marie-Louise with all the comforts she wanted. She had therefore taken the practical, time-honoured and mutually beneficial step of acquiring a rich lover or protector. No, she could not say if she loved him or not. In respect of that particular verb she was as perplexed as Ashton.

Marie-Louise and Ashton had begun their guilt-less enjoyment of each other about ten days after his arrival. Having slipped naturally into the famil-iar and friendly intimacy already described, Ashton had found that he was always welcome at her rooms in the evening if the marvels of Paris theatre or opera had not lured him. She had made it clear in her frank way that he was to 'take her as he found her' but providing the spectacle of her sewing feathers onto a hat or attending to some aspect of her toilette did not offend him then her door was always open. When her protector returned from the trip to Marseilles which had engaged him for several weeks this arrangement would need to adhere to a somewhat less flexible timetable, but they had already enjoyed several happy evenings together

On the occasion in question Ashton had arrived just as his good-natured friend had begun to wash her hair. Of course he did not mind. It would be a new experience for him – and so indeed it was.

Marie-Louise had glowing auburn hair and the milky skin which often accompanies that colour-ing. She was wearing a loosely-fitting silk gown and had already put out water and the other things she would need on the washstand.

'Are you to lie a spectator or will you help me?'

'I will help of course.' Ashton was amazed at the

OPPOSITE and ABOVE *At the end of the nineteenth century photography was still imitating art, as in* The Blue Veil. *Meanwhile some artists had been influenced by photography to produce idealized wonders like this painting entitled* Voluptuousness, *which was reproduced in sepia monochrome as a postcard.*

A French postcard printed at the turn of the century.

A coloured lithograph illustrating the maxim 'Early to bed, and up with the cock'.

length of her hair, unpinned she could have sat upon it.

She bent over the bowl. 'Pour the water now.'

He did so, and also followed her other directions. As Marie-Louise bent forward her gown hung away from her, revealing milky white breasts and nipples so intense in colour they almost looked sore.

Ashton, who was already suffering from the misery of sexual abstinence, was transfixed. He had of course been very aware of Marie-Louise, who was as attractive as she was cheerful, but for some reason had not considered making love to her a possibility. Consideration of that very possibility now animated both his mind and his body. The raging erection struggling to assert itself within the confines of his trousers was not pacified when he noticed that below the glorious breasts an equally glorious belly and froth of red hair was visible.

Ashton may have gasped, perhaps his eyes betrayed him when her own hot green orbs confronted him. The more prosaic bulge in his trousers could have given the clue. Whatever the

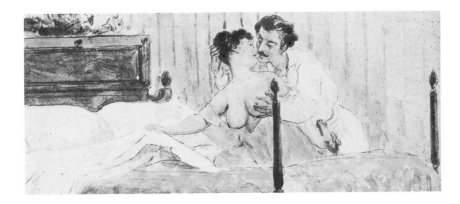

reason, when Marie-Louise had finished drying with the towel and stood supporting herself on her hands against the mantelpiece, head dropped forward so that her damp hair was in front of the fire, she suddenly said: 'I want it as badly as you. Why don't we do it?'

Hast du die Lippen mir wund geküsst,
So küsse sie wieder heil.

You who bruised my lips with kissing
Kiss them well again.

HEINRICH HEINE
(1797–1856)

For a moment all was silence. Ashton was not sure he had understood: then he did. Staying in the same position she loosened her gown with one hand and let it slip to the floor.

Instantly he was behind her, lifting the soft weight of her breasts with one hand, and exploring between her legs with the other. She remained as she was before the fire. He tore off his clothes and dropped to his knees behind her. She bent her legs a little and pushed out her buttocks so that he could lick her. Her body perfume was intense, the taste of her scarlet sex like ripe fruit that has burst open.

He stood now and slowly pushed his throbbing penis where his tongue had been. She gave a long moan; supported by him and with him still inside her, she sank to her knees. Rutting her now with a fury, he drove in and out until there was a lather which sucked and slapped between belly and buttocks. At the finish she shouted 'Yes, yes, yes!' as if to confirm her pleasure. Her sex gripped him then, milking the last seed from his manhood.

Ashton and Marie-Louise took such pleasure in each other that it made them reckless. To risk being together on the very day her protector returned was ill-considered enough, to ignore the chiming of the clock was madness. Fate was not slow to rebuke them for this self-indulgence.

*Bedroom frolics – an engraving
from the turn of the century.*

The returning merchant could not have guessed at the extraordinary and immediate effect of his thunderous knock upon the door. Within, and mercifully hidden from his eyes, the sound drove Ashton to the only possible exit and Marie-Louise into a fury of tidying. Four strides took Ashton from the couch and out onto the tiny balcony. Ashamed that he had shown no presence of mind beyond the selfish impulse of snatching off the table cover when the freezing night air first struck his naked body, he watched the meticulous preparations of Marie-Louise with admiration. Before her protector had time to knock again she called out that she was washing and would be finished in a moment. This was indeed true. Stooping over the wash bowl to freshen herself after many hours of lovemaking with Ashton took only a moment. As there was no slop pail it took only another moment to open the narrow doors of the balcony, fling out the tell-tale water, kiss her lover, re-close the doors and draw the curtains.

Through the narrow chink which remained, Ashton saw her put his clothes and boots under the large chair. Calling out all the time to her protector in mock chiding tones, she upbraided him for being so impetuous. 'Surely he was very early?' At this time she was smoothing the bed which had been so deliciously rumpled. 'Did he not know that there were little things a lady must do before receiving her lover?' Now she was removing the boots from beneath the chair which prevented it from resting flat and sliding them under the curtain. 'Was he very passionate today?' Until now she had been naked. After a visit to her perfume bottle she took a fresh silk gown from the armoire and slipped it on. 'If passion had made him forget his manners then she forgave him.'

All this had taken less time than it takes to tell it. Finally, the extraordinary girl went to her lover's hiding place to check on his condition. At the sight of Ashton, naked except for the table cover which concealed only his upper torso and which he wore in the manner of an old lady's shawl, she could not control her laughter.

This was too much for her protector. His knocking became furious and he called out to her angrily. For the first time a look of fear swept over her beautiful face. After all he paid for all her luxuries, her clothes,

Gudewife, when your gudeman's frae hame,
Might I but be sae bauld,
As come to your bed-chamber,
When winter nights are cauld;
As come to your bed-chamber,
When nights are cauld and wat,
And lie in your gudeman's stead,
Wad ye do that?

Young man, an ye should be so kind,
When our gudeman's frae hame,
As come to my bed-chamber,
Where I am lain my lane;
And lie in our gudeman's stead,
I will tell you what,
He fucks me five times ilka night,
Wad ye do that?

Wad Ye Do That?
FROM *THE MERRY MUSES OF CALEDONIA*
ROBERT BURNS (1759–96)

The suggestive keyhole motif was popular with publishers of erotic postcards in fin-de-siècle Paris.

for this apartment. He was not a bad man, indeed he was kind and sometimes generous. But his good nature would not countenance this ghastly disclosure! The stakes could not have been higher. Ashton knew what was going through her mind, but she bravely suppressed the dark thoughts and even managed a smile and a wink for him. She re-closed the curtains carefully. Not only to conceal her lover and his boots, but also to protect him from whatever scene was to be enacted in the room.

In this last intention she was unsuccessful. A narrow chink remained, imperceptible from within but enough to reveal the entire brightly lit room to Ashton. He saw Marie-Louise cross to the door, pausing momentarily by the pier glass to check her hair and face. She opened the door and a tall man entered clutching an assortment of parcels. Evidently annoyed, he ignored her kiss and strode towards the window.

Filled with horror, Ashton turned and pressed against the iron railings. Far below, invisible in the murky blackness, was an alleyway. To jump was certain death. A sickly glow above the rooftops was a mocking reminder of the busy streets close by. But no one in the great city of Paris could help him now.

He turned to confront his fate, assuming – by what lunatic rules he knew not – what seemed an appropriate expression. The doors did not open. He moved nearer to the glass and saw the man's back. On the table to the right were a hat and the parcels. He almost cried out with relief.

Her protector's anger had evidently blown itself out, but Marie-Louise fell to her knees before him. He said nothing. She said nothing. Ashton was

OPPOSITE *After the party: a late nineteenth-century lithograph.*

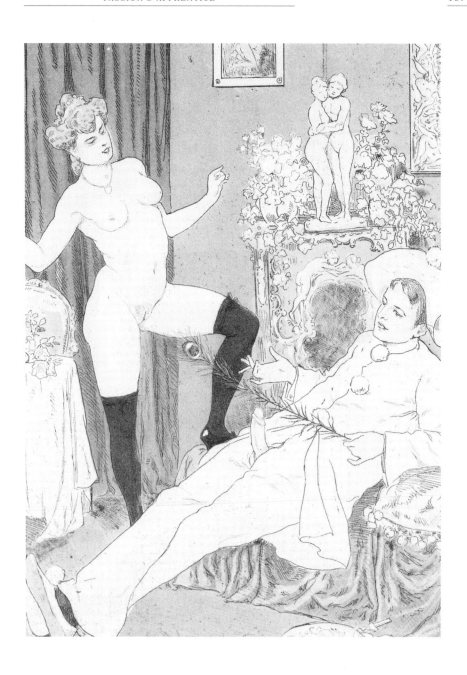

Late Victorian coloured engravings.

perplexed. Still nothing was said. What was the meaning of this silent tableau when all had been so noisy a few moments before? The man made a strange sound and with difficulty stooped and helped Marie-Louise to her feet. In doing so he turned. Then Ashton understood. A penis, fiery red and glistening, stuck out from his trousers.

The unwilling voyeur turned his back on the disturbing scene. In fairness he had to accept that the only person with any cause for complaint in this situation was the protector of Marie-Louise. And he remained in blissful ignorance. For once, only the guilty suffered. Marie-Louise knew mental torment because of the fear of discovery. Ashton's punishment, he now realized, was that reserved by Dante for the very worst sinners – cold.

The night was so cold that splashes from the wash bowl had already turned to ice at his feet. This made movement dangerous, but move he must if he was not to perish on his frozen perch. Clutching the table cover around him he hopped from one bare foot to the other, trying to avoid the iron railing which had become sticky with frost. He could not prevent his teeth from chattering and feared it might have been audible in the room. But their attention was on other things.

Marie-Louise's protector had removed his clothes and sat crushing Ashton's under the armchair. She was leaning over the arm sucking and tonguing his penis, while tugging and fondling his testicles with her long white fingers. Standing up, and slipping out of her gown, she knelt on the arms of the chair and lowered herself slowly on to him. In any other circumstances the sight of his long stalk appearing and disappearing between the white orbs of her bottom would have excited a saint to lust. But a clutch icier than piety had hold of Ashton's vitals which had shrunk to a sad vestige resembling a frozen gooseberry. The gooseberry fool! He laughed despite himself.

It was no gooseberry, but some rude and brightly coloured tropical fruit which appeared as the merchant slipped down onto the floor until his face rested between the thighs of Marie-Louise. Now his tongue took up the work. Her movements became more erratic, breathing the tide of familiar little gasps. When the hair of the man's beard permitted Ashton could see his tongue lapping at the long, glistening inner lips of her sex.

Now the merchant stood up behind her. She dropped forward against the back of the chair and reaching back with both hands pulled her bottom cheeks apart. Ashton gasped, or the merchant did, he could not tell. Nothing was more beautiful than the gaping sex of Marie-Louise at that moment.

She groaned as he buried himself in her. Foam hung about the long brown shaft as he worked in and out with a fury. Ashton saw her white fingers reach back and grasp his testicles. It was too much for her protector. With a shout he gave a final thrust and fell forward onto her.

Ashton's passions were in turmoil. He wanted to laugh and cry, all at once. He looked to his own frozen assets and laughed bitterly.

Suddenly the door opened. Involuntarily he pressed back against the iron rail which scared his skin. 'He has gone to the closet. Quickly" He was stupid, numb with the cold. He took the bottle of brandy and the blanket without speaking. There was a sound behind her. She kicked his boots out

Sex, like Justice, should where possible be seen to be done. At the time when these girls were photographed, Alice was having her own rather different adventures through a looking-glass.

onto the balcony and was gone again, the curtain closed.

The sound of a boot striking the ground far below echoed forlornly between the walls. With difficulty he pulled on the other with frost-bitten fingers and wrapped the blanket around him. He consumed the brandy with painful gulps until he had nearly finished the bottle. At a whim he poured some over his manhood and tried to rub some life into it, but it was hopeless.

Inside, Marie-Louise was riding her protector on the bed. Ashton thought how beautifully her breasts moved. How he should like to feel the weight of them and unpin her hair.

Even with the stimulus of the brandy, everything was becoming very slow. Ashton moved into a kind of dream state where events were jumbled. He saw most of what they did to each other, but

Soixante-neuf: a contemporary drawing with flesh and linen made luminous in the colouring.

with increasing detachment. When Marie-Louise masturbated her protector their observer was merely curious at the amount of semen which still spurted from the man. She massaged it into her breasts and nipples. She had never done that for him, he reflected.

He then lost all sense of time. Finally the doors opened. Propped on the one leg which had a boot, somehow holding the coverings around his upper body, he looked like a rather miserable stork.

Marie-Louise slowly brought her lover back to life in front of the fire. It is not easy to speak with your mouth full – even when it is only a morsel blighted by the frost – but her words were just intelligible. 'Cheri, you taste of brandy.' Ashton did not explain.

A couple enjoy some cuissade lovemaking, drenched in reflected, nocturnal light: a contemporary colour study.

In the theatre of erotica we, the readers, have the title 'principal voyeur'. We are, after all, spying upon the real or imagined sexual encounters of others for our own enjoyment. In presenting us with these scenes writers of erotica often introduce secondary voyeurism, as we have seen. The anonymous author of the next excerpt invents the clever idea of making the secondary voyeur, and narrator, a flea. Who better to hop promiscuously from one sexual skirmish to another, taking plot, narrative (and reader) with him? *Souvenirs d'une Puce* ('Memoirs of a Flea') is a brilliantly salacious literary device. We have of course jumped species rather dramatically. But what intimacies and secrets the reader can enjoy vicariously from a flea's-eye view in exchange for the willing suspension of disbelief!

I will not say I followed, but I 'went with her,' and beheld the gentle girl raise one dainty leg across the other and remove the tiniest of tight and elegant kid-boots.

I jumped upon the carpet and proceeded with my examinations. The left boot followed, and without removing her plump calf from off the other, Bella sat looking at the folded piece of paper which I had seen the young fellow deposit secretly in her hand.

Closely watching everything, I noted the swelling thighs, which spread upwards above her tightly fitting garters, until they were lost in the darkness, as they closed together at a point where her beautiful belly met them in her stooping position; and almost obliterated a thin and peach-like slit, which just shewed its rounded lips between them in the shade.

Presently Bella dropped her note, and being open, I took the liberty to read it.

'I will be in the old spot at eight o'clock to night,' were the only words which the paper contained, but they appeared to have a special interest for Bella, who remained cogitating for some time in the same thoughtful mood.

My curiosity had been aroused, and my desire to know more of the interesting young being with whom chance had so promiscuously brought me in pleasing contact, prompted me to remain quietly ensconced in a snug though somewhat moist hiding place, and it was not until near upon the hour named that I once more emerged in order to watch the progress of events...

It has been said, *'ce n'est que le premier coup qui coute'* ['it is only the first blow which costs'], but it

OPPOSITE *The same artist, and the same couple, as on page 171 but this time cunnilingus.*

The last in a series of brilliant drawings of lovemaking postures: here the couple and their bed glow like an island that is caught in a lighthouse beam.

may be fairly argued that it is at the same time perfectly possible that *'quelquefois il coute trop'* ['sometimes it costs dear'], as the reader may be inclined to infer with me in the present case.

Neither of our lovers, however, had, strange to say, a thought on the subject, but fully occupied with the delicious sensations which had overpowered them, united to give effect to those ardent movements which both could feel would end in ecstasy.

As for Bella, with her whole body quivering with delicious impatience, and her full red lips giving vent to the short excursive exclamations which announced the extreme gratification, she gave herself up body and soul to the delights of coition. Her muscular compressions upon the weapon which had now effectually gained her, the firm embrace in which she held the writhing lad, the delicate grip of the moistened, glove-like sheath, all tended to excite Charlie to madness. He felt himself in her body to the roots of his machine, until the two globes which tightened beneath the foaming champion of his manhood, pressed upon the firm cheeks of her white bottom. He could go no further and his sole employment was to enjoy – to reap to the full the delicious harvest of his exertions.

But Bella, insatiable in her passion, no sooner found the wished for junction completed, than relishing the keen pleasure which the stiff and warm member was giving her, became too excited to know or care further aught that was happening, and her frenzied excitement, quickly overtaken again by the maddening spasms of completed lust, pressed downwards upon the object of her pleasure, threw up her arms in passionate rapture, and then sinking back in the arms of her lover, with low groans of ecstatic agony and little cries of surprise and delight, gave down a copious emission, which finding a reluctant escape below, inundated Charlie's balls.

No sooner did the youth witness the delivering enjoyment he was the means of bestowing upon the beautiful Bella, and became sensible of the flood which she had poured down in such profusion upon his person, than he was also seized with lustful fury. A raging torrent of desire seemed to rush through his veins; his instrument was now plunged to the hilt in her delicious belly, then, drawing back, he extracted the smoking member almost to the head. He pressed and bore all before him. He felt a tickling, maddening feeling creeping

An etching by Leon Richet which was made to illustrate Jules Barbey d'Aurévilly's collection of Decadent tales, Les Diaboliques.

Erotic shadowplay: an early twentieth-century watercolour.

upon him; he tightened his grasp upon his young mistress, and at the same instant that another cry of rapturous enjoyment issued from her heaving breast, he found himself gasping upon her bosom, and pouring into her grateful womb a rich tickling jet of youthful vigour.

A low moan of salacious gratification escaped the parted lips of Bella, as she felt the jerking gushes of seminal fluid which came from the excited member within her; at the same moment the lustful frenzy of emission forced from Charlie a sharp and thrilling cry as he lay with upturned eyes in the last act of the sensuous drama.

Male interest in female masturbation has no real counterpart in women. The ragtime song of the Twenties is right – everybody's doin' it. Or, more precisely, eighty-five per cent of females and ninety-five per cent of males are doin' it, doin' it. But it seems that males also have a tendency to include masturbation among their spectator sports. 'Pauline Réage' explores the topic in *Story of O*.

Then Sir Stephen approached and, taking her by the shoulders, made her lie down upon the carpet: she found herself on her back, her legs drawn up, her knees flexed. Sir Stephen had seated himself on the same spot where, a moment ago, she had been leaning upon the couch; he caught her right knee and dragged her to him. As she was squarely opposite the fireplace, the nearby fire shed an intense light upon the two well-opened

Her father gave her dildos six,
Her mother made 'em up a score;
But she loves nought but living pricks,
And swears by God she'll frig no more.

JOHN WILMOT, EARL OF ROCHESTER
(1647–80)

cracks of her womb and her behind. Without let- *'Nudo Seduto Addormentato' by*
ting go of her, Sir Stephen curtly bade her caress *the contemporary photographer*
herself, but not to close her legs back together. *Giovanni Zuin.*
Numb, she obediently stretched her right hand
down towards her sex and her fingers encountered, between the already parted fleece, the
already burning morsel of flesh placed above
where the fragile lips of her sex joined together.
She touched that morsel of flesh, then her hand
fell away, she stammered: 'I can't.' And she actually could not. She had never caressed herself except
furtively, in the warmth and covering obscurity of
her bed, when she had been alone; and never had
she pursued her pleasure through to a crisis. She'd

stopped, gone to sleep, sometimes found the crisis in an ensuing dream, and had waked, disappointed that it had been simultaneously so strong and so transitory. Sir Stephen's stare was obstinate, compelling. She couldn't withstand it and, repeating her 'I can't,' shut her eyes. For she saw it again, and couldn't get it out of her head, and every time she saw it she had the same nauseous sensation she'd had when she'd actually witnessed it when she was fifteen years old: Marion slumped in a leather armchair in a hotel room, Marion, one leg flung over an arm of the chair and her head sagging down towards the other arm: caressing herself, and moaning, in front of O. Marion had told her that she'd once caressed herself that way in the office where she worked and at a time when she thought there was no one else there; and the boss had suddenly walked in and caught her smack red-handed in the middle of the act. O had a recollection of Marion's office: a room, a bare room, pale

'Donna Addormentata' by Giovanni Zuin.

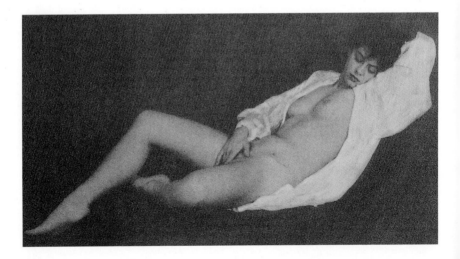

green walls, light coming in from the North through dusty windows. One chair in the room, it was intended for visitors and was opposite the table. 'Did you run away?' O had asked. 'No,' Marion had replied, 'he asked me to go ahead and start again, but he'd locked the door and had made me take off my panties and he'd moved the chair over by the window.' O had been overwhelmed with admiration for what she'd considered Marion's courage, and with horror, and had shyly but stubbornly refused to caress herself in front of Marion, and had sworn that she'd never caress herself in front of anyone else. Marion had laughed and said: 'You'll see when your lover asks you to.'

Dildo in a basket: – the ultimate take-away. An early twentieth-century etching.

The candid heroine of *Memoirs of a Venetian Courtesan* gives a consumer's report on that aid to female masturbation and object of male fantasy, the dildo. In this extract the only voyeurism is ours.

Her description of buying it from the shop where all Murano glass products are sold had us both curled-up with mirth. The shop-keeper asked her what size she required and she was so startled by the question that she blurted out 'the largest you have.'

This extraordinary erotic artefact was made for the wife of a wealthy merchant. Venetian, eighteenth-century.

He then re-appeared from the storeroom with a corked receptacle of such proportions that Alina could not believe her eyes. She said it was more like something designed to warm the feet, and fashioned in the shape of a penis for whimsical reasons, than a dildo. She then told the shop-keeper that she had not asked for the tower of San

An amusing artistic conundrum: has she been discovered, or spied upon masturbating among the scatter cushions? Is the figure of a powerful Renaissance man the focus of her excitement?

Giorgio and would he bring one of the small to middle size.

It is lying on the table beside me and even this size looks daunting. It is beautifully fashioned in strong smooth glass with a life-like helmet and a small testicle-like protruberance to hold it by where the cork is inserted.

Most women piss into them. But Alina has brought me hot water instead. We laughed again when she told me she had added the provision of hot water for my dildo to the list of daily tasks she personally undertakes. Dear Alina. Faustolla has a whole collection of these things, made in wood, leather and ivory as well as glass. But she still prefers her hand when a cock is not available

– which is not often.

Well, I have twice masturbated with my glass dildo. The first time I enjoyed the novelty and the feel of something hard in my sex again. I even gave a little cry when my crisis came, the pleasure was so intense.

Later, I wanted it again. This time I pissed into it: difficult to achieve without accident even if the sex is held open.

Dildos are not for me. There is something I do not care for in the use of one. Not only are the preparations absurd, there is a sadness in it which is not there when you use your hand.

The device of the two copper plums
With silver in them
Slowly and very slowly
Satisfies.
Just as all finishes
Dew falls on my clenched hand.
I would rather the bean flowered yellow
And he were here!

GEISHA SONG
ANONYMOUS
EIGHTEENTH-CENTURY

The eponymous hero of *Gus Tolman* – a rattling yarn written in America early in the twentieth century – makes his own observations on, and of, female auto-erotism.

I entered my room and for the first time noticed the very thin partition between it and Miss Taylor's room. I later heard strange sounds like moans from a woman in distress. Then I distinctly heard a one-sided conversation; she was apparently talking to herself and this is what I heard: 'Oh – Oh – if I could only have a lover like that man,' she said trembling. 'He – he – is so big and handsome.'

I could hear her voice shake, as if she was under some great strain or emotion. I remember the sensual expres-

The convention of introducing animals as mute observers, particularly when auto-eroticism is the subject, increases the erotic charge in some mysterious way. For the same reason the Old Masters usually press-ganged petulant cherubs into watching the lovemaking of the gods in mythological paintings.

Pencil sketch by an unknown artist: early twentieth-century.

sion on her face as the dreamy, pathetic eyes swept over me. Surely, I thought, the poor girl is in heat and apparently craves relief. While I was preparing for bed, and removing my shoes, my eye caught sight of a register in the partition, evidently used in the winter to allow a circulation of warm air. Upon examining it, I found that it opened very easily and through the grill frame I had a wide view of Miss Taylor's room. In my range of vision I saw the bed and an upholstered chair of generous capacity. Opposite this was a bureau with a large tilting mirror.

Miss Taylor was standing before the mirror, slowly removing the belt from her waist and gazing intently with that same languorous look at some pictures on the wall on either side of the mirror. Peering intently, I discovered that they were pictures of men, three of a stalwart pugilist in different poses stripped, but with a sash to hide his bulging genitals. Other pictures were of actors, presumably matinee idols, but the girl's eyes lingered on the muscular figure of the pugilist.

I saw her full red lips move as if she were talking to the fighter. Lifting up a pair of pretty white bubbies out of her corset, she bounced them up and down, then spoke in a low hysterical voice: 'Oh, Jack, see my titties – come – to – me – and – fondle them.'

I was no longer puzzled. The girl was hot and she was calling to Jack, the pugilist, as an imaginary lover. Her thoughts were lustily centred on the fleshy pleasures such a body would impart if she could but hold it in her arms and feel the strong sexual embrace and enjoyment that might result. In her impulsive emotions the girl tore off her corsets and then slipped out of her dress and

An imaginative use of watercolour technique: our eyes respond strongly to the dark areas of stocking and hair, so that the search for the other pigments which define the moulding of her body is almost like tactile exploration.

drawers. She stood there revealed in nothing but her stockings and under-vest, which she quickly removed. When I saw what a finely built young girl she was, that settled it. She had to be gratified. I lay on my back so I could better contemplate with ease what might transpire in the girl's room.

She was about twenty and I could plainly see her white nude body, rich in lovely contours and graceful curves, together with a very disturbing view of her dark thickly haired pussy and her white cherry-tipped bubbies. They made me rampant, and my tool was standing straight up. I doubtless would have made a rush through the door to the girl if my curiosity had not gotten the better of me. I gasped when I saw her press her hand to her pussy and insert a finger and again gaze at the picture of the pugilist as she vigorously rubbed and worked her finger in and out.

Her feelings were getting the better of her and as she worked herself up to a pitch of passionate frenzy, a wave of erotic emotion spread a lovely glow over her shapely charms. As if suddenly thinking of something, she unlocked the bureau drawers and extracted a book and a small packet from which she selected several pictures, evidently an obscene book, as I later discovered.

Reclining on the edge of the bed, with one leg hanging over the side, she switched on a reading lamp over her head, which gave me a brilliantly lighted view of the girl's tempting and sensual body in a voluptuous pose. The line of my vision took in every detail of a plump and well defined cunnie between a pair of lovely white thighs. The contrast of the dark thick curls made her belly and thighs appear like alabaster.

OPPOSITE *The Tribades, a coloured lithograph by Andre Provot.*

An illustration of a Venetian Carnival from Casanova's History of My Life.

Adjusting her pillow, the girl began reading, holding two of the pictures on the edge of the book, leaving her right hand free. Occasionally she would gloat on her own charms reflected in the tilting mirror. At the same time she would pinch and titillate the stiff red nipples of her firm round bubbies.

The swelling, curly mound and pretty round belly began to rise and fall with convulsions and erotic longings as she gloated over the book and pictures. Inflamed to a frenzy the girl's hand slipped down and covered the restless pussy. Then with her middle finger she sought to appease her passions with a rapid nervous thrust and pressure on the burning clitty. Suddenly, apparently coming to a passage in her book which inflamed the poor girl, she gasped aloud. I heard a smothered cry – 'Oh, how lovely – how I'd – like – to – be – in her place.' Then holding the pictures close she gazed with languorous eyes and clasped the whole of the plump curly cunnie in her hand with two fingers in it, squeezing it hard.

The heavy breathing and groans told me of her approaching crisis. Dropping the pictures, her head went back to the pillows. Her limbs twitched and quivered. The pretty bubbies trembled. Then with a convulsive heave and choking expressions of pleasure, as '– Oh – Oh – how – good,' spasm after spasm of voluptuous ecstasy swept over her in a thrilling orgasm.

The ultimate expression of voyeurism is the orgy. Indeed that is specifically what Angela Ruberta is commissioned to provide in *Memoirs of a Venetian Courtesan*.

Carnival is not only a time when every licence is permitted, it is a time when those with a taste for such things plan new excesses and delights which they can enjoy.

The orgy which the senator wished me to arrange was to know no limitations in behaviour. His only stipulations were that four others, two men and two women, whose integrity I could vouch for, would be involved in addition to himself and his wife. Naturally all would remain masked throughout.

Before agreeing, and before indicating the price of such lavish entertainments, I outlined certain rules of my own. The orgy would take place in my house. It would be restricted to the large room and would begin at sunset and end at dawn. No servants but mine would be allowed to enter and my own would be restricted to the other floors. Lastly, although no other control would be exercised, nothing violent or cruel in any way would be permitted.

An engraving that could only be by Franz von Bayros.

The senator agreed to both rules and price – which was considerable – without quibble.

My chosen participants were Faustolla and her lover, a nobleman who owned a theatre; myself, the senator and his wife of course; and Fabrizio. Although he had taken to drink since his marriage Fabrizio was a loyal friend; he was also a considerable asset in an enterprise of this sort! During the days before the orgy I was frequently moved to mirth at the thought of Fabrizio and the senator's slight, blonde wife.

The preliminary meal was, as I had feared, a little strained. The wine helped and I was very attentive to the glasses. The inevitable result was

A finely executed drawing by an unknown artist.

frequent traffic to the chamberpots which I had had situated at the far end of the room. The men, as ever, were less decorous than the ladies in this procedure, and we were treated to several glimpses of those parts which were later to perform their other and more enjoyable function.

It was after just such an incident that the senator's wife grew suddenly more attentive to Fabrizio. She repeatedly caught his glance across the table, smiling and hooding her blue-grey eyes. This was all very well, but as director and *première danseuse* this seemed to me to be a slow beginning. I was reflecting on various ways to warm-up the proceedings when the senator's wife became the spark which started a conflagration.

Fabrizio was moved to walk once again to the chamber pot. The sight of his gigantic penis, turgid with its present activity, was too much for the senator's wife. The stream had barely ceased when she rushed across the room and crammed what she could of him into her mouth. Frigging and sucking him in a frenzy, she soon had Fabrizio's cock looming over her like the arm of a crane. Whimpering in her excitement, and still kneeling, she tore off her clothes and presented her naked posterior to him.

Fabrizio's clothes followed hers and he was soon rutting on her like a wild animal. How she was receiving the full length of this monster in her delicate body was a mystery to all of us, but her squeals were not those of discomfort or disapproval.

The effect of this tableau on the rest of the gathering was immediate and surprising. It seemed we had all chosen not only the subject but also the manner of our first encounter. There was no disagreement and the minimum of confusion. In a span of time so short as to seem almost instantaneous, clothes were removed and the coupling achieved.

Faustolla's lover had his head between my legs and his cock in my mouth. The senator was already clenching and unclenching his buttocks between Faustolla's open legs in a manner allowing no ambiguity of interpretation.

The more leisurely beginning which my partner and I had made meant that we had only begun to enjoy the main course when the others were already searching for sweet meats. The consequence of this was that they gathered

The orgy takes its name from a Greek word meaning 'secret rites'. Orgies are religious in origin: in the Ancient World there were many cults, especially those associated with Dionysus, where worship involved drinking, dancing and group sex. Drawing by an unknown artist.

*In this anonymous watercolour the
participants have readied that
moment in their group encounter
when each couple no longer cares
what anyone else is doing.*

around us just as he began his first long strokes
into me.

The senator's wife, who proved to have the
appetites and sensuality of a feral cat, seized upon
my partner's sex as he thrust into me. When he
withdrew I could feel her fingers around my lips
and his slippery shaft.

Faustolla was not slow to investigate the
mystery between the senator's wife's legs as an
opportunity now presented itself. I could see her
exploring with fingers and tongue. As the senator
and Fabrizio were momentarily at a loss to know
quite where to join the game I took matters in hand:
the one new, and interesting for that reason, the
other familiar but having lost none of its charm.
Having been prepared by me for further adven-

tures the senator then knelt behind his former partner and began fucking her again. I have no doubt that he was moved to do this not only by a wish to explore the beauty of Faustolla's arse but by the novelty of her having her auburn head buried in the more familiar contours of his wife's bottom.

At this point my intrepid partner reached his crisis, each spasm of which was also enjoyed by the senator's wife who had one hand down between his buttocks and the other clutching his testicles.

As he softened and withdrew the senator's wife hungrily took him in her mouth. Soon he was lying on his back beside me, begging her to let him recover a little. She silenced him by straddling his face and pressing her sex down onto his mouth. Then, leaning forward, she resumed her sucking.

My own pleasure was not complete. Sensing this, Fabrizio knelt between my legs and pushed slowly into me. I begged him not to thrust too hard. He whispered in my ear that he had locked-up often enough to know how to insert the key. Nor did he need to use up his oil, a few movements were all it took to make the mechanism work.

Soon after there began what resembled a children's game more closely than anything else. As soon as Faustolla's lover was ready to participate, the men coupled with us, but changed partners after only a few thrusts. Men retain more of the child in them than us, and this new game was more to their taste than ours.

We tried to make of it what we could while we waited for our turn with Fabrizio. Then there was always one indignant man standing for his turn

Lesbianism takes its name from the Greek island of Lesbos, home of the poet Sappho and her followers around 600 BCE. Sappho's sexual tastes have tended to obscure the fact that she was one of the greatest poets of the classical world. Plato – who also suffered at the hands of dictionary compilers – called her 'The Tenth Muse'. Unsigned watercolour, early twentieth-century.

while the next woman complained that her time with Fabrizio had come. As this was leading to disharmony Fabrizio suggested a variation where all lights were extinguished and we had to guess which man we were receiving each time. We told him not to be foolish.

This and similar games took us through to the dawn, sustained by periods of rest and refreshment. All possible groupings of men with women and women with women were tried, but not men with men. Except that the senator asked if he might masturbate Fabrizio. By this time Fabrizio was quite drunk. He agreed, provided he was all the while given clear view of the senator's wife and Faustolla who were then enjoying each other before the fire.

There were no other noteworthy revelations, except perhaps that Faustolla's lover took great delight in watching the women make water. We all indulged him in this innocent pleasure, and tried to make it as interesting as possible for him. The women agreed that the activity seemed to us to lack the spectacle which is the essence of theatre. But he seemed pleased enough.

An orgy is both voyeuristic and atavistic: an erotic group encounter, a sexual package holiday to a primitive animalistic past. We are back at our beginning. The distance from the sophistication and decadence of an elegant Venetian palazzo on the Grand Canal to the Rift Valley, a million years of human evolution, is rather less than we might suppose.

Troilism, where three people make love simultaneously, is also known as triolism: the vowels mimicking the reversal of positions available in triangular sex. This drawing is by an unknown artist, early twentieth-century.

OPPOSITE *A lithograph from Memoires d'une Chanteuse, published in Paris in 1933.*

CHAPTER FIVE
Shades of Light and Dark

🍃

... he above the rest
In shape and gesture proudly eminent
Stood like a tower; his form had yet not lost
All her original brightness, nor appeared
Less than archangel ruined, and the excess
Of glory obscured: as when the sun new risen
Looks through the horizontal misty air
Shorn of his beams, or from behind the moon
In dim eclipse disastrous twilight sheds
On half the nations, and with fear of change
Perplexes monarchs. Darkened so, yet shone
Above them all the archangel: but his face
Deep scars of thunder had intrenched, and care
Sat on his faded cheek, but under brows
Of dauntless courage, and considerate pride
Waiting revenge...

FROM *Paradise Lost, Book I*
JOHN MILTON

An engraving from the series
Les Diaboliques: neither technique
nor catch will be found in The
Compleat Angler.

A paradox is not in itself an answer, but in wrestling with a paradox – as Luther wrestled with the Devil – we may find our own answers. In *Paradise Lost* Milton presents us with a magnificent paradox (so magnificent that the anti-hero almost gets up and walks off with the greatest religious poem in the English language): a Prince of Darkness who is also Lucifer, the 'Light-Bringer'.

At the beginning of this erotic part, we visited the geographical Garden of Eden, the Rift Valley

OPPOSITE *A nineteenth-century oil*
painting imaginatively reconstructs
the in-flight entertainment of the
rebel angels after they had been
'hurled headlong flaming from
the ethereal sky'.

In 1514, when Hans Baldung Grien made this magnificent drawing, it was advisable for artists wishing to deal with sexual subjects to ascribe to witches the activities depicted – in this case a young witch is enjoying cunnilingus as only the Devil can do it. Artists failing to follow the convention of blaming witches for everything were liable to share their unpleasant fate.

which was home to the first of our species. Let us now visit the mythological Eden: a place no less important. Satan has of course been to the Garden before us: his horticultural contribution was to plant sin and to scatter the seeds of guilt. We would like to think that it was not all gardening for Adam and Eve before his visit, but only afterwards is there any mention of sex. By then, sex is inextricably bound up with the concept of good and evil.

This unfortunate confusion, this bundle of paradoxes, is our erotic inheritance. Sex is good but it can also be evil: the misuse of sexuality, the misuse of power, is a serious issue. Sex is creative but some psychologists maintain that it is ultimately the same as violence. We enjoy sex, as we should, but it does not take much to make us ashamed of it. One thing is certain: sex is the *sine qua non* of human existence and we cannot understand it by ignoring it. It is our ambivalence towards sex – and the ambiguity of sex itself – that makes it useful to explore the literature and art of sex in terms of black and white or 'shades of light and dark'.

One aspect of the dark side of erotic literature concerns the personage who hauled sex into the good-versus-evil debate in the first place: Satan. Surely the Prince of Darkness has no more loyal follower than the vampire: certainly none more sensitive on the issue of light versus dark. Bram Stoker's novel *Dracula* began the modern myth and unknowingly founded a major industry. This extract lays bare the erotic symbolism of vampirism in what amounts to a fairy tale about oral sex.

I suppose I must have fallen asleep; I hope so, but I fear, for all that followed was startlingly real – so real that now, sitting here in the broad, full sunlight of the morning, I cannot in the least believe that it was all sleep.

I was not alone. The room was the same, unchanged in any way since I came into it; I could see along the floor, in the brilliant moonlight, my own footsteps marked where I had disturbed the long accumulation of dust. In the moonlight opposite me were three young women, ladies by their dress and manner. I thought at the time that I must be dreaming when I saw them, for, though the moonlight was behind them, they threw no shadow on the floor. They came close to me and looked at me for some time, and then whispered together. Two were dark, and had high aquiline noses, like the Count, and great dark, piercing eyes, that seemed to be almost red when contrasted with the pale yellow moon. The other was fair, as fair as can be, with great, waxy masses of golden hair and eyes like pale sapphires. I seemed somehow to know her face, and to know it in connection with some dreamy fear, but I could not recollect at the moment how or where. All three had brilliant white teeth, that shone like pearls against the ruby of their voluptuous lips. There was something about them that made me uneasy, some longing and at the same time some deadly fear. I felt in my heart a wicked, burning desire that they would kiss me with those red lips. It is not good to note this down, lest some day it should meet Mina's eyes and cause her pain; but it is the truth. They whispered together, and then they all three laughed – such a silvery, musical laugh, but

A steel engraving after William Blake's illustration of Adam and Eve, when everything in the garden was lovely.

Sometimes, after an hour of apathy, my strange and beautiful companion would take my hand and hold it with a fond pressure, renewed again and again; blushing softly, gazing in my face with languid and burning eyes, and breathing so fast that her dress rose and fell with the tumultuous respiration. It was like the ardor of a lover; it embarrassed me; it was hateful and yet overpowering: and with gloating eyes she drew me to her, and her hot lips traveled along my cheek in kisses; and she would whisper, almost in sobs, 'You are mine, you shall be mine, and you and I are one forever.' Then she has thrown herself back in her chair, with her small hands over her eyes. leaving me trembling.

FROM *CARMILLA*
JOSEPH SHERIDAN LE FANU
(1814–73)

as hard as though the sound never could have come through the softness of human lips. It was like the intolerable, tingling sweetness of water-glasses when played on by a cunning hand. The fair girl shook her head coquettishly, and the other two urged her on. One said:–

'Go on! You are first, and we shall follow; yours is the right to begin.' The other added:– 'He is young and strong; there are kisses for us all.' I lay quiet, looking out under my eyelashes in an agony of delightful anticipation. The fair girl advanced and bent over me till I could feel the movement of her breath upon me. Sweet it was in one sense, honey-sweet, and sent the same tingling through the nerves as her voice, but with a bitter underlying the sweet, a bitter offensiveness, as one smells in blood.

I was afraid to raise my eyelids, but looked out and saw perfectly under the lashes. The fair girl went on her knees, and bent over me, fairly gloating. There was a deliberate voluptuousness which was both thrilling and repulsive, and as she arched her neck she actually licked her lips like an animal, till I could see in the moonlight the moisture shining on the scarlet lips and on the red tongue as it lapped the white sharp teeth. Lower and lower went her head as the lips went below the range of my mouth and chin and seemed about to fasten on my throat. Then she paused, and I could hear the churning sound of her tongue as it licked her teeth and lips, and could feel the hot breath on my neck. Then the skin of my throat began to tingle as one's flesh does when the hand that is to tickle it approaches nearer – nearer. I could feel the soft, shivering touch of the lips on the super-sensitive skin of my throat, and the hard dents of two sharp teeth, just touching and pausing there. I closed my eyes in a languorous ecstasy and waited – waited with beating heart.

The elements of the vampire story which appeal to us are worth examining individually. There is of course the perverse glamour of evil. A decade before the publication of *Dracula*, in 1886, Robert Louis Stevenson wrote about this in *The Strange Case of Dr Jekyll and Mr Hyde*.

There was something strange in my sensations, something indescribably new, and, from its very novelty, incredibly sweet. I felt younger, lighter, happier in body; within I was conscious of a heady

A disturbing drawing of the predator and his prey. The artist and the date are unknown.

recklessness, a current of disordered sensual images running like a mill-race in my fancy, a solution of the bonds of obligation, an unknown but not an innocent freedom of the soul. I knew myself, at the first breath of this new life, to be more wicked, tenfold more wicked, sold a slave to my original evil; and the thought, in that moment, braced and delighted me like wine.

Stevenson understood that the thrill of evil can come from abandoning ourselves to the animal and primitive forces within our own natures.

... I learned to recognise the thorough and primitive duality of man; I saw that, of the two natures that contended in the field of my consciousness, even if I could rightly be said to be either, it was only because I was radically both... I had learned to dwell with pleasure, as a beloved daydream, on the thought of the separation of these elements.

Rapunzel, *drawn by Rudolph Keller,* died 1890.

The abandonment of ourselves to animality is – not surprisingly – a recurring motif in erotic literature. The metaphor of a tiger or panther is often used to denote a voracious woman. This sexual safari is by Anaïs Nin.

His room was like a traveler's den, full of objects from all over the world. The walls were covered with red rugs, the bed was covered with animal furs. The place was close, intimate, voluptuous like the rooms of an opium dream. The furs, the deep-red walls, the objects, like the fetishes of an African priest – everything was violently erotic. I wanted to lie naked on the furs, to be taken there lying on this animal smell, caressed by the fur.

I stood there in the red room, and Marcel undressed me. He held my naked waist in his hands. He eagerly explored my body with his hands. He felt the strong fullness of my hips.

'For the first time, a real woman,' he said. 'So many have come here, but for the first time here is a real woman, someone I can worship.'

As I lay on the bed it seemed to me that the smell and feel of the fur and the bestiality of Marcel were combined. Jealousy had broken his timidity. He was like an animal, hungry for every sensation, for every way of knowing me. He kissed me eagerly, he bit my lips. He lay in the animal furs, kissing my breasts, feeling my legs, my sex, my buttocks. Then in the half-light he moved up over me, shoving his penis in my mouth. I felt my teeth catching on it as he pushed it in and out, but he liked it. He was watching and caressing me, his hands all over my body, his fingers everywhere seeking to know me completely to hold me.

The tactile qualities of flesh and fur are explored in this photograph from the 1920s.

I threw my legs up over his shoulders, high, so that he could plunge into me and see it at the same time. He wanted to see everything. He wanted to see how the penis went in and came out glistening and firm, big. I held myself up on my two fists so as to offer my sex more and more to his thrusts. Then he turned me over and lay over me like a dog, pushing his penis in from behind, with his hands cupping my breasts, caressing me and pushing me at the same time. He was untiring. He would not come. I was waiting to have the orgasm with him, but he postponed and postponed it. He wanted to

Of lust frightful, past belief,
Lurking unforgotten,
Unrestrainable endless grief
In breasts long rotten.

A song? What laughter or what song
Can this house remember?
Do flowers and butterflies belong
To a blind December?

FROM *THE HAUNTED HOUSE*
ROBERT GRAVES (1895–1985)

'Donna con Capello Nero' by Giovanni Zuin.

linger, to feel my body forever, to be endlessly excited. I was growing tired and I cried out, 'Come now, Marcel, come now.' He began then to push violently, moving with me into the wild rising peak of the orgasm, and then I cried out, and he came almost at the same time. We fell back among the furs, released.

The other feature of the vampire myth which strikes a chord in the dark side of our personality is the idea of enslavement, the willing subordination of self to another. Count Dracula demands everything of his female victims and – although he must have been one of the worst halitosis sufferers of all time – he usually gets it. The same is true of his equally unpleasant fellow-aristocrat in *Story of O*.

He followed her; but, on the other side of the door, immediately thrust up against the wall, her sex and breasts seized by Sir Stephen, her mouth forced open by his tongue, O moaned from happiness and deliverance. The tips of her breasts stiffened beneath Sir Stephen's hand. He dug his other hand so roughly into her belly that she thought she might faint. Would she ever dare tell him that no pleasure, no joy, nothing she even imagined ever approached the happiness she felt before the freedom wherewith he made use of her, before the idea that he knew there were no precautions, no limits he had to observe in the manner whereby he sought his pleasure in her body. Her certitude that when he touched her, whether it be to caress or beat her, that when he ordered her to do something it was uniquely because he wanted her to do

it and for his sole pleasure, the certitude that he
made allowances for nothing, was concerned for
nothing but his own desire, so overwhelmed O
that, every time she had proof of it, and often even
when she simply thought about it, a fiery vest-
ment, a red-hot corselet extending from shoulders
to knees seemed to descend over her. As she was
there, standing pinned against the wall, eyes shut,
murmuring I love you, I love you when there was
breath in her to murmur, Sir Stephen's nevertheless cool hands, cool as well-water in contact with
the fire consuming her, the fire which traveled up
and down within her, burned her still more. He
quit her gently, smoothing the skirt down over her
wet thighs, shutting the bolero over her quivering
breasts.

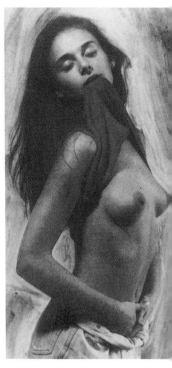

Seminudo in Piedi' by
Giovanni Zuin.

O is of course masochistic and it is that element
within a balanced personality which may resonate to Pauline Réage's simple but powerful
writing. But there is something else which dis-
turbs about this novel, which appeared mysteriously in Paris in 1954 and which Graham Greene
described as 'a rare thing, a pornographic book
well written and without a trace of obscenity'. Let
us look at the clues: the subordination of self;
total obedience; O's serenity, which is constantly
echoed in the writing. At the beginning of the
novel O is prepared for her new life.

And then I know that they released O's hands, until
that point still tied behind her back, and told her
to undress. They were going to bathe her and
make her up. But they made her stand still; they
did everything for her, they stripped her and laid

her clothes neatly away in one of the cupboards. They did not let her do her own bathing, they washed her themselves and set her hair just as hairdressers would have, making her sit in one of those big chairs that tilt backwards when your hair is being washed and then come up again when the drier is applied. That took at least an hour. She was seated nude in the chair and they prohibited her from either crossing her legs or pressing them together. As, on the opposite wall, there was a mirror running from floor to ceiling and straight ahead of her, in plain view, every time she glanced up she caught sight of herself, of her own body.

When she was made up, her eyelids lightly shadowed, her mouth very red, the point and halo of

her nipples rouged, the sides of the lips of her sex
reddened, a lingering scent applied to the fur of
her armpits and her pubis, to the crease between
her buttocks, to beneath her breasts and the palms
of her hands, she was led into a room where
a three sided mirror and, facing it, a fourth mirror
on the opposite wall enabled, indeed obliged, her
to see her own image reflected. She was told to sit
on a hassock placed between the mirrors, and
to wait.

Story of O is not an unpleasant parody of a nun's
initiation. It is a novel full of cruelty but it is not
anti-religious or blasphemous. It is simply the
dark equivalent of what happens in the light.

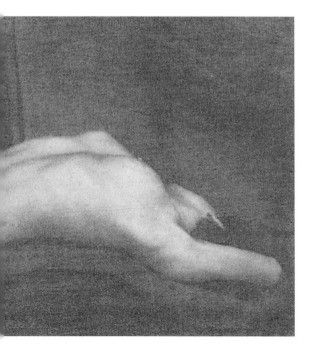

'Nudo in Rosso': yet another
magnificent nude by Giovanni Zuin.

An illustration from Erotici, *published by Quintieri in Milan in 1921. Drawn by Adolfo Magrini.*

Much of the anti-clerical erotica produced from the Age of Enlightenment onwards makes poor reading. The frequently used fomula which combined cruel invective and crueller sexual deviation automatically excludes it from this book. More interesting is the far older, and more success- ful, tradition which uses humour to lampoon the excesses of the ecclesiastical establishment

Boccaccio di Chellino di Buonaiuto was born in 1313, probably in Paris where his father, who was to become Prior of Florence in 1321, first seduced and then abandoned his mother. Apprenticed to a merchant at the age of ten, Boccaccio soon rebelled. His father then tried to interest him in canon law, but this too failed. A period in Naples at the tolerant and enlightened court of King Robert allowed Boccaccio's genius to flourish. His most famous work, *The Decameron*, was written under the patronage of Queen Joan after 1348, although he had been gathering material for some time. This extraordinary work was to have a huge influence on European literature (Chaucer borrowed widely from it). Many stories ridicule contemporary Church morals.

As he and Boccaccio shared a common agenda, it is ironic that *The Decameron* was among the 'vanities' consigned to the flames by the pious reformer Savonarola in 1497 (also that his own bonfire was arranged by indignant Church officials only a year later, when he was burnt at the stake). 'The Tale of Masetto', who pretends to be a dumb simpleton in order to work in a nunnery, is typical of Boccaccio's humour.

Now it so befell that after a hard day's work he was taking a little rest, when two young nuns, who were walking in the garden, approached the spot where he lay, and stopped to look at him, while he pretended to be asleep. And so the bolder of the two said to the other:– 'If I thought thou wouldst keep the secret, I would tell thee what I have sometimes meditated, and which thou perhaps mightest also find agreeable.' The other replied:– 'Speak thy mind freely and be sure that I will never tell a soul.' Whereupon the bold one began:– 'I know not if thou hast ever considered how close we are kept here, and that within these precincts dare never enter any man, unless it be the old steward or this mute: and I have often heard from ladies that have come hither, that all the other sweets that the world has to offer signify not a jot in comparison of the pleasure that a woman has in connexion with a man. Whereof I have more than once been minded to make experiment with this mute, no other man being available. Nor, indeed, could one find any man in the whole world so meet therefor; seeing that he could not blab if he would; thou seest that he is but a dull clownish lad, whose size has increased out of all proportion to his sense; wherefore I would fain hear what thou hast to say to it.' 'Alas!' said the other, 'what is 't thou sayst? Knowest thou not that we have vowed our virginity to God?' 'Oh,' rejoined the first, 'think but how many vows are made to Him all day long, and never a one performed: and so, for our vow, let Him find another or others to perform it.' 'But,'

Dô hete er gemachet also riche von
  bluomen eine bettestat.
des wirt noch gelachet innecliche
  kumt iemen an daz selbe pfat.
bî den rosen er wol mac tandaradei,
  merken wâ mirz houbet lac.

I watched him
As he made a bed
From sweetest meadow flowers.
Now anyone who finds the place,
Our blissful place,
Will laugh:
Seeing from the roses
Where we lay!

FROM *UNDER THE LINDEN TREE*
WALTHER VON DER VOGELWERDE
(1170?–1230)

ABOVE, BELOW and OPPOSITE
More illustrations from the
collection Erotici.

said her companion, 'suppose that we conceived, how then?' 'Nay but,' protested the first, 'thou goest about to imagine evil before it befalls thee: time enough to think of that when it comes to pass; there will be a thousand ways to prevent its ever being known, so only we do not publish it ourselves.' Thus reassured, the other was now the more eager of the two to test the quality of the male human animal. 'Well then,' she said, 'how shall we go about it?' and was answered:– 'Thou seest 'tis past none; I make no doubt but all the sisters are asleep, except ourselves; search we through the kitchen-garden, to see if there be any there, and if there be none, we have but to take him by the hand and lead him hither to the hut where he takes shelter from the rain; and then one shall mount guard while the other has him with her inside. He is such a simpleton that he will do just whatever we bid him.' No word of this conversation escaped Masetto, who, being disposed to obey, hoped for nothing so much as that one of them should take him by the hand. They, meanwhile, looked carefully all about them, and satisfied themselves that they were secure from observation: then she that had broached the subject came close up to Masetto, and shook him; whereupon he started to his feet.

So she took him by the hand with a blandishing air, to which he replied with some

clownish grins. And then she led him into the hut,
where he needed no pressing to do what she
desired of him. Which done, she changed places
with the other, as loyal comradeship re-quired; and
Masetto, still keeping up the pretence of simplicity,
did their pleasure. Wherefore before they left, each
must needs make another assay of the mute's powers of riding; and afterwards, talking the matter
over many times, they agreed that it was in truth
not less but even more delightful than they had
been given to understand; and so, as they found
convenient opportunity, they continued to go and
disport themselves with the mute.

Church morals had clearly not improved three
centuries later when Casanova visited Spain and
wrote the following.

At Saragossa I saw the great devotion paid to
Nuestra Senora del Pilar. I saw processions in
which gigantic wooden statues were carried. I was
taken to receptions where I found monks. I was
introduced to a very fat lady who, I was told, was
a cousin of the Blessed Palafox, at which I was
expected to fall into a transport of reverence;
and I made the acquaintance of a
Canon Pignatelli, who was
the presiding judge of the

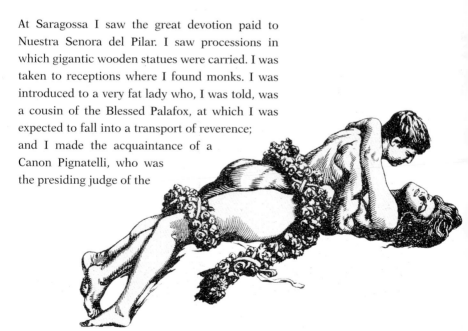

Rembrandt's famous Monk in a Cornfield: made with no particular anti-clerical intention that we know of, it probably records an incident that he had witnssed during his walks in the countryside.

Inquisition and who every morning sent to prison the bawd who on the previous evening had arranged for him to sup with a whore, who had then spent the night with him. He woke up, and, after thus exercising his judicial authority, he went to confession, he said mass, then he dined, the devil in the flesh overcame him, another girl was procured for him, he enjoyed her, and the next morning he did over again what he had done the day before; and it was the same thing every day. Always struggling between God and the devil, the Canon was the happiest of men after dinner and the unhappiest in the morning.

One of the most remarkable and successful anti-clerical erotic works is *Thérèse Philosophe,* written by the Marquis d'Argans and published with numerous highly explicit engravings in 1748. This urbane creation of the Enlightenment is a highly spiced amalgam of sexual instruction and libertine propaganda served up as a picaresque novel. This extract is a clever but disgraceful satire on holy relics in which Thérèse spies upon her friend. Her homily at the end of the chapter is typical of the tone of the book.

... I suddenly noticed to my utter surprise that the venerable Father Dirrag opened his fly. A throbbing arrow shot out of his trousers which looked exactly like that fateful snake about which my former father confessor had warned me so vehemently.

The monster was as long and as thick and as heavy as the one about which the Capuchine monk had made all those dire predictions. I shuddered with delightful horror. The red head of this snake seemed to threaten Eradice's behind which had taken on a deep pink colouration because of the blows it had received during the Bible recitation. The face of Father Dirrag perspired and was flushed a deep red.

Scenes from Thérèse philosophe, first published in 1748.

'And now,' he said, 'you have to transport yourself into total meditation. You must separate your soul from the senses. And if my dear daughter has not dis-

---

*Q: The Abbess woke up frantic after she
Had dreamed all night of eating gooseberry fool,
To find her mouth full of the abbot's tool,
How had she sinned, though?
Greed? Or lechery?*

*A: She didn't sin, as far as we make out,
In either way. It was an accident –
Although, if she had found it in her cunt
Or up her arse, there might have been a doubt.*

PIETRO ARETINO (1492–1557)

appointed my pious hopes, she shall neither feel, nor hear, nor see anything.'

And at that very moment this horrible man loosened a hail of blows, letting them whistle down upon Eradice's naked buttocks. However, she did not say a word: it seemed as if she were totally insensitive to this horrendous whipping. I noticed only an occasional twitching of her bum, a sort of spasming and relaxing at the rhythm of the priest's blows.

'I am very satisfied with you,' he told her after he had punished her for about five minutes in this manner. 'The time has come when you are going to reap the fruits of your holy labours. Don't question me, my dear daughter, but be guided by God's will which is working through me. Throw yourself, face down, upon the floor; I will now expel the last traces of impurity with a sacred relic. It is a part of the venerable rope which girded the waist of the holy Saint Francis himself.'

The good priest put Eradice in a position which was rather uncomfortable for her, but extremely fitting for what he had in mind. I had never seen my girl friend in such a beautiful position. Her buttocks were half-opened and the double path to satisfaction was wide-open.

After the old lecher had admired her for a while, he moistened his so-called rope of Saint Francis with spittle, murmured some of the priestly mumbo-jumbo which these gentlemen generally use to exorcise the devil, and proceeded to shove the rope into my friend.

I could watch the entire operation from my little hideout. The windows of the room were opposite

BELOW and OPPOSITE *The libertine literature of the eighteenth century was often lavishly illustrated. The centre for this flourishing industry was Paris, where engravers from all over Europe were employed to produce a wealth of erotic art varying from simple illustration to exquisite roccoco masterpieces.*

the door of the alcove in which Eradice had
locked me up. She was kneeling on the floor,
her arms were crossed over the footstool and
her head rested upon her folded arms. Her
skirts, which had been carefully folded
almost up to her shoulders, revealed her
marvellous buttocks and the beautiful
curve of her back. This exciting view did
not escape the attention of the venerable
Father Dirrag. His gaze feasted upon the
view for quite some time. He had clamped
the legs of his penitent between his own legs,
and he dropped his trousers, and his hands
held the monstrous rope. Sitting in this position
he murmured some words which I could not
understand.

He lingered for some time in this devotional
position and inspected the altar with glowing eyes.
He seemed to be undecided how to effect his sacrifice, since there were two inviting openings. His
eyes devoured both and it seemed as if he were
unable to make up his mind. The top one was a
well-known delight for a priest, but, after all, he
had also promised a taste of Heaven to his penitent. What was he to do? Several times he knocked
with the tip of his tool at the gate he desired most,
but finally he was smart enough to let wisdom triumph over desire. I must do him justice: I clearly
saw his monstrous prick disappear the natural
way, after his priestly fingers had carefully parted
the rosy lips of Eradice's lovepit.

The labour started with three forceful shoves
which made him enter about halfway. And suddenly the seeming calmness of the priest changed
into some sort of fury. My God, what a change!

Restoration comedy: *Samuel Pepys (1633–1703) witnessed a riot in Bow Street when Sir Charles Sedley, nude, urinated on a watching crowd after enacting 'all the postures of lust and buggery that could be imagined, and abusing of Scripture... preached a mountebank sermon from that pulpit, saying that there he hath to sell such a powder as should make all the cunts run after him – a thousand people standing underneath to see and hear him. And that being done he took a glass of wine and drank the King's health.'*

Imagine a satyr. Mouth half-open, lips foam-flecked, teeth gnashing and snorting like a bull who is about to attack a cud-chewing cow. His hands were only half an inch away from Eradice's full behind. I could see that he did not dare to lean upon them. His spread fingers were spasming; they looked like the feet of a fried capon. His head was bowed and his eyes stared at the so-called relic. He measured his shoving very carefully, seeing to it that he never left her lovepit and also that his belly never touched her arse. He did not want his penitent to find out to whom the holy relic of Saint Francis was connected! What an incredible presence of mind!

I could clearly see that about an inch of the holy tool constantly remained on the outside and never took part in the festivities. I could see that with every backward movement of the priest the red lips of Eradice's love-nest opened and I remember clearly that the vivid pink colour was a most charming sight. However, whenever the good priest shoved forward, the lips closed and I could only see the finely curled hairs which covered them. They clamped around the priestly tool so firmly that it seemed as if they had devoured the holy arrow. It looked for all the world like both of them were connected to Saint Francis' relic and it was hard to guess which one of the two persons was the true possessor of this holy tool.

What a sight, especially for a young girl who knew nothing about these secrets. The most amazing thoughts ran through my head, but they all were rather vague and I could not find proper

A Russian snuff box which was made in about 1830.

words for them. I only remember that I wanted to throw myself at least twenty times at the feet of this famous father confessor and beg him to exorcise me the same way he was blessing my dear friend. Was this piety? Or carnal desire? Even today I could not tell you for sure.

But, let's go back to our devout couple! The movements of the priest quickened; he was barely able to keep his balance. His body formed an 'S' from head to toe whose frontal bulge moved rapidly back and forth in a horizontal line.

'Is your spirit receiving any satisfaction, my dear little saint?' he asked with a deep sigh. 'I, myself, can see Heaven open up. God's infinite mercy is about to remove me from this vale of tears, I...'

An engraving by an unknown artist, probably Antoine Borel, c. 1780.

'Oh, venerable Father,' exclaimed Eradice, 'I cannot describe the delights that are flowing through me! Oh, yes, yes, I experience Heavenly bliss. I can feel how my spirit is being liberated from all earthly desires. Please, please, dearest Father, exorcise every last impurity remaining upon my tainted soul. I can see... the angels of God... push stronger ... ooh... shove the holy relic deeper... deeper. Please, dearest Father, shove it as hard as you can ... Ooooh!: ooh!!! dearest holy Saint Francis... Ooh, good saint... please, don't leave me in the hour of my greatest need... I feel your relic... it is sooo good... your... holy... relic... I can't hold it any longer... I am... dying!'

The priest also felt his climax approach. He shoved, slammed, snorted and groaned. Eradice's last remark was for him the signal to stop and pull out. I saw the proud snake. It had become very meek and small. It crawled out of its hole, foam-covered, with hanging head.

ABOVE, BELOW and OPPOSITE
*Woodcuts by Italo Zetti designed
to be used as bookplates.*

Our last anti-clerical piece is from *Josefine Mutzenbacher (oder Jugent-Geschichte einer wienerischen Dirne* ['Story of a Young Viennese Maiden']). This novel, written in the Viennese vernacular – which includes borrowings from Serbian and Yiddish as well as Bavarian – is generally thought to be the work of Felix Salten (1869–1945), and he certainly never denied authorship. Born in Hungary, Salten was working as a journalist in Vienna in 1906 when *Josefine Mutzenbacher* was first published. Josefine is the archetypal heroine of the dark erotic novel: a voracious nymphomaniac who proceeds through a catalogue of sexual encounters and perversions 'with the inevitability of a sleepwalker' to borrow a phrase from her Viennese contemporary, Adolf Hitler. In the following episode Josefine's confessor exacts a form of penance which will come as no surprise.

Still standing he advanced his sacred candle, all warm, to the opening. Feeling this I could not resist thrusting myself towards him. Slowly, very slowly he penetrated me. He groaned loudly but I

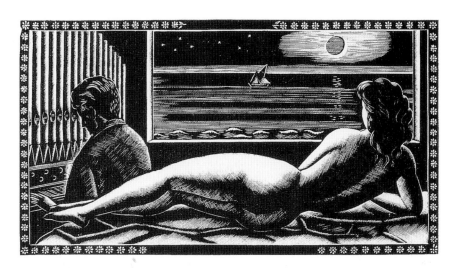

couldn't see his face. I clasped his stalk – which had penetrated quite a long way – firmly in my mussel.

By now I wanted to be fucked properly. Especially as it wasn't a sin. I lay there feeling a mixture of amazement, desire, pleasure and the urge to laugh which finally dissolved my inhibitions. I began to realize that the Kooperator was play-acting and had all along had the intention of powdering me. But I resolved to play along and not give the game away – I still believed the priest had the power to grant absolution. He stayed with his pole lodged in my flesh without moving, breathing heavily. I began to waggle my popo up and down, which made him groan.

'Father,' I whispered. 'What?' 'It wasn't like this,' I said softly. 'How was it then?' 'Back and forth, in and out, that's how he went.' He started pushing careful-

Vows can't change nature, priests are only men,
And love likes stratagem and subterfuge

FROM *THE RING AND THE BELL*
ROBERT BROWNING (1812–89)

ABOVE *A bookplate designed especially for a library of 'Galant 'literature.*

OPPOSITE *'Donna che solleva la Gonna' by Giovanni Zuin.*

ly but fast and strong. 'Like that, maybe?' 'Ah, ah, yes,' I cried, shuddering in an ecstasy of pleasure, 'but faster, Father, faster!' 'Good girl, good girl,' he roared, 'tell me exactly how it was... tell me...,' he couldn't carry on speaking, he was breathing so stormily and ramming so violently.

I needed no further encouragement. 'Ah, ah, that's how it was, it's good like this, better; Father, shoot now, I'm coming, I'm coming, I can't help it, oh Father your cock is so good – it's so very good!'

After a brief spell in the light we are now back in the dark, or in the darkroom at least. In the late nineteenth and early twentieth centuries the elitist collectors of erotica – although they never disappeared – were gradually marginalized by the supply and demand of a new mass market in sexual material. New technology, especially the camera, accelerated the process and a division opened up between literary erotica and erotic art on the one hand, and photographs, magazines and mass-market fiction on the other. There are, of course, numerous important exceptions (several in this part of the book), but the general trend in the creation of 'forbidden' material can be described in this way. Some dealers and publishers of 'gallant' material have always supplied both markets. Leonard Smithers (1861–1907), whom Oscar Wilde described as 'the most learned erotomaniac in Europe', published and numbered among his circle a host of literary figures including Sir Richard Burton, Algernon Swinburne and André Gide, but he also dealt in photographs. In his entertaining book *Memoirs of an Erotic*

Bookseller, Armand Coppens describes a visit to a Paris bookshop in 1948.

'A useful book,' remarked Leclercq. 'I'll just put it aside for a moment.'

While I was looking through the rest of the books in that suitcase, I considered my financial position. Would the Carmelites expect me to pay for my stay or not?

Meanwhile, Leclercq was busily unpacking the second case from which he took an enormous number of pornographic photographs and some films.

'I'm more interested in this sort of thing,' I said, indicating the Forberg.

'It takes all kinds to make a world,' he replied.
Then, tapping the second suitcase, continued:

'But this is the stuff that makes the money. God
knows, if I had to depend on the few customers with
your tastes, I should have starved long ago. Well,
since you're a compatriot, I'll let you have it cheap.
You can have it for 10,000 francs (about £7).'

I could hardly believe my ears. This was a very
rare book indeed and could easily have fetched
fifty pounds at any auction. Ironically, even seven
pounds was a lot of money to me at that time.

OPPOSITE and ABOVE *More
bookplates made by Italo Zetti
in the 1940s and 50s.*

While I pretended to look through the other books
and make up my mind, the door suddenly opened
and a tiny Vietnamese girl came into the room.

'Bonjour, cherie,' said Leclercq. And then,
'You're late. We only have an hour and a half now.'
Turning to me he said, 'This is Mr...'

'Coppens,' I supplied.

'... Mr Coppens, a Belgian customer. At least, I
hope he's going to he a customer. Would you like
to look through the books again, sir?' Leclercq
obviously knew my type. One looks again and
again at some odd piece in a collection and
increasingly realizes its beauty, rarity or value
until, eventually, it is impossible not to buy.

I persuaded myself that the Carmelites simply
could not demand money for their hospitality.
Suddenly, I became aware of Leclercq saying:

'Just a moment, please.' He reached over and
took away my Forberg.

'But I'm going to buy it,' I protested.

'Of course. At that price, who wouldn't? But I
need to borrow it for a couple of minutes.'

Then turning to the boy and speaking in French,
he said:

'Clear the table a bit, Henri. I'll have to use it for a while.'

The boy sighed but obediently removed some of the books. As soon as he had cleared about two-thirds of the table for his employer, he returned to his own work.

An engraved bookplate by Rudolf Koch.

Meanwhile, Leclercq was showing the

Vietnamese girl – who turned out to be his model – some of Forberg's postures. He seemed particularly interested in one which showed a girl kneeling on a couch while a man made love to her from behind. In the background, a naked servant girl watches, a bottle of wine in her hand.

'We'll start with this pose,' Leclercq said to the girl and, turning to me, explained:

'I do hope you don't mind, hut we are in rather a hurry. I've got to have this order ready for tonight and your book really inspires me. Please, have another look at the collection while I borrow it.'

He then produced three or four lamps which he positioned around the table. The Vietnamese girl, meanwhile, had undressed and was shivering slightly with the cold. Leclercq assured her that she would soon feel warmer under the lamps and then ordered Henri to make more room on the table.

The boy uttered another of his exasperated sighs, removed more books from the table and immediately returned to his packing. Leclercq seemed content with the preparations then and began to explain to the girl exactly what he wanted.

'Up on the table now and down on all fours. That's right. Now raise your behind a bit. Wonderful! Thighs a bit further apart. That's right. You are getting a belly, dear. You'll have to lay off the absinthe.'

The girl protested vehemently at this criticism of her charms.

'Any girl would have a belly in this position. When I'm standing up, I have a perfectly nice belly. Anyway, I hate this position. It makes me feel like a cow.'

'You should worry,' retorted Leclercq. 'Where

Bibliophiles have always commissioned bookpates for their private collections; the work of artists such as Franz von Bayros adorns many rare items of erotica. This fine example is one of a series of woodcuts made by Italo Zetti in the 1940s and 50s.

you come from, the cow is a sacred animal.'

At this moment, the preoccupied Henri made his one and only interruption.

'Do the parcels to Germany have to be registered, sir?'

'How the hell do I know?' Leclercq barked. 'Stop interrupting. Only this gentleman,' he said, pointing to me, 'seems to understand the necessity for calm, concentration.'

In silence he undressed and climbed on to the table.

'Right,' he commanded. 'As soon as I'm in her and we are moving, press the button, Henri.'

'You can forget about the moving,' the model remarked drily. 'It won't show in the pictures. Just pretend.'

This remark obviously touched the artist in Leclercq who immediately demanded:

'And what about our expressions? How are we going to look like lusting lovers if we're not actually doing anything? Who do you think we are, members of the *Comédie Française*? No, we'll do it properly or not at all.'

At the end of his tirade, he entered the girl and began moving vigorously. I found the spectacle so absorbing that I immediately forgot both the Carmelites and the precious books in the suitcase. Henri, however, was still occupied with his parcels.

'Hurry up, Henri,' Leclercq suddenly shouted. 'This isn't the only picture we've got to take.'

Henri did not seem in the least affected by or interested in the scene. His attitude, rather, seemed to be one of intense irritation at having his own work interrupted. As soon as the button had

OPPOSITE *'Nudo Maschile alla Finestra'; this superb contemporary nudes has been coloured and finished by the photographer, Giovanni Zuin.*

Do not confuse the priesthood with the Church or there is no hope for the world!

AGATHIAS
(SIXTH CENTURY CE)

*Children are dumb to say
how hot the day is,
How hot the scent is of the
summer rose,
How dreadful the black
wastes of evening sky,
How dreadful the tall
soldiers drumming by.*

*But we have speech, to
chill the angry day,
And speech, to dull the
rose's cruel scent.
We spell away the
overhanging night,
We spell away the soldiers
and the fright.*

*There's a cool well of
language winds us in,
Retreat from too much joy
or too much fear ...*

FROM *THE COOL WEB*
ROBERT GRAVES
(1895–1985)

been pressed, Leclercq took a chair and placed it on the table. He sat down and pulled the girl on to his lap, facing him.

'This is what we call the romantic study,' he explained. 'We've got to look both sexy and serene. There must be tenderness in the way we touch each other.'

Fitting his actions to his words, Leclercq tenderly caressed the girl's breasts and laid his cheek gently against hers. The result was undeniably charming.

'O God!' he exclaimed. 'I've forgotten all about the lighting.'

'I know quite a bit about photography, sir,' I said. 'Let me take care of it.'

'Marvellous!' exclaimed Leclercq. 'The Belgians really are practical. Look at the mess the French are making of Indo-China while the Congo, which is much bigger, is a peaceful, smooth-running country.'

'Don't start talking about war, darling,' said the girl. 'I can't act tenderly while you talk about atrocities.'

Leclercq quickly reminded her that she should not find it necessary to act in her present situation. It seemed to me that the girl was getting far more enjoyment out of the session than she cared to admit.

'Everything's all right,' I reported.

'Henri!' Leclercq shouted.

At this I simply had to laugh. I was so strongly reminded of Pavlov and his dogs. I was all ready to push the button and take the photograph but practice made it inconceivable to Leclercq that the process could be satisfactorily concluded without Henri's grudging aid. Henri did respond, at length, and grumbling quietly to himself, pushed the button.

'*Salauds*', he muttered. 'You can't work properly in this bloody place. People have paid for these books and they've got to be sent off tonight. But everything has to stop because some old bastard can't get sexed up without a pile of photographs. And the string's disappeared, too.'

Despite Henri's protests, the session continued and, if I remember correctly, another eighteen photographs were taken. Not once did Henri lose his air of irritated indifference. As far as he was concerned the whole spectacle might have been happening on another planet. I am certain that both Leclercq and the girl must have reached orgasm more than once. But since Leclercq was constantly changing the pose and the props, carefully consulting the Romano illustrations in my book and checking the lighting, it was impossible to observe him closely. I do remember that his erection, however, never flagged and the Vietnamese girl's radiant face bore witness to the pleasure she received. After an hour and a half, as Leclercq had predicted, the session was over.

When Leclercq and the girl were dressed, I was at last able to pay for my copy of the Forberg.

'I'm sorry you had to wait so long,' said Leclercq. 'But the circumstances really were exceptional.'

One photographic darkroom is much like another, except that the darkroom in this scene from *Suburban Souls* first published in 1901 – could symbolize the novel: claustrophobic and black.

A dilemma: a study which is both dark and fetishistic – and beautiful. Paris, c. 1910.

Fellatio: French engraving c. 1930.

> All this the world well
> knows yet none know
> well,
> To shun the heaven that
> leads men to this hell.
>
> FROM *SONNET 128*
> WILLIAM SHAKESPEARE
> (1564–1616)

*Drawing of unknown origin
c. 1930.*

... Lily [told] me to follow her into the dark-room immediately after breakfast, as she wanted to show me something there. We left Papa eagerly discussing the Dreyfus case in German, and as usual he was all in favour of the generals, as was the Teutonic guest. I had refused to join in the discussion, although Mamma, knowing my opinions, tried to get me to talk on the subject by telling the stranger that I held contrary views to his! I preferred to slip away with Lilian and we were no sooner inside the little cabin than after a long sweet kiss from her fevered lips, she plainly informed me that she wanted me to give her pleasure with my finger as she felt very 'naughty'. Nothing loth, I put my hand up her clothes, as she stood up, leaning against the sink, and my finger immediately touched the spot. I was very surprised to see her start and draw back, with a rapid movement, dislodging my hand completely. I saw at once what had happened. She knew, of course, that she was no longer a virgin, but her great preoccupation was to make me still believe in her virtue. In her excitement, she had presented herself in quite an easy position, the knees half-bent, eager to be manipulated, and I, full of lust and luncheon, had pushed my finger in too far, as I could tell by the soft warmth and moisture. I asked why she drew away from my touch.

'Oh, that is nothing. Don't be offended! Surely you can excuse an instinctive movement of shame?'

I was too clever, and at the same time too excited myself, to do anything but agree with her, and I was content to do my best to bring about the crisis, as she stood bolt upright now, her thighs pressed together. After the usual expressions of pleasure, she suddenly broke away from me, exclaiming that she had spent, and I said to myself that she had been remarkably quick about it. She now made a dive for my neglected organ, which she found quite ready to her hand, as it was all prepared, sticking out of the drawers, as I have explained. She caressed it a little, telling me to keep a sharp eye for fear any of the workgirls should come along, and bending down, took it in her hot mouth, rolling her agile tongue round its swollen head. She had not been sucking me for two seconds, when she got uneasy, and left off. I begged her to continue and finish me, as she stood by my side laughing and looking,

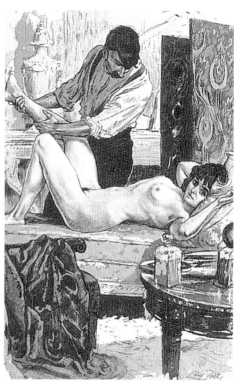

An original illustration of 'Jacky S.' and 'Lily'.

and admiring my sign of virility, and she bent down again, once more popping it into the velvety seclusion of her warm mouth. But directly she felt that I was about to ejaculate, she left off suddenly, exclaimed that she heard footsteps, and fled rapidly from the tiny building, leaving me all alone with my stiff rod sticking up out of my trousers. The disappointment was so great that my erection soon passed off, and I was too much in love with the coquette to feel any anger with her.

Suburban Souls is an obsessional account, complete with facsimile telegrams, letters and even a

Compare this pretty, doll-like image of a woman with the photograph on page 227. Could they be more different? One is 'dark', the other sweet: yet both are depersonalized, male views of women and in that sense fetishistic and the same.

floor plan, of an obsessional affair. It is well written and the characters come to life to the extent that we are left with the suspicion that the deceitful 'Lily' and the stockbroker, 'Jacky', did exist. Here Jacky embarks on a journey which will take him and the reader through three volumes of morbid jealousy and curiously oppressive sexual encounters.

November 26, 1897

Everyone knows the feverish excitement experienced by an eager lover, when awaiting his mistress at the first appointment. I felt hot and excited, and gave a great sigh of relief, when Lilian slowly lifted the *portière* and advanced towards me in the tawdrily furnished bedroom of the mysterious *pavillon* of the Rue de Leipzig. I quickly bolted the door, and drew her to me, placing her on my knees, as I sat on the inevitable *chaise-longue*. She seemed worried and frightened, and told me that she had great trouble in getting away from home. There was a tremendous struggle to get her dress unfastened, and she studiously avoided looking towards the large curtained bed that occupied the middle of the room. She hoped I would not touch it, as if I did, people of the house would guess we had been using it! I tried by my kisses to warm her blood, and I think I succeeded, for she grew more and more bold, and I was able to undo her dress, and feast my eyes on her tiny breasts, which were like those of a girl of fifteen. Nevertheless, the size of the red and excited nipples proved her real age. I sucked and nibbled them greedily, and her pretty ears and neck also came in for a share of attention from my eager lips and tongue. I begged her to let me take off all her garments, but she wanted me to be satisfied with her small, but beautifully made breast. I pretended to be deeply hurt and she excused herself. I must have patience. This was the first time. She would be more yielding when she knew me better. I replied by boldly throwing up her skirts, and after admiring her legs, in their black stockings, and her coquettish be-ribboned drawers, I, at last, placed my hand on the mark of her sex. It was fully covered with a thick, black undergrowth and quite fleshy. The large outer lips were fatter and more developed than we generally find them among the women of France. Her legs, though slim, were well-made, and her thighs of fair proportions. I began to explore the grotto.

'You hurt me,' she murmured.

And as far as I could tell, she seemed to lie intact, or at any rate had not been often approached by a man. I could feel that my caresses delighted her

This photograph is of the same period as the one on page 227, but it is quite different. Fetishists need not despair: it is an image, not a woman — but it is an image of a woman, not a toy. Across time and through lenses, photographic emulsion and printer's ink she makes us aware of her personality. We are in the main thoroughfare of erotica with her, one step away from life, not in a dark alley or prettified dead end.

A lithograph from the series The
Beauty and the Little Monkey,
published in the 1920s.

greatly and she gave way a little. At last, I persuaded her to take off her petticoat and drawers.
She consented, on condition that I would not look
at her. I acquiesced and she dropped her skirt and
took off her bodice, standing before me in her petticoat and stays. She wore a dainty cambric
chemise, tied with cherry ribbons, and I enjoyed
the sight of my love thus at last in my power. I
gloated over her naked shoulders; the rosy nipples,
stiff, and glistening with my saliva: and the luxuri-
ant black tufts of hair beneath the armpits.

She consented now to drop her petticoat, and as
I leant back on the sofa, she placed one soft, cool
hand over my eyes, and with the other, undid
everything, until she stood in her chemise. She
would not go near the bed and struggled to get
away from me. Indeed, she would not let me touch
her, until I closed the window-curtains. We were in
the dark. I placed her on the *chaise-longue*, and

going on my knees, I tried to part her thighs and kiss her mossy cleft. With both hands, she tried to push me away.

'You hurt me!' she said again, but I licked her as well as I could, and feeling the warmth of my mouth, she opened her thighs a little, and I managed to perform my task. It was difficult, as she writhed about, uttered pretty little cries, and would not sufficiently keep her legs apart. But I was not to be dislodged. I was not comfortably installed. My neck was wellnigh broken. The room too was very hot; but I remained busily licking, sucking, perspiring, and my member, bursting with desire, already let a few drops of the masculine essence escape from its burning top. I am certain she experienced a feeling of voluptuousness, by the shuddering of her frame at one moment, and by the peculiar taste that I could not mistake. At last, she thrust my head away. And I rose to my feet, greatly pleased at leaving the prison of her soft thighs. I got my handkerchief, wiped my mouth, and returning to her, as she still laid motionless and silent on the couch, I threw myself upon her without ceremony. I inserted the end of my turgescent weapon between the hairy lips of her lower mouth, and forgetting all prudence, I pushed on. She shrieks and dislodges me. I try to regain my position, but I cannot succeed. She was a virgin; there was no doubt about it.

Lilian is half-seated on the narrow sofa, and I have no way of getting to her, unless I pull her flat down on her back. I am tired too, and very hot. I have twisted my neck and it is painful. So I relent and give up active warfare for the present.

Bird sighs for the air,
Thought for I know not where,
For the womb the seed sighs.
Now sinks the same rest
On mind, on nest,
On straining thighs.

THE LOVER'S SONG
W. B. YEATS (1865–1939)

Photograph taken in a Paris brothel in the early twentieth century.

'Take it in your hand yourself,' I say, 'and do what you like with it.'

She does so, and leaning over her, I find she lets the tip go a little way in. Now all was dry and far from agreeable. I suppose I had done wrong to suck her so long. She had no more feeling of lust. So I moved up to her face, as she reclined with her head on a cushion, and straddling across her, rubbed my arrow and the appendages gently on her face and mouth. She did not move. I took her hand and placed it on my staff of life. She started and roughly drew her hand away. Strange inconsistency. She had placed it herself at the entrance of her virgin cleft; she had allowed me to caress her lips and cheeks with it, but now she recoiled at the idea of grasping it.

So I resolved to overcome any disgust she might feel, and putting the end between her lips, I told her rather roughly to suck it at once. She tried to, timidly; I could see she did not know how.

'Tell me, show me, and I will do all you wish.'

I took her hand, and sucked and licked one of her fingers by way of example.

She took to it readily, and I tried to excite her and keep her up to her work by talking to her as she sucked me awkwardly. But the soft warm caress of her capacious mouth and the clinging grasp of her luscious lips excited me to madness. I moved in and out, slowly, saying:

'Darling! Lilian! It is delicious! Not your teeth, Lily. You must not let your teeth touch it! So! Lick it nicely! Let me feel your tongue! Do not move! Do not go away. I am going to enjoy in your mouth, and you must remain as you are until I tell you.'

With angelic docility, she continues the play of

tongue, and to my great surprise and delight I feel her hands gently caressing my reservoirs. And the crisis comes too soon. The pleasure I had was beyond words. I had kept back the moment of joy as long as I could, but now the charge exploded with violence, and I could feel that a very large quantity gushed into her mouth. I thought I should never cease emitting. Lilian did not stir until I slowly withdrew, having exhausted the pleasure until there was not a throb left, and my organ had begun to soften. Then she sat up and uttered inarticulate cries.

Suburban Souls ends abruptly with a curious note from the author.

And now, Mr Prompter, please ring down the curtain. This drama is finished.

The actors wash off their paint; the brown holland is put over the boxes. We go home, and all is dark until the next night.

So it is on the mimic stage, but in life there is no ending to the long succession of comedy and tragedy which is played out in many acts, and is never ended.

Death now and then calls at the stage-door, and one of the players: poor, painted, false villain, or roguish clown; tragedy queen, or meretricious dancing girl; is carried away in the black hearse, but the universal spectacle of love and hate goes on all the same.

Thus with my most vile story. I must break off here, hut there is no finish to a real book, such as this is.

When the novel is a mere phantasy, it is easy to

ABOVE and OPPOSITE *A boisterous series of Italian nineteenth-century lithographs featuring some inventive gymnastic routines.*

dispose of the characters. But this tale being a true one, I can only bow and go, making way for some fresh actor, who is waiting in the wings to caper in the light, when I shall have disappeared, whether I will or no; for I am, and so are you, Reader, in the hands of the Great Scene-Shifter.

July 1899 – January 1900

Was this postscript a hint as to the real identity of the author? Perhaps, but this part could do with some light comedy after the gloomy melodrama of Jacky and Lilian. This cheerful extract comes from *Passion's Apprentice*.

The irresistible mutual attraction between human beings which – mercifully for the stability of society – is a once-in-a-lifetime event for most people can, like lightning, strike some individuals with greater frequency. It has other characteristics in common with lightning such as heat, sudden and spectacular displays, and a close association with danger and disaster.

However, that gentler expression of electricity, magnetism, best describes the first exchanges between Ashton and Mrs Van Houtte in the dark intimacy of the theatre box. His foot showed a marked tendency to push against hers. Her arm pressed gently but unmistakably against his. Finally their hands, the conductivity no doubt aided by the damp condition of them, found themselves locked together between their chairs.

Lightning struck for the first time in the interval after Act One when Mrs Van Houtte's companion had been despatched to search for her glove at the

A nicely composed Parisian postcard, c. 1900.

entrance. Had he been successful in his chivalrous quest and returned early (which was unlikely since the missing article was in her purse) he would have been surprised to find his inamorata and the Englishman locked together, the tongue of each urgently exploring the mouth of the other.

An early return from the equally impossible task he was given during the second interval would have surprised him even more: he would have found the impetuous Mrs Van Houtte sucking noisily and vigorously at the straining red organ of her new friend which she had just released from his trousers. As it was she could not immediately thank her escort for his concern over her flushed appearance as she was still swallowing the thick seed of Mr Ashton. The Third Act was the most tense of the drama for Ashton, not so much because of any skill on the part of the dramatist but because any request for the programme would have revealed the still partially turgid member which he had not had time to put away.

He eventually managed to make this small but essential adjustment to his evening dress while the only one of their party with any interest in the play was enthusiastically applauding the end of the Third Act (on stage). Had the young Sampson wielding the jawbone of an ass climbed into their box at the beginning of the third interval (it was a four-act play) he is unlikely to have driven Mrs Van Houtte's escort from it. So on this occasion he was left behind while the others went out to 'seek refreshment'.

Finding an unoccupied box immediately adjacent to their own, and having taken the precaution of propping a chair against the door handle, they took this hurried hut delicious refreshment against the plush-covered wall. Little more than a partition, this structure moved under the rhythmic pressure of Mrs Van Houtte's bottom and thighs which were crushed against it as her lover thrust into her. Nor did it in any significant way baffle the gasping cry she uttered at the consummation of her pleasure.

Returning at last to their own box they found their companion in sullen mood. 'Could they not have shared their refreshment with him?' He also confided morbidly that he fully expected to read in the morning's paper that a violent murder had taken place in the next box but was 'damned if he cared' since to intervene would have meant leaving his seat again.

An illustration from Mémoires d'une Chanteuse

Is the actress-courtesan Nana of Emile Zola's magnificent novel, his 'golden fly', a creature of the light or of the dark? Or, like a goddess, or a real person, is she composed of both? In 1878 Zola finished his *ébauche*, or outline, for *Nana*. Of the book's theme he wrote:

The philosophical subject is as follows: A whole society hurling itself at the cunt. A pack of hounds after a bitch, who is not even on heat and makes fun of the hounds following her. The poem of male desires, the great lever which moves the world. There is nothing apart from the cunt and religion.

Later, Zola began to flesh out the characters for the novel. About Nana he said:

Her character: good-natured above all else. Follows

her nature, but never does harm for harm's sake, and feels sorry for people. Bird-brain, always thinking of something new, with the craziest whims. Tomorrow doesn't exist. Very merry, very gay. Superstitious, frightened of God. Loves animals and her parents. At first very slovenly, vulgar; then plays the lady and watches herself closely. – With that, ends up regarding man as a material to exploit, becoming a force of Nature, a ferment of destruction, but without meaning to, simply by means of her sex and her strong female odour, destroying everything she approaches, and turning society sour just as women having a period turn milk sour. The cunt in all its power; the cunt on an altar, with all the men offering up sacrifices to it. The book has to be the poem of the cunt, and the moral will lie in the cunt turning everything sour. As early as Chapter One I show the whole audience captivated and worshipping; study the women and the men in front of that supreme apparition of the cunt. – On top of all that, Nana eats up gold, swallows up every sort of wealth; the most extravagant tastes, the most frightful waste. She instinctively makes a rush for pleasures and possessions. Everything she devours; she eats up what people are earning around her in industry, on the stock exchange, in high positions, in everything that pays. And she leaves nothing but ashes. In short a real whore. – Don't make her witty, which would be a mistake; she is nothing but flesh, but flesh in all its beauty. And, I repeat, a good-natured girl.

In *Nana* the men are the obvious victims. But is it not true that the women, Nana herself, are victims too? Perhaps it is society which is at fault,

OPPOSITE *A coloured engraving made to illustrate Paul Verlaine's* Oeuvres Libres.

or rather unable to cope, with the potentially destructive power within our sexuality.

The predatory element within male sexuality stalks the dark side of erotic literature just as the fictional Mr Hyde or the all too real Jack the Ripper prowled the dark alleyways of London. Let us follow an earlier prowler through the familiar streets of the West End. It is in many ways a journey of discovery.

These are extracts from the 1763 diary of a man with a strict Calvinist background. He is James Boswell, a friend of Voltaire (François-Marie Arouet) and of Jean-Jacques Rousseau, as well as being the scrupulous biographer of Dr Samuel Johnson.

Drawing of a brothel scene by an unknown artist.

25th March
As I was coming home this night, I felt carnal incli-
nations raging through my frame. I determined to
gratify them. I went to St James's Park and picked
up a whore.

10th May
At the bottom of Haymarket I picked up a strong,
jolly young damsel, and taking her under the arm
I conducted her to Westminster Bridge and there
in armour complete did I engage her upon this
noble edifice. The whim of doing so there with the
Thames rolling below us amused me much. Yet
after the brutish appetite was sated, I could not
but despise myself for being so closely united with
such a low wretch.

17th May
I picked up a fresh, agreeable young girl called
Alice Gibbs. We went down a lane to a snug place,
and I took out my armour, but she begged that I
might not put it on, as the sport was much pleas-
anter without it, and as she was quite safe. I was
so rash as to trust her and had a very agreeable
congress.

4th June
I went to the Park, picked up a low brimstone vira-
go, went to the bottom of the Park, arm-in-arm
and dipped my machine in the Canal and performed most manfully. I then went as far as St
Paul's Churchyard, roaring along, and then came
to Ashley's Punch-house and drank three penny
bowls. In the Strand, I picked up a little profligate
wretch and gave her sixpence. She allowed me

Detail from an oleograph used to decorate a tobacco box.

entrance. But the miscreant refused me performance. I was much stronger than her, and pushed her up against the wall. She, however, gave a sudden spring from me; and screaming out, a parcel of more whores and soldiers came to her relief. 'Brother soldiers,' said I, 'should not a half-pay officer roger, for sixpence? And here has she used me so and so.' I got them on my side, and I abused in blackguard style, and then left them. At Whitehall I picked up another girl to whom I called myself a highwayman and told her I had no money and begged she would trust me. But she would not.

Boswell's journal continues in much the same vein until:

13th July
Since my being honoured with the friendship of Mr Johnson I have more seriously considered the duties of morality. I have considered that promiscuous concubinage is certainly wrong. Sure it is that if all the men and women in Britain were merely to consult an animal gratification, society would be a most shocking scene. Nay, it would cease altogether. Notwithstanding of these reflections, I have stooped to mean profligacy even yesterday. Heavens, I am resolved to guard against it.

But Boswell's good intentions cannot long control his appetite. Admittedly, here it is the prostitute who does the importuning.

3rd August
... I should have mentioned that on Monday night,

coming up the Strand, I was tapped on the shoulder by a fine fresh lass. I went home with her. She was an officer's daughter and born at Gibraltar. I could not resist indulging myself with the enjoyment of her. Surely, in such a situation, when the woman is already abandoned, the crime must be alleviated, though in strict morality, illicit love is always wrong.

Poor Boswell, he began to drink heavily after that, in the forlorn hope that the demon of alcohol might subdue the demon of sexuality, prevailing where he had failed. Poor Boswell, but what of the women he used? It is amusing for us – as it was for him – to think of copulating on Westminster Bridge, but what of the poverty that drove the girl to acquiesce? And what tale of misery could the officer's daughter from Gibraltar have told?

The oleograph technique which was used to produce this miniature allowed the reproduction of coloured erotic images on mass market items such as snuff boxes and cigar cases.

In a section which is all about ambivalence – shades of light and dark – Boswell gives us a few problems to resolve in the penultimate extract of the anthology. First, there are the issues raised by that oldest of games, Love For Sale. What can we say about that? Can the winners and losers be predicted by gender: is it that simple? Not really, but as in all games of chance the odds favour the House and the manager is generally male.

The second problem which Boswell's candid diary gives us is his terminology. A highly literate man who knew the value of

ABOVE and OPPOSITE *Details from a series of French coloured engravings dealing with incidents during the time of the Revolution.*

words, he nevertheless describes episodes of random coupling for money as 'illicit love'. The confusion of love with sex is one of the most poisonous of all the hardy perennials planted by the adversary of mankind, Satan, in the Garden of Eden. Eating the fruit of that particular tree is the surest way to taste hell while yet alive.

The final issue which the tormented Boswell raises takes us back to the very beginning of this book, to the real 'Garden of Eden' of our species in the African Rift Valley. It is an issue which has kept history's prophets and philosophers almost as busy as contemporary divorce lawyers: monogamy. How did Boswell, the archetypal male – a sexual predator addicted to casual encounters – cope with marriage? We have only to turn the pages of his blisteringly honest diary: 'from henceforth I shall be a perfect man; at least I hope so.'

Boswell put up a good fight. He was faithful for almost three years until his wife's aversion 'to hymenal rites' tried him beyond endurance. Boswell was to practise what he called 'Asiatic multiplicity' until the end of his life. In common with most of us Boswell washed to remain 'faithful' in a monogamous relationship while at the same time wanting sexual variety and adventure. It is another paradox within our sexual inheritance which each must work out in his or her own way. Some societies seek to replicate the sexual possibilities available to our palaeolithic forbears in other forms of 'marriage' such as polygamy. But in monogamous cultures other solutions must be sought.

Nature usually provides her own compensations. Along with infinitely larger penises than our nearest simian cousins we can also boast much larger brains. We can satisfy our need for erotic variety by using our imagination and by raising 'love'-making to an art rather than a repetitive animal function. This, of course, is where erotica comes in. Kalyana Malla, medieval author of the Indian sex manual *Ananga-Ranga*, describes his purpose in writing: 'I have in this book shown how the husband, by varying enjoyment of his wife, may live with her as with thirty-two different women, ever varying enjoyment of her,, and rendering satiety impossible for both.' It takes two to tango, however, and the good Mrs Boswell may have found the multiform delights of Hindu erotology as alien as the thought of copulating on Westminster Bridge.

In the last extract in this part we join another frequenter of the dark byways, who nevertheless had a knack for shedding light on the subject of sex. His city was Paris, and Restif de la Bretonne discovers that the perusal of erotica is not always a useful antidote for infidelity.

I have said I was faithful to Zéphire with her companions. That truth might lead you into error. I must tell all, if I am not to deceive you. Here is another of my turpitudes, all the more surprising in that it took place in a time of virtue, and that nothing seemed to foreshadow it. I was respecting

An early nineteenth-century watercolour illustration from an erotic book.

my intended and abstaining from other women: I was living more virtuously than I had ever done before, and I was beginning to imagine that one could become accustomed to it. But what is going to show the danger of books such as the *Le Portier des Chartreux, Thérèse Philosophe, La Religieuse en chemise*, and others like them, is the sudden and terrible eroticism which they aroused in me after long abstinence. A great libertine, that Molet whom I have already mentioned and who was a fellow-lodger of mine at Bonne Sellier's, had come to see me one Sunday morning when I was still in bed, and had brought me the first of these books, which I had only glimpsed at La Mace's. Filled with a lively curiosity, I took it eagerly and started reading in bed; I forgot everything, even Zéphire. After a score of pages, I was on fire. Manon Lavergne, a relative of Bonne Sellier, came on behalf of my former landlady to bring my linen and Loiseau's, which Bonne continued to wash for us. I knew what Manon's morals were like. I threw myself upon her. The young girl did not put up very much resistance.

I resumed my reading after she had gone. Half an hour later there appeared Cécile Decoussy, my sister Margot's companion, who came on her behalf to ask why she no longer saw anything of me. Without any regard for this young blonde's position (she was about to be married), or for the atrocious way in which I was bringing shame on my sister in the person of her friend, I put so much fury into my attack that, alarmed as much as surprised, she thought that I had gone mad. I returned to my baneful reading.

About three quarters of an hour later Thérèse

Courbisson arrived, laughing and bantering. 'Where is he, that lazy scamp? Still in bed!' And she came over to tickle me. I was waiting for her. I seized her almost in the air, like a feather, and with only one hand I pulled her under me. 'Oh! After what you've just done to Manon? A fine man you are!' She was caught before she could finish; and, as she was very partial to phys-

An anonymous French etching, c. 1920.

ical pleasure, she did nothing more but help me. At last she tore herself from my arms because she heard my landlord coming upstairs. She went out, leaving the door open. I finished my book.

The bed had warmed me up; the three pleasures I had enjoyed were just a spur to my senses: I got up with the intention of going to fetch Zéphire, of bringing her to my room, and of abandoning

Inspecting the troops: French engraving, c. 1930.

A drawing by an uknown artist.

myself with her to my erotic frenzy. At that moment someone scratched at my door, which I had only pushed to. I started, thinking it was Zéphire. 'Who is it?' I cried. 'Come in.' 'Séraphine,' said a voice which I thought I recognized. I trembled, thinking it was Séraphine Destroches who had come to scold me for my behaviour with her companion Decoussy. 'Who is it?' I repeated. 'Séraphine Jolon.' The only person I had ever known by that name was the housekeeper of a painter who was our neighbour in the Rue de Poulies, and I had whispered sweet nothings to her once or twice; but then Largeville had turned up, and Jeannette Demailly, and I had left the house. Reassured. I opened the door. It was she. 'I have come,' the pretty girl said to me, 'on behalf of Mademoiselle Fagard, now Madame Jolon, my sister-in-law, who begs you to introduce me and recommend me to Mademoiselle Delaporte, who thinks highly of you and can render me a great service.' 'Immediately,' I said; 'sit down, pretty neighbour.' She was charming. As she turned round, she showed me a perfect figure. I seized her, and pushed her back on to the bed. She tried to defend herself. That was adding fuel to the fire. I did not even take time to shut the door. I finished, I began again. 'I... did... not... tell... you,' gasped Séraphine, 'that... my sister Jolon... was waiting for me.' This thought spurred me on towards a treble. I was like a madman, when the door opened. It was Agathe Fagard. 'Help! Help!' cried Séraphine. I left her uncovered; I jumped up, kicked the door to, threw the lovely brunette on to my bed, and submitted her to a sixth triumph no less vigorous than the first, carried away as I was by the force of my imagination. Agathe Fagard had not yet recovered from her surprise when, appeased by an almost simultaneous triple effort, I blushed at my frenzy and apologized to the two sisters-in-law. 'He has to be seen to be believed!' said Séraphine. I used all the arguments I could to calm them and only just succeeded. Such is the effect of erotic literature.

The reactions of the retainers in this French engraving are interesting. The man on the floor seems depressed at the enormity of the affair; the younger man rises in sympathy.

PART THREE

Our Wildest Dreams

This part follows the development of sexual art and literature through four centuries and more, from the pyrotechnic creations of the Earl of Rochester and the sophisticated paintings of the French and Italian Renaissance to the art and writing of men and women in our own time. Like the 'Grand Tour' enjoyed by a privileged few during the Age of Enlightenment, this is a journey full of incident. There are extracts from the libertine literature which sizzled in the secret library drawers of the eighteenth-century aristocracy, and selections from the best examples of the erotic novels which their Victorian great-grandchildren took in Gladstone bags to every corner of the British Empire. The images which accompany these texts are just as varied: there are prints and drawings by numerous artists, known and unknown, celebrating the many delights of human sexuality. The development of photography in the mid-nineteenth century opened up an exciting new world of possibilities for the erotic imagination, and we have included a unique collection of rare and beautiful early daguerreotypes as well as many later photographs.

The forbidding shadow of Queen Victoria stretched far into our own century. But sex is too insistent and too important to be denied, and there have always been those who have chosen it

The Abbé, from Under the Hill *by Aubrey Beardsley (1872–98).*

OPPOSITE *Photograph by China Hamilton, Suffolk, England.*

as their subject despite the risk of disapproval or even prosecution. In a new millennium, it seems incredible that as fine and well-intentioned a book as *Lady Chatterley's Lover* or that cheerful classic *Fanny Hill* could have been hauled through the English courts – but they were. While England struggled to clear its air of the fog from nineteenth-century industries and its mind of murky Victorian hypocrisy, Paris shone like a beacon of reason in the gloom: much of the twentieth-century material we have included was created there. Of course, bright lights will attract vicious things as well as beautiful and interesting ones, but then it is the job of anthologists to sort out the glamorous moths from among the mosquitoes and midges.

ABOVE and OPPOSITE *Watercolours attributed to the German artist Johann Heinrich Romberg (1763–1840).*

The creators of erotica have no choice but to tap their own reservoir of sexuality in order to achieve that reciprocal excitement in the viewer or reader which is the whole point of erotic art and literature. This means digging deep into the unconscious and far below experience, however wide and varied that may be. Erotic art and literature can then be regarded as akin to dreams: idealized expressions of their creator's urges, obsessions and preoccupations. Dreams – both the profound, sleeping kind and waking fantasies – are of course immensely potent. Fuelled by the limitless power of the unconscious, they can – if they resonate in the imagination of others – go forth into the world like the Golem, full of potential for either good or evil.

If erotica is indeed the stuff of dreams it makes the anthologist's job – choosing a selection of this volatile material – a task requiring care. Are we perhaps taking this task a little too seriously? Let

*Learning by example, watercolour
by Georg Emmanuel Opitz
(1775–1841).*

us consult a couple of dreamers. In the summer of 1908 Sigmund Freud wrote the second preface to one of the most important books of the twentieth century, his *The Interpretation of Dreams*: a work which was the foundation stone of psychoanalysis. To complete this project Freud chose to retreat high in the glorious mountains of the Tyrol. Freud did not know – and it would certainly have spoiled his vacation if he had known – that thirty years later another man who understood how to use dreams would make his home on the very same spot. This man once said that he moved towards his destiny 'with the inevitability of a sleep-walker'; he demonstrated to the world that mad and evil dreams can wield power if you can make them echo in the minds of others. The place was Berchtesgaden, of course; the man, Adolf Hitler.

The point of this Alpine excursion was to show that a genre which operates at a dream level needs to be properly considered – not banned, but taken seriously. Erotica plugs deep into the psyche of both creator and user and is potentially powerful stuff. In making this selection we have therefore endeavoured to choose material which celebrates life and gives something back to it. That does not mean the erotic 'dreams' we have included are always cheerful. Some are dark and disturbing – sex has many faces. In one respect this selection of erotic material is clear-cut and unambiguous: the Marquis de Sade and other prophets of cruelty have been left to sweat in their own nightmares.

CHAPTER SIX
The Libertine Imagination

Naked she lay, clasped in my longing arms,
I filled with love, and she all over charms;
Both equally inspired with eager fire,
Melting through kindness, flaming in desire.
With arms, legs, lips close clinging to embrace,
She clips me to her breast, and sucks me to her face.
Her nimble tongue, Love's lesser lightning, played
Within my mouth, and to my thoughts conveyed
Swift orders that I should prepare to throw
The all-dissolving thunderbolt below.
My fluttering soul, sprung with the pointed kiss,
Hangs hovering o'er her balmy brinks of bliss.
But whilst her busy hand would guide that part
Which should convey my soul up to her heart,
In liquid raptures I dissolve all o'er,
Melt into sperm, and spend at every pore.
A touch from any part of her had done't:
Her hand, her foot, her very look's a cunt.

The Feeling, an engraving by the Dutch artist Heinrich Goltzius (1558–1617).

The unmistakable voice of John Wilmot, second Earl of Rochester (1647–80), echoes down the years: the first, and one of the very few, poets writing in English to make sex his principal subject. It is true that Robert Herrick (1591–1674) had already explored every inch of his delicious mistress Julia in verse before Rochester was born, and there is wonderful erotic verse by earlier poets including John Donne, Thomas Carew and of course Shakespeare. But these men had other subjects too, while for Rochester there was really only sex. Three centuries have not dulled his ability to shock and sting us: the words, from his poem *The Imperfect Enjoyment*, still explode like Chinese crackers at a court ball.

One of the brightest stars in the dissolute court of Charles II, Rochester took only 33 years to burn himself out with drink and debauchery. His love lyrics are some of the most beautiful in the English language, but it is for his bawdy work that he is chiefly remembered. Such was the reputation of this brilliant rake that the Victorian pornographer William Dugdale even produced a phony biography detailing court intrigues and 'the amatory adventures of Lord Rochester in Holland, France and Germany'. Why did he bother? The truth needed no embellishment.

The word 'lechery' is derived from the verb 'to lick': this powerful evocation of both is by Artur Fischer (1872–1948).

Having offended different individuals with his erotic satires at various times, Rochester decided to mark the marriage of the Italian princess Mary of Modena to the Duke of York (later James II) by comprehensively slandering almost every woman in the court. *Signior Dildo* is one of the most outrageous poems ever written, and not the kind of wedding present the Duke and Duchess might have hoped for:

You ladies all of merry England
Who have been to kiss the Duchess's hand,
Pray, did you lately observe in the show
A noble Italian called Signior Dildo
This signior was one of Her Highness's train,
And helped to conduct her over the main;
But now she cries out, 'To the Duke I will go!
I have no more need for Signior Dildo.'

Priapus, the tireless patron of debauchery, receives an unexpectedly intimate tribute during a parkland orgy. Eighteenth-century sepia print.

Rochester then proceeds to describe the intimate sexual practices of his aristocratic circle:

That pattern of virtue, Her Grace of Cleveland,
Has swallowed more pricks than the ocean has sand;
But by rubbing and scrubbing so large does it grow,
It is just fit for nothing but Signior Dildo!

The unofficial marriage-song ends with the unfortunate Dildo ('... sound, safe, ready and dumb/As ever was candle, carrot, or thumb') being chased down Pall Mall by a crowd of jealous penises:

Leather dildos were an important hidden export for Italy during the seventeenth and eighteenth centuries; a contemporary engraving.

The good lady Sandys burst into laughter
To see how the bollocks came wobbling after,
And had not their weight retarded the foe,
Indeed't had gone hard with Signior Dildo.

Rochester's own end came seven years later. Bishop Burnet maintained that he repented of his wicked ways on his deathbed; visitors to London can see his face in the National Portrait Gallery and judge for themselves if England's first and finest libertine was a man to abandon his principles. Afterwards, if pilgrimages appeal, it is a short walk to the royal park Rochester immortalized in *A Ramble in St James's Park*:

Much wine had passed, with grave discourse
Of who fucks who, and who does worse....
When I, who still take care to see
Drunkenness relieved by lechery,
Went out into St James's Park
To cool my head and fire my heart.
But though St James has th'honour on't,
'Tis consecrate to prick and cunt.
There, by a most incestuous birth,
Strange woods spring from the teeming earth....

Each imitative branch does twine
In some loved fold of Aretine,
And nightly now beneath their shade
Are buggeries, rapes, and incests made.
Unto this all-sin-sheltering grove
Whores of the bulk and the alcove,
Great ladies, chambermaids, and drudges,
The ragpicker, and heiress trudges.
Carmen, divines, great lords, and tailors,

Prentices, poets, pimps, and jailers,
Footmen, fine fops do here arrive,
And here promiscuously they swive.

On 13 January 1668, Samuel Pepys wrote in his famous diary: 'Thence homeward by coach and stopped at Martin's, my bookseller, where I saw the French book which I did think to have had for my wife to translate, called *L'escholle des filles*, but when I came to look in it, it is the most bawdy, lewd book that I ever saw.' Nevertheless, by 8 February Pepys had returned 'to the Strand to my booksellers and there staid an hour, and bought the idle roguish book *L'escholle des filles...*' Curiosity had clearly got the better of Pepys, and whether to appease his conscience in purchasing the book, or because he had read more on his second visit, he had moderated his opinion of the work. But the judgement is still unfair. *L'Ecole des filles* is a charming, elegant book and a minor masterpiece.

It employs the dialogue form common to many erotic books of the period, and first used by Pietro Aretino in his *Ragionamenti*. But how different *L'Ecole des filles* is from all the other seventeenth- and eighteenth-century Aretino clones. It takes the woman's view of sex so convincingly, and offers such sound and practical advice to the uninitiated, that it may indeed have been written by a woman. Michel Millot and Jean L'Ange were certainly involved in its publication in 1655,

Have you beheld (with much delight)
A red rose peeping through a white?
Or else a cherry (double graced)
Within a lilly? Centre placed?
Or ever marked the pretty beam,
A strawberry shows half drowned in cream?
Or seen rich rubies blushing through
A pure smooth pearl, and orient too?
So like to this, nay all the rest,
Is each neat niplet of her breast.

UPON THE NIPPLES ON JULIA'S BREASTS
ROBERT HERRICK
(1591–1674)

The digéstif, *anonymous English copper engraving, eighteenth century.*

but a rumour has persisted that the real author was Françoise d'Aubigné (c. 1635–1719), better known as Madame de Maintenon, bride of Louis XIV! In reading the following extracts you can make your own decision as to the gender of the writer. The sexually experienced Susanne establishes some first principles with her young cousin Fanchon:

FANCHON: And now that we're on the subject, tell me why on most nights I feel a certain agitation just here – I mean in my cunny – which hardly lets me sleep. I toss and turn from one side to the other without being able to soothe it. What should I do?

SUSANNE: All you need is a big, sinewy yard to penetrate your femininity, to make the sweet sap flow there and soothe the inflammation. Or alternatively, when this happens you should rub it with your finger for a while and then you'll taste all the pleasures of an orgasm.

FANCHON: With a finger? Impossible!

SUSANNE: With your middle finger, using it on the edge, like this.

FANCHON: All right, I'll keep it in mind. But to return to what we were talking about, love, haven't you told me that you sometimes experience this enjoyment with men?

SUSANNE: Certainly, when I feel like it. I owe it all to a boy whom I love very much.

FANCHON: Just as I thought. It must be true that you love him because otherwise, according to you, he wouldn't be able to do it. I'm surprised, though! Has he given you a lot of pleasure like this?

SUSANNE: So much that I can hardly bear it!

FANCHON: And how am I going to find someone who will do this for me?

SUSANNE: Well, you must choose someone who really loves you and who has enough discretion not to say a word about it to anyone.

The importance of love and trust is stressed throughout *L'Ecole des filles*. The practical advice is as systematic as that given in *Kama Sutra*, and in many ways superior. This is what Susanne has to say about touching, male psychology, the sensitivity of the perineum and masturbation:

FANCHON: I never talk to you without learning something... But can't you tell me why men seem to get more pleasure from having their yards caressed by our hands than by any other part of the body? When they have their yards right inside us during intercourse, they still enjoy feeling our hands stroking their stones.

SUSANNE: It's not easy to give an absolute answer. One of the greatest pleasures which they can ever experience is some sign of gratitude from us for what they are doing to us, as I've already mentioned. That's where love's greatest happiness lies, it longs to divide pleasure equally between two lovers, so that one doesn't have more than the other. What better way is there, then, of letting them know how they are exciting us than by using our hands to attend to the instrument which serves us so well? When we caress them, it makes them see that we are in no way half-hearted about it and that we say to our-

Wo'd ye oyle of blossomes get?
Take it from my Julia's sweat:
Oyl of lillies, and of spike,
From her moysture take the like:
Let her breath, or let her blow,
All rich spices thence will flow.

UPON JULIA'S SWEAT
ROBERT HERRICK (1591–1674)

Riding St George, *anonymous English copper engraving, eighteenth century.*

Engraving of a drawing attributed to Antoine Borel (1743–1810). In illustrating erotica, the prodigious Parisian artist often strayed from the text, using scenes from other books which were graphically more exciting or creating sexual tableaux of his own invention.

selves as they watch us doing it: 'I enjoy touching this with my hand because it is an emblem of all my pleasure and happiness, because I have it as it is, and because from this organ I must receive my greatest satisfaction'. This pleases them especially and the touch of the hand is more exciting, a more womanly examination, as with all due care she explores the nature of the instrument, as though it were a limb that seemed strange to her and of which she was going to make use for the first time. This caressing is both pleasurable and soothing for men, thrilling them through and through. The simple, willing grasp of a white, delicate hand which closes round their shepherd's staff is enough to reveal to them the thought of their mistress's heart. The hand working gently on its object is like the symbol of the love which it embodies, just as when it is used too harshly it is a symbol of hostility. As a rule we use the hand to touch those things we love. Two friends seal their friendship by clasping hands, when it's a purely platonic relationship which permits no other kind of contact. Yet contact between a man and a woman should be natural and complete, with body and soul taking part in it. They caress one another's organs as a way of showing their mutual love. A woman who does such things to a man and allows him to do such things to her, shows him more clearly that she loves him than if they had merely shaken hands! There is nothing more precious to us than the stones and I can tell you, what's more, that if she permits kissing, embracing, mounting, riding, insertion – in short, discharging the yard in the cunny – but yet refuses to touch his instrument, she doesn't show her love as clearly as if she had simply put her hand on it out of affection and was too frightened to let him go any further. In fact, this is the summit of love's pleasure: when the woman cannot touch the man's instrument because it is completely engulfed in hers, she can at least caress the nearest thing to it which remains free during intercourse, and stroke the stones which are the source of her pleasure. No form of familiarity is greater than the hand's. Nature, having seen to it that a man can enjoy two pleasures at once, those of the cunny and

OPPOSITE *Copy of the oil painting*
A Bed in the Corn Field,
attributed to Michael Martin
Drolling (1786–1851).

One of a series of erotic miniatures
satirizing French influence in the
Catholic cantons; gouache on ivory,
Switzerland, c. 1800.

the hand, has also left a good length and expanse of the yard behind the stones which cannot enter the woman but runs round almost to the rump, so that the woman can caress it, put her hand on it and fondle it during intercourse. This shows clearly that there is nothing in the creation of men and women which was unintentional and nothing which doesn't have its reasons, if one is curious enough to discover them. It follows from this that it must be a clear abuse of those means of satisfaction which nature has given us not to put them to the purpose for which they were intended. I'm rather preoccupied by this argument because it concerns me in one respect. One of my lover's greatest joys, when we are naked under the sheets, is to see how white my hands are, as I use them in that place which it is absurd to call indecent. (After all, it's the hidden temple of the greatest pleasure in the world, and often makes us flush with excitement just to touch it.) In the same way, I experience a double pleasure when he shows himself eager to bestow the same kind of caresses on me. I ask you, love, what greater happiness is there than to see a little length of limp flesh hanging at the base of your lover's belly – a thing which we take in our hands and which gradually grows stiff and becomes so large that you can hardly get your hand round it. The skin of it is so delicate that it almost makes you swoon with delight just to touch it. After you've squeezed it gently, you find it becomes stiff enough, and then it seems

An illustration from the 1784 French edition of Fanny Hill, entitled 'Woman of Pleasure or Fille de Joye'. The drawing by Antoine Borel was engraved by F. R. Elluin.

feverish with heat and crimson in colour, which is quite intriguing to watch. You bring your lover to this ecstasy by stroking him and then you see the yard ejaculate a whitish liquid between your fingers, quite opposite in colour to the yard, which is so inflamed. Then we let it fall again as quickly as we took it up, until after a while we begin again.

Another landmark of libertine literature – and probably the most famous erotic novel there has ever been – was *Fanny Hill*. This minor masterpiece was written in Fleet Prison between 1748 and 1750 by John Cleland, a journalist and former diplomat whose debts had finally caught up with him. *Fanny Hill* is a charming work: a unique combination of vivid descriptions and shrewd insights into human nature, expressed in ornate language encrusted with metaphors. Despite the restrictions of the genre, Cleland even manages to breathe life into some of the minor characters. As for Fanny herself, she is one of those archetypal characters who escape from books and inhabit the realm of imagination and dreams.

We may say what we please, but those we can be the easiest and freest with are ever those we like, not to say love, the best.

With this stripling, all whose art of love was the action of it, I could, without check of awe or restraint, give a loose to joy, and execute every scheme of dalliance my fond fancy might put me on, in which he was, in every sense, a most exquisite companion. And now my great pleasure

lay in humouring all the petulances, all
the wanton frolic of a raw novice just
fleshed, and keen on the burning scent
of his game, but in broken to the sport:
and, to carry on the figure, who could
better THREAD THE WOOD than he, or
stand fairer for the HEART OF THE HUNT?

He advanc'd then to my bedside, and
whilst he faltered out his message, I
could observe his colour rise, and his
eyes lighten with joy, in seeing me in a
situation as favourable to his loosest
wishes, as if he had bespoke the play.

I smiled, and put out my hand
towards him, which he kneeled down to
(a politeness taught him by love alone, that great
master of it) and greedily kiss'd. After exchanging
a few confused questions and answers, I ask'd him
if he could come to bed to me, for the little time I
could venture to detain him. This was like asking
a person, dying with hunger, to feast upon the dish
on earth the most to his palate. Accordingly, without further reflection, his clothes were off in an
instant; when, blushing still more at this new liberty, he got under the bedclothes I held up to
receive him, and was now in bed with a woman for
the first time in his life.

Here began the usual tender preliminaries, as
delicious, perhaps, as the crowning act of enjoyment itself; which they often beget an impatience
of, that makes pleasure destructive of itself, by
hurrying on the final period, and closing that
scene of bliss, in which the actors are generally too
well pleas'd with their parts, not to wish them an
eternity of duration.

Nanny blushes, when I woo her,
And with kindly chiding eyes,
Faintly says, I shall undo her,
Faintly, O forbear, she cries.

But her breasts while I am pressing,
While to her's my lips I join;
Warmed she seems to taste the blessing,
And her kisses answer mine.

Undebauched by rules of honour,
Innocence, with nature, charms;
One bids, gently push me from her,
T'other take me in her arms.

NANNY BLUSHES
MATTHEW PRIOR (1664–1721)

Another illustration from the 1784 French edition of Fanny Hill, *drawing by Antoine Borel engraved by F. R. Elluin.*

When he had sufficiently graduated his advances towards the main point, by toying, kissing, clipping, feeling my breasts, now round and plump, feeling that part of me I might call a furnace-mouth, from the prodigious intense heat his fiery touches had rekindled there, my young sportsman, embolden'd by every freedom he could wish, wantonly takes my hand, and carries it to that enormous machine of his, that stood with a stiffness! a hardness! an upward bent of erection! and which, together, with its bottom dependance, the inestimable bulse of lady's jewels, formed a grand show out of goods indeed! Then its dimensions, mocking either grasp or span, almost renew'd my terrors.

I could not conceive how, or by what means I could take, or put such a bulk out of sight. I stroked it gently, on which the mutinous rogue seemed to swell, and gather a new degree of fierceness and insolence; so that finding it grew not to be trifled with any longer, I prepar'd for rubbers in good earnest.

Slipping then a pillow under me, that I might give time the fairest play, I guided officiously with my hand this furious battering ram, whose ruby head, presenting nearest the resemblance of a heart, I applied to its proper mark, which lay as finely elevated as we could wish; my hips being borne up, and my thighs at their utmost extension, the gleamy warmth that shot from it, made him feel that he was at the mouth of the indraught, and driving foreright, the powerfully divided lips of that pleasure-thirsty channel receiv'd him. He hesitated a little; then, settled well in the passage, he made his way up the straits of it, with a difficulty

A watercolour attributed
to Johann Heinrich Romberg
(1763–1840).

nothing more than pleasing, widening as he went,
so as to distend and smooth each soft furrow: our
pleasure increasing deliciously, in proportion as
our points of mutual touch increas'd in that so
vital part of me in which I had now taken him, all
indriven, and completely sheathed; and which,
crammed as it was, stretched, splitting ripe, gave it
so gratefully straight an accommodation! so strict
a fold! a suction so fierce! that gave and took unutterable delight. We had now reach'd the closest
point of union; but when he backened to come on
the fiercer, as if I had been actuated by a fear of
losing him, in the heights of my fury, I twisted my
legs round his naked loins, the flesh of which, so
firm, so springy to the touch, quiver'd again under
the pressure; and now I had him every way en-
circled and begirt; and having drawn him home to
me, I kept him fast there, as if I had sought to
unite bodies with him at that point. This bred a
pause of action, a pleasure stop, whilst that delicate glutton, my nethermouth, as full as it could
hold, kept palating, with exquisite relish, the

morsel that so deliciously engorged it. But nature could not long endure a pleasure that so highly provoked without satisfying it: pursuing then its darling end, the battery recommenc'd with redoubled exertion; nor lay I inactive on my side, but encountering him with all the impetuosity of motion I was mistress of. The downy cloth of our meeting mounts was now of real use to break the violence of the tilt; and soon, too soon indeed! the high wrought agitation, the sweet urgency of this to-and-fro friction, raised the titillation on me to its height; so that finding myself on the point of going, and loathe to leave the tender partner of my joys behind me, I employed all the forwarding motions and arts my experience suggested to me, to promote his keeping me company to our journey's end. I not only then tighten'd the pleasure-girth round my restless inmate, by a secret spring

The Hayloft, *a watercolour by an unknown artist, French, twentieth century.*

of friction and compression that obeys the will in those parts, but stole my hand softly to that store bag of nature's prime sweets, which is so pleasingly attach'd to its conduit pipe, from which we receive them: there feeling, and most gently indeed, squeezing those tender globular reservoirs, the magic touch took instant effect, quicken'd, and brought on upon the spur the symptoms of that sweet agony, the melting moment of dissolution, when pleasure dies by pleasure, and the mysterious engine of it overcomes the titillation it has rais'd in those parts, by plying them with the stream of a warm liquid, that is itself the highest of all titillations, and which they thirstily express and draw in like the hot-natured leech, which to cool itself, tenaciously attracts all the moisture within its sphere of exsuction. Chiming then to me, with exquisite consent, as I melted away, his oily balsamic injection, mixing deliciously with the sluices in flow from me, sheath'd and blunted all the stings of pleasure, it flung us into an ecstasy that extended us fainting, breathless, entranced.

Prisoners have no choice but to dream: waking and sleeping they must inhabit their own internal landscape. Deprived of contact, they find their dreams are often sexually charged; if they can give form to those dreams, that writing becomes a kind of sexual act in itself. Honoré Gabriel Riquetti, Comte de Mirabeau (1749–91), inhabited several famous prisons – the Ile de Ré; the Château d'If; Fort de Joux; and the Château de Vincennes – and while there he produced some famous erotica. Mirabeau's voice is the last great shout of the libertine soul in Europe. His

Midday, *after Pierre-Antoine Baudoin by Emmanuel de Ghendt (1738–1815). It is interesting to speculate which particular erotic book has excited the imagination of the Rococo lady in this copperplate engraving.*

erotica gave him a means of sexual expression, but it is also full of anger and is therefore uncompromising and powerful stuff. Here is an example of Mirabeau's style: a pitiless description of a prolonged sexual encounter between a society lady and a gigolo, from *Ma Conversion.*

A few days later, I run into Madame de Confroid ['cold cunt'], whom I have had before and who I heard had come into some money. She is petite with a rather nice figure, but there is nothing striking about her face. Although her love grotto is as cold as an icy cavern, she does have a remarkable and extraordinary talent for sucking pricks.

I have never come across any woman even remotely approaching her skill in this art. In my time, I have permitted myself to be fellated by members of the third sex who certainly are no amateurs, but Confroid puts the best of them to shame.

At her coquettish glance, I follow her home

OPPOSITE The Broken Fan, *French eighteenth-century colour print.*

Cupid looks on nervously at the erotic gymnastics he has instigated in this eighteenth-century sepia print. Unable to join the action, the other spectator has decided to take matters into her own hands.

where we get into bed. There she sucks me continually for two hours without taking the organ out of her mouth. While she drains me, she masturbates and I fondle her pointed breasts, which is about all I can do.

That is the only way she can get pleasure – sucking a man and playing with herself at the same time. It takes her at least an hour at this activity before she can come to a climax.

I have had normal intercourse with her in every conceivable position without producing any reaction. Once I brought two of my friends with me and we had her simultaneously in all three orifices, but when it was over, she was still as motionless as a rock.

There is nobody like her to get my prick standing up. First she grazes it with her delicate fingers, and then she breathes on it.

Her lips wander over my stomach and groin.

She nuzzles her nose in my pubic hair, gets close to my sex, teases it with her blowing, and finally gives it a fugitive kiss. She is driving me out of my mind.

When she sees how my prick is throbbing, she knows the precise spot where I am most sensitive. She can judge perfectly the rise of my seminal fluid, for she stops just when I am ready to explode.

After letting it calm down for several moments, her mouth grazes the gland again. She gives it little darts with her tongue. Then her mouth is wide open to take each of my testicles in turn.

Then she quickly turns her attention back to my virility, running her tongue up and down it, and bestowing little kisses on it. I am trembling through and through and I feel the sperm rising like the mercury in a thermometer on a hot day.

The vixen senses it. She swallows the tip of my prick for just a moment before spitting it out. A second later I would have come. My prick is in agony from this abortive frustrating pleasure, but it is an agony that I could endure forever.

All this time she is masturbating, violently. Furiously her busy fingers open the lips of her cunt as wide as possible. She squashes her clitoris that springs up red and hard and then scratches it with her fingernails.

Because the gland has quietened down, Confroid renews her oral caresses, inserting it in her mouth down to the very bottom of her throat. Again she rejects it just before the supreme moment to pay attention to her own pleasure. Finally, she is becoming aroused.

This succession of suctions sends delicious shiv-

Erotic pillboxes became popular in the eighteenth century, often with ladies. This pair is French.

ABOVE AND OPPOSITE *Etchings by Denon Vivant, c. 1790.*

ers running up and down my spine. They are a series of voluptuous vibrations which make me shudder like a palsy sufferer. I hear the rattles in my throat.

This time, I think she has made up her mind. The gland is all the way in her mouth. The tip is touching her tonsils while her tongue is all over it.

I can't stand it any more... Now... I'm coming.

But again the same confounded frustration. With her extraordinary prescience, she ceases her activities a fraction of a second before my ejaculation.

I remain in that suspended state for I don't know how long. I twitch exquisitely with my nerves taut from the interrupted voluptuousness. It lasts interminably. During one of the pauses, Confroid masturbates even more vigorously. She passes her thigh on my breast so that the cunt with the busy finger in it is only a few inches from my eyes.

She once told me that she had been playing with herself since she was four years old and has been doing it three or four hours every day since then.

While she is thus engaged with herself, I feel the urge to return the homage she pays my sexuality, but she does not let me, saying it would ruin her pleasure. I content myself by stroking her bottom and sticking my finger in her rear aperture.

Waves of passion rush through my nerves, muscles and veins. My entire body is on fire. I fidget and quiver like a woman in heat. I think my organ is going to expire from the raptures.

Suddenly, my whole being is concentrated in a wild torrent rushing across my stomach and through my prick like an unleashed wild river. It is a marvellous fireworks exploding in a thousand spangles that her mouth avidly gulps down...

Indefatigably, Gonfroid continues to suck while she thrusts her fingers in her cunt more enthusiastically than ever. I see her wrist and fingers dance in a mad twirl. Her irritated hardened clitoris is a purplish blue.

Again I ejaculate. Two times, three times. And each sensation is more rapturous and more grievous. She never ceases her implacable sucking. I clench my teeth in order not to scream.

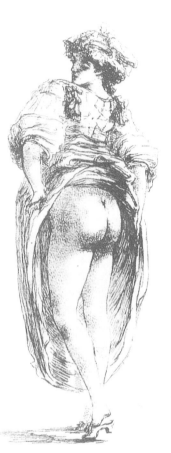

I no longer have any control over myself. Again I spurt. Writhing in delirious spasms, I think I am going out of my mind. Now pleasure and pain are inextricably blended, and I no longer know if I ejaculate or not. Finally, I am out of sperm.

Confroid is now near the zenith. Her body throbs, her bosom heaves, and her thighs open and close spasmodically.

Now is the time. Brutally I insert one hand in her cunt and the other in her rear – three fingers in the vagina and two in the anus.

She gives a convulsive jolt. Finally releasing my lifeless sex, she gives a yelp like a mortally wounded animal. Her body becomes taut, arches, relaxes … and collapses. Her screech of rapture is muted and prolonged.

Confroid has reached the climax.

When I take my leave of her, she, knowing my insatiable thirst and need for money, gives me a purse containing a hundred louis.

The 'libertine of quality' and hero of the French Revolution spared no one with the salvoes he fired into contemporary society. In another extract from *Ma Conversion*, Mirabeau's *alter ego* spies on two young nuns in the cell they inhabit.

The door opened and in stepped Angela, one of the more delicious of the novices, who was warmly welcomed with a kiss.

'What lovely hair you have,' Stephanie remarked.

'And how about yours, Sister Stephanie?'

'I am rather vain about it.'

'But I thought when you took your vows, you had to have your head shaved.'

'Yes, you do. But if you get on the good side of the Mother Superior, she gives you permission to let it grow and fix it any way you like. It goes without saying that you can't let it show. Certain nuns would understand these special marks of favour.'

'Show me your hair,' Angela demanded.

Without any hesitation, the woman removed her wimple, and a cascade of tresses tumbled down over her shoulders. Silky curls, elegant waves fell on the white starched collar that formed a part of her costume.

After a gasp of unfeigned admiration, Angela asked permission to brush it.

The girl sat down facing the sister and began to brush the hair with measured strokes. Suddenly, Stephanie kissed Angela's lips with her moist mouth. At first, the girl shrank back but then surrendered her lips and tongue. In a trice her body was embraced. I could see that her sex was being ignited. The sensation must have become even more unbearable when Stephanie caressed the yearning breasts through the blouse. Then, baring them, she took the nipples in her mouth and sucked them slowly and avidly.

'I think I have wet myself,' Angela murmured.

Finally, Sister Stephanie disrobed, exhibiting

OPPOSITE *Nuns have featured in both the literary and visual erotica of the West since the Middle Ages. The eighteenth century saw the appearance of politically motivated anti-religious erotica such as Voltaire's* La pucelle d'Orléans *(1762), but this watercolour by C. Bernard (1870) draws on the much older tradition deeply rooted in male sexual fantasies.*

So, when my days of
impotence approach,
And I'm by pox and wine's
unlucky chance
Forced from the pleasing
billows of debauch
On the dull shore of lazy
temperance,

I'll tell of whores attacked,
their lords at home;
Bawds' quarters beaten up,
and fortress won;
Windows demolished,
watches overcome;
And handsome ills by my
contrivance done.

Nor shall our love-fits,
Chloris, be forgot,
When each the well-looked
linkboy strove t'enjoy.
And the best kiss was the
deciding lot
Whether the boy fucked
you, or I the boy.

FROM *THE DISABLED*
DEBAUCHEE
JOHN WILMOT, EARL OF
ROCHESTER (1647–80)

her nude body with arrogance and hauteur. She possessed opulent round breasts, a thick fleece, smooth thighs, and delicious buttocks.

With deft nimble hands, she quickly divested the girl of her clothing, pushed her back on the bed and began to fondle her ardently.

I could see that Angela had lost touch with reality and I surmised that this was the first time she was experiencing true voluptuousness. Her twitches soon became violent convulsions.

She sank back in a faint from the force of the sensations. But she recovered under the tingling caresses that the sister was bestowing between her open thighs with her agile darting tongue. Then I heard the enamoured sighs, the squeals of joy, and the prolonged moans of pleasure which announced the arrival of the supreme sensation.

Mirabeau spent his last years respectably, as the much-loved Deputy for Aix-en-Provence. The passions he had once channelled into the writing of illicit erotica found expression in public oratory, and he died a popular hero.

Libertinism did not long outlive the eighteenth century. The idea that an individual could be devoted entirely to pleasure, unrestricted by any moral laws, was essentially aristocratic. 'Madame Guillotine' played her part in trimming the loose ends of the old order, but it was less gruesome machines which really marked the finish. The new Railway Age was about efficiency and straight lines: libertinism detested the straight and narrow, its devotees enjoyed being off the rails.

CHAPTER SEVEN
Dreams of Empire

O nce the political aftershocks from the upheavals at the end of the eighteenth century had subsided, the nineteenth century could concentrate on trade and imperial expansion. Powerful new printing presses, trains and eventually steamships rushed erotica to an expanding bourgeois market, which was as eager to consume sex as it was everything else. An early piece of imperial erotica was a slightly absurd book entitled *The Lustful Turk*, published in

The Harem by the great London caricaturist Thomas Rowlandson (1756–1827). Rowlandson's art epitomizes the uniquely English tradition of satire: moral and idealistic at heart, but taking a ribald, almost affectionate delight in detailing the very sins and excesses it mocks and denounces.

1828. Although it contains some cruel and unpleasant material, it is all so over the top that it has a certain period charm. After the intrepid Emily Barlow finally falls for her abductor the wicked Dey of Algiers – a kind of fierce prototype for Rudolph Valentine's Sheikh – she is rather badly let down by her chum and fellow captive: 'The first object that met my eyes was a naked female, half reclining on a table, and the Dey with his noble shaft plunged up to the hilt in her... Imagine to yourself... what must have been my emotions on my beholding in his arms my friend Silvia!'

The Dey eventually suffers a fate appropriate to his crimes when a spirited Greek girl – baulking at one of his more exotic sexual ideas – delivers the unkindest cut of all. It was of course only four years since the 'mad and bad' Lord Byron had died at Missolonghi, and the popular imagination was filled with the heroic struggle of the Greeks against the Turks in their War of Independence. The book was even said to have been written by a Greek: a theory borne out by the pickling of the Dey's testicles in glass jars after his emasculation, in a manner normally reserved for Kalamata olives. This extract is typical of the rather overheated style:

... After refreshing myself with a few hours' rest, I returned to my captive with recruited strength for the night's soft enjoyment. The smile of welcome was on her lovely countenance; she was dressed from a wardrobe I had pointed out to her, containing every-

So, we'll go no more a-roving
So late into the night,
Though the heart be still as loving,
And the moon be still as bright.

For the sword outwears its sheath,
And the soul wears out the breast,
And the heart must pause to breathe,
And love itself have rest.

Though the night was made/or loving,
And the day returns too soon,
Yet we'll go no more a-roving
By the light of the moon.

WE'LL GO NO MORE A-ROVING
LORD BYRON (1788–1824)

thing fit for her sex. With grateful pleasure I instantly perceived that her toilet had not been made for
the mere purpose of covering her person, but
every attention had been paid in setting off her
numerous charms. The most care had been
given to the disposing of her hair, whilst the
lawn which covered her broad voluptuous
breasts was so temptingly disposed that it
was impossible to look on her without burning desire. She sprang off the couch to meet
me; for a moment I held her from me in an
ecstasy of astonishment, then drawing her to
my bosom, planted on her lips a kiss so long and
so thrilling, it was some moments before we recovered from its effects. My passions were instantly in
a blaze. I carried her to the side of the couch,
placed her on it, and while sucking her delicious
lips, uncovered her neck and breasts, then seizing
her legs lifted them up, and threw up her clothes.
A dissolving sentiment struggled with my more
amorous desires. I stooped down to examine the
sight! Every part of her body was ivory whiteness,
everything charming; the white interspersed with
small blue veins showed the transparency of the
skin whilst the darkness of the hair, softer than velvet, formed most beautiful shades, making a delicious contrast with the vermilion lips of her new-
stretched love sheath...

Tired of admiring without enjoyment, I carried
my mouth and hand to everything before me, until
I could no longer bear myself. Raising myself from
my sloping position, I extended her thighs to the
utmost, and placed myself standing between them,
letting loose my rod of Aaron, which was no sooner at liberty but it flew with the same impetuosity

In the bathhouse, *painted in
gouache on card, French school.*

So I determined to write
my private life freely as
to fact, and in the spirit
of the lustful acts done
by me, or witnessed;
it is written therefore
with absolute truth
and without any regard
whatever for what the
world calls decency.

FROM THE PREFACE TO
MY SECRET LIFE
'WALTER'

Candlelight, *a watercolour by Georg Emmanuel Opitz (1775–1841).*

with which a tree straightens itself when the cord that keeps it bent towards the ground comes to be cut; with my right hand I directed it towards the pouting slit, the head was soon in; laying myself down on her, I drew her lips to mine; again I thrust, I entered. Another thrust buried it deeper; she closed her eyes, but tenderly squeezed me to her bosom; again I pushed – her soft lips rewarded me. Another shove caused her to sigh deliciously – another push made our junction complete. I scarcely knew what I was about, everything now was in active exertion, tongues, lips, bellies, arms, thighs, legs, bottoms, every part in voluptuous motion until our spirits completely abandoned every part of our bodies to convey themselves into the place where pleasure reigned with so furious but still with so delicious a sentiment. I dissolved myself into her at the very moment Nature had caused her to give down her tribute to the intoxicating joy. My lovely prey soon came to herself, but it was only to invite me by her numberless charms to plunge her into the same condition. She passed her arms round my neck and sucked my lips with dove like kisses. I opened my eyes and fixed them on hers; they were filled with dissolving languor; I moved within her, her eyes closed instantly. The tender squeeze of her love-sheath round my instrument satisfied me as to the state she was in. Again I thrust. 'Ah!' she sighed. 'The pleasure suffocates me – I die! – ah, me.' I thrust furiously; her

A coloured daguerreotype from the studio of the French photographer Bruno Braquehais, c. 1858. The fact that he could not speak, and therefore could not communicate with his models, gives his nude studies a uniquely intimate, almost voyeuristic quality. The colourist was the daughter of the photographer Alexis Gouin, and later became Mrs Braquehais.

I love prostitution in and for itself... In the very notion of prostitution there is such a complex convergence of lust and bitterness, such a frenzy of muscle and sound of gold, such a void in human relations, that the very sight of it makes one dizzy! And how much is learned there! And one is so sad! And one dreams so well of love!

GUSTAVE FLAUBERT (1821–80)

Felix Jacques-Antoine Moulin (active in Paris 1849–61) liked to work with amateur models. In this image we can see Moulin's special ability of capturing nuances of mood. Coloured daguerreotype, Paris, 1851–4.

limbs gradually stiffened, she gave one more movement to the fierce thrusts made into her organ; we both discharged together.

The courtesans of the Second Empire held sway in Paris like despotic queens: their hunger for luxury and money was exceeded only by their ability to squander and spend it. On their chosen battlefields – their beds – and with the politicians, bankers and aristocrats who kept them, these warrior queens were invincible. But each secretly feared the prowess of her fellow courtesans and the rivalry between them was intense.

In *The Memoirs of Cora Pearl*, the famous English courtesan recalls her irritation on hearing that Anne de Chassigne had received a coterie of important admirers while bathing luxuriously in asses' milk. Commenting that cows' milk would have been more appropriate, Cora prepares a suitable response.

A week later I invited six gentlemen to dinner. The irritating but indispensable M. Goubouges was one, for his tattle I was in need of; then came the Duc de Treage, the Prince C—, Colonel Marc Aubry, M. Paul of the Banque National, M. Perriport (the brother of the owner of the Restaurant Tric), and the actor Georges Gapillon, a friend of Henri Meilhac, Offenbach's librettist, on whom I was eager to make an impression. I let it be known that the chief purpose of the occasion was to display the talents of my chef, Salé, formerly with the Prince d'Orléans, but I hinted to Goubouges that the final dish was likely to be one of an unusual nature.

I received the gentlemen in my finest style, and entertained them to a dinner of excellent quality; the conversation was agreeable, the wines accomplished. When we had finished all but the final course, I excused myself, in order to supervise its presentation. Slipping to the kitchen, I stepped out of my gown (when entertaining gentlemen it is never my habit to wear quantities of underclothing, and especially was this the case on this occasion) and mounting a chair lay upon a vast silver dish which Salé had borrowed for me from the Prince d'Orléans' kitchen. I lay upon my side, my head upon my hand.

Salé stepped forward, accompanied by Yves, a footman I had employed only recently, carrying as it were his palate [sic] – a large tray upon which was a set of dishes filled with marzipans, sauces and pastes, all of different colours. With that deftness and artistry for which he was so famed, Salé began to decorate my naked body with rosettes and swathes of creams and sauces, each carefully composed so that the heat of my body would not melt them before I came to table.

As Salé was laying long trails of cream across my haunches and applying wreaths of tiny button flowers to the upper sides of my breasts, I could not help noticing that Yves, chosen like all my servants for a combination of personal charm and accomplishment, and a young man of obvious and ever-increasingly virile promise, was taking a peculiar interest in the chef's work. The knuckles

Many of the photographers working in Paris during the 1850s had trained as painters or miniaturists. Alexis Gouin, who produced this daguerreotype, was one of the first to experiment with the new process and was famous for the delicacy of his colouring.

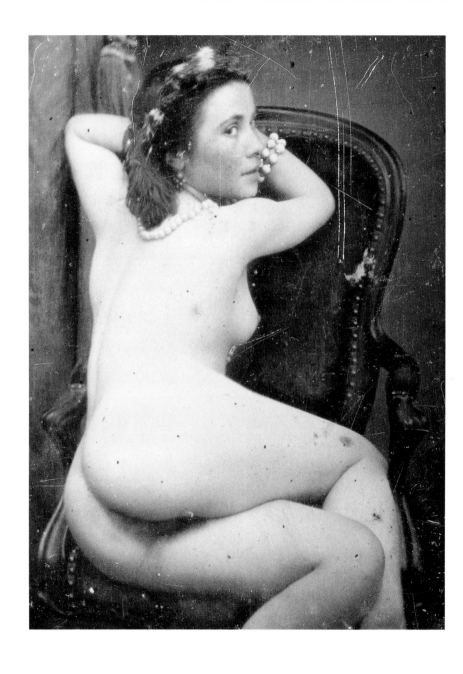

of his hands were whiter than would have been the case had the tray been ten times as heavy, and the state of his breeches proclaimed the fact that his attitude to his employer was one of greater warmth than respect. Having finished the decoration by placing a single unpeeled grape in the dint of my navel, Salé piled innumerable meringues about the dish, completing the effect with a dusting of icing sugar. The vast cover which belonged to the dish was then placed over me, and I heard Salé call the other two footmen into the room. Shortly afterwards I felt myself being raised, and carried down the passage to the dining-room. I heard the door opened, and the chatter of voices cease as the dish was carried in and settled upon the table.

When the lid was lifted, I was rewarded by finding myself the centre of a ring of round eyes and half-open mouths. M. Paul, as I had expected, was the first to recover, and with an affectation of coolness reached out, removed the grape, and slipped it slowly between his lips. Not to be outdone, M. Perriport leant forward and applied his tongue to removing the small white flower that Salé had placed upon my right tit; and then all, except for M. Goubouges, who as I expected was as usual content simply to observe and record, were at me, kneeling upon their chairs or upon the table, their fingers and tongues busy at every part of me as they lifted and licked the sweetness from my body. The Prince was so inflamed by the circumstances that nothing would content him other than to have me there and then upon the table, to the ruination of the remaining decoration upon my body, and the irritation of the other gentlemen, in whom

'I wish I had feathers,
  a fine sweeping gown,
And a delicate face, and
  could strut about Town!'
'My dear – a raw country
  girl, such as you be,
Cannot quite expect that.'
  'You ain't ruined,'
  said she.

FROM *THE RUINED MAID*
THOMAS HARDY
(1840–1928)

OPPOSITE *This superb daguerreotype by an unknown photographer achieves a perfect balance between beauty and eroticism.*

> I have never deceived anybody, because I have never belonged to anybody; my independence was all my fortune, and I have known no other happiness...
>
> CORA PEARL (1837–86)
> FROM HER FIRST
> AUTOBIOGRAPHY

An oil painting by an unknown German artist. By the time of the Weimar Republic, German Art's cheerful bawdy tradition had turned into the bitter nightmare world of George Grosz.

only reverence for rank restricted violence.

So speedily did the Prince fetch off that they had not to wait long – *le laurier est tot coupé*, as my friend Theo used to say. Since the centre of a dining-table and a mess of meringues together with wine-glasses and forks is not the most convenient nor comfortable of pleasure-beds, the price of my comforting the other members of the party was that they should give me time at least to dispose myself on one of the nearby couches, where the Duc continued where the Prince had left off; M. Capillon as was his wont contented himself with an energetic frigging (often the taste of members of his profession, I have frequently been disappointed to observe), while M. Paul offered his shaft to my lips and Colonel Aubry his to my sufficiently practised manual manipulation. Finally, M. Perriport, in a desperate fit of agitation, was attempting to displace the Due when his ecstasy overflowed, together with an excess of language which seemed to me to betray a youth spent in less than polite circles.

Cora Pearl's own youth had also been spent in less eminent, though perfectly respectable circles: she had been born Eliza Emma Crouch at 5 Devonshire Place, Plymouth, in 1837. The witty account of her rise (some might say descent) to being a courtesan who could command the equivalent of £10,000 a night makes enjoyable reading. It glosses over the less savoury aspects of high-class prostitution but appears to be a reasonably reliable account – except in relation to her rivals. Cora maintains that she alone among les grandes horizontales was allowed to drive her carriage through the enclosure at Baden races – in fact Hortense Schneider shared that privilege. She also suggests that she was the model for Zola's Nana, which is downright silly since she herself is referred to in the novel (in less than flattering terms); and Blanche d'Antigny is generally regarded as the original Nana. In most matters, however, we can rely on the book's accuracy.

It is a matter of record that Cora Pearl included among her lovers Prince Napoléon, Prince Achille Murat, Prince William of Orange, the Duc de Morny, and Khalil Bey. It is also a possibility – though she never claimed it – that the Emperor himself was no stranger to her bed. In this episode, the Emperor's cousin – His Imperial Highness Prince Napoléon – arranges a little entertainment for Cora, having annoyed her by falling asleep on the previous evening.

Louis Jules Duboscq-Soleil impressed Queen Victoria at the Great Exhibition of 1851 with a photograph he had made especially for her. It is unlikely to have been this particular image from his studio.

'My dear,' said the Prince, 'I am sorry that my conduct last night left you unsatisfied; but as you see I have brought you two of my best beasts, and I hope that they will provide some compensation. Look!' said he, wacking Brunet lightly upon the buttocks with his cane, 'Charles here is fine enough for any filly, while André' (making a gesture in the direction of Hurion's already swelling person) 'has flanks and loins only less formidable than mine own once were. Gentlemen, please don't mind me...' At which he took himself off to an armchair with a bottle of brandy and a glass, to watch events.

First the two men, with infinite solicitude and many murmurs of appreciation, undressed me. By the time they had completed their task, Hurion's manhood stood out proudly, an enormous tool not as massive perhaps as the Prince's, but evidently much more vigorous and ready for the fray. Sturdy and thick, with the bag beneath supporting two stones of concomitant size, it rose from a belly thickly matted in black, curly hair, the line of which was continued to sprout across his chest. Brunet on the other hand was of a small but perfect frame, so that he looked the very model of a Greek statue, the hair of his body so light that it was almost invisible, lying in tight curls around the root of his tool, which was classically shaped rather than large, an object of beauty which could have failed to attract the admiration only of the insensitive...

At first somewhat deterred by the Prince's suavity, when his two friends showed themselves so eager to enjoy me at his command, it would have been ill-natured of me not to show my gratitude for his solicitude. So I led both men to the bed, where they lay one on either side of me, toying with tenderness with my breasts and thighs, while I enjoyed the play of candlelight upon the skin of their bodies, one so dark that it might almost have been that of an Indian, the other utterly pale and white, almost that of a young girl. At last, Hurion placed himself between her thighs and slowly

pressed himself into me, filling me with the utmost
pleasure. As he moved gently and in a full, plunging motion, he raised his chest so that Brunet
could kiss my breasts, running his tongue about
my nipples while I stroked his back and buttocks,
feeling what I could not see, the light down upon
his body. Presently, I felt his fingers as they moved
between my body and Hurion's, to caress us both
at the extreme point of pleasure.

After a while, careful to afford Brunet the
pleasure that his friend and I already enjoyed,
I encouraged Hurion to raise himself upon
his knees, so that while I still lay impaled,
my thighs supported on his own, he was in
an   upright   position,   allowing
Brunet to throw his leg over
and kneel in front of his
friend, presenting my lips
with the opportunity of
embracing him. By this
time we were all three

*The influence of Ingres and the
other great painters of the female
nude is clearly evident in the
lighting and poses of many of
the finest daguerreotypes. This
magnificent study is unattributed.*

La Diligence de Lyon, *a*
watercolour by Henri Monnier
(1799–1875).

Prostitution is essentially
a matter of lack of choice.

CHARLES BAUDELAIRE
(1821–67)

at a pitch of pleasure, and within a moment we
together reached our goals and spent our passion
in mutual delight. So caught up were we that we
were equally startled at the applause with which
the Prince, observing us from across the room,
greeted our endeavours. We now fell into a pleasant lethargy, and then into a doze; from which,
when I woke perhaps an hour later, I saw the chair
across the room to be empty, but three glasses of
brandy placed upon the bedside table. Waking my
two companions, I handed them each a glass, and
we toasted our past pleasure and our coming
delights, the glass warming us to these, for Hurion
immediately took my hand and placed it between
his thighs, in the hairy coverts of which a limber
something was already astir. A moment's stroking,
without even the application of my lips, restored
him to full life. Brunet, however, showed no sign of
recovery, and even my careful mumbling of his
perfect tool had no effect; whereupon to my surprise Hurion bent to do my office with his friend,
and the first touch of his tongue performed that
office so effectively that Brunet was restored to a
pitch of excitement in so brief a time that it was
only a moment before I invited him to claim me.
Taking my legs behind the knees, the beautiful boy
pulled me to the side of the bed, where standing he
shot the mark, throwing my legs over his shoulders and leaning his hands behind my head. The
perfection of his form had quite a different effect
upon me than Hurion's animal strength, and I
closed my eyes for a moment in ecstasy when, feeling a tension in Brunet's body, I opened them to
see with surprise Hurion's face peering over his
friend's shoulder, his hands clutching his fore-

arms, and his body moving in an unmistakable motion. He had entered his friend from behind, and the three of us were moving as one creature. Placing my hands between us, it was with the strangest sensation that I felt two pairs of stones moving in enthusiastic concert, while the ecstatic expressions on my lovers' faces showed that they were fully in accord as to the pleasure of the occasion. I was to learn that Hurion in fact had no special bent towards the enjoyment of boys, nor Brunet towards the enjoyment of women; in fact upon one occasion when at my own request I made love with Brunet alone, I was unable to rouse him sufficiently to employ himself conventionally with me, and it was only by encouraging him to come at me from behind (though still conventionally) that we were able to achieve a conclu-

An illustration by Achille Deveria (1800–57) from Gamiani ou Deux Nuits d'excès.

There are only nine original humorous stories in the world, eight of which you cannot tell to a lady.

RUDYARD KIPLING

(1865-1936)

sion. Both men, however, were so devoted friends that they were willing to support each other in roles which some men would have considered strange or even improper. Upon this occasion, it was the Prince's offer of his services in obtaining promotion for Brunet which had encouraged him to engage his friend on my behalf, which, though he loved him, he knew was his natural bent.

Originally published in four volumes between 1873 and 1876, *The Romance of Lust* is the erotic equivalent of a patchwork quilt: diverse material sewn together to form a whole. And like a patchwork quilt it travelled in cabins and sleeping cars to every corner of the British Empire. *The Romance of Lust* tells the story of Charlie – or rather the editor/author William Simpson Potter uses the priapic Charlie like a needle to stitch together different tales. Apart from this remorseless and unsympathetic character, the fundamental link between the parts is just that – links between fundaments and parts. However, *The Romance of Lust* did represent extraordinary value for money; the ratio of couplings (orifice optional) to pages was unbeatable. During the last quarter of the century this action-packed novel, written in vigorous language, was an underground bestseller.

OPPOSITE *A Victorian mass-produced erotic postcard. During the Belle Epoque rival companies vied to produce 'souvenirs' that were beautiful as well as sexy.*

Miss Evelyn at last concentrated all her attention on my well-developed member, which she most endearingly embraced and fondled tenderly, very quickly putting him into an ungovernable state of erection. I was lying on my back, and she partially raised herself to kiss my formidable weapon; so

An example from a series of drawings by the Viennese artist 'AL', published in Vienna in 1935.

gently putting her upon me, I told her it was her turn to do the work. She laughed, but at once mounted upon me, and bringing her delicious cunt right over my prick, and guiding it to the entrance of love's grotto, she gently sank down upon it and engulphed it until the two hairs pressed against each other. A few slow up and down movements followed, when becoming too libidinous for such temporizing delays, she sank on my belly, and began to show most wonderful activity of loins and bottom. I seconded her to the utmost, and finding she was so excited, I slipped my hand round behind and introduced my middle finger in the rosy and very tight orifice of her glorious backside. I continued to move in and out in unison with her up and down heavings. It seemed to spur her on to more vigorous actions, and in the midst of short gaspings and suppressed sighs, she sank almost senseless on my bosom, I, too, had quickened my action, and shot into her gaping womb a torrent of boiling sperm...

'Oh! my beloved Charlie, what exquisite delight you have given me; you are the most delicious and loving creature that ever could be created. You kill me with pleasure, but what was that you were doing to my bottom? What put such an idea into your head?'

'I don't know,' I replied. 'I put my arm round to feel the beautiful globes of your bottom, and found in grasping one that my finger was against a hole, all wet with our previous encounters, and pressing it, found that my finger slipped in; you gave it such a delicious pressure when in that the idea entered into my head that, as it resembled the delicious pressure your enchanting other orifice gives my shaft when embracing you, this orifice would like a similar movement to that which my shaft exercised in your quim. So I did so, and it seemed to add to your excitement, if I may judge by the extraordinary convulsive pressures you gave my finger when you died away in all the agony of our final rapture. Tell me, my beloved Miss Evelyn, did it add to your pleasure as much as I fancied?'

'Well, my darling Charlie, I must own it did, very much to my surprise; it seemed to make the final pleasure almost too exciting to bear, and I can only account it a happy accident leading to an increase to pleasure I already thought beyond the power of nature to surpass. Naughty boy, I feel your great instrument at full stretch again, but you must moderate yourself, my darling, we have done enough for to-night. No, no, no! I am not going to let him in again.'

Passing her hand down, she turned away its head from the charming entrance of her cunt, and began handling and feeling it in apparent admiration of its length, thickness, and stiffness. Her gentle touch did anything but allay the passion that was rising to fever heat; so sucking one of her bubbies, while I pressed her to me with one arm under her, and embracing her on the other side, I passed my hand between our moist and warm bodies, reached her charming clitoris, already stiff with the excitement of handling my prick. My titillations soon decided her passions, and gently prompting her with the arm under her body, I turned her once more on the top of me. She murmured an objection,

She arrived at his apartment moist and trembling. The lips of her sex were as stiff as if they had been caressed, her nipples hard, her whole body quivering, and as he kissed her he felt her turmoil and slipped his hand directly to her sex. The sensation was so acute that she came.

FROM *DELTA OF VENUS*
ANAÏS NIN (1903–77)

> It would have been good to die at any moment then, for love and death had somewhere joined hands.
>
> FROM *THE ALEXANDRIA QUARTET*
> LAWRENCE DURRELL (1912–90)

but offered no resistance; on the contrary, she herself guided my throbbing and eager prick into the voluptuous sheath that was longing to engulph it. Our movements this time were less hurried and more voluptuous. For some time she kept her body upright, rising and falling from her knees. I put my finger to her clitoris, and added to the extatic pleasure she was so salaciously enjoying. She soon found she must come to more rapid and vigorous movements, and lying down on my belly embraced and kissed me. Toying with our tongues I put an arm round her waist, and held her tight, while her glorious buttocks and most supple loins kept up the most delicious thrust and pressures on my thoroughly engulphed weapon. I again stimulated her to the highest pitch of excited desire by introducing my finger behind, and we both came to the grand crisis in a tumultuous state of enraptured agony, unable to do ought, but from moment to moment convulsively throb in and on our engulphed members. We must have lain thus languidly, and deliciously enjoying all the raptures of the most complete and voluptuous gratification of our passions, for fully thirty minutes before we recovered complete consciousness. Miss Evelyn was first to remember where she was. She sprang up, embraced me tenderly, and said she must leave me at once, she was afraid she had already stayed imprudently long. In fact, it was near five o'clock in the morning. I rose from the bed to fling my arms round her lovely body, to fondle and embrace her exquisite bubbies. With difficulty she tore herself from my arms. I accompanied her to the door, and with a mutual and loving kiss we parted, I to

A nineteenth-century postcard, artist unknown.

return and rapidly sink into the sweetest slumber after such a delicious night of most voluptuous fucking.

In the 1870s and 1880s a plethora of new magazines and periodicals were published, reflecting both technical advances in printing and the development of a widening middle-class market. These periodicals covered a wide range of subjects, but just as erotica had been represented among the first lithographs and one of the earliest of all photographs was a nude, so sex reared its head among the new journals. The first and most notorious of these was *The Pearl – a Journal of Facetiae and Voluptuous Reading*. Eighteen volumes were published between July 1879 and December 1880 when it finally disappeared.

'Loo'd', a drawing by the artist Rojan or Rojankowski (active 1930–50).

Although it was an urban and elitist production, scattered with literary references and Latin phrases, which no doubt pleased its university readership, its largest market was in the new middle-class suburbs. Goodness knows what they made of its subversive tone. The editor explains his choice of *The Pearl* as the title:

... in the hope that when it comes under the snouts of the moral and hypocritical swine of the world, they may not trample it underfoot, and feel disposed to rend the publisher, but that a few will become subscribers on the quiet. To such better disposed piggy wiggys, I would say, for encouragement, that they have only to keep up appearances by regularly attending church, giving to charities, and always

> Eroticism is assenting to life even up to the point of death.
>
> GEORGES BATAILLE (1897–1962)

More nineteenth-century French postcards.

appearing deeply interested in moral philanthropy, to ensure a respectable and highly moral character, and that if they only are clever enough never to be found out, they may, *sub rosa*, study and enjoy the *philosophy of life* till the end of their days, and earn a glorious and saintly epitaph on their tombstone, when at last the Devil pegs them out.

There was something for everyone in *The Pearl*, although the comprehensive sexual menu had a bias towards maidenheads and bottoms. Readers in service could confirm their worst suspicions with 'Belgra-vian Morals': 'The Countess's dress was raised to her navel and I could see the jewelled hand of Miss Courtney groping between her lovely thighs.' Readers who had not travelled could read 'The Sultan's Reverie' and be transported to some very exotic places: 'not there, not there, I never would allow the Sultan to do that!'

The Pearl's largely urban readership were offered an alternative *Country Life* in 'Sub-Umbra, or sport among the She-noodles'; the following extract gives some idea of the journal's torrid style:

For fear of damaging her dress, or getting the

green stain of the grass on the knees of my light trousers, I persuaded her to stand up by the gate and allow me to enter behind. She hid her face in her hands on the top rail of the gate, as I slowly raised her dress; what glories were unfolded to view, my prick's stiffness was renewed in an instant at the sight of her delicious buttocks, so beautifully relieved by the white of her pretty drawers; as I opened them and exposed the flesh, I could see the lips of her plump pouting cunny, deliciously feathered, with soft light down, her lovely legs, drawers, stockings, pretty boots, making a *tout ensemble*, which as I write and describe them cause Mr. Priapus to swell in my breeches; it was a most delicious sight. I knelt and kissed her bottom, slit, and everything my tongue could reach, it was all mine, I stood up and prepared to take possession of the seat of love – when, alas! a sudden shriek from Annie, her clothes dropped, all my arrangements were upset in a moment; a bull had unexpectedly appeared on the opposite side of the gate, and frightened my love by the sudden application of his cold, damp nose to her forehead. It is too much to contemplate that scene even now.

Annie was ready to faint as she screamed, 'Walter! Walter! Save me from the horrid beast!' I comforted and reassured her as well as I was able, and seeing that we were on the safe side of the gate, a few loving kisses soon set her all right.

Not long after the disappearance of *The Pearl* from London's streets *The Oyster* mysteriously appeared. Although some of the same contributors may have been involved in this production, it was quite different, less abrasive and

A French sepia postcard, late nineteenth century. The creators of 'naughty postcards' used the latest developments in photography and printing techniques to produce erotic ephemera which has never been surpassed.

subversive than its predecessor. The preface to the first edition of *The Oyster* suggests a change of editor:

What is it that causes my lord to smack his chops in that wanton, lecherous manner, as he is sauntering up and down Bond Street, with his glass in hand, to watch the ladies getting in and out of their carriages? And what is it that draws together such vast crowds of the holiday gentry at Easter and Whitsuntide to see the merry rose-faced lassies running down the hill in Greenwich Park? What is it causes such a roar of laughter when a merry girl happens to overset in her career and kick her heels in the air? Lastly, as the parsons all say, what is it that makes the theatrical ballet so popular?

There is a magic in the sight of a female leg, which is hardly in the power of mere language to describe, for to be conceived it must be felt...

Your editor never sees a pretty leg but feels certain unutterable emotions within him, which as the poet puts it:

Should some fair youth,
  the charming sight explore,
In rapture he'll gaze,
  and wish for something more!

Whether by popular demand or because its production was a rich man's fun, *The Oyster* continued publication until 1889. In this extract a pastiche of John Cleland's erotica raises a fever which even an improbable glass of lemonade cannot cool:

'Her secret orifice opened to the probing of my ardent tongue. Her rounded bottom began to move in rhythm with the explorations of my own. Sensing that it was time to leave off this occupation, pleasurable though it was, I retraced my steps, kissing again the delicate outer lips, the still-wet moss, the bluish-white skin of her inner thighs, and concentrated myself upon the main enjoyments. Inch by inch, I impaled her with my sturdy rod, now grown to even greater dimensions by preceding excitations. This time with her mount of pleasure fully receptive to the aggressions of my member, she did not gasp with pain but moaned with pleasure.

An illustration by Félicien Rops (1833–98) from The Lesbians. This Belgian artist's strict Catholic upbringing, eclipsed by ideas from Baudelaire and his own sexual appetite, produced a technically brilliant, darkly erotic œuvre that was to influence Beardsley, von Bayros and many other artists. Rops has been called 'the last painter of sins'.

'I thrust; she answers; I stroke, she heaves; our rhythms join and our passions grew. I push so deep into her that I think I must rend the wench in twain but her sole response is yet another moan, this low in the throat as our breathing deepens to a growl, then, in unison, to a roar. The bed shudders with the weight and fury of our entwined violence. Then with a shriek she adds her juices to my own and I discharge in an enormity of passion, my

Au bois, a coloured lithograph
from Gamiani by Louis André
Berthomme-Saint-André (1905–77).

juices boiling over, searing her deepest vitals'...

I ended my reading and sipped slowly at my glass of cool lemonade. The passionate words of Mr Gleland had certainly achieved the desired effect. Louella and Lucy were entwined in a passionate embrace and their mouths met as Lucy's hands examined the large breasts of the dark-haired Louella who unbuttoned her blouse to let Lucy enjoy free play with her plump bubbies. She continued to play with those magnificent breasts while Louella's hands were under Lucy's skirts doing all kinds of things to her clitty. Louella eased down her partner's underdrawers and Lucy's rounded bottom cheeks were naked to my eyes, which feasted upon them as Louella's hands probed the cleft between them, making the blonde girl gasp with joy.

During the 1880s *The Oyster* had to compete with a rival publication: *The Boudoir*. Although a superior publication – or perhaps for that reason – *The Boudoir* lasted for only six issues before sinking without trace. The editorial style is quite different from its crustacean rivals – *The Pearl* and *The Oyster* – and although some of the contributors may be the same, it is a more literary production which is full of classical allusions and cheerful anecdotes and less reliant on four-letter words for its pyrotechnics. This extract from the serial 'Voluptuous Confessions of a French Lady of Fashion' is, despite its title, a very English piece of erotic writing:

Mrs Drummond, the famous preacher among the Quakers, on being asked by a gentleman if the spirit had ever inspired her with thoughts of marriage, 'No, friend,' says she, 'but the flesh often has.'

FROM *THE BOUDOIR*

Yet, I was far from depraved! I loved my husband as a sure friend, as the companion of my existence, and if he had possessed the manly vigour that was necessary for me, or if even he had known how to subdue my clever caresses, I should never have dreamt of being unfaithful to him! I resolved to spare him all sorrow and I have fully succeeded, as he has never had the least suspicion!

This revolution demanded much care, trouble, and even privation; the town I inhabited was much inclined to scandal, and it was very difficult for me to hide my connection, so I had to take endless precautions.

I warned my lover, who, wishing above all to save my reputation, promised to do all in his power not to excite suspicion, and I knew I could rely on his honour.

A few days went by without our meeting; I suffered greatly and he as much as I! A sign, a look during our walks was our only consolation for eight long days!

At last F. could bear it no longer, and came to pay us a visit; we chatted in an ordinary friendly way; someone else called, F. went away; my husband showed him out and returned to the room. I know not what instinct warned me that F. had not left the house! I got up, with some excuse that seemed all the more reasonable as the visitor was keeping up a technical conversation with my husband, and went into the vestibule. I was not mistaken; F., seeing no servants about, was waiting by the street-door.

As soon as he saw me, he threw

> The daughter of Pythagoras used to say that the woman who goes to bed with a man must put off her modesty with her petticoat, and put it on again with the same.
>
> FROM *THE BOUDOIR*

An illustration of a scene from
Gamiani by Berthomme-Saint-André.

himself upon me, clasped me in his arms
and with violent passion exclaimed:
'Darling angel, how I suffer!'

'And I?...'

We were once again between the double doors. Before I knew where I was,
our mouths were glued together, my petticoats were up to my navel, his finger
pushed itself into my burning slit, that
opened beneath its pressure. My hand
had seized the darling object.

What more can I say? In a second or
two – a few movements of our hands
took place – I swooned with joy, and
drew away my hand, bathed all over
with an abundance of the warm liquid.

Yet a few moments went by without our being
able to meet, till at last a happy moment of liberty
was granted to us. A whole hour was ours.

Ah, how we profited by it! My lover came into
my boudoir. I rushed to receive him, and I
devoured him with caresses...

I tore myself from him, pulled up my clothes
behind, and, getting onto the sofa on my knees,
presented my bottom.

He put it in at once, and I very soon swooned
beneath his copious discharge.

We then sat down, but my lover was not satisfied, and despite my fears I could not refuse. He
went on his knees between my legs, then he made
me stretch wide apart. I took his vigorous firebrand
in my hand; it was already as hard as ever. I stroked
it a second, then pushed it gradually into myself,
while I savoured slowly the delightful pleasure...

I used to vastly like to change the way of doing

it. For instance, sometimes when plugged from behind, one of my favourite positions, would unhorse my cavalier, turn round quickly, give a kiss to my rosy conqueror, wet with my spendings, and escape to the other end of the room, I would place myself in an easy chair, my legs upraised, and my pussy quite open, while I gave it a provoking twitching movement. My lover was hardly in me again, when by a fresh whim I would draw it out, make him sit on a chair, get on his knees, my back turned towards him, and taking his courser, plunging in my body to the very hilt, let his burning jet finish our sweet operation.

An unknown Victorian artist has fun with an adult version of an old children's game.

My dear Minet, as I generally called the splendid instrument of my joy, had become my passion, the object of real worship. I was never tired of admiring its thickness, its stiffness, and its length, all equally marvellous. I would dandle it, suck it, pump at it, caress it in a thousand different ways, and rub it between my titties, holding it there by pressing them with both my hands. Often when captive in this voluptuous passage, it would throw out its dew.

My lover returned all my caresses with interest. My pussy was his god, his idol. He assured me that no woman had ever possessed a more perfect one. He would open it, and frig it in every conceivable way. His greatest delight was to apply his lips there-to, and extract, so to speak, the quintessence of voluptuousness, by titillations of the tongue, that almost drove me mad.

CHAPTER EIGHT

Decadent Visions

... *'Sweet youth*
Tell me why, sad and sighing, thou dost rove
These pleasant realms? I pray thee speak me sooth
What is thy name?' He said, 'My name is Love!'
Then straight the first did turn himself to me
And cried, 'He lieth, for his name is Shame,
But I am Love, and I was wont to be
Alone in this fair garden, till he came
Unasked by night; I am true Love, I fill
The Hearts of boy and girl with mutual flame.'
Then sighing said the other, 'Have thy will,
I am the Love that dare not speak its name.'

These lines, taken from 'Two Loves' by Lord Alfred Douglas, were read aloud by the prosecution at the trial of his friend Oscar Wilde. Asked to explain the love that dare not speak its name, Wilde (1854–1900) said it was 'a great affection of an elder for a younger man such as there was between David and Jonathan, such as Plato made the very basis of his philosophy, and such as you find in the sonnets of Michelangelo and Shakespeare. It is that deep, spiritual affection that is as pure as it is perfect... on account of it I am placed where I am now... the world mocks at it... puts one in the pillory for it.' The world has indeed mocked Oscar for his sexual orientation. It mocked him in the savage sentence of two years' hard labour, which ruined his health. It mocked him with a premature death in exile, living in poverty ('I am dying above my means') with – thank God – his old love Robbie Ross there to hold his hand at the end ('either that wallpaper goes or I do'). And the world still remembers Oscar Wilde as much for his homosexuality as for his astonishing brilliance as a wit, dramatist, and poet.

The decision to include extracts from *Teleny* – the homosexual novel written by Wilde and others – could be criticized for perpetuating the link. After all, the year 1995 marked the anniversary of his trial and the placing of a long overdue memorial in Westminster Abbey. However, there was a powerful self-destructive tendency in Oscar, embodied in his own paradoxical asser-

'Then afterwards came Egypt, Antinoüs and Adrian. You were the Emperor, I was the slave … Who knows, perhaps I shall die for you one day' (Teleny). A lithograph, hand-coloured in watercolour, by the French artist Paul Avril (1849–1928).

We two boys together clinging,
One the other never leaving,
Up and down the roads going,
*   North and South excursions making,*
Power enjoying, elbows stretching,
*   fingers clutching*
Arm'd and fearless, eating, drinking,
*   sleeping, loving...*

FROM *CALMUS*
WALT WHITMAN (1819–92)

tion that 'each man kills the thing he loves'. If he did not seek martyrdom, he certainly did not avoid it as many others had done, and his actions were often those of a man courting disaster. Oscar took the original risk of involving himself in the creation of *Teleny*: it seems fair to include it. Published in 1893, *Teleny* is arguably the first modern homosexual novel. The pity is, of course, that it is not the novel it would have been if Wilde had written it all. Yet his voice is there, and worth hearing on a subject with which he will for ever be associated.

The main character, Des Grieux, first falls under the spell of Teleny at a concert. The young pianist's playing stimulates vivid hallucinations of Ancient Egypt, Greece and, portentously, 'the gorgeous towns of Sodom and Gomorrah'. That night Des Grieux has a dream that Teleny is his own sister, and not a man, yet he desires her. The forbidden passion in this piece of *grand guignol* is all the more disturbing (and Freudian) since Des Grieux does not actually have a sister!

A coloured engraving by an unknown artist which was made to illustrate an edition of Verlaine's Oeuvres Libres.

'One night, unable to overcome the maddening passion that was consuming me, I yielded to it and stealthily crept into her room.

'By the rosy light of her night-lamp, I saw her lying, or rather, stretched across her bed. I shivered with lust at the sight of that pearly-white flesh. I should have liked to have been a beast of prey to devour it.

'Her loose and dishevelled golden hair was scattered in locks all over the pillow. Her lawn chemise scarcely veiled part of her nakedness, whilst it enhanced the beauty of what was left bare. The ribbons with which this garment had been tied on her shoulder had come undone, and thus exhibited her right breast to my hungry, greedy glances. It stood up firm and plump, for she was a very young virgin, and its dainty shape was no bigger than a large-sized champagne bowl...

'I quietly drew near the bed on the tip of my toes, just like a cat about to spring on a mouse, and then slowly crawled between her legs. My heart was beating fast, I was eager to gaze upon the sight I so longed to see. As I approached on all fours, head foremost, a strong smell of white heliotrope mounted up to my head, intoxicating me.

'Trembling with excitement, opening my eyes wide and straining my sight, my glances dived between her thighs. At first nothing could be seen but a mass of crisp auburn hair, all curling in tiny ringlets, and growing there as if to hide the entrance of that well of pleasure. First I lightly lifted up her chemise, then I gently brushed the hair aside, and parted the two lovely lips which opened by themselves at the touch of my fingers as if to afford me entrance.

'This done, I fed my greedy eyes upon that dainty pink flesh that looked like the ripe and luscious pulp of some savoury fruit appetizing to behold, and within those cherry lips there

A Rococo fantasy by Franz von Bayros (1866–1924).

Of man's delight and man's desire
In one thing is no weariness –
To feel the fury of the fire,
And writhe within the close caress
Of fierce embrace, and wanton kiss,
And final nuptial done aright,
How sweet a passion, shame, is this,
A strong man's love is my delight!

To feel him clamber on me, laid
Prone on the couch of lust and shame,
To feel him force me like a maid
And his great sword within me flame,
His breath as hot and quick as fame;
To kiss him and to clasp him tight;
This is my joy without a name,
A strong man's love is my delight.

FROM *WHITE STAINS*
ALEISTER CROWLEY (1875–1947)

nestled a tiny bud – a living flower of flesh and blood.

'I had evidently tickled it with the tip of my finger, for, as I looked upon it, it shivered as if endowed with a life of its own, and it protruded itself out towards me. At its beck I longed to taste it, to fondle it, and therefore, unable to resist, I bent down and pressed my tongue upon it, over it, within it, seeking every nook and corner around it, darting into every chink and cranny, whilst she, evidently enjoying the little game, helped me in my work, shaking her buttocks with a lusty delight in such a way that after a few minutes the tiny flower began to expand its petals and shed forth its ambrosial dew, not a drop of which did my tongue allow to escape.

'In the meanwhile she panted and screamed, and seemed to swoon away with joy.'

We may feel instinctively – and we may be right – that Oscar Wilde did not write that piece. But deciding what he did contribute to the book is difficult: the nicely crafted but over-embellished links which carry the plot forward, heavy with the scent of heliotrope and anguished passion? Or the compelling and fearful brothel scene, like the drawings of Félicien Rops transformed into words? Perhaps it was the descriptions of passionate, physical love between two men. These are probably the best thing in *Teleny* or *The Reverse of the Medal* – a suggestive subtitle which also reminds us that here is simply another face of love.

'... our knees were pressed together, the skin of our thighs seemed to cleave and to form one flesh.

'Though I was loath to rise, still, feeling his stiff and swollen phallus throbbing against my body, I was just going to tear myself off from him, and to take his fluttering implement of pleasure in my mouth and drain it, when he – feeling that mine was now not only turgid, but moist and brimful to overflowing — clasped me with his arms and kept me down.

'Opening his thighs, he thereupon took my legs between his own, and entwined them in such a way that his heels pressed against the sides of my calves. For a moment I was gripped as in a vice, and I could hardly move.

'Then loosening his arms, he uplifted himself, placed a pillow under his buttocks, which were thus well apart – his legs being all the time widely open.

The Phallacy, *a watercolour sketch by a contemporary artist.*

'Having done this, he took hold of my rod and pressed it against his gaping anus. The tip of the frisky phallus soon found its entrance in the hospitable hole that endeavoured to give it admission. I pressed a little; the whole of the glans was engulfed. The sphincter soon gripped it in such a way that it could not come out without an effort. I thrust it slowly to prolong as much as possible the ineffable sensation that ran through every limb, to calm the quivering nerves, and to allay the heat of the blood. Another push, and half the phallus was in his body. I pulled it out half an inch, though it seemed to me a yard by the prolonged pleasure I felt. I pressed forward again, and the whole of it, down to its very root, was all swallowed up. Thus wedged, I vainly endeavoured to drive it higher up

An allegorical self-portrait of Aubrey Beardsley published in The Savoy magazine. Tethered to the phallic god Priapus, is the artist carrying a pen or a whip to flog us with? Perhaps for him they are one and the same thing?

– an impossible feat, and, clasped as I was, I felt it wriggling in its sheath like a baby in its mother's womb, giving myself and him an unutterable and delightful titillation.

'So keen was the bliss that overcame me, that I asked myself if some ethereal, life-giving fluid were not being poured on my head, and trickling down slowly over my quivering flesh.

'Surely the rain-awakened flowers must be conscious of such a sensation during a shower, after they have been parched by the scorching rays of an estival [summer] sun.

'Teleny again put his arm round me and held me tight. I gazed at myself within his eyes, he saw himself in mine. During this voluptuous, lambent feeling, we patted each other's bodies softly, our lips cleaved together and my tongue was again in his mouth. We remained in this copulation almost without stirring, for I felt that the slightest movement would provoke a copious ejaculation, and this feeling was too exquisite to be allowed to pass away so quickly. Still we could not help writhing, and we almost swooned away with delight. We were both shivering with lust, from the roots of our hair to the tips of our toes; all the flesh of our bodies kept bickering luxuriously, just as placid waters of the mere do at noontide when kissed by the sweet-scented, wanton breeze that has just deflowered the virgin rose.

'Such intensity of delight could not, however, last very long; a few almost unwilling contractions of the sphincter brandle the phallus, and then the first brunt was over; I thrust in with might and main, I wallowed on him; my breath came quickly; I panted, I sighed, I groaned. The thick burning fluid was spouted out slowly and at long intervals.

'As I rubbed myself against him, he underwent all the sensations I was feeling; for I was hardly drained of the last drop before I was likewise bathed with his own seething sperm. We did not kiss each other any further; our languid, half-open, lifeless lips only aspired each other's breath. Our sightless eyes saw each other no more, for we fell into that divine prostration which follows shattering ecstasy.

'Oblivion, however, did not follow, but we remained in a benumbed state of torpor, speechless, forgetting everything except the love we bore each other, unconscious of everything save the pleasure of feeling each other's bodies, which, however, seemed to have lost their own individuality, mingled and confounded as they were together.'

Another drawing from Aubrey Beardsley's Lysistrata. After the Oscar Wilde scandal of 1895, the Decadents rushed to death before the century from which they were forever alienated: Beardsley in March and Rops in August 1898.

After his release from prison in May 1897, Oscar Wilde went to live in the village of Berneval in Normandy. Close by was Dieppe, a favourite resort for the English, who could combine the joys and economies of France with the familiar comforts of an expatriate community. While Oscar was engaged in the therapy of writing *The Ballad of Reading Gaol* he hoped, therefore, to receive visits from old friends who were holidaying in Dieppe. Some came, but some did not. Among those who did not come, for fear of further scandal, was the brilliant young artist Aubrey Beardsley, who had done the illustrations for Wilde's *Salome*. After his arrest it was reported that Wilde had been carrying a copy of *The Yellow Book*, the controversial magazine Beardsley had helped to found. As a result the

*'The Toilet of Lampito', from
Lysistrata by Aubrey Beardsley
(1872–98).*

artist lost his job and found employment difficult. Beardsley's avoidance of Wilde might then have been entirely understandable but for their friendship. In a letter from Reading, Wilde wrote of Beardsley's deteriorating health: 'Poor Aubrey: I hope he will get alright... Behind his grotesques there seems to lurk some curious philosophy.' On hearing that Beardsley had avoided him in Dieppe, Oscar said simply: 'That was cowardly of Aubrey.' It was, especially as the main concern of Beardsley's art was to explore the ambiguities of gender while attacking Victorian sexual hypocrisy. His own sexuality was unconventional in the extreme, and perhaps that was the main reason for his cowardice. Beardsley was visiting Dieppe with his sister Mabel, whose close relationship with the artist was already the subject of unpleasant rumour. He was to die from tuberculosis in the following year, before his twenty-sixth birthday. So little time and so much still to do – no time for the distractions of scandal? Perhaps; we shall never know.

In his short life Aubrey Beardsley produced a large body of extraordinary art. Largely self-taught, he took what he needed from a wide range of artistic traditions: the erotic art of Japan, Shunga; Greek vase decoration; eighteenth-century masters such as Gillray and contemporaries including Félicien Rops. The unique and highly innovative style which Beardsley developed is instantly recognizable as his own. It was also the ideal vehicle for his exploration of his special subject: sex.

We know from his contemporaries that the

prodigiously talented erotomane also wanted to become a writer. From the experimental work that remains, some poems and the unfinished novel *Under the Hill* – a version of the *Tannhäuser* story – it is fair to assume that his graphic art would have remained the best expression of his genius. The poems are complicated erotic cyphers, as dull as his drawings are exciting. Beardsley said that *Under the Hill* was an exercise in 'rococo eroticism with peeps into the exotic underworld of amorous fantasy'. In this extract the draughtsman uses language to make us see, forming words with a drawing pen:

A print from a series by 'Jean le Pêcheur'. The artist's name is a pun on a word which can mean both 'sinner' and 'fisher'.

Poor Adolphe! How happy he was, touching the Queen's breasts with his quick tongue tip. I have no doubt that the keener scent of animals must make women much more attractive to them than to men; for the gorgeous odor that but faintly fills our nostrils must be revealed to the brute creation in divine fullness. Anyhow, Adolphe sniffed as never a man did round the skirts of Venus. After the first interchange of affectionate delicacies was over, the unicorn lay down upon his side, and, closing his eyes, beat his stomach wildly with the mark of manhood. Venus caught that stunning member in her hands and laid her cheek along it; but few touches were wanted to consummate the creature's pleasure. The Queen bared her left arm to the elbow, and with the soft underneath of it made amazing movements upon the tightly strung instrument. When the melody began to flow, the unicorn offered up an astonishing vocal accomplishment. Tannhäuser was amused to learn that the etiquette of Venusberg compelled everybody to await the outburst of those venereal sounds before they could sit down to *déjeuner*.

The nineteenth century closed, but the party went on. Edward VII presided over the feast like a reformed satyr, eager to prove – as he did – that he could be a king as well. Most of the important guests – Wilde, Verlaine, Beardsley, Rops – had already left, but in the heat and clamour of the moment they were hardly missed. With the benefit of hindsight, knowing that young men were rushing towards Passchendaele and the Somme, we are tempted to read into their gaiety some unconscious understanding that the end was near. We are probably wrong. Of course, erotica flourishes in so humid an atmosphere – and it did. Like lewd orchids raised secretly in the conservatories of the middle classes, a whole crop of colourful erotic novels appeared.

This Edwardian erotica was literate, but not much of it was literature. It was as if the well-educated, robust journalists who wrote quality boys' magazines such as *The Captain* had turned their hands (anonymously) to a different genre; perhaps they had. *Eveline* was first published in 1904. The aristocratic, very English heroine of this fast-moving adventure has trouble keeping her hands off the servants:

I rang the bell.
    'I want some tea, John. What time is it?'
    'It's not ten yet, miss.'
    'Where is the butler?'
    'Sir Edward has sent him out, miss, to see the

The Lovers, *a coloured print by the Danish artist Gerda Wegener (b. 1889).*

painter. He is not to send his men in the morning unless it is quite fine.'

'How is poor Robin, John? I am afraid he is drooping.'

The footman came closer. He bent cautiously down to me.

'Drooping? Miss Eveline, I wish he was! Why he stands up in the mornings and looks at me in the face. It's shocking how he suffers. I'm quite ashamed to look at him, miss.'

'So am I, John. All the same, let me see the poor thing. I might be able to do him some good.'

The door was shut. John looked all round. He listened. All seemed in order and quiet. He saw his chance. In another instant, he had opened his flap. He twisted his big limb out from under his shirt. My hand closed on it. It was already stretching itself out, and half erect. I loved to feel it thus – so warm, so soft!

The Unexpected Gift, *a coloured lithograph of a drawing by 'Onyx'.*

I bent my head over it as I sat. I kissed the red tip. The impulse was too strong for my resistance in the condition in which I was. I opened my moist lips. I let the big nut pass in. I sucked it. It swelled and stiffened. John involuntarily moved himself backwards and forwards. It very quickly attained its extreme stiffness and dimensions. I withdrew my face a little to look at it. The big round top shone as if it had been varnished.

'Take care what you do, miss. He's not to be trusted. He's in such a condition. What you have just done has made him more rampageous than ever.'

> You cannot expect a boy to be depraved until he has been to a good school.
>
> SAKI (H. H. MUNRO) (1870–1916)

ABOVE AND OPPOSITE *Two prints from the series by 'Jean le Pêcheur'. The caricatures of knowing ways which the artist creates lend a curious atmosphere to this strange group of erotic prints.*

I rubbed his member up and down quickly. He put down his hand and stopped me.

'Oh, Miss Eveline, mind your dress, miss.'

'Is it so near, John? Poor Robin! He must have all the pleasure I can give him to make him more tractable.'

I put down my head. I applied my lips again. I only released his limb to whisper:

'Let it come so, John! I want it!'

The idea made him mad. He pushed forward, breathing hard. He moved his loins again. I took into my mouth the whole of the big nut. I tickled it with my tongue. I moved both hands in little jerks upon the white shaft.

'Oh, Miss Eveline! Oh, my good Lord! I shall come! Oh!'

He discharged. My mouth was instantly filled with a torrent of his sperm. I swallowed as much as I could. It flew from him in little jets. It must have given him immense pleasure. Soon all was over.

'Now fetch the tea, John. I hope Robin will be better. If it had not been a cock – your Robin – I should have said it had laid an egg and broken it.'

Edwardian London saw the publication of a group of erotic novels which were evidently the work of the same anonymous writer: *The Confessions of Nemesis Hunt, Pleasure Bound Afloat, Pleasure Bound Ashore* and *Maudie*. Who this man was is uncertain, but he seems to have had links with the theatre. Not only is the heroine of *Nemesis Hunt* an actress, and the novel full of background detail; but all the books are theatrical both in their presentation and their pacing. *Pleasure Bound Afloat* even has pirates to provide some action, as did J. M. Barrie's *Peter Pan*, which had first appeared four years earlier, in 1904; but John Tucker, ex-MD of Edinburgh, who left 'for an unmentionable offence in Princes Street Gardens', has none of Captain Hook's problems with foreplay.

John Tucker began to think: he must show his manhood. He pulled her over him as tenderly as he knew how, and swept his strong hand over her deliciously rounded breasts to the opening in her drawers. He knew all the time that he was thinking about the boat coming in, and he knew that Helena knew it, but his penis stiffened automatically.

She, always all readiness, guided his great prick, not without some difficulty, into her moist little cunt. She wriggled delightedly, closed her eyes, and bit him savagely on the check. Then she flung herself violently up and down on his vibrating cock, uttering little cries of joy. Her fingers dug into his ribs, her naked legs clasped in a vice-like grip round his, her little tongue darted in and out of his mouth, and together they spent voluminously and savagely. For those few seconds all thoughts of mines and dividends had fled from John's brain; he saw only the lovely angel face pressed close to his, felt only the vicious clasp of her cunt muscles. It was the first time she had been so madly passionate with him. Perhaps, he thought, that little talk had done good. He made up his mind to keep her straight.

'Promise me, little angel,' he whispered as she slowly raised her cunt from off his cock, and looked down with those lovely turquoise eyes into his, 'promise me to be true.'

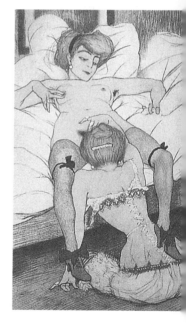

'If you can always do it like that, I'll think it over.'
They strolled on, hand in hand, the lovely, semi-
naked girl, and the brutally strong-looking bucca-
neer, through the soft groves.

The dialogue in all the books is also handled in
a way that suggests familiarity with scripts, and
much attention is given to costume and the
appearance of each erotic tableau.

The Sisters Lovett were just his style: they made
him remember with a sigh the jolly chorus girl
supper parties of the old days, the merry moments
in the dressing-rooms, and the frank impropriety
of the conversation.

ABOVE and OPPOSITE *Etchings by
an unknown German artist
illustrating the* Steps of Love *by
the playwright Frank Wedekind
(1864–1918). He was famous for
his plays* Pandora's Box *and* Spirit
of the Earth, *on which Alban Berg
based his opera* Lulu; *the heroine
is the spirit of destructive sexuality.*

He was rather sorry just now to find the sisters
nude; he would have liked them better in their dar-
ingly suggestive music hall frocks, he liked to see
pretty legs emerging from a sea of fluff. He apologized with a laugh for his unannounced intrusion.

'We are rather free and easy here, you know,' he
said.

'Oh, don't mind us,' said Tilly, 'we've soon tumbled to your habits.'

'And we like 'em,' added Cissie.

Mike knew his girl, and had not come empty-
handed.

'I know you theatre girls like jewels and pretty
things,' he said, and emptied his pockets.

They were pretty things with a vengeance, and
the sisters went into openly expressed raptures.
Bracelets, rings, necklaces, all of beautiful designs,
mingled with brooches, combs, jewelled garters,
and a score of dainty ornaments.

'You'd best just divvy 'em up equally,' said Mike,

A studio photograph, Paris, early
twentieth century.

'only you ought to have your clothes on to show
'em off.'

'Shall we dress, then, in our music hall frocks?'
asked Tilly, 'and after that we'll thank you ever so
prettily.' She was clever enough to see that this was
just the way the young man wanted to be made
randy, and didn't attempt to kiss him.

They chose rather simple dresses, those in which
as *les deux demi-vierges* they had electrified even
Paris.

Firstly they had to do their hair, which now was
all flowing loose. In two twin plaits it went, with a
little bow at the end. In front a deep wave swept

their foreheads. The corsage was not very *décol-letée* in front, but at the back the V cut down to the waist. They wore no corsets.

The skirts were short, well above the knee, distended by a mass of under skirts. They had very short drawers, and very long black stockings with a golden stripe down the side: the whole note of the costumes was black and gold. Their shoes were golden, with very high black heels.

'Well?' said Tilly, when the attire was complete.

'Like to kiss us?' said Cissie.

'Wait till I put all the pretty things on, and then you'll see what I want to do,' answered the young earl excitedly.

He just loved them like this, and all the old *joie de théâtre* came back to him. When Cissie did a high kick and Tilly slipped gracefully into the 'splits' he was in a seventh heaven.

'We oughtn't to have 'em on with those clothes,' said Cissie, 'we're supposed to be dear little darlings who've never had our windows broken. We ought to keep 'em for our second costumes, but we'll do that when we give our real show at the theatre.'

The jewels pretty well smothered the girls, and they danced for delight before the long cheval glass.

'Now then, you darling,' said Tilly, 'we've both got to thank you, but you can't have us both at once; which'll you have first?'

It was an *embarras de richesses*, and Mike looked uncomfortable.

Eventually the toss up made it Cissie.

'Do you want me to undress?' she asked.

'No, no, I'm sick of naked women.'

'Well, *you* must undress,' said Tilly. 'I'll boss this

fuck, Cis, you just go and lie on that couch.'

Cissie obeyed, and lay back, her legs wide apart, a ravishing vision.

Tilly undressed Mike to the buff. She did it slowly, for she was very randy, and took an especially long time in undoing his fly.

He was a finely made young fellow and his cock stood proudly up. Tilly took it in her mouth for a moment, then kissed him, smacked his bottom and told him to do his duty.

He dived lasciviously into Cissie's mass of *dessus*, his white naked body making a wicked contrast to the black and gold of the girl's clothes.

It was a couch that could be raised at either end, and Tilly, knowing the joy for a man of fucking a really acrobatic girl when her head is on a lower level than her body, raised the front of the couch.

Cissie curved up her legs right round his shoulders, and a very loving fuck began. She kissed and bit him and squeezed him and they finished in a frenzy, Cissie giving a piercing scream as she felt the juice spurt into her.

Although all the erotic books in what we might call the 'Edwardian Theatrical' series are pure escapism and were written to order for an eager public, they are still good examples of their kind. The books are humorous and well-paced; it is even true to say that some of the characters occurring in the books give a strange impression that they are drawn from life. However, who was their creator? The biography of 'Charlie Osmond' in *Maudie* is written as something of a joke, but is it only that?

OPPOSITE *A French erotic postcard of the Belle Epoque. The care and imagination with which much of this erotic ephemera was produced raised the status of the postcard to a new art-form.*

ABOVE AND BELOW *Two etchings by an unknown German artist illustrating* Wedekind's The Steps of Love. *Both the technique and the composition are daring and original.*

A gentleman by birth, he had most of the right instincts and perversions. He had left Eton for the usual reason, and he regretted it. He did not want to bugger other boys, but some did, and he somehow hated to be out of the fashion. Unfortunately, he was found out.

At Oxford his career had been meteoric. He could not go to a very good college, owing to his school troubles, and his good allowance made him a star at – (we will suppress the name). He did many things he should not have, and his final exploit of sowing the word 'CUNT' in mustard and cress in the front quad grass, which came up under the astonished eyes of the dean's daughter, led to his final exit. His defence – that he had meant the word as a moral admonition to those of the Varsity who had leaned to malpractices in the sodomitical line – was not accepted, and he went.

The home-coming was as usual – nobody to meet him at the station but the chauffeur, and father in the gun-room.

> Your son's devotion to landscape gardening [ran the dean's note] is undoubtedly commendable, but we must remind you that the grass in the front quadrangle at — has for 500 years preserved its virginity, and the word inscribed makes not only a blemish on the grass, but conveys a reflection on the locality. We are only pleased that no word has found its way to the American papers. – We are, etc.,
>
> HY. CHARTERIS (DEAN)

Charlie Osmond came to town with £300 a year, and a paternal kick on the arse.

It has been suggested by P. J. Kearney, the
authority on erotic literature, that the true identity of the writer who produced this cheerful cor-
pus of erotic work in the decade before World
War I was the journalist George Reginald
Bacchus (1873–1945). He certainly seems to fit
the evidence. Bacchus had been a close friend of
Leonard Smithers, the well-connected publisher
of erotica whom Oscar Wilde called 'the most
erudite erotomane in Europe'. He had been
at Oxford ('the homecoming was as usual').
Improbably, Bacchus wrote for a weekly religious paper ('Biblical subjects were quite preva-

*Another French erotic postcard
of the Belle Epoque.*

lent there') and, most important of all, he was married to Isa Bowman (1874–1958), the well-known actress. Bacchus certainly had the right name for the job: wine and other delights of the table abound in the novels. But if he was the author, what did his wife – one of the theatrical Bowman Sisters – make of it all?

One evening, during Christmas 1914, Lytton Strachey (1880–1932) read his novel *Ermyntrude and Esmeralda* to his friend David Garnett. The book had been written two years earlier for the artist Henry Lamb, with whom Strachey was then very much in love. Garnett saw at once that the light comedy – delivered in Strachey's piping falsetto voice – disguised a stinging satire on contemporary attitudes to sex and sex education.

Ermyntrude and Esmeralda is written as an exchange of letters between two privileged

A studio photograph, Paris, early twentieth century.

Half of a stereoscopic photograph taken by Eugène Agelou and reprinted in 1910.

young ladies whose sexual education has been sadly neglected. By pooling their experiences – Ermyntrude lives in London, her friend in the country – they hope to solve the mystery.

In an early letter Ermyntrude reports on the questioning of her governess, Simpson, and decides on an absurd nomenclature for the sexual organs, which both girls adopt.

I've tried to go on with our enquiries about love and babies, but I haven't got much further. The other day I began edging round the conversation in that direction with old Simpson, and naturally that didn't succeed. She shut me up when I was still miles

The Western custom of one wife and hardly any mistresses.

SAKI (H. H. MUNRO) (1870–1916)

ABOVE and OPPOSITE *Two etchings by an unknown German artist for the edition of Wedekind's The Steps of Love. Expensively produced limited editions of illustrated erotica have always found a small, discriminating connoisseur market.*

A woman whose dresses are made in Paris and whose marriage has been made in Heaven might be equally biased for and against free imports.

SAKI (H. H. MUNRO) (1870–1916)

off. Everyone always does – that is, everyone who knows. What can it mean. It is very odd. Why on earth should there be a secret about what happens when people have babies? I suppose it must be something appallingly shocking, but then, if it is, how can so many people bear to have them? Of course I'm quite sure it's got something to do with those absurd little things that men have in statues hanging between their legs, and that we haven't. And I'm also sure that it's got something to do with the thing between our legs that I always call my Pussy. I believe that may be its real name, because once when I was at Oxford looking at the races with my cousin Tom, I heard quite a common woman say to another 'There, Sarah, doesn't that make your pussy pout?' And then I saw that one of the rowing men's trousers were all split and those things were showing between his legs; and it looked most extraordinary. I couldn't quite see enough, but the more I looked the more I felt – well, the more I felt my pussy pouting, as the woman had said. So now I call ours pussies and theirs bow-wows, and my theory is that people have children when their bow-wows and pussies pout at the same time. Do you think that's it? Of course I can't imagine how it can possibly work, and I daresay I'm altogether wrong and it's really got something to do with W.C's.

As the correspondence develops Ermyntrude asks if the bow-wow of her brother's tutor, Mr Mapleton, 'pouts' for Esmeralda. Alas for the eager young lady, we soon learn that it does not:

There has been the most awful row. Papa went in by accident yesterday morning to get a shoe-horn,

ABOVE and OPPOSITE Les
Délassements d'Eros, a suite
of twelve 'pochoir' prints by the
Danish artist Gerda Wegener
(b. 1889), a popular commercial
artist, who worked in Paris
between the wars.

He belonged to that race of beings
who are in effect, since it is precisely
because their temperament is
feminine that they worship manliness,
at cross-purposes with themselves.

MARCEL PROUST (1871–1922)

and found Mr. Mapleton in Godfrey's bed. He was most fearfully angry, told Mr. Mapleton that he would have to go away out of England and live abroad for ever and ever, or he would have him put in prison, and stormed at Godfrey like anything, and said he would flog him, only he was too old to be flogged, but he ought to be flogged, and that he had disgraced himself and his family, and that it could never be wiped out, never, and that he couldn't hold up his head again with such a son, and that as Godfrey wasn't to be flogged he would have to be punished in some even worse way – but none of us know what yet. It was too dreadful for words. Godfrey told me all about it. Mr. Mapleton went away that very morning, immediately after breakfast, but he didn't come down to it, so perhaps he didn't have any, and Mama has been almost in tears ever since, and Papa has hardly spoken to anyone. The Dean has been looking very grave... Poor Godfrey is in such dreadful disgrace, and I am very sorry for him. I suppose it was a frightfully wicked thing to do, but the curious thing is he doesn't seem at all wicked, and I really do believe I'm fonder of him than I've ever been before. I talked to him for quite a long time yesterday before dinner. I went into the morning room, and he was there, so I began to say how sorry I was. But before I'd said very much he turned round and walked towards the window, and then I saw that he was crying. I hardly knew what to do, so I went on talking for a little, and at last I threw my arms round his neck and kissed him a great many times, which seemed to comfort him although he began to cry harder

than ever at first. But in the end he
told me all about Mr. Mapleton, and
how fond he was of him, and how
unhappy he was to think he'd never
see him again, and when I asked him
whether he was in love with him, he
said yes, he was, and why not? – that
he loved him better than anyone in the world and
always would as long as he lived, and then he
began crying again. And he said he didn't think
he'd done anything wicked at all, and it seems the
Greeks used to do it too – at least the Athenians,
who were the best of the Greeks – which is very
funny, don't you think?

How different, how very different from
the home life of our own dear Queen.

AN OVERHEARD REMARK BY AN
ANONYMOUS BRITISH MATRON DURING A
PERFORMANCE OF *ANTHONY AND CLEOPATRA*

CHAPTER NINE
After the Nightmare

A fter the world's first technological war nothing was, or could ever be, the same again.
Empires, classes, political systems: all the old
structures were either fractured or had collapsed
altogether. In art and literature new voices said
new things, and old voices said different things.
Sex became a subject which mainstream writers
demanded freedom to explore. It was a freedom
which had to be fought for – there are still skir-
mishes – but sex was in the open. While writers
like James Joyce pushed language to its limits to
explore new aspects of conventional sexuality, in
Ulysses (first published in Paris in 1922), other
writers used conventional language to explore

*This reclining nude by the
Cordoban artist Julio Romero de
Torres captures the melancholy
mood which lay beneath the brittle
glamour of the roaring twnties,
following the apocalypse of the
Great War.*

the extreme limits of sexuality itself. The American writer Edith Wharton (1862–1937) took one of the darkest of all sexual topics, incestuous love, as the subject for her short story *Beatrice Palmato*.

Then suddenly he drew back her wrapper entirely, whispered: 'I want you all, so that my eyes can see all that my lips can't cover,' and in a moment she was free, lying before him in her fresh young nakedness, and feeling that indeed his eyes were covering it with fiery kisses. But Mr Palmato was never idle, and while this sensation flashed through her one of his arms had slipped under her back and wound itself around her so that his hand again enclosed her left breast. At the same moment the other hand softly separated her legs, and began to slip up the old path it had so often travelled in darkness. But now it was light, she was uncovered, and looking downward, beyond his dark silver-sprinkled head, she could see her own parted knees, and out-stretched ankles and feet. Suddenly she remembered Austin's rough advances, and shuddered.

Eve by Eric Gill (1882–1940), first-class artist, typographer and, so it appears, practitioner of a wide variety of sexual activities, both legal and illegal.

The mounting hand paused, the dark head was instantly raised. 'What is it, my own?'

'I was—remembering—last week—' she faltered, below her breath.

'Yes, darling. That experience is a cruel one – but it has to come once in all women's lives. Now we shall reap its fruit.'

But she hardly heard him, for the old swooning sweetness was creeping over her. As his hand stole higher she felt the secret bud of her body swelling, yearning, quivering hotly to burst into bloom.

In the bath, *a book illustration
by G. de Sainte-Croix (active
1949–59 in France); drypoint,
hand-coloured in aquatint.*

Ah, here was his subtle forefinger pressing it, forcing its tight petals softly apart, and laying on their sensitive edges a circular touch so soft and yet so fiery that already lightnings of heat shot from that palpitating centre all over her surrendered body, to the tips of her fingers, and the ends of her loosened hair.

The sensation was so exquisite that she could have asked to have it indefinitely prolonged; but suddenly his head bent lower, and with a deeper thrill she felt his lips pressed upon that quivering invisible bud, and then the delicate firm thrust of his tongue, so full and yet so infinitely subtle, pressing apart the close petals, and forcing itself in deeper and deeper through the passage that glowed and seemed to become illumined at its approach...

'Ah—' she gasped, pressing her hands against her sharp nipples, and flinging her legs apart.

Instantly one of her hands was caught, and while Mr Palmato, rising, bent over her, his lips on hers again, she felt his fingers pressing into her hand that strong fiery muscle that they used, in their old joke, to call his third hand.

'My little girl,' he breathed, sinking down beside her, his muscular trunk bare, and the third hand quivering and thrusting upward between them, a drop of moisture pearling at its tip.

She instantly understood the reminder that his words conveyed, letting herself downward along the divan until her head was in a line with his middle she flung herself upon the swelling member, and began to caress it insinuatingly with her tongue. It was the first time she had ever seen it actually exposed to her eyes, and her heart swelled excitedly: to have her touch confirmed by sight enriched the sensation that was communicating itself through her ardent twisting tongue. With panting breath she wound her caress deeper and deeper into the thick firm folds, till at length the member, thrusting her lips open, held her gasping, as if at its mercy; then, in a trice, it was withdrawn, her knees were pressed apart, and she saw it before her, above her, like a crimson flash, and at last, sinking backward into new abysses of bliss, felt it descend on her, press open the secret gates, and plunge into the deepest depths of her thirsting body...

If Frank Harris had not published *My Life and Loves* (in Paris in 1925) the world of letters would have been poorer (and duller), but the author's reputation would have stood rather higher. This was after all the radical editor of the *Saturday Review* who defended the Boers, who spoke out against the war with Germany, who went to Brixton Prison fighting for the freedom of the press. Harris (1856–1931) was also the loyal ally of Oscar Wilde and a close friend of Bernard Shaw for forty years. Shaw's perceptive assessment of him ran as follows:

An illustration in watercolour over sepia ink by an unknown Italian artist, c. 1935.

Harris suffered deeply from repeated disillusions and disappointments. Like Hedda Gabler he was tormented by a sense of the sordidness in the commonplace realities which form so much of the stuff of life, and was not only disappointed in people who did nothing splendid, but savagely contemptuous of people who did not want to have anything splendid done...

Frank, too, was a man of splendid visions, unreasonable expectations, fierce appetites which

A book illustration by G. de Sainte-Croix (active 1949–59 in France); drypoint, hand-coloured in aquatint.

he was unable to relate to anything except to romantic literature, and especially to the impetuous rhetoric of Shakespear. It is hardly an exaggeration to say that he ultimately quarrelled with everybody but Shakespear...

It was Harris's tendency to romanticize and idealize everything – especially what he called 'the greatest of all influences', sex – which has led some people to dub him a liar, or at the very least a fantasist. As we have seen, remembered sexual incidents, even when the intention is to be truthful, hover between reality and the world of dreams. Did Frank really talk to his young lover Grace about Montaigne? Yes, he probably did.

I put my arms round her legs and, lifting her up, carried her to the bed. The next moment I had thrown up her clothes and buried my face between her thighs.

'What are you doing?' she cried, but as I began kissing love's sweet home and the little red button, involuntarily she opened her thighs and gave herself to the new sensations. As I felt her responding, I drew her nearer to me a little roughly and opened her thighs fully. There never was a more lovely sex, and already the smaller inside lips were all flushed with feeling, while soon pearling love-drops oozed down on my lips.

I kept on, knowing that such a first experience is unforgettable and soon she abandoned herself recklessly, and her hand came down on my head and directed me now higher, now lower, according to her desire.

A niece of the late Queen of Sheba
Was promiscuous with an amoeba.
This queer blob of jelly
Would lie in her belly
And, quivering, murmur, 'Ich liebe!'

NORMAN DOUGLAS (1868–1952)

When the love-play had gone on four or five times and I stood up to rest, she said gravely: 'You are a dear and gave me great pleasure, but do you like it?'

'Of course,' I said. 'Even old Montaigne knew that the pleasure we give the loved one is more than that we get.'

> The only woman I really love, is the Unknown who haunts my imagination – seduction in person, for she possesses all the incompatible perfections I've never yet found in any one woman. She must be intensely sensuous, yet self-controlled; soulful, yet a coquette: to find her, that's the great adventure of life and there's no other.
>
> GUY DE MAUPASSANT (1850–93)
> SPEAKING TO FRANK HARRIS

'Oh, that's my feeling,' she said, 'but how am I to give you pleasure?' In answer, I took out my sex. She touched it curiously, drawing back the skin and pushing it forward: 'Does that give you pleasure?'

I nodded. 'But this,' and I put my hand on her sex, 'could give me much more.'

My Life and Loves may be 'lascivious' (and a lot more besides), but it is certainly not 'obscene', 'lewd' or 'indecent'. Two paragraphs after the last extract, Harris makes a very revealing comment about himself: 'Dimly I became conscious that if this life were sordid and mean, petty and unpleasant, the fault was in myself and in my blindness. I began then for the first time to understand that I myself was a magician and could create my own fairyland, ay, and my own heaven, transforming this world into the throne-room of a god.'

Frank Harris was no ordinary romantic in search of perfection: he sought it in every sphere of his life – as an editor, as a writer, and of course in bed. A *ménage à trois* with a mature French

ABOVE and OPPOSITE *More illustrations in watercolour over sepia ink by an unknown Italian artist, c. 1935.*

woman and her adopted daughter affords him a glimpse, at least, of sexual perfection.

I gave a big lunch to people of importance in the theatre and journalism and invited Jeanne and referred everything to her and drew her out, throning her, and afterwards returning to her house to dinner. While she was changing and titivating, I took Lisette in my arms and kissed her with hot lips again and again while feeling her budding breasts, till she put her arms round my neck and kissed me just as warmly; and then I ventured to touch her little half-fledged sex and caress it, till it opened and grew moist and she nestled up to me and whispered: 'Oh! how you excite me!'

'Have you ever done it to yourself' I asked. She nodded with bright dancing eyes. 'Often, but I prefer you to touch me.' For the first time I heard the truth from a girl and her courage charmed me. I could not help laying her on the sofa, and turning up her clothes: how lovely her limbs were, and how perfect her sex. She was really exquisite, and I took an almost insane pleasure in studying her beauties, and parting the lips of her sex [with] kisses: in a few moments she was all trembling and gasping. She put her hand on my head to stop me. When I lifted her up, she kissed me. 'You dear,' she said with a strange earnestness, 'I want you always. You'll stay with us, won't you?' I kissed her for her sweetness.

When Jeanne came out of the cabinet, we all went into the dining-room, and afterwards Lisette went up to her room after kissing me, and I went to bed with Jeanne, who let me excite her for half an hour; and then mounting me milked me with

Another in the series of watercolour and sepia illustrations by an Italian artist of c. 1935.

such artistry that in two minutes she brought me to spasms of sensation, such as I had never experienced before with any other woman. Jeanne was the most perfect mistress I had met up to that time, and in sheer power of giving pleasure hardly to be surpassed by any of western race.

An unforgettable evening, one of the few evenings in my life when I reached both the intensest pang of pleasure with the even higher aesthetic delight of toying with beautiful limbs and awakening new desires in a lovely body and frank honest spirit.

A true obsessive in his search for sexual perfection, Frank is mortified by any flaw.

'It's your naughtiness saves you,' I responded, 'and your wonderful beauty of figure; your little breasts are tiny-perfect, taken with your strong hips and the long limbs and the exquisite triangle with the lips that are red, crimson-red as they should be, and not brown like most, and so sensitive, curling at the edges and pearling with desire.'

Suddenly she put her hand over my mouth. 'I won't listen,' she pouted, wrinkling up her nose – and she looked so adorable that I led her to the sofa and soon got busy kissing, kissing the glowing crimson lips that opened at once to me, and in a minute or two were pearly wet with the white milk of love and ready for my sex.

But in spite of the half-confession, the antagonism between us continued, though it was much less than it had been. I could not get her to give herself with passion, or to let herself go frankly to love's ultimate expression, even when I had reduced her to tears and sobbings of exhaustion. 'Please not, boy! Please, no more,' was all I could get from her, so that often and often I merely had her and came to please myself and then lay there beside her talking, or threw down the sheets and made her lie on her face so that I could admire the droop of the loins and the strong curve of the bottom. Or else I would pose her sideways so as to bring out the great swell of the hip and the poses would usually end with my burying my head between her legs, trying with lips and tongue and finger and often again with my sex to bring her sensations to ecstasy and if possible to love-speech and love-thanks! Now and again I succeeded, for I had begun to study the times in the month when she was most easily excited. But how is it

*The first of a sequence of studies
of a young woman, Paris,
c. 1930; photographer unknown.*

that so few women ever try to give their lover the utmost sum of pleasure?

In giving an account of Frank Harris in an anthology of erotica, the thumbnail sketch of the man which emerges is, perhaps, less sympathetic than it should be, especially to women. Some of his lovers became lifelong friends, like Enid Bagnold, who said 'his talk made you feel as though you were living in heaven'. Many other women, who were not lovers, regarded Harris as a loyal and devoted friend. As usual, it is better to leave the last word on the subject to Frank: 'All that is amiable and sweet and good in life, all that ennobles and chastens I have won from women. Why should I not sing their praises, or at least show my gratitude by telling of the subtle intoxication of their love that has made my life an entrancing romance?'

For more than thirty years after its first publication in 1928 an English person wishing to read *Lady Chatterley's Lover* had to purchase a copy abroad. The famous trial in which the jury – to their eternal credit – decided that the book was not obscene had several positive results. Among these, and by no means the least important, was the extraordinary publicity the case received. As a direct result the book became a bestseller overnight and was read by countless thousands of people who would not otherwise have done so. If D. H. Lawrence's vast new readership expected smut they were mistaken. *Lady Chatterley's Lover* is a tender, moral book and – for all its idiosyncrasies and quaintness – one of the finest books about sexual love ever written. In the foreword to the Paris edition of 1928, D. H. Lawrence (1885–1930) said that the point of his novel was to enable 'men and women to be able to think sex, fully, completely, honestly and cleanly. Even if we cannot act sexually to our complete satisfaction, let us at least think sexually, complete and clear.' Lawrence was in fact rather prudish about sex: he loathed bawdiness and anything which (as he saw it) detracted from the sacredness of our sexuality.

Lady Chatterley's Lover is the story of Connie, who finds true love and fulfilment with her husband's gamekeeper. In this extract Connie summarizes her frustration, and her past sexual experience. Michaelis is her former lover.

Another in the sequence of studies of a young woman, Paris, c. 1930.

When Connie went up to her bedroom she did what she had not done for a long time: took off all her clothes, and looked at herself naked in the huge mirror. She did not know what she was looking for, or at, very definitely, yet she moved the lamp till it shone full on her.

And she thought, as she had thought so often, what a frail, easily hurt, rather pathetic thing a human body is, naked, somehow a little unfinished, incomplete!

She had been supposed to have rather a good figure, but now she was out of fashion: a little too female, not enough like an adolescent boy. She was not very tall, a bit Scottish and short; but she had a certain fluent, down-slipping grace that might have been beauty. Her skin was faintly tawny, her limbs had a certain stillness, her body should have had a full, down-slipping richness;

but it lacked something.

Instead of ripening its firm, down-running curves, her body was flattening and going a little harsh. It was as if it had not had enough sun and warmth; it was a little greyish and sapless.

Disappointed of its real womanhood, it had not succeeded in becoming boyish, and unsubstantial, and transparent; instead it had gone opaque.

Her breasts were rather small, and dropping pear-shaped. But they were unripe, a little bitter, without meaning hanging there. And her belly had lost the fresh, round gleam it had had when she was young, in the days of her German boy, who really loved her physically. Then it was young and expectant, with a real look of its own. Now it was going slack, and a little flat, thinner, but with a slack thinness. Her thighs, too, they used to look so quick and glimpsy in their female roundness, somehow they too were going flat, slack, meaningless...

She looked in the other mirror's reflection at her back, her waist, her loins. She was getting thinner, but to her it was not becoming. The crumple of her waist at the back, as she bent back to look, was a little weary; and it used to be so gay-looking. And the longish slope of her haunches and her buttocks had lost its gleam and its sense of richness. Gone! Only the German boy had loved it, and he was ten years dead, very nearly. How time went by! Ten years dead, and she was only twenty-seven. The healthy boy with his fresh, clumsy sensuality that she had then been so scornful of! Where would she find it now? It was gone out of men. They had their pathetic, two-seconds spasms like Michaelis; but no healthy human sensuality, that warms the blood and freshens the whole being.

OPPOSITE and ABOVE *Two more studies of a young woman, Paris, c. 1930, by an unknown photographer.*

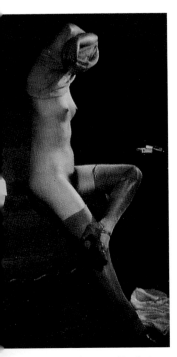

ABOVE and OPPOSITE *Two further studies from the sequence of a young Parisian woman, c. 1930.*

Still she thought the most beautiful part of her was the long-sloping fall of the haunches from the socket of the back, and the slumberous, round stillness of the buttocks. Like hillocks of sand, the Arabs say, soft and downward-slipping with a long slope. Here the life still lingered hoping. But here too she was thinner, and going unripe, astringent.

In writing *Lady Chatterley's Lover* Lawrence created a new language to describe sex: he needed to. No one had ever written like that before, no novelist of genius had ever been brave enough to describe the things he describes, and bring such creative insights to the subject.

After Lawrence the floodgates opened and the bad and the mediocre swept in along with the good, but he was the first. And even now he moves us with the truth of what he says. We can smile at the naïvety and what now seems in some senses old-fashioned, but still he moves us.

The erotica of the 1930s and early 1940s was dominated by two writers: the Frenchwoman Anaïs Nin and the American Henry Miller. They were friends, and together with several other members of their bohemian expatriate circle they wrote erotica for 'a dollar a page' to make ends meet. They lived in Paris, and the city exerted such a strong influence on both writers that it is almost like a character in their work. Here is Anaïs Nin:

It was a soft rainy afternoon, with that gray Parisian melancholy that drove people indoors, that created an erotic atmosphere because it fell

The final photograph from the sequence of studies of a young woman in Paris, c. 1930.

like a ceiling over the city, enclosing them all in a nerveless air, as in an alcove; and everywhere, some reminder of the erotic life – a shop, half-hidden, showing underwear and black garters and black boots; the Parisian woman's provocative walk; taxis carrying embracing lovers.

Balzac's house stood at the top of a hilly street in Passy, over-looking the Seine. First they had to ring at the door of an apartment house, then descend a flight of stairs that seemed to lead to a cellar but opened instead on a garden. Then they had to traverse the garden and ring at another door. This was the door of his house, concealed in the garden of the apartment house, a secret and mysterious house, so hidden and isolated in the heart of Paris.

The woman who opened the door was like a ghost from the past – faded face, faded hair and clothes, bloodless. Living with Balzac's manuscripts, pictures, engravings of the women he had loved, first editions, she was permeated with a vanished past, and all the blood had ebbed from her. Her very voice was distant, ghostly. She slept in this house filled with dead souvenirs. She had become equally dead to the present. It was as if each night she laid herself away in the tomb of Balzac, to sleep with him.

She guided them through the rooms, and then to the back of the house. She came to a trap door, slipped her long bony fingers through the ring and lifted it for Elena and Pierre to see. It opened on a little stairway.

This was the trap door Balzac had built so that

the women who visited him could escape from the surveillance or suspicions of their husbands. He, too, used it to escape from his harassing creditors. The stairway led to a path and then to a gate that opened on an isolated street that in turn led to the Seine. One could escape before the person at the front door of the house had enough time to traverse the first room.

> We fucked a flame into being. Even the flowers are fucked into being between the sun and the earth.
>
> FROM *LADY CHATTERLEY'S LOVER*
> D. H LAWRENCE (1885-1930)

For Elena and Pierre, the effect of this trap door so evoked Balzac's love of life that it affected them like an aphrodisiac. Pierre whispered to her, 'I would like to take you on the floor, right here.'

The ghost woman did not hear these words, uttered with the directness of an apache, but she caught the glance which accompanied them. The mood of the visitors was not in harmony with the sacredness of the place, and she hurried them out.

The breath of death had whipped their senses. Pierre hailed a taxi. In the taxi he could not wait. He made Elena sit over him, with her back to him, the whole length of her body against his, concealing him completely. He raised her skirt.

Elena said, 'Not here, Pierre. Wait until we get home. People will see us. Please wait. Oh, Pierre, you're hurting me! Look, the policeman stared at us. And now we're stopped here, and people can see us from the sidewalk. Pierre, Pierre, stop it.'

But all the time that she feebly defended herself, and tried to slip off, she was conquered by pleasure. Her efforts to sit still made her even more keenly aware of Pierre's every movement. Now she feared that he might hurry his act, driven by the speed of the taxi and the fear that it would stop soon in front of the house and the taxi driver

OPPOSITE and ABOVE *Two of a series of thirty lithographs, entitled* Idylle Printanière, *hand-coloured in crayon by the artist Rojan or Rojankowski, 1933.*

would turn his head towards them. And she wanted to enjoy Pierre, to reassert their bond, the harmony of their bodies. They were observed from the street. Yet she could not draw away, and he now had his arms around her. Then a violent jump of the taxi over a hole in the road threw them apart. It was too late to resume the embrace. The taxi had stopped. Pierre had just enough time to button himself. Elena felt they must look drunk, disheveled. The languor of her body made it difficult for her to move.

Pierre was filled with a perverse enjoyment of this interruption. He enjoyed feeling his bones half-melted in his body, the almost painful withdrawal of the blood. Elena shared his new whim, and later they lay on the bed caressing each other and talking.

Miller's Paris is a very different place from the city Anaïs Nin has just described. In *Tropic of Cancer* (1934), although he concedes it is exciting he calls it 'a foul sink' and a 'whore', and is eternally ambivalent about it:

The world of Matisse is still beautiful in an old-fashioned bedroom way. There is not a ball bearing in evidence, nor a boiler, plate, nor a piston, nor a monkey wrench. It is the same old world that went gaily to the Bois in the pastoral days of wine and fornication. I find it soothing and refreshing to move amongst these creatures with live, breathing pores whose background is stable and solid as light itself. I feel it poignantly when I walk along the Boulevard de la Madeleine and the whores rustle beside me, when just to glance at them causes me to tremble. Is it because they are exotic or well-nourished? No, it is rare to find a beautiful woman along the Boulevard de la Madeleine. But in Matisse, in the exploration of his brush, there is the trembling glitter of a world which demands only the presence of the female to crystallize the most fugitive aspirations. To come upon a woman offering herself outside a urinal, where there are advertised cigarette papers, rum, acrobats, horse races, where the heavy foliage of the trees breaks the heavy mass of walls and roofs, is an experience that begins where the boundaries of the known world leave off... Even as the world falls apart the Paris that belongs to Matisse shudders with bright, gasping orgasms, the air itself is steady with a stagnant sperm, the trees tangled like hair. On its wobbly axle the wheel rolls steadily downhill; there are no brakes, no ball bearings, no balloon tires. The wheel is falling apart, but the revolution is intact...

It is worth exploring the differences between these two pieces of writing before comparing their treatment of explicitly sexual scenes. Paris is an eroticized city for both of them, a place where the ghosts of the great affect the living. That is enough for her; she catches the mood and follows its influences. Miller, in contrast, has to analyse and dissect, hacking at the idea with robust prose that is almost poetry. Her prose never shocks – it glides like silk across the idea, defining it that way.

Tropic of Cancer is an erotic book in that one of its main topics is sex, but it is not intended to excite the reader sexually. To compare the two

Two more of the series Idylle Printanière, *hand-coloured lithographs by Rojan or Rojankowski, 1933.*

writers – and a woman's erotica with a man's – it is better to look at the work each of them produced for a dollar a page. In both extracts, the subject of the erotic writing is the effect of visual erotica. Here is Anaïs Nin.

She could think only of erotic images in connection with him, his body. If she saw a penny movie on the boulevards that stirred her, she brought her curiosity or a new experiment to their next meeting. She began to whisper certain wishes in his ear.

Pierre was always surprised when Elena was willing to give him pleasure without taking it herself. There were times after their excesses when he was tired, less potent, and yet wanted to repeat the sensation of annihilation. Then he would stir her with caresses, with an agility of the hands that approached masturbation. Meanwhile her own hands would circle around his penis like a delicate spider with knowing fingertips, which touched the most hidden nerves of response. Slowly, the fingers closed upon the penis, at first stroking its flesh shell; then feeling the inrush of dense blood stretching it; feeling the slight swell of the nerves, the sudden tautness of the muscles; feeling as if they were playing upon a stringed instrument… Then he would be drugged by her hands, close his eyes and abandon himself to her caresses. Once or twice he would try, as if in sleep, to continue the motion of his own hands, but then he lay passively, to feel better the knowing manipulations, the increasing tension. 'Now, now,' he would murmur. 'Now.' This meant that her hand must become swifter to keep pace with the fever pulsing within him. Her fingers ran in rhythm with the quicken-

ing blood beats, as his voice begged,
'Now, now, now.'

Blind to all but his pleasure,
she bent over him, her hair
falling, her mouth near his
penis, continuing the
motion of her hands and at
the same time licking the
tip of the penis each time it
passed within reach of her
tongue – this, until his body
began to tremble and raised
itself to be consumed by her hands
and mouth, to be annihilated, and the
semen would come, like little waves breaking
on the sand, one rolling upon another, little waves
of salty foam unrolling on the beach of her hands.
Then she enclosed the spent penis tenderly in her
mouth, to cull the precious liquid of love. His pleasure gave her such a joy that she was surprised
when he began to kiss her with gratitude, as he
said, 'But you, you didn't have any pleasure.'

'Oh, yes,' said Elena, in a voice he could not
doubt.

*The warm tones and sensitive
lighting heighten the erotic impact
of this photograph, one of a series
of exceptionally fine studio nudes
by an unknown photographer,
Paris, c. 1930.*

In this extract from *Opus Pistorum*, Henry
Miller shows a visiting American his Paris flat.

Ann thinks that my apartment is very quaint and
very cozy. Everything about it is so private, she
says... she doesn't know about the parades that
troop in and out of here at the most inappropriate
times. Such a place would be just the thing for a
woman who wished to conduct an affair, wouldn't
it? And are there many such in the neighborhood?

Of course she was merely wondering...

Ann wants to know Paris better, and she has a list of questions as long as your arm. Where is this? Where does one find that? Which is the best neighborhood for thus and so? And for this first half hour that she's in my place she sits and scribbles into a note-book all the answers. She still has a lot of Paris to see before she goes home, she exclaims, and she wants to know the city from all angles. Now, where does one buy those awful post-cards?

I tell her where she can buy dirty pictures... Although how she's been here as long as she has and not met the hawkers I don't know. Then she wants to know if they are actually as bad as they're supposed to be... or are they just... risqué? She's never seen any, of course... Well, would she like to see some. Oh, I have some? Now, that's embarrassing... but she supposes that it's part of life. Yes, she ought to see them; one's education should be well rounded...

I show her the ones of Anna, give her the whole handful of them and let her go through them. She blushes as soon as she glances at the first one. Oh ... they are rather strong, aren't they? She looks at them all very quickly and then looks at them all again, very slowly... She becomes warm, glances at the fireplace, and loosens her sweater. She drinks many glasses of wine...

Getting her out of her clothes after that isn't very hard at all. A few feels and she's ready for anything ... or so she thinks. Once I've got my hand under her skirt it's clear sailing. She spreads her thighs when I feel them up and lets me take off her pants without as much as a raised eyebrow. And she's

OPPOSITE and ABOVE *Two further photographic studies in the series by an unknown Parisian photographer of c. 1930.*

Sid has a dong on that looks like something you ought to go after with a horse and a lariat, but that's just the kind Ann is looking for.

FROM *OPUS PISTORUM*
HENRY MILLER
(1891–1980)

really gotten into the spirit of those pictures, the bitch... she's so juicy between the legs that her pants are soaked, and that big cunt of hers is like a firebox...

Ann rolls back and forth on the couch while I feel her up. Oh, what would Sam think, what would he do, if he saw her now! She sticks her fist into my pants and grabs my dick. What would Sam think! This is really shameful of her... coming here to be fucked by me, leaving poor Sam to himself. She ought to be at home screwing her husband rather than here giving it to me...

Finally I let her get a taste of what she wants to feel. I kiss her squarely on the cunt, slide my tongue over the lips and in... her thighs swing wide, like a double gate that will never close again, and she gasps when I suck the juicy, hot fruit... Oh, what a feeling!... My tongue can go in deeper ... I can suck harder... she'll spread her legs further...

While Miller uses strong language and staccato rhythms to achieve his effect, Anaïs Nin moves the action forward gently, with long, dreamily orchestrated sentences. Both writers create an artificial world, but whereas Miller wants the sex scenes to be immediate and 'real', it is always clear in the writings of Anaïs Nin that we are stepping into never-never land. Her erotica is an invitation to share in her fantasies. Dreaming and sleep are recurring motifs in *Delta of Venus*: 'the dream that had grown between them', 'a dream of enveloping caresses', or more explicit fantasies.

Which of the two writers produced the better erotica? That can only be a matter of individual taste. It has to be said that as magnificent as *Tropic of Cancer* and *Tropic of Capricorn* were, some of Miller's hack work, written in difficult times, was not. But whether it was written for 'a dollar a page' or because he wanted to, his work is always bursting with humour and life. Anaïs Nin wrote some beautiful erotica but humour was not among the ingredients she used. She could also write powerfully when she wanted.

> Martha, completely naked, was behaving like a demon, climbing over him, in a frenzy of hunger for his body.
>
> FROM *DELTA OF VENUS*
> ANAÏS NIN (1903–77)

LEFT and OPPOSITE *Two more of the imaginative and effective studio photographs by an unknown Parisian photographer, c. 1930.*

CHAPTER TEN
Fantasy or Reality?

A happier face of sexuality reveals itself in *Initiation Amoureuse*, published with charming illustrations by Suzanne Ballivet in 1943. The anonymous author of this novella describes the gentle wooing of a young bride by her intelligent (and preternaturally patient) husband. This hymn to foreplay proceeds as gently as we would expect.

Two of the series of thirty lithographs, Idylle Printunière, by Rojan or Rojankowski, 1933.

I repeat my caresses of the night before on the stunning beauty of her naked bosom: gentle manual pressure, multiple fondling with my fingers, teasing with my tongue and sucking with my lips. And these caresses, emboldened by a new conquest, venture as far as her stomach, which quivers under my lips; like a minuscule lake, a little saliva shines in the hollow of her navel. Thérèse lets me do this, her arms inert, indifferent in appearance; but when my tongue, sliding across her stomach, slowly climbs towards her breasts, I see them swell with voluptuous expectation, heave with increased respiration and raise their hardened tips...

Languidly, her lips and tongue trace a thousand interweaving arabesques on my body. Then, with the supple grace of a wild animal, she comes close enough to me to press her breasts against my stomach and takes pleasure in brushing their two pointed tips against my body. Their delicate flesh feels slightly cooler than the rest of her skin.

Sometimes she brings them up as far as my mouth
and holds them there a moment to let me taste
their flushed sweetness. Sometimes she retreats as
far as my navel where she hides the little red fruit
for a second; then it's back to my lips to tirelessly
continue her game. But when she slithered
towards me on her stomach, across the bed, the
sheet slid off her rump, within close range of my
hand. It is still only partly naked, however enough
to reveal the small of her back in its harmonious
entirety and the beginning of a narrow valley.
Soon I push the sheet back; the double profile
emerges entirely in its abundant, but svelte fullness. Will Thérèse protest against the inquisitive-
ness of this action? For a moment, I fear that she
will, since right away her bottom has tensed, ready
to refuse me; but almost as soon, it relaxes, accepting its nudity under my gaze. All the same, I don't
wish to abuse my victory. Resisting the urge to
grab my voluptuous prize, I content myself with
greedily eyeing the perfection of its curves and its
mysterious line of shadow. Eventually tiring of
stroking me, Thérèse has allowed her head to fall
on to my stomach. This movement of a broken,
but somewhat erratic doll has pushed her bottom
towards me. So adjusting my position a little in
order to reach, with both hands, the coveted riches, I begin to stroke them as lightly as possible
with my fingers. The same reflex as before: the
tensing action of a modesty that would still deny
me, followed by the relaxation of a body which is
accepting of – and curious about – new sensual
delights. My hands, now bolder, knead the yielding
amplitude of her twin buttocks.

At first I follow the length of her bottom.

An original illustration by the
French artist Suzanne Ballivet
(active 1930–45) from Initiation
Amoureuse: etching with aquatint.

Another illustration by the French artist Suzanne Ballivet (active 1930–45) from Initiation Amoureuse: *etching with aquatint.*

Leaving the small of her back, my hands climb the double hill, coming down again towards the dimples which denote the beginning of her thighs. And once there, I often let my errant finger brush against the silky fleece, so close to her warm sex. But fearing my impatience, just as soon I flee this provoking contact and return to the small of her back in order to resume my amorous comings and goings. At other times, my hands move from left to right and back again, squeezing and releasing the twin globes of flesh. Flesh which is both firm and pliable at the same time and whose texture is infinitely soft to the touch. Flesh which is cooler at its peaks but warmly perspiring in its shadowy crevice. Flesh that comes alive as I stroke it, which sometimes tightens to protect the intimacy of its secret valley, but which, by contrast, relaxes in confident and visible sensuality when my hands bring these matching spheres together. In my ardent love for my wife, her enjoyment under my touch is as sweet to me as if it were my own; tirelessly I multiply my caresses. Evening is almost here when Thérèse asks me to stop, her eyes heavy with a voluptuous weariness.

Initiation Amoureuse succeeds as erotica by herding its readers together like voyeuristic old goats and leading them into the bedroom of two newly-weds. Nevertheless the book has a serious point, which it makes well, and in this respect it is in the tradition of *L'Ecole des filles*: titillation with education.

In 1945, refusing to walk any further after a two-day forced march towards Kiel, Maurice

Sachs and his male lover were shot by an SS officer. He had played many parts in his time: novitiate for the priesthood, chronicler of Paris in the Twenties, husband, collaborator, Gestapo spy. Sachs considered himself 'thoroughly defiled'. It was the right time to bring down the curtain. Maurice Sachs had been a friend of Jean Cocteau in Paris, and of many of the other homosexuals who contributed so much to the world of art and letters. This extract from his autobiography speaks for all of them.

... I knew of no more subtle master under heaven
Than is the maiden passion for a maid.

FROM *GUINEVERE*
ALFRED LORD TENNYSON (1809–92)

An etching by Suzanne Ballivet (active 1930–45) from Initiation Amoureuse.

ABOVE and BELOW *Two more original etchings by Suzanne Ballivet (active 1930–45) from* Initiation Amoureuse.

It was at this period that I experienced the first strong passion of my life. It was for a boy whom I shall call Octave. We had met at the Collège de Luza. At home, my good behavior astonished everyone; there was no need to forbid me anything now. Indeed, as soon as dinner was over, I locked myself in my room and wrote enormous letters to Octave. I was happy: he loved me too…

Blond, muscular, covered with freckles, Octave had something rather animal about him; he was if not younger, at least shorter than I, but I showed utter submission toward him, for unconsciously I had perhaps already developed a certain inferiority complex that has hampered my emotional involvements ever since, leading me to that victimization to which those who must buy love are subjected.

How had this affair begun? I no longer remember very clearly. It seems to me that I took the first step, I mean, that I wrote first. He answered, even before we had made any gesture toward each other more affectionate than those customary among schoolmates. And that was the paradoxical thing about our situation: we treated each other as 'comrades' and wrote each other so passionately that anyone would have assumed, had they read what we wrote, that we were making love every day; for we used a conventional vocabulary, as children and uneducated people always do when they are surprised by their own feelings. But such pleasures preoccupied us singularly little. Doubtless they seemed the necessary fulfillment to such ardor, but we were not in any hurry to achieve it.

During recess periods, we kept apart from the others and talked endlessly (and it seems to me today, quite intelligently for our age). Sometimes we held hands, and given our extreme youth, this did not seem at all improper. Soon, the tone of our letters mounting, Octave got in the habit of spending an hour at my house in the afternoon.

We lay together on the couch in my bedroom, rather like puppies, while playing in the fashion of lovers. I remember those afternoons with deep emotion. Enthusiasm and innocence sorted well together, and so deep was the wellspring of tenderness we felt that I don't recall we felt any real guilt at all. And if I kept the door shut, it was rather out of modesty, out of respect for this emotion which I thought deserved secrecy, and out of fear that I would be accused of laziness, for my love in itself seemed innocent and beautiful. And if I felt some sense of inferiority, it was only toward

An illustration for his autobiographical account of homosexuality Le Livre Blanc *by Jean Cocteau (1889–1963).*

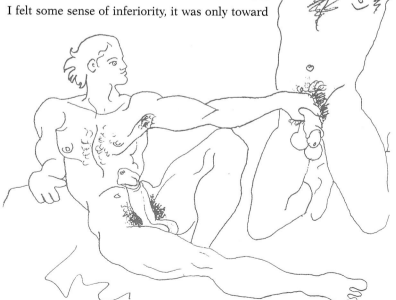

this friend of whom I considered myself unworthy, for I thought him more handsome, more charming, more sensitive than myself.

I shall not claim that this relationship was entirely chaste. But I recall that we were not at all eager to seal it in the pleasure of the flesh, so greatly did we enjoy the exaltation of those embraces without any declared purpose, without ulterior motive. The day we touched each other more intimately we added nothing to our happiness, for at that age tenderness can still do without possession.

If the reader grants with me that the whole of our life is nothing more than an attempt to fulfill the dreams of our youth, he will understand that it is possible to search throughout the whole of one's life for a happiness one has enjoyed as a child.

For me, the memory of Octave and the endless, perhaps futile search for another Octave all too like the original confirmed me in my homosexual appetites and I no longer believe myself capable of other pleasures of the heart and of the body. Doubtless there is some infantilism in this, as the psychiatrists call it, and doubtless I would have rediscovered these innocent pleasures that Octave afforded me, so gentle yet so sensual, much more certainly in the arms of a woman my own age twenty years later.

But this is beyond my powers. I do not *believe*, in other words I do not believe that a woman can ever be Octave. She cannot even pretend to be.

A drawing by Jean Cocteau (1889–1963).

The writing of Violette Leduc (1907–72) is fierce, sad stuff. But it is a voice which Albert Camus – publisher of her first novel –

thought we should hear. This extract from her autobiographical novel *La Bâtarde*, although it takes place in a girls' dormitory, is a very long way from the jolly hockey-sticks world of Angela Brazil.

Abbandono, *contemporary photograph by Giovanni Zuin.*

Her hand undressed my arm, halted near the vein in the crook of the elbow, fornicated there among the traceries, moved downward to the wrist, right to the tips of the nails, sheathed my arm once more in a long suede glove, fell from my shoulder like an insect, and hooked itself into the armpit. I was stretching my neck, listening for what answers my arm gave the adventuress. The hand, still seeking to persuade me, was bringing my arm, my armpit, into their real existence. The hand travelled over the chatter of white bushes, over the last frosts on the meadows, over the first buds as they swelled to fullness. Spring that had been chirping with impatience under my skin was now bursting forth into lines, curves, roundnesses. Isabelle, stretched out upon the darkness, was fastening my feet with ribbons, unravelling the swaddling bands of my alarm. With hands laid flat upon the mattress, I was immersed in the self-same magic as she. She was kissing what she had caressed, and then, lightly, her hand ruffled and whisked with the feathers of perversity. The octopus in my entrails quivered. Isabelle was drinking at my breast, the right, the left, and I drank with her, sucking the milk of darkness when her lips had gone. The fingers were returning now, encircling and testing the warm weight of my breast. The fingers were pretending to be waifs in a storm; they were taking shelter inside me. A host of slaves, all with the face of Isabelle, fanned my brow, my hands.

A brilliantly executed drawing by Mario Tauzin, active in Paris in the 1920s. The artist's controlled use of line, careful exaggeration, and stylistic tricks such as luring the viewer's eye to the erotic focus with shading, owe much to the shunga tradition of Japan.

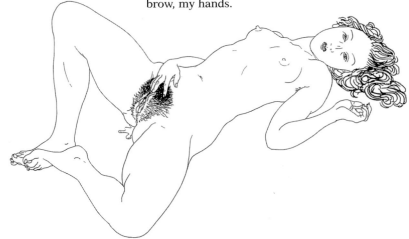

She knelt up in the bed.

'Do you love me?'

I led her hand up to the precious tears of joy.

Her cheek took shelter in the hollow of my groin, I shone the torch on her, and saw her spreading hair, saw my own belly beneath the rain of silk. The torch slipped, Isabelle moved suddenly toward me.

As we melted into one another we were dragged up to the surface by the hooks caught in our flesh, by the hairs we were clutching in our fingers; we were rolling together on a bed of nails. We bit each other and bruised the darkness with our hands.

Slowing down, we trailed back beneath our plumes of smoke, black wings sprouting at our heels. Isabelle leaped out of bed.

I wondered why Isabelle was doing her hair again. With one hand she forced me to lie on my back, with the other, to my distress, she shone the pale yellow beam of the torch on me. I tried to shield myself with my arms. 'I'm not beautiful. You make me feel ashamed,' I said. She was looking at our future in my eyes, she was gazing at what was going to happen next, storing it in the currents of her blood.

She got back into bed, she wanted me.

I played with her, preferring failure to the preliminaries she needed. Making love with our mouths was enough for me: I was afraid, but my hands as they signalled for help were helpless stumps. A pair of paint brushes was advancing into the folds of my flesh. My heart was beating under its molehill, my head was crammed with damp earth. Two tormenting fingers were exploring me. How masterly, how inevitable their caress

ABOVE and OPPOSITE
Contemporary photographs by
China Hamilton, Suffolk, England.

... My closed eyes listened: the finger lightly touched the pearl. I wanted to be wider, to make it easier for her.

The regal, diplomatic finger was moving forward, moving back, making me gasp for breath, beginning to enter, arousing the tentacles in my entrails, parting the secret cloud, pausing, prompting once more. I tightened, I closed over this flesh of my flesh, its softness and its bony core. I sat up, I fell back again. The finger which had not wounded me, the finger, after its grateful exploration, left me. My flesh peeled back from it.

'Do you love me?' I asked.

I wanted to create a diversion.

'You mustn't cry out,' Isabelle said.

I crossed my arms over my face, still listening under my lowered eyelids.

Two thieves entered me. They were forcing their way inside, they wanted to go further, but my flesh rebelled.

'My love... you're hurting me.'

She put her hand over my mouth.

'I won't make any noise,' I said.

The gag was a humiliation.

'It hurts. But she's got to do it. It hurts.'

I gave myself up to the darkness and without wanting to, I helped. I leaned forward to help tear myself, to come closer to her face, to be nearer my wound: she pushed me back on the pillow. She was thrusting, thrusting, thrusting... I could hear the smacking noise it made. She was putting out the eye of innocence. It hurt me: I was moving on to my deliverance, but I couldn't see what was happening.

We listened to the sleeping girls around us, we

sobbed as we sucked in our breath. A trail of fire still burned inside me.

'Let's rest,' she said.

The *Story of O* appeared in Paris in 1954. Its origins are still unclear, but we know that it was written by a woman who used the pseudonym 'Pauline Réage'. Uniquely, for a book dealing with bondage, flagellation and the outer limits of sexual behaviour, *Story of 0* has received serious critical attention and praise. A lot of this has to do with the cool, elegant prose which distances the novel from obscenity.

Her lover one day takes O for a walk, but this time in a part of the city – the Parc Montsouris, the parc Monceau – where they've never been together before. After they've strolled awhile along the paths, after they've sat down side by side on a bench near the grass, and got up again, and moved on towards the edge of the park, there, where two streets meet, where there never used to be any taxi-stand, they see a car, at that corner. It looks like a taxi, for it does have a meter. 'Get in,' he says; she gets in. It's late in the afternoon, it's autumn. She is wearing what she always wears: high heels, a suit with a pleated skirt, a silk blouse, no hat. But she has on long gloves reaching up to the sleeves of her jacket, in her leather handbag she's got her papers, and her compact and lipstick. The taxi eases off, very slowly; nor has the man next to her said a word to the driver. But on the right, on the left, he draws down the little window-shades, and the one behindtoo; thinking that he is about to kiss her, or so as to caress him, she has slipped off her

gloves. Instead, he says: 'I'll take your bag, it's in your way.' She gives it to him, he puts it beyond her reach; then adds: 'You've too much clothing on. Unhitch your stockings, roll them down to just above your knees. Go ahead,' and he gives her some elastics to hold the stockings in place. It isn't easy, not in the car, which is going faster now, and she doesn't want to have the driver turn around. But she manages anyhow, at last; it's a queer, uncomfortable feeling, the contact of silk of her slip upon her naked and free legs, and the unattached garters are sliding loosely back and forth across her skin. 'Undo your garter-belt,' he says, 'take off your panties.' There's nothing to that, all she has to do is get at the hook behind and raise up a little. He takes the garter-belt from her hand, he takes the panties, opens her bag, puts them away inside it; then he says: 'You're not to sit on your slip or on your skirt, pull them up and sit on the seat without anything in between.' The seat-covering is a sort of leather, slick and chilly; it's a very strange sensation, the way it sticks and clings to her thighs. Then he says: 'Now put your gloves back on.' The taxi goes right along and she doesn't dare ask why Rene is so quiet, so still, or what all this means to him: she so motionless and so silent, so denuded and so offered, though so thoroughly gloved, in a black car going she hasn't the least idea where. He hasn't told her to do anything or not to do it, but she doesn't dare either cross her legs or sit with them held together. One on this side, one on that side, she rests her gloved hands on the scat, pushing down.

'Here we are,' he says all of a sudden. Here we are: the taxi comes to a stop on a fine avenue,

ABOVE and OPPOSITEE *Two more images in the sequence of contemporary photographs by China Hamilton.*

A photograph by China Hamilton, Suffolk, England.

under a tree – those are plane trees – in front of a small mansion, you could just see it, nestled away between courtyard and garden, the way the Faubourg Saint-Germain mansions are. There's no streetlight nearby, it is dark inside the cab, and outside rain is falling. 'Don't move,' said Rene. 'Don't move a muscle.' He extends his hand towards the neck of her blouse, unties the ribbon at the throat, then unbuttons the buttons. She leans forward ever so little, and believes he is about to caress her breasts. But no; he's got a small penknife out, he's only groping for the shoulder-straps of her brassiere, he cuts the straps, removes the brassiere. He has closed her blouse again and now, underneath, her breasts are free and nude, like her belly and thighs are nude and free, like all of her is, from waist to knee.

'Listen,' he says. 'You're ready. Here's where I leave you. You're going to get out and go to the door and ring the bell. Someone will open the door, whoever it is you'll do as he says. You'll do it right away and willingly of your own accord'...

And so O enters an alternative world, a novitiate, abandoning one life and all its trappings, to wear new clothes and live by strict newrules: she does this of her own free will and all because of love. Or, since this famous erotic novel has alternative beginnings, O steps through the looking glass into a sado-masochistic pantomime, produced in a madhouse and utterly devoid of humour.

The costumes and rituals, which are such an essential part of the sexuality explored in the *Story of O*, are described with scrupulous attention to detail: colours, textures and shapes are all defined, all carefully chosen. After an elaborate toilette O learns that concepts such as jealousy and possession have no place in her new world. As each new dignity and supposed right is stripped away from our heroine, with only love remaining at the centre and that always untouched, we become aware that a curious sense of morality pervades the book.

> The bonds of wedlock are so heavy that it takes two to carry them – sometimes three.
>
> ALEXANDRE DUMAS
> (1802–70)

Erica Jong has said: 'I wrote *Fear of Flying* in a mad rush, heart racing, adrenaline pumping, wanting to tell the truth about women whatever it cost me.' Millions of readers are very happy that Erica Jong (b. 1942) took that chance in 1973. In a preface written to mark twenty years of continual reprinting the author said that her novel 'had become a rallying cry for women who wanted the right to have fantasies as rich and raunchy as those of men'. The heroine of *Fear of Flying*, the intrepid Isadora Wing, explores every aspect and application of erotic fantasy in her search for fulfilment.

A drypoint etching from France, c. 1960.

I shut my eyes tightly and pretended that Bennett was Adrian. I transformed B into A. We came – first me, then Bennett – and lay there sweating on the awful hotel bed. Bennett smiled. I was miserable. What a fraud I was! Real adultery couldn't be worse than these nightly deceptions. To fuck one man and think of another and keep the deception a secret – it was far, far worse than fucking another man within your husband's sight. It was as bad as any betrayal I could think of. 'Only a fantasy,' Bennett would probably say. 'A fantasy is only

Curiosita, *a photograph by Giovanni Zuin.*

a fantasy, and everyone has fantasies. Only psychopaths actually act out all their fantasies; normal people don't.'

But I have more respect for fantasy than that. You are what you dream. You are what you daydream. Masters and Johnson's charts and numbers and flashing lights and plastic pricks tell us everything about sex and nothing about it. Because sex is all in the head. Pulse rates and secretions have nothing to do with it. That's why all the best-selling sex manuals are such gyps. They teach people how to fuck with their pelvises, not with their heads.

What did it matter that technically I was 'faithful' to Bennett? What did it matter that I hadn't screwed another guy since I met him? I was unfaithful to him at least ten times a week in my thoughts – and at least five of those times I was unfaithful to him while he and I were screwing.

Maybe Bennett was pretending I was someone else, too. But so what? That was his problem. And doubtless 99 per cent of the people in the world were fucking phantoms. They probably were. That didn't comfort me at all. I despised my own deceitfulness and I despised myself. I was already an adulteress, and was only holding off the actual consummation out of cowardice. That made me an adulteress and a coward (cowardess?). At least if I fucked Adrian I'd only be an adulteress (adult?).

Erica Jong's achievement in cramming so many facets of the sexual debate into such a readable, funny novel should not be underestimated. Furthermore, in creating a heroine with whom readers can identify she has made it a genuinely enabling book. In this final extract, male writing about female sexuality receives close scrutiny, as do sex education and Steve Applebaum.

Nay, slay me now; nay, for I will be slain
Pluck thy red pleasure/rom the teeth of pain,
Break down thy vine 'ere yet grape-gatherers prune,
Stay me 'ere day can slay desire again;
Ah God, ah God, that day should be so soon.

FROM *THE ORCHARD*
ALGERNON SWINBURNE (1837-1909)

SEX. I was terrified of the tremendous power it had over me. The energy, the excitement, the power to make me feel totally crazy! What about that? How do you make that jibe with 'playing hard to get'?

I never had the courage to ask my mother directly. I sensed, despite her bohemian talk, that she disapproved of sex, that it was basically unmentionable. So I turned to D. H. Lawrence, and to *Love Without Fear*, and to *Coming of Age in Samoa*. Margaret Mead wasn't much help. What did I have in common with all those savages? (Plenty, of course, but at the time I didn't realize it.) Eustace Chesser, M.D., was good on all the fascinating details ('How to Manage the Sex Act,' penetration, foreplay, afterglow), but he didn't seem to have much to say about my moral dilemmas: how 'far' to go? inside the bra or outside? inside the pants or outside? inside the mouth or outside? When to swallow, if ever. It was all so complicated. And it seemed so much more complicated for women. Basically, I think, I was furious with my mother for not teaching me how to be a woman, for not teaching me how to make peace between the raging hunger in my cunt and the hunger in my head.

So I learned about women from men. I saw them through the eyes of male writers. Of course, I didn't think of them as male writers. I thought of

Sogno *a photograph by*
Giovanni Zuin.

them as writers, as authorities, as gods who knew and were to be trusted completely.

Naturally I trusted everything they said, even when it implied my own inferiority. I learned what an orgasm was from D. H. Lawrence, disguised as Lady Chatterley. I learned from him that all women worship 'the Phallos' – as he so quaintly spelled it. I learned from Shaw that women never can be artists; I learned from Dostoyevsky that they have no religious feeling; I learned from Swift and Pope that they have too much religious feeling (and therefore can never be quite rational); I learned from Faulkner that they are earth mothers and at one with the moon and the tides and the crops; I learned from Freud that they have deficient superegos and are ever 'incomplete' because they lack the one thing in this world worth having: a penis.

But what did all this have to do with me – who went to school and got better marks than the boys and painted and wrote and spent Saturdays doing still lifes at the Art Students League and my weekday afternoons editing the high-school paper (Features Editor; the Editor-in-Chief had never been a girl – though it also never occurred to us then to question it)? What did the moon and tides and earth-mothering and the worship of the Lawrentian 'phallos' have to do with me or with my life?

I met my first 'phallos' at thirteen years and ten months on my parents' avocado-green silk living-room couch, in the shade of an avocado-green avocado tree, grown by my avocado green thumbed mother from an avocado pit. The 'phallos' belonged to Steve Applebaum, a junior and art major when I was a freshman and art major, and it had a most memorable abstract design of blue veins on its Kandinsky-purple underside. In retrospect, it was a remarkable specimen: circumcised, of course, and huge (what is huge when you have no frame of reference?), and with an impressive life of its own. As soon as it began to make its drumlin-like presence known under the tight zipper of Steve's chinos (we were necking and 'petting-below-the-waist' as one said then), he would slowly unzip (so as not to snag it?) and with one hand (the other was under my skirt and up my cunt) extract the huge purple thing from between the layers of his shorts, his blue Brooks-Brothers shirttails, and his cold, glittering, metal-zippered fly. Then I would dip one hand into the vase of roses my flower-loving mother always kept on the coffee table, and with a right hand moistened with water and the slime from their stems, I would proceed with my rhythmic jerking off of Steve. How exactly did I do it? Three fingers? Or the whole palm? I suppose I must have been rough at first (though later I became an expert). He would throw his head back in ecstasy (but controlled ecstasy: my father was watching TV in the dining room) and would come into his Brooks-Brothers shirttails or into a handkerchief quickly produced for the purpose. The technique I have forgotten, but the feeling remains. Partly, it was reciprocity (tit for tat, or clit for tat), but it was also power. I knew that what I was doing gave me a special kind of power over him – one that painting or writing couldn't approach. And then I was coming too – maybe not like Lady Chatterley, but it was something.

An illustration by G. de Sainte-Croix (active 1949–59 in France); drypoint, hand-coloured in aquatint.

Today there is an explosion of new erotic fiction. A thousand voices, beautiful and thrilling, vicious and tuneless, clamour to be heard. Pens explore every erogenous crevice, word processing facilitates the birth of the good, the bad and the ugly without discrimination.

Subniv Babuta's first novel, *The Still Point*, was published in 1991. An extract from it makes a fitting conclusion to this book, pointing as it does to a hopeful future for erotic literature while recalling that the first humane writing about sexuality came out of India. Two young Westerners make love in today's India, while nine centuries

RIGHT and OPPOSITE *Illustrations by G. de Sainte-Croix (active 1949–59 in France); drypoint, hand-coloured in aquatint.*

earlier the old temple architect and sculptor Srivastava has a vision of their lovemaking.

Max knew he was being watched. But he often had this feeling when making love to Imogen, and it was never anything more than a figment of his imagination. He was, once again, above her. He could see her perfectly, his own shadow shielding her face from the fierce sun above them. Max bent down and kissed her, searching her mouth with his tongue. Moments later, he pulled away, and let his tongue begin to explore her neck, which Imogen stretched to its full length as she arched her body backwards.

She tasted bitter, and the saline savour, coupled with the aroma rising from lower down, quickened Max's desire. As he traced a path with his tongue between her breasts, he slid his whole body down. Over the ridges he continued, sucking the skin until the blood rose to the surface. Imogen held onto Max's shoulders, restraining him. Then she released him, and he worked his way down, pushing his tongue into the crevices formed beneath each

Anja, a sculpture in alabaster by the contemporary German artist Arpad Safranek.

breast, then going on to trace intricate invisible patterns on Imogen's stomach. He felt her hands urging him to go lower, but he waited, resting his cheek on her waist. Max closed his eyes, breathing in the juices deeply, feeding on their promise. Then, almost imperceptibly, he began to descend. Max's tongue moved from the smooth surface of Imogen's womb, into a tiny thicket of soft hair. Slowly and deliberately, he licked each strand dry. Eventually, he reached the crevice between his lover's legs and, frantically, Imogen pressed his head into her, twisting strands of his hair in her fingers. With his tongue, Max pushed aside the soft folds of flesh, feeling at last the warm fluid flowing over his lips.

Imogen relaxed. As soon as she relinquished her hold over herself, the tiny disparate fires that the firefly had set alight inside her suddenly gathered force, and exploded. Wave after wave of fire rushed through Imogen's body. She held Max's head down, drawing it in with her thighs. As he sucked deeper and deeper, so Imogen surrendered to the raging within her.

Srivastava felt the dream slipping from him. The image of the lovers was beginning to fade, and he knew that soon he must leave this place and return to the world of his labours. He was satisfied that he now possessed the visions he would sculpt. He turned to leave the hall through the archway he had entered. But something held Srivastava back. On an impulse, the old man turned back again, and keeping his eyes fixed on the empty alcove on the wall, walked over to it. He touched the smooth plaster. It was still soft and supple, and the sculptor's finger left a tiny trench where he had traced it. Srivastava caressed the wet wall softly, as if stroking a delicate

Torso *by A. Klinkenberg,*
contemporary.

animal. As his eyes looked down, he noticed a pebble at its base. Instinctively, he bent down and picked it up. Its sharp point formed a perfect nib with which to inscribe the plaster. Srivastava smoothed the wall with his hand just below the base of the alcove. Here, deliberately, and with a craftsman's practised care, he took the pebble and began to cut the intricate outlines of Sanskrit characters into the stonework. The pebble sliced easily through the smooth skin. One by one the shapes appeared. Srivastava knew that such a liberty with the Prince's temple would be forbidden him in reality, but here, in his sleeping vision, the old man was master. With a steady hand, Srivastava finished off the word that he had been compelled to write. VIDHI. As the sculptor stepped back to examine his handiwork, his lips formed the sound. 'Vidhi,' he whispered silently to himself. Destiny.

Max pushed further and further into the soft flesh. Imogen had begun to convulse gently, pulling him in, then pushing him away in a regular rhythm. Her hands grasped Max firmly, afraid that he might withdraw. He could feel her gasping for breath. But now Imogen pulled him up sharply, guiding his head the full length of her body, forcing him to shift his body awkwardly and rise once more onto her. As he covered her, Max felt Imogen pull his still glistening mouth hungrily onto her own. At the same time, her hand searched lower down, beneath their waists. Gradually, her firm sensitive fingers tightened on Max, guiding him once again inside her. He felt her thighs shuddering against him. Her gasping became desperate, yet she refused to release her lover's mouth. Her heart pounded with a deafening rhythm.

As Max thrust, and thrust again, Imogen rushed to the edge of the precipice, and looked down into the chasms of fire at her feet. Yet she clung for a moment longer. Together, they would plunge into the inferno. Each tiny movement brought Max closer. He felt her waiting for him. Higher and higher he pushed. Still she waited. Finally, Max too could see the edge of the precipice: as he caught sight of the blazing sea beneath the cliff, he rushed forward with a final explosion of energy, grabbed Imogen as she waited on the edge, and leapt into the chasm.

> *Out of a misty dream*
> *Our path emerges for a while, then closes*
> *Within a dream.*
>
> FROM *VITAE SUMMA BREVIS*
> ERNEST DOWSON (1867–1900)

For a moment, the two bodies, fused together on the dusty patch of grass, stopped. All sound ceased. The breeze did not blow, the dust froze. Even the birds, hiding from the sun in shady nooks, arrested their fidgeting. The shadows on the ground, lengthening each second, held their shapes one instant longer. Into the stillness a shot was fired. The noise tore through the silence, and sound rushed back in through the hole in the vacuum. Birds, startled by the explosion, took off, flapping their wings frantically. The sand began its meanderings once more, blown into flurries and eddies by a new wind. The sun continued on its relentless journey, and the shadows lengthened once more.

Imogen felt the surge deep inside her, and screamed silently. Though audible to no human ear, her cry reached every corner of the derelict temple. The carvings, motionless and inert, safe within their alcoves, heard the song, and for a moment their own sculpted passion came to life.

COLLECTING EROTIC ART

By James Maclean

At its best, erotic art is one of the most direct manifestations of our response to the life force. It is a celebration of our most fundamental and enjoyable instincts; a celebration which can enhance the experience of those fortunate enough to have access to it.

This genre of art is the only surviving area of man's creativity in which objects of exceptional power and beauty have been secreted away – for diverse cultural reasons – from the scrutiny of the vast majority of people. It has an earthy candour not often found in other, more formal artistic categories such as portraiture or still-life; it can give us a valuable insight into the sexual politics of the day or afford access to the secret world of an artist's innermost thoughts.

Because of censorship and repression, much erotic art has been destroyed; the rest usually remains hidden from public view. In the nineteenth century, rich individuals such as the Russian Prince Galitzin accumulated such a magnificent hoard of erotic works that it occupied two catalogues and several hundred pages when dispersed by auction sale in 1887. The widow of the great explorer and collector of erotica, Sir Richard Burton, on the other hand, incinerated his important collection when he died in 1890, and only two years earlier a London publisher, Henry Vizctelly, had been imprisoned as an old man for printing Zola's La Terre, despite the protests of the artistic and literary world of the time. The Royal Collection, the Vatican and a number of major museums around the world have great but concealed collections. The sub rosa, under-the-counter attitudes

that persist in most museums about their erotic trea-
sures are therefore doubly infuriating. Few, if any,
major museums would have the bravery to put on a
comprehensive exhibition of erotic works.

Historically, the market for erotic art has been
clandestine and all but non-existent; the market-
place remains tiny thanks to a noticeable reluctance
on the part of most media to let their readers or
viewers be exposed to this sort of thing. But there are
ways to build a collection. It is worth viewing auction sales when possible, but this is a time-consum-
ing, though pleasant, occupation: very few auction
houses have specialist sales of erotica.

Some picture dealers and antiquarian book-sellers
specialize in erotic art, but these again need to be
winkled out. Some publishers of facsimile prints
spend years of research assembling enough material
to grant their membership access to limited editions
of the world's finest existing erotica.

These are produced, often in small numbers, using
the newest technology but with faithfulness to the
quality and character of the originals. The prints
offered by The Erotic Print Society, for example,
span a period from the sixteenth century to the present day. Their first portfolio of prints by a contemporary artist, Monica Guevara (*see right*), has proved
to be an enormous success. The majority of the
drawings and prints in this part are from the collection of The Erotic Print Society.

Another way of collecting erotica is to buy high-
quality prints of the work of contemporary photographers from specialist photographic galleries such
as the Akehurst Bureau in London. Finally, you can
of course become part of the age-old – and very
important – system of artistic patronage by simply

buying the work of young artists. Arpad Safranek of Viersen in Germany produces bronzes (*see left*) of the exquisite alabaster sculpture on page 388. Only if contemporary artists of talent are encouraged will our culture leave a legacy of erotic art for future generations to enjoy.

The Erotic Print Society's website is:
http://www.eroticprints.org
Email: eps@leadline.co.uk
Freephone orderline: (UK only) 0800 026 25 24
Fax: 0044 (0)871 575 0080
Post: EPS, 54 New Street, Worcester WR1 2DL
Their 172-page colour catalogue costs £10.00
including p&p plus a free copy of the Society's
literary and arts erotic magazine SEx.

James Maclean, formerly of Sotheby's, is a leading
expert on erotic art.

ACKNOWLEDGEMENTS

The material in this volume has been compiled from a series of three original volumes, and the organization of the acknowledgements reflects this. Bibliographical details of the excerpts are given with copyright notices and permissions indicated. Every effort has been made to acknowledge the copyright of the material used but where this has proved impossible the copyright owner is invited to contact Eddison Sadd Editions.

Part One

Authors

Wystan Hugh Auden (1907–73) English (later naturalized American) poet.

William Blake (1757–1827) English poet and artist.

Giovanni Boccaccio (1313–75) Italian writer, wrote the *Decamaron* in 1348–53.

Giovanni Giacomo Casanova, *Chevalier de Seingalt* (1725–98) Italian adventurer, gambler, spy, writer and librarian.

C. P. Cavafy (1863–1933) Greek poet who lived mainly in Alexandria.

Nicolas Chorier (late seventeenth–early eighteenth century) French writer.

John Cleland (1709–89) English novelist; he wrote *Fanny Hill*.

e. e. cummings (1894–1962) American poet whose work experimented with typographical effects.

Ernest Dowson (1867–1900) English poet, friend of Yeats.

Sigmund Freud (1856–1939) Austrian psychiatrist and psychoanalyst.

Robert Graves (1895–1985) English poet and novelist, author of *The White Goddess*.

Frank Harris (1856–1931) Writer and newspaper editor; born in Ireland; lived in London and USA.

Robert Herrick (1591–1674) English poet.

James Joyce (1882–1941) Irish novelist; he wrote *Ulysses* in 1922.

David Herbert Lawrence (1885–1930) British novelist; wrote *Lady Chatterley's Lover*.

Henry Miller (1891–1980) American novelist, author of *Tropic of Cancer* and *Tropic of Capricorn*.

Pablo Neruda (1904–73) Chilean poet and diplomat who won the Nobel Prize in 1971.

Anais Nin (1903–77) French writer, brought up in New York.

Octavio Paz (b. 1914) Mexican poet and diplomat.

Pierre de Ronsard (1524–85) French poet.

Christina Rossetti (1830–74) English poet; sister of Dante Gabriel.

Robin Skelton (b. 1925) Canadian poet.

Algernon Charles Swinburne (1837–1909) English Decadent poet.

Paul Verlaine (1844–96) French poet, leading light of the Symbolists.

Oscar Wilde (1854–1900) English dramatist of Irish ancestry, born in Dublin; imprisoned for homosexuality.

John Wilmot, Earl of Rochester (1647–80) English poet at court of Charles II.

Artists

Franz von Bayros (1866–1924) German painter and illustrator.

Aubrey Beardsley (1872–98) English Decadent

illustrator, contributor to the *Yellow Book*.

Antoine Borel (1743–1810) French artist.

Carl Breuer–Courth Early twentieth- century German painter and illustrator.

Jaques Philippe Caresme (1734–96) French artist.

Agostino Carracci (1557–1602) Italian painter and engraver.

Louis Corinth (1858–1925) German painter.

Theo van Elsen Indonesian-born illustrator working in Paris in the 1930s.

Peter Fendi (1796–1842) Austrian artist.

Henry Fuseli (1741–1825) Swiss-born British artist.

Paul Gavarni (1804–66) French illustrator.

Giulio Romano (1492/9–1546) Italian Mannerist painter and architect.

Julius Klinger Twentieth-century German artist.

Henry Lemort Early twentieth-century Freneli artist.

Martin van Made Early twentieth-century Belgian engraver.

Johannes Martini (1866–early twentieth- century) German artist.

Louis Morin (1851– early twentieth- century) Belgian painter.

Joseph Ortloff Early twentieth-century German artist.

Paul Paede (1868–1929) German artist.

Georges Pavis Early twentieth-century French artist.

M. E. Phillipp German

engraver active at the beginning of the twentieth century.

Leon Richet Late nineteenth-century French artist.

Félicien Rops (1835–98) Belgian painter, engraver and illustrator.

Thomas Rowlandson (1756–1827) English painter, illustrator and caricaturist.

Mario Tauzin (b. 1910) Parisian artist.

Utamaro Utagawa (1753–1806) Japanese woodcut artist.

Marcel Vértes (1895–1961) French artist.

Mihály Ziehy (1827–1906) Hungarian painter.

Sources

Poems of Amaru and Mayura from the Sanscrit; Geisha Songs from the Japanese; song from French Indo–China, trails. E. Powys Mathers in Eastern Love, privately printed in London, 1920s.

W. H. Auden, Lullaby. From *Collected Shorter Poems 1927–57*, © 1940, 1968. By permission of Faber and Faber Ltd, London.

William Blake, Visions of the *Daughters of Albion*. c. 1793.

Boccaccio, *Decameron*. Trans. J. M. Rigg for Navarre Society. (Also published by Penguin Books.)

The Boudoir: Voluptuous Confessions of a French Lady of Fashion. British Library. (Also published by Star Books/W. H. Allen, London; Grove Press, Inc, New York.)

Casanova, *History of My Life (Memoirs)*. Trans. W. R. Trask. By permission of Penguin Books Ltd and Harcourt Brace Jovanovich, New York.

C. P. Cavafy, *One Night*. Trans. John Mavrogordato. By permission of the C. P. Cavaty Estate and The Hogarth Press, London. Also *He Came to Read*. Trans. John Mavrogordato. Reprinted by permission of the C. P. Cavafy Estate and The Hogarth Press, London.

Chin P'ing Mei, trans. as *The Golden Lotus* by Clement Egerton, 1939. By permission of Penguin Books Ltd, London.

Nicolas Chorier, *Satyra Sotadica*. 1660. English trans. in British Library, 1682, 1740, 1786; original in Bibliothèque Nationale, Paris.

John Cleland, *Fanny Hill – Memoirs of a Woman of Pleasure*. British Library. (Also published by Penguin Books/ Mayflower.)

e. e. cummings, *may i feel said he*. From *Complete Poems 1913–1962*. By permission of MacGibbon & Kee, an imprint of HarperCollins Publishers Limited, and Liveright Publishing Corporation, USA.

Ernest Dowson, *Days of Wine and Roses*.

Sigmund Freud, from *Complete Works*, trans. and ed. James Strachey. W. W. Norton Co., New York.

Robert Graves, *Down, Wanton, Down!* From *Collected Poems 1975*. By permission of A. P. Watt Ltd, London, on behalf

of the Trustees of the Robert Graves Copyright Trust, and Oxford University Press. New York.

Frank Harris, *My Life and Loves*. © 1925 Frank Harris, © 1953 Nellie Harris, © 1963 by Arthur Leonard Ross as Executor of the Frank Harris Estate. Copyright renewed © 1991 by Ralph d. Ross and Edgar M. Ross. Used by permission of Grove Press, Inc., New York.

Ikkyu, *Kyounshu*. Trans. Don Sanderson.

James Joyce, *Ulysses*. Copyright 1934 and renewed 1962 by Lucia and George Joyce. Reproduced by permission of Random House Inc.

D. H. Lawrence, *Lady Chatterley's Lover*. Reprinted by permission of Laurence Pollinger Ltd, London, and the Estate of Frieda Lawrence Ravagli. Published by Penguin Books. Also *New Year's Eve*. By permission of Laurence Pollinger Ltd, London, and the Estate of Frieda Lawrence Ravagli. Also *Fidelity*. By permission of Laurence Pollinger Ltd, London, and the Estate of Frieda Lawrence Ravagli.

Kalyana Malla, *Ananga– Ranga*. Trans. Burton and Arbuthnot for the Kama Shastra Society, London. (Also published by Hamlyn.)

Henry Miller, *Plexus*. Copyright © The Estate of Henry Miller. Reproduced with permission of Grove Press, Inc., New York, and Curtis Brown group Ltd, London. Also *Tropic of Cancer*. Copyright © the Estate of Henry Miller. Reproduced with

permission of Grove Press, Inc, New York, and Curtis Brown Group Ltd, London.

Pablo Neruda, *Lone Gentleman*. Trans. N. Tarn. From *Selected Poems by Pablo Neruda*, ed. Nathaniel Tarn, © 1970, by permission of Jonathan Cape Ltd, London.

Sheikh Nefzawi, *The Perfumed Garden*. Trans. Richard Burton for the Kama Shastra Society, London. (Also published by Hamlyn.)

Anais Nin, *Delta of Venus*, © Anais Nin 1969, © The Anais Nin Trust, 1977. By permission of Penguin Books Ltd, London and Harcourt Brace Jovanovich Inc, New York. Published 1990 by Penguin Books.

Octavio Paz, *Touch*. From *Configurations*, trans. Charles Tomlinson. © 196S Octavio Paz and Charles Tomlinson. Reprinted by permission of Laurence Pollinger Ltd, London.

Pauline Réage, *Story of O*. Published by Société Nouvelle des Editions J.–J. Pauvert, Paris, 1954. (Also published by Corgi, London.)

Pierre de Ronsard, *Corinna in Vendome*. Trans.Robert Mezey. From *The Penguin Rook of Love Poetry*, 1973, by permission of Penguin Books Ltd.

Christina Rossetti, *Goblin Market*. 1862.

Edward Sellon, Letter to H. S. Ashbee. From *Index Librorum Prohibitorum* by Pisanus Fraxi, ed. H. S. Ashbee. British Library.

Robin Skelton, *Because of Love*. By permission of the author and McClclland & Stewart, Inc, Canada.

The Song of Songs (The Song of Solomon). From The Bible.

Algernon Charles Swinburne, *Love and Sleep*.

Vatsyayana, *Kama Sutra*. Trans. Burton and Arbuthnot for the Kama Shastra Society, London. (Also published by Unwin & Hyman, and Hamlyn.)

Paul Verlaine, *Anointed Vessel*. From *Femmes Hommes/ Women Men*, trans. Alistair Elliot, published in 1979 by Anvil Press Poetry, London; Sheep Meadow Press, New York. Also, *A Brief Moral*. From *Femmes Hommes/ Women Men*, trans. Alistair Elliot, published in 1979 by Anvil Press Poetry, London; Sheep Meadow Press, New York.

'Walter', *My Secret Life*. British Library; reprinted by Grove Press, Inc, New York.

Oscar Wilde et al., *Teleny or The Reverse of the Medal*. 1893. British Library. (Also published by Grove Press Inc, New York.)

John Wilmot, Earl of Rochester, *A Ramble in St James's Park*.

Thanks are also due to the staff of the British Library and the Bodleian Library, Oxford.

The majority of the illustrations in this part are reproduced by kind permission of the Klinger Collection, Nuremburg, Germany. Eddison Sadd is also grateful to: the Akehurst Gallery © Giovanni Zuin (page 6); the Naturhistorisches Museum, Vienna, for the Venus of Willendorf (page 9); the Noel Rands Collection (page 116).

Part Two

Authors
Agathias (sixth century AD) Byzantine Greek poet and philosopher.
Pietro Aretino (1492–1557) Italian playwright and poet.
Marquis d'Argans Jean–Baptiste de Boyer (1704–71) French writer and political pamphleteer.
John Berger (b. 1926) British novelist and art critic.
Giovanni Boccaccio (1313–75)
James Boswell (1740–95) Scottish writer and lawyer, author of biography of Dr Samuel Johnson.
Restif de la Bretonne (1734–1806) French novelist and diarist.
Robert Browning (1812–89) English poet.
Robert Burns (1759–96) Scottish poet, regarded as the national poet.
Giovanni Giacomo Casanova, Chevalier de Seingalt (1725–98)
Armand Coppens (mid-twentieth–century) Belgian writer and bookseller.
Johann Wolfgang von Goethe (1749–1832) German scholar, poet and statesman; his greatest work, *Faust*, was published 1808.
Robert Graves (1895–1985)
Frank Harris (1856–1931)
Heinrich Heine (1797–1850) German Romantic poet.
Erica Jong (b. 1942) American novelist and poet; author of *Fear of Flying*.
Joseph Sheridan Le Fanu (1814–73) Irish writer.
Henry Miller (1891 1980)
John Milton (1608–74) English poet; he

published *Paradise Lost* in 1667.
Comte Gabriel Honoré Riqueti de Mirabeau (1749–91) French writer; political figure of the Revolution.
Adrian Mitchell (b. 1932) English poet.
Anais Nin (1903–77).
Paulos (sixth century AD) Byzantine poet and aphorist.
Samuel Pepys (1633–1703) English diarist and political figure.
Dante Gabriel Rossetti (1828–82) English painter and poet.
Rufinus (c. second century AD) Greek poet and aphorist.
Felix Salten (1869–1945) Austro-Hungarian writer; best-known work is the story of *Bambi*.
William Shakespeare (1564–1616) English playwright and poet; greatest dramatist in the English language.
Robert Louis Stevenson (1850–94) Scottish writer and traveller, author of *Treasure Island*, *Kidnapped* and *The Strange Case of Dr Jekyll and Mr Hyde*.
Bram Stoker (1847–1912) Irish novelist who published *Dracula* in 1897.
Paul Verlaine (1844–96)
Walther von der Vogelweide (1170?–1230) German courtly poet.
Mae West (1892–1980) American film actress.
Oscar Wilde (1854–1900)
John Wilmot, Earl of Rochester (1647–80)
William Butler Yeats (1865–1939) Irish poet and playwright.
Emile Zola (1840–1902) French novelist.

Artists
Hans Baldung Grien (c. 1484–1545) German painter and engraver.
Franz von Bayros (1866–1924) German painter and illustrator.
William Blake (1757–1827) English mystic poet and artist.
Margit Gaal Early twentieth-century German artist.
Rudolf Koch German illustrator of the mid-twentieth century.
Adolfo Magrini Italian artist of the early twentieth century.
Cesare Peverulli Mid-twentieth-century Italian artist.
André Provot Nineteenth-century French illustrator.
Rembrandt Harmensz van Rijn (1606–69) Dutch painter and engraver, the most outstanding of the seventeenth century in Holland.
Leon Richet Late nineteenth-century French artist.
Auguste Rodin (1840–1917) French sculptor, whose works are among the most highly regarded of his time.
Italo Zetti Mid-twentieth-century Italian illustrator.
Giovanni Zuin Italian photographer of the late twentieth century.

Sources
Anonymous Geisha song of the eighteenth century.
Anonymous, Greek, 'I wish I were the wind', trans. Barriss Mills, *The Greek Anthology* (Allen Lane, 1973: Penguin Classics, 1981).
Pietro Aretino, extracts, trans. © Alistair Elliot.

Also *Sonnet No 4*, trans. Oscar Wilde.
Marquis d'Argans, *Therese Philosophie*. 1748.
John Berger, *G* (n.e. Hogarth Press, 1989), reprinted by permission of Random House UK.
Boccaccio *The Decamaron*, trans. © J. M. Rigg (Everyman's Library, 1979.
James Boswell, *Diaries*.
Restif de la Bretonne, *Diary*.
Robert Browning, *In a Gondola; The Ring and the Book*.
Robert Burns, 'Wad Ye Do That?' from *The Merry Muses of Caledonia*.
Giacomo Casanova, *History of My Life*, trans. Willard R. Trask. © 1966 Hareourt Brace Jovanovich, Inc., reprinted by permission of the publisher.
Armand Coppens. *Memoirs of an Erotic Bookseller*, © Armand Coppens, 1969.
Eskimo Nell, anonymous poem.
Johann Wolfgang von Goethe, 'Gretchen at the Spinning Wheel' from *Faust* Part 1, trans. © 1993 Fiona Ford.
Robert Graves. extracts from 'The Haunted House' and 'The Cool Web' from *Collected Poems 1975*. Reprinted by permission of A. P. Watt Ltd on behalf of the Trustees of the Robert Graves Copyright Trust.
Anthony Grey, *A Gallery of Nudes*. Star Books, 1987.
Heinrich Heine, fragment of a poem.
Erica Jong, 'The Wingless & the Winged' from *Selected Poems*, © Erica Jong 1977.
Joseph Sheridan Le Fanu, *Carmilla: Memoirs of a Venetian Courtesan*.©

L.O.E.C.

Henry Miller, *Black Spring*. © The Estate of Henry Miller. Reprinted by permission of Curtis Brown Ltd and Grove Weidenfeld.

John Milton, *Paradise Lost*, Book 1.

Gabriel Honoré de Mirabeau. *The Lifted Curtain*, trans. Howard Nelson, © Holloway House Publishing, 1972, reprinted W. H. Allen, 1956.

Adrian Mitchell, 'Celia Celia' from *For Beauty Douglas* © 19S2 Adrian Mitchell. Reprinted by permission of Peters Fraser & Dunlop Group Ltd. Note: neither this nor any other of Adrian Mitchell's poems is to he used in any examination whatsoever.

Anais Nin, *Delta of Venus* (Penguin Books, 1990), © Anais Nin 19d9. © The Anais Nin Trust, 1977, reprinted by permission

of Penguin Books Ltd and of Hareourt, Brace & Company.

O My Darling Flo, anonymous English poem.

Passion's Apprentice. © L.O.E.C.

Paulos, 'Our kisses Rodope', trans. Alan Marshfield, *The Greek Anthology* (Allen Lane, 1973: Penguin Classics, 1981).

Samuel Pepys, excerpt from his *Diaries*.

Pauline Réage, *Story of O*, © Editions Pauvert, 1954.

The Romance of Lust, ed. William Simpson Potter, 1873–6.

Dante Gabriel Rossetti, *Jenny*.

Rufinus, 'A silvertoed virgin', 'Rhodope, Melite and Rhodoklea', 'I do not enjoy', trans. Alan Marshfield, *The Greek Anthology* (Allen Lane, 1973; Penguin Classics, 1981).

Felix Salten, *Josefine Mutzenbacher*, 1906.

William Shakespeare, excerpt from *King Lear* (1605/6); *Sonnet 128*.

Souvenirs d'une Puce ('Memoirs of a Flea').

Robert Louis Stevenson, *The Strange Case of Dr Jekyll and Mr Hyde*, 1880.

Bram Stoker, *Dracula*.

Gus Tolman, early twentieth-century American.

Suburban Souls.

Paul Verlaine. extracts from 'At the Dance', 'Now, Poet, Don't be Sacrilegious', 'Even Without Presenting Arms . . .' and 'The Way the Ladies Ride' from *Femme/Hombres*, trans. Alistair Elliot, published 1979 by Anvil Press Poetry. London, and Sheep Meadow Press, New York.

Walther von der Vogelweide, 'Under the Linden Tree', trans. © 1993 Fiona Ford.

'Walter', *My Secret Life*. British Library; reprinted by Grove Press Inc., New York.

Oscar Wilde et al., *Teleny or The Reverse of the Medal*, 1893. British Library. (Also published by Grove Press Inc., New York.)

W. B. Yeats, *The Lover's Song*.

Emile Zola, *Nana*, trans. © George Holden 1972 (Penguin Classics, 1972), reprinted by permission of Penguin Books Ltd.

The majority of the illustrations in this part are reproduced by kind permission of Il Collezionista, Italy. Eddison Sadd is also grateful to the following for permission to reproduce: © Giovanni Zuin. Courtesy of Akehurst Gallery (pages 177, 178, 202, 203, 204–205, 219, 225).

Part Three

Authors

Subniv Babuta (b. 1958) Indian novelist.

Georges Bataille (1897–1962) French writer and librarian.

Charles Baudelaire (1821–67) French poet, author of *Les Fleurs du Mal*.

Aubrey Beardsley (1872–98).

William Blake (1757–1827)

George Gordon, Lord Byron (1788–1824) British poet, author of *Childe Harold* and *Don Juan*.

Nicolas Chorier (late seventeenth–early eighteenth century)

John Cleland (1709–89)

Leonard Cohen (b. 1934) Canadian poet and singer.

Aleister Crowley (1875–1947) English magician.

Lord Alfred Douglas (1870–1945) 'Bosie', son of the Marquess of Queensberry and lover of Oscar Wilde.

Norman Douglas (1868–1952) British novelist who settled in Italy.

Ernest Dowson (1867–1900)

Alexandre Dumas *père* (1802–70) French novelist; author of *The Three Musketeers*.

Lawrence Durrell (1912–90) British novelist and poet.

Gustave Flaubert (1821–80) French novelist, author of *Madame Bovary*.

John Fletcher (1579–1625) English dramatist

who may have collaborated with Shakespeare.

Thomas Hardy (1840–1928) English poet and novelist, author of the 'Wessex' novels.

Frank Harris (1856–1931)

Robert Herrick (1591–1674)

Erica Jong (b. 1942)

Rudyard Kipling (1865–1936) British writer and poet; author of the *Jungle Books*.

D. H. Lawrence (1885–1930)

Violette Leduc (1907–72) French writer.

Guy de Maupassant (1850–93) French short story writer and novelist.

Henry Miller (1891–1980)

Comte Gabriel Honoré

Riqueti de Mirabeau (1749–91)

Anaïs Nin (1903–77)

Sir Thomas Overbury (1581–1613) English poet and essayist.

Cora Pearl (1837–86) English courtesan who lived in Second Empire Paris.

Matthew Prior (1664–1721) English diplomat and poet.

Marcel Proust (1871–1922) French novelist; author of *Remembrance of Things Past*.

Pierre de Ronsard (1524–85)

Maurice Sachs (d. 1945) Parisian writer.

Saki (H. H. Munro) (1870–1916) English writer of sardonic short stories.

William Shakespeare (1564–1616).

George Bernard Shaw (1856–1950) Irish playwright and theatre critic.

Edmund Spenser (1552–99) Elizabethan poet.

Lytton Strachey (1880–1932) English biographer; author of *Eminent Victorians*.

Algernon Charles Swinburne (1837–1909) British poet.

Alfred Lord Tennyson (1809–92) British poet; he became Poet Laureate in 1850.

Edith Wharton (1862–1937) American writer, later resident in France; author of *The Age of Innocence*.

Walt Whitman (1819–92) American poet, author of *Leaves of Grass*.

Oscar Wilde (1854–1900)

John Wilkes (1727–97) English journalist and politician.

John Wilmot, Earl of Rochester (1647–80)

Artists

Eugène Agelou Late nineteenth-century French photographer.

A1 (active 1930s) Viennese illustrator.

Paul Edouard-Henri Avril (1849–1928) French artist, born in Algeria.

Suzanne Ballivet (active 1930–15) French book illustrator.

Franz von Bayros (1866–1924)

Aubrey Beardsley (1872–98)

C. Bernard Late nineteenth-century French watercolourist.

Louis André Berthomme Saint-André (1905–77) French illustrator.

Antoine Borel (1743–1810)

Bruno Braquehais Mid-nineteenth-century French photographer.

Carl Breuer-Courth Early twentieth-century.

Jean Cocteau (1889–1963) French novelist, dramatist, film-maker and poet.

Achille Deveria (1800–57) French painter and illustrator.

Michael Martin Drolling (1786–1851) Parisian painter, pupil of J.L. David.

Louis-Jules Duboscq-Soleil Late nineteenth-century French photographer.

Alexandre Dupouy Contemporary Parisian photographer.

Peter Fendi (1796–1842) Austrian artist, court painter at Vienna.

Artur Fischer (1872–1948) German painter.

Emmanuel de Ghendt (1738–1815) French engraver.

Eric Gill (1882–1940) British graphic artist and typographer.

Heinrich or Hendrick Goltzius (1558–1617) Dutch engraver and painter.

Alexis Gouin Mid-nineteenth-century French photographer.

Monica Guevara Contemporary graphic artist.

China Hamilton (b. 1946) English photographer, graphic designer, painter, musician and healer.

A. Klinkenberg Contemporary German artist and sculptor.

Henri Monnier (1799–1875) French watercolourist.

Felix Jacques-Antoine Moulin (active from 1849–61) Parisian photographer.

Georg Emmanuel Opitz (1775–1841) Austrian painter and illustrator.

Rojan or Rojankowski (active 1930–50) Polish-French illustrator.

Johann Heinrich Romberg (1763–1840) German watercolourist.

Félicien Rops (1833–98)

Thomas Rowlandson (1756–1827)

Arpad Safranek Contemporary German sculptor and photographer.

G. de Sainte-Croix (active 1949–59) French book illustrator.

Mario Tauzin (active 1910/20) Parisian draughtsman.

Denon Vivant Late eighteenth-century French etcher and engraver.

Gerda Wegener (b. 1889) Danish commercial artist.

Giovanni Zuin Contemporary Italian photographer.

Sources

Subniv Babuta, *The Still Point*. © The Author, 1991. Reproduced by permission of Weidenfeld & Nicolson, London.

Aubrey Beardsley, *Under the Hill*. British Library.

The Boudoir: Voluptuous Confessions of a French Lady of Fashion, early 1880s. British Library. (Also published by Star Books/W. H. Allen, London; Grove Press Inc., New York.)

Lord Byron, *We'll Go No More A-roving*.

Nicolas Chorier, *Satyra Sotadica*, 1660. English trans. in British Library, 1682, 1740, 1786; original in Bibliothèque Nationale, Paris.

John Cleland, *Fanny Hill – Memoirs of a Woman of Pleasure*, 1749. British Library. (Also published by Penguin Books/ Mayflower.)

Leonard Cohen, 'A Long Letter from F', from *Beautiful Losers*, ©

Leonard Cohen 1967. Reproduced by permission of Black Spring Press Ltd, London, and Stranger Music Inc., Los Angeles. All rights reserved.

Aleister Crowley, *White Stains*.

Lord Alfred Douglas, *Two Loves*.

Norman Douglas, limerick.

Ernest Dowson, *Vitae Summa Brevis*.

Lawrence Durrell, *The Black Book*, 1938. Copyright © The Estate of Lawrence Durrell 1938, 1973, reproduced with permission of Faber and Faber Ltd, London, and Curtis Brown Ltd, London, on behalf of The Estate of Lawrence Durrell. *The Alexandria Quartet*, 1957–60.

L'Ecole des filles ('School of Venus'), 1655. Trans. © 1972 Donald Thomas, Panther. Reproduced by permission of Harper Collins Publishers Ltd, London.

Eveline, 1904. British Library. (Also published by Star Books/W. H. Allen, London.)

John Fletcher, *Love's Emblems*.

Thomas Hardy, *The Ruined Maid*.

Frank Harris, *My Life and Loves*. Copyright © 1925 Frank Harris, © 1953 Nellie Harris, © 1963 by Arthur Leonard Ross as Executor of the Frank Harris Estate. Copyright renewed © 1991 by Ralph G. Ross and Edgar M. Ross. Used by permission of Grove Press Inc., New York.

Robert Herrick, *Upon the Nipples of Julia's Breast; Upon Julia's Sweat*.

Initiation Amoureuse, Buenos Aires, 1943. Reproduced by courtesy of The Erotic Print

Society, London.
Erica Jong, *Fear of Flying*.
© Erica Mann Jong
1973. Reproduced by
permission of Reed
Books Ltd, UK, and
Henry Holt & Co., New
York.
D. H. Lawrence, *Lady
Chatterley's Lover*, 1928.
Reprinted by permission
of Laurence Pollinger
Ltd, London, and the
Estate of Frieda
Lawrence Ravagli.
Published by Penguin
Books Ltd, London, and
Penguin USA, New York.
Violette Leduc, *La Batarde*,
trans.Derek Coltman. ©
The Author's Estate.
Reproduced by
permission of Peter
Owen Publishers,
London, and Gallimard,
Paris.
The Lustful Turk, 1828.
British Library.
Henry Miller, *Tropic of
Cancer*. Copyright ©
1934 The Estate of
Henry Miller.
Reproduced with
permission of Grove
Press Inc., New York.
Opus Pistorum. © 1983
The Estate of Henry
Miller. Reproduced with
permission of Grove

Press Inc., New York.
Honoré Gabriel Riquetti,
Comte de Mirabeau, *Ma
Conversion*. Trans. ©
Holloway House
Publishing Co., Los
Angeles, 1972. (Also
published by Star
Books/W. H. Allen,
London.)
Anaïs Nin, *Delta of Venus*,
Erotica. Copyright © The
Anais Nin Trust, 1977,
reprinted by permission
of Penguin Books Ltd
(publ. 1990) and of
Harcourt, Brace &
Company, USA.
The Oyster magazine,
c. 1880.
Cora Pearl, *The Memoirs
of Cora Pearl*. © 1983
William Blatchford,
Granada. Reproduced by
permission of Harper
Collins Publishers Ltd,
London.
The Pearl magazine,
1879–80.
Pleasure Bound Afloat,
1908; *The Confessions of
Nemesis Hunt*, 1910;
Maudie, 1909. British
Library.
Matthew Prior, *Nanny
Blushes*.
Pauline Réage, *Story of O*.
Published by Société
Nouvelle des Editions

J.-J. Pauvert, Paris, 1954.
(Also published by Corgi,
London, and Ballantine,
New York.)
The Romance of Lust, ed.
William Simpson Potter,
4 vols., 1873-6.
Pierre de Ronsard, *A son
Ame* ('To his Soul').
Maurice Sachs, *Witches'
Sabbath*, © 1965 Stein &
Day, trans. Richard
Howard.
William Shakespeare,
excerpt from *Othello*.
l604.
George Bernard Shaw,
from the Preface to the
Grove Press edition of
*The Collected Works of
Frank Harris*.
Edmund Spenser, *The
Faerie Queen*, 1589–96.
Lytton Strachey,
*Ermyntrude and
Esmeralda*, 1912.
Reproduced by
permission of The
Society of Authors,
London, as agents of the
Strachey Trust.
Algernon Charles
Swinburne, *The Orchard;
Dolores*.
Alfred Lord Tennyson,
Guinevere.
'Walter', *My Secret Life*,
1850s. British Library.
Reprinted by Grove

Press Inc., New York.
Edith Wharton, *Beatrice
Palmate* (short story). ©
The Author's Estate.
Walt Whitman, *Calamus*.
Oscar Wilde et al, *Teleny
or The Reverse of the
Medal*, 1893. British
Library. (Also published
by Grove Press Inc., New
York.)
John Wilkes, *An Essay on
Women*.
John Wilmot, Earl of
Rochester, *The Imperfect
Enjoyment; Signior
Dildo; A Ramble in St
James's Park; Love and
Life; The Disabled
Debauchee*.

Most of the art used to
illustrate this part is
reproduced by kind
permission of The Erotic
Print Society, London. For
the exceptions Eddison
Sadd would like to thank
and acknowledge the
following: The Klinger
Collection (pages 258, 300,
323, 326, 327, 336, 337,
343, 346, 347 and 348); Il
Collezionista (page 272).
All the photographs are
reproduced courtesy of
the Akehurst Bureau,
London.

EDDISON•SADD EDITIONS
Editorial Director Ian Jackson
Art Director Elaine Partington
Mac Designer Malcolm Smythe
Design Assistant Freddie Godfrey-Smythe
Production Cara Herron

Eddison Sadd acknowledge with grateful thanks
the contribution of SP Creative Design to this edition